ODDLY ENOUGH VOL. 2

MORE TALES OF THE UNORDINARY

KIM M. WATT

CONTENTS

To you, magical readers,
who have put up with multiple platform changes,
a weird fixation on tentacles,
and far too many author asides.
These stories wouldn't exist without you.
Thank you.

AN OPENING NOTE

In looking back at the first *Oddly* collection, I see that I started with "I don't normally go in for forewords, or introductions, or prefaces or preludes or any of that stuff that happens before we get to the good bits."

Unfortunately, subsequent books seem to have proved me wrong, as it seems I often feel the need to ramble on about something or other, which may or may not be relevant to the book, and quite likely has no bearing on your (hopeful) enjoyment of it at all.

But given that you can just skip this part should you wish (there are no penalties, and no one will feed you to the shed), I shall try to offer a small introduction for those who fancy it.

Firstly, the majority of these stories have already been shared with (and are possible due to) the wonderful members of what is now The Familiar Society over on Circle. Their support has enabled me to write a brand new tale every month, and this collection is very much thanks to them. However, I have also popped a couple of extra, new ones in, and there is a final brand-new story to download from the link at the end of the book. It was meant to be included, but with true Kim style it grew and sprawled and crawled up the wall, and in the end I couldn't squish it in. It would've made this volume *way* too full. So it awaits you at the end.

Secondly, there are no rules as to how this book works. There's no order to the stories, and in fact I haven't even presented them in the order in which they were written. So feel free to dip in and out at your leisure, to choose what takes your fancy. The only exception is that the last three stories are linked, and do build on each other a little. But only a little.

Thirdly … Well. There is no thirdly. Here are some stories, little snippets of worlds and lives and possibilities, glimpses of magic and mystery and mayhem, from me to you. I hope very much that you enjoy them.

Just do watch the jam. Bad things can happen in the jam …

Happy reading!
Kim

SOMEONE DID SOMETHING

I often think I would like to write some sci-fi, then realise that I am not very clear on many technical details that are probably required for the whole 'sci' part. And also that all the proper sci-fi readers would likely be very displeased, because I would write things like this ...

SOMEONE HAD DONE SOMETHING.

Of course they had. Someone *always* does something. If the history of sentient life can be boiled down to one phrase, it's that: Someone did something.

Usually something unwise, often something unexpected, and generally speaking always something unwelcome.

Such was the life philosophy of Carolina Ruiz (Lina to her crew, *bloody nightmare* to her superiors in The Fleet, such as they were, and *that woman* to quite a lot of other people, usually embellished with some colourful language), who currently had her forehead resting against the nav console in the bridge and her hands set widely on either side of it.

"Tell me again, Rikki," she said.

"The engines won't work," the young engineer said, fiddling with the neck of their overalls.

Lina turned her head without lifting it, eyeing them. Rikki was new, but had come with impeccable references, other than the note that they didn't *integrate* well. Lina wasn't bothered by integrating – what that tended to mean was that some human captain didn't like the fact their whole crew didn't get down to ancient Earth music and stuff themselves with Sunday roasts. Or they had tails. People got really weird about tails.

Rikki flicked their tongue nervously, testing the air, and Lina wondered what her stress pheromones tasted like. Oily, she imagined. It had been a busy week, what with the capture of four fugitive rock climbers in the orbit of Ephemeroptera (rock climbers being a slang term for smugglers of Blackpool rock, which had gained an astonishing value on the black market over the last century) and their delivery to the citrus orchards of Caelestra to work off their punishment; then refuelling in Tarsius, which had somehow turned into a chase for three illegally bred unicorn foxes (Tarsius being a known haunt of rogue geneticists); and finally the whole thing with the poker game in Numididae, in which her first officer Claudette had lost an eye. Lina looked at Claudette, who shrugged. She had a Band-Aid over the missing eye, which would be regenerating already. She could see fine out of the other six, anyway.

Lina shifted her gaze back to her new engineer. "I rather gathered that the engines aren't working, Rikki, love, based on the fact we're currently drifting. My question is why, and how long until they will be?"

"Right," Rikki said. "Of course." They fiddled in their pockets, coming out with a piece of string and some sockets, then put them away again. "Ah … I don't know."

Claudette chortled. "Told you those new drives were a bad idea, Lina."

Lina went back to staring at the console from very close range. "Gloating doesn't become you, Claud."

"Rubbish. I'm great at gloating. Aren't I, Rikki?"

"Um," Rikki said, checking their pockets again as if there might be a good answer hidden inside.

"Don't harass the crew," Lina said, pushing herself upright and rubbing a hand over her close-shaven head. "That's why Steve left."

"No, you fired Steve because of the shark," Claudette said.

"There was that," Lina admitted, and looked out at the void that surrounded the ship, pocked with the scattered glitter of distant suns and planets, and smeared with the paths of galaxies. At least the engines had chosen an empty bit to stop in. Although it was all pretty empty, Lina supposed. Non-travellers were always convinced that you spent the whole time thrashing through asteroid fields and having narrow escapes with black holes, but if that was happening on a regular basis you were a pretty poor pilot. Or had bought your charts from X'atat, which used inverted ratios and right-angled physics, and made no sense to anyone except X'atatians.

"What shark?" Rikki asked.

"Steve sneaked one on," Claudette said. "Not big." She waved vaguely. "A metre or so long, maybe."

Rikki blinked. "But why?"

"That was Steve," Claudette said cheerfully, and popped a couple of live crickets into the mouth on the back of her neck, still speaking out of the other. "Couldn't have a mouse when a carnivorous boar rat would do."

"But on a ship ..." Rikki trailed off, lifting their hands slightly. They were scaled and palely luminescent, colours rising and falling in them like a cuttlefish. "Where did he keep it?"

"It was an air-shark," Lina said. "Modded, you know. So it didn't need water, and sort of wriggled about on its fins. Only then it couldn't keep up with him, so Steve gave it some wheels, and it scooted into the bridge and bit a sodding customs agent. So I had to fire him on the spot or have the ship seized for a full investigation."

Rikki looked around as if wondering if the shark was still lurking in the corridors somewhere. "You'd have let him stay on otherwise?"

"Not the shark," Lina said. "Steve, maybe."

"He dropped hair a lot, though," Claudette said. "It was gross."

"The shark?" Rikki asked, their eyes wide.

"Steve." They stared at each other, and Lina pulled her fluffy boots on.

"Enough of this. Rikki, let's go and see if we can figure out what's happening with the engines."

"Together?"

Lina grinned at them, a small, rounded woman with broad shoulders, wearing a floral housecoat with a tool belt strapped over it. "You're not on The Fleet cruisers now, you know. We specialist services have broader job descriptions than you're used to."

"And smaller budgets," Claudette said, going back to gluing bits of the nav station back on. A rogue gremlin had bounced across it a few days ago and chipped pieces off everywhere. Lina wasn't sure Claudette was getting all the bits back in the right places, but as long as it worked, it hardly mattered.

Lina was still considering her *someone's done something* life philosophy as she led the way through the narrow, metal-walled corridors of the ship, the floor plates clanking beneath her soft boots. She supposed it should be *someone's done something, or someone **hasn't** done something that they really should have done*, but that was a bit more of a mouthful. She had the feeling that life philosophies should be short and pithy, not that she was much of an expert in that.

She *was* an expert in quite a lot of other things, though, which was why, even if her ship was currently being held together with duct tape and superglue, she was the least likely member of The Fleet to be pulled in front of her superiors (most of whom had been in test tubes when she already had her first command). And also why there were no questions asked over things like rogue sharks and missing eyes. She was just *there*, taking her miserly specialist's ship budget and stashing her (now rather considerable) pay cheque away after each trip. She knew there were generals who'd kill for her salary, and would probably like a chance to try, but also that they'd never actually dare. She was an expert in not getting killed, too.

So she picked and chose the jobs that interested her, made sure her crew had decent food and comfortable beds and enough cash to buy modded bloody sharks, and just got on with things, and The Fleet let her do so. Some new young lieutenant with creaky, barely worn boots had come on the ship a few tours back and suggested she must be thinking of retirement soon. She'd taken him as an unwilling guest on a couple of jobs, and the last she'd heard he was pouring clam juice martinis on Io.

She glanced back at Rikki as she walked (the halls were too narrow to walk abreast) and said, "How're you finding it, then? Everything okay?"

"Um, yes?" they said.

"You don't sound very sure."

"No," they agreed, and little pulses of pale blue alarm from their skin reflected off the walls around them.

"Look, we're not big and shiny, but you tell me what you need and I'll get it," Lina said.

"Well, I can just do the requisition—"

"No. You tell me."

"Yes, Captain," they said, a little squeak creeping into their voice.

Lina stopped and examined her new engineer curiously. "What's up? You've been on board for what, sixty days now?"

"Sixty-three," Rikki said, giving the impression they were counting them carefully.

"How are you still this nervous? We can't be doing with nervous. I told you, we all have wide job descriptions here. You're going to need to get your hands dirty."

Rikki looked at their immaculate hands. "I'm okay with that."

"Then what is it?"

"Well …" They took a breath. "You have a … reputation."

Lina tipped her head. "Which one?"

"Um …"

"Does it relate to drinking, fighting, or shag—"

"*No!*" Rikki yelped. "No, not any of those. Work."

"Oh, right." She shrugged. "That's my least interesting reputation, really."

"Um … okay." Rikki looked vaguely confused. Lina wasn't sure (and it seemed a bit rude to ask), but she thought they might've been brought up in one of those morality farms. She hadn't seen them touch a drop of alcohol, and anytime she or Claudette swore it was like disco lights on Rikki's skin.

Lina gave them the most encouraging smile she could

manage. "Go on, then. What about my professional reputation is currently worrying you, and why?"

They scrunched their face up, revealing a few rows of hefty teeth that would've made Steve's shark a bit insecure, then said, "That it's not, exactly. Professional, I mean."

Lina pressed one hand to her chest in mock horror. "*Excuse* me?"

"I mean … I just … they said … and I … because …" Rikki's skin was incandescent, drowning the low lighting of the corridor, and Lina looked around, impressed.

"That's beautiful, that is."

"What?" There were so many flashes of light on the engineer's skin that Lina could barely look at them.

"Calm down, poppet. Here's the thing." She leaned forward a little, as if to whisper a secret in the empty ship. "In very ancient Earth times, women like me were thought to be witches."

"Women like you?"

"Older. A bit weird. Good at what we do. Disinclined to tolerate nonsense." She grinned, wide and wolfish. "And The Fleet, you see, for all its *all galaxies together* and pretty wording and all that, is very much made up of the sort of people who still think women like me are …" She considered it. "*Unwanted. Unnecessary.* So they say things about me. Whisper behind my back. Tell stories to scare the children. Like you." She winked at them. "And they send me out here where they don't have to look at me. Keep me out of the way."

Rikki blinked at her. "But doesn't that upset you?"

Lina chuckled. "Why would it? They give me plenty of money to stay out of sight, and I get to do what I want. And somewhere there will be another woman who looks at that and thinks, *Yes, I'm a bit of a witch too.* And that, dear Rikki, makes me happy. The old and the weird live on, even in our shiny new universe."

Rikki considered it, then said, "Was I sent here as a punishment?"

"Probably," Lina said, examining the engineer's smooth skin and meticulously rolled hems and the small flowers they'd embroidered on the chest pocket of the overalls. Not very *Fleet,* that. "Does it feel like one?"

"Not exactly." They hesitated. "So you won't throw me out of the airlock, then?"

"Only did it once, and he was *handsy.*"

Rikki's mouth twisted. "Ew. But still—"

"Not handsy to me. Handsy to young females who thought they had to put up with it."

"Ah. What about feeding me to the maw of Jern?"

"Stole from the other crew." She shrugged. "Also I just didn't like him much. Anyway, the maw just makes you kind of snotty all over for the next ten years. It doesn't kill you."

"Stranding me on an asteroid of Pith?"

"Bad jokes. I can't abide bad jokes."

"An *asteroid* for bad jokes?"

"He was picked up in like a month. And I mean *bad* jokes, not just unfunny ones."

Rikki was quiet for a moment, and Lina knew they were going through all the stories they'd no doubt been told when their new assignment was announced. There were plenty of stories, and she supposed they weren't *all* justified, but she regretted none of them. If one wanted to keep one's reputation intact, one had to keep up a good level of strandings and crew ejections.

"Now are you going to tell me why I should do any of that to you?" she asked.

Rikki sighed. "I'll show you. But please don't feed me to the maw of Jern. That sounds … icky."

"Right. No ickiness."

Rikki shuddered, somehow without it seeming theatrical, and set off little bright green flares on their cheeks. "I really can't abide ickiness."

"Noted. I shall reserve ickiness for only the worst of transgressions." She raised her hands instantly as Rikki's mouth fell open. "Joke. *Joke.*"

"You deserve an asteroid for that," Rikki said, and Lina grinned as she waved to them to lead on.

RIKKI STOPPED outside the engine room and looked at Lina. It was ominously silent, and she put a hand on the heavy door, feeling for the slightest vibration, but there was nothing. Her ship was dead in space, and a sudden sickness seesawed in her belly. Would they give her another ship, if this one was beyond resuscitation? Was this yet another attempt at forced retirement, only with no way to run away from it this time?

She looked up at Rikki, eyebrows raised.

"I'm really sorry," they said, swallowing so hard she could hear it in the dull, flat silence of her lifeless ship. "They … they made it sound like it'd be the end of my career, joining your crew."

"It probably is," she said. "They never send me *their* best. The brightest, yes, because The Fleet doesn't want those. They just want tidy little drones. That's what they call best."

Rikki twitched, and nodded. "They said this wasn't a punishment, but a way to prove myself. That if I did … something, they would reinstate me in a cruiser. With a promotion."

"I see." Lina kept her voice as calm as she could, then nodded. "The engine upgrade. When you first arrived."

"Yes."

"You sabotaged it."

"Not exactly."

She looked at them narrowly. "*Not exactly?* It's a Devious NX-23-5J9. It's a bloody workhorse, and completely over-specced for this size ship. We should be skipping across galaxies like a damn cirrus-snake, and you're saying you *didn't exactly* sabotage it? I helped you install it, for the Bang's sake! It was *fine.*"

"You're not an engineer," they pointed out.

"In a small ship—"

"You have broad job descriptions, I know." They sighed. "The night we installed it, when you and Claudette went out … carousing."

"Carousing?" She almost grinned, then remembered her broken ship and scowled instead. "You were going to some bloody trans-dimensional meditation thing."

"I didn't." Rikki looked pained. "I made some … *tweaks* to the cat converter."

"*Tweaks?*" Lina took a breath, ready to tell them exactly what she thought of unauthorised tweaks, then stopped, suddenly recalling a bit of cross-universe gossip that had been drifting in the bars last month. It had concerned a Fleet ship corralling refugee vessels fleeing the war-torn planet of Mutos for the safer but unwelcoming skies of Panarch. It was well-known that The Fleet's official role was to turn the boats back. The exact manner in which it did that was a matter of nods and winks, and also the reason why Lina had ended up nearly being retired the last two times, since she didn't hold with nodding, winking, or official roles, and had escorted several refugee ships to more sympathetic landing spots while on her days off.

But this particular Fleet ship … "You were on *The Welcomer,*" she said. "You *tweaked* the feral phase wave cannons."

Rikki didn't say anything, but their skin was suddenly clammily pale.

"You tweaked the cannons and they fired roses and waterlilies and *banana muffins.*"

"I like banana muffins," they mumbled.

"You fired them at ships. In space. What was that meant to do?"

"They took some on board," they said, twisting their fingers together. "Maybe they like banana muffins too."

Lina stared at the engineer, then burst out laughing. "You're a *genius.* How did you not get court-martialled?"

"They couldn't prove I did anything. It was just a programming thing and I changed it back. No trace, but they had enough suspicions to … this." They waved around vaguely, encompassing Lina and the creaking old ship.

"I would love to know what sort of *programming thing* replaces feral phase waves with banana muffins." Lina leaned against the engine room door, listening to the silence, then said, "You are a very interesting person, our Rikki. So tell me, why do you want to go back and work with the murdering b-"—she swallowed, remembering the engineer's neon flashes—"blighters?"

"I have to send money home," they said quietly, and Lina watched them for a moment, her heart suddenly tired. Of course. Of course they did, because their family was caught in some other world that maybe wasn't Mutos, but it was the same. It was rendered barren by overpopulation, or raging with war, or torn by storms or pollution or just the collapse of a dying, overexploited planet, and this creature, this *child,* because however old they were, Rikki felt like a child to her (most people did), was out here working for an organisation that might very well destroy the exact ship their family was scraping and saving to make their escape on, but it was the only hope they had. And even such a desperate and crumbling hope was better than none at all, because hope is life and life is hope, and someone should do something, but no one ever did. Or not the right somethings, anyway.

She sighed and dug in her tool belt, coming out with a small package of fudge. She offered Rikki a piece, who took it with a bemused look on their face, then she took one herself and popped it in her mouth. "So you sabotage my ship, they retire me, you get reinstated, and maybe you can save your family."

They nodded.

"Why tell me?"

Rikki considered that, sucking on the fudge. Then they said, "I only knew stories before. They're not … well, they're true, but not how they tell them."

"Truth's tricky," Lina agreed.

"I programmed the tweak into the install," they said. "That was when I first got on board, and now … well, I was kind of hoping it hadn't worked."

"Can you un-programme it?"

"That'd be like turning the banana muffins back into feral phase waves. Once they're created they're just … there."

"Right." Lina ran her hands back over her head. "Let's see, then."

Rikki took a deep breath, and spun the round handle that opened the engine room door. There was the whisper of the seal opening, releasing a whiff of grease and fuel and gases, but not the usual rush of heat. Lina stepped inside. The floor was cleaner than the bridge floor, and the engine looked as if Rikki had been polishing it like their aunt's favourite silverware. It was cramped, though, not one of the big ships with their walkways and workshops, and she had to squeeze around the belly of the engines to where the catalytic converter … wasn't. She stared at the blank space, pipes sheared as neatly as if someone had been running about down here with a laser cutter, and looked at Rikki.

"What happened to the cat converter? Where is it?"

"Them," they said.

"Sorry?"

Rikki turned away from her and bent to a tool cabinet that was bolted to the floor. They opened the front, reached inside, then hesitated for a moment before turning back. "Them."

Lina stared at the two large and slightly disgruntled ginger cats dangling from the engineer's hands and said, "Sorry?" again.

"Cat converter," Rikki whispered.

By the time Lina had finished laughing, and had called Claudette down from the bridge (she hit Rikki around the head with her tail a few times, then claimed the cats to snuggle), Rikki had resorted to sitting on the floor in the hall with their forehead on their knees, both hands clutched over their head.

"I'm so sorry," they said again. "If I'd known … I mean, they made you sound like a monster!"

"She is," Claudette said. "Shall I call this one Fred and this one M'Ng'th'cal-y'thu?"

"No Aitch names," Lina said. "Someone'll just mispronounce it and we'll end up with a dimensional tear as well as no engine."

"Fred and Ginger?"

"Uninspired, but better." She sat down next to Rikki. "Can you fix it?"

"Maybe," they said, and gave her a timid look. "What're you going to do to me?"

"Make you clean their litter boxes," she said, pointing at the cats.

Rikki blinked at her. "I sabotaged your ship."

"Yes, but I think the best punishment for that is that you have to stay here and clean up your mess," she said. "No promotion for you. *Bad* engineer."

Claudette laughed. "Look at them go!"

Lina glanced at her first officer, but she was entirely taken up with flashing a laser pointer around the engine room for the cats to chase.

"So I stay here?" Rikki asked. "Really?"

"I like inventive people," Lina said. "If you'd just cut a couple of wires I'd've been like, off with your head! But the cats were funny. Even better than banana muffins."

"Really?" they said again, and there was a wobble in their voice.

"Sure. We've not sent out any SOS. No traffic in the area. When The Fleet get in contact, you tell them I busted you and won't let you leave."

"They'll try something else," Rikki said. "They really don't like you."

"I *know*," Lina said, with that wolfish grin. "Isn't it marvellous?"

And when she laughed this time, Rikki joined in a little hesitantly, but it was drowned out by the sudden groan of the engines turning over. Lina stared at Rikki, and they stared back, and Claudette popped her head out of the engine room door.

"Um, that dimensional tear thing?"

"No," Lina said.

"Can cats run fast enough to cause one?"

"*No.*"

Rikki dived into the engine room, and came out a moment later with a cat in each hand and a bewildered look on their face. "There's still no cat converter," they said. "But the laser pointer and the cats and … it's like a plasma ball, but not, and …"

"Do we have power?" Lina asked.

"Yes, but …"

"You are a clever sod," she said. "Onward! We've got a …" She trailed off, trying to remember.

"Stolen shipment of yams to catch," Claudette supplied, and pointed at the cats. "Are you done with them?"

"I don't know," Rikki said, looking at Fred and Ginger. Their fur was standing up in all directions, static leaping from the tips of their ears and tails, but they were both purring so loudly Lina wasn't sure if it was the engine or the cats she could hear.

"Figure it out, then meet me on the bridge," Lina said. "I want to know what tweaks you can make in the galley." She turned and strode off, Claudette pattering behind her and occasionally using the wall or the ceiling instead when it suited her. Lina wondered where the kid's home planet was, and how big their family was.

Now that would *really* twist the knickers of The Fleet, wouldn't it? If someone *did something.*

She grinned, wide and wolfish, and at least a little witch-like.

2

READY. STEADY. BAKE

Of course I love Bake Off. *Who doesn't love a show full of cakes and bright moments and niceness? It's the best sort of refuge from the world.*

But then my subconscious gets involved, and things get weird.

Like, really weird ...

Do mind the jam.

JADE SMOOTHED HER APRON DOWN WITH SHAKING HANDS, THE bright blue plaster on her index finger an exclamation against the grimy beige cloth. Flour still dusted the dark skin of her forearms, and she wondered vaguely how much she'd inhaled during the incident with the mixer. That hadn't been ideal. But at least she'd got everything back under control in time to finish, even if it had been messy. Some chopped nuts had found their way into her socks, and there was a large splodge of batter on the toe of one trainer.

The details loomed large, as if sucking all the colour out

of the world, and she struggled not to look at the cameras. They lurked like spindly, headless beasts along one side of the big marquee, the jeans-clad legs of their operators emerging smug and stain-free beneath them. Even when she kept her gaze carefully directed elsewhere she could feel the all-seeing eyes of the lenses, blank and hungry, gobbling up the row of bakers perched on stools around her. Rain streaked the plastic windows of the tent, the bunting soggy and limp outside, and the green fields and graceful trees that surrounded them were drowning in the grey day.

She swallowed hard, her throat clicking, and in front of her one of the judges leaned on the table, supporting himself with his large hands placed wide, pale eyes narrowed.

"I like this one," he said, straightening up to poke one of the cakes with the tip of a knife. There were eight of them, studded with fruit and nuts, all rendered in varying degrees of elegance and precision. "Nice structure." He sliced into it, the knife catching the lights from the cameras and winking like a cheeky aside.

Next to him, an older woman in a luminously bright shirt and chunky earrings made an encouraging noise, flashing a smile at the row of contestants. "I rather think you're right, Don," she said. "A lovely colour to it, too."

"Maybe a bit too much colour," Don countered, and Jade felt the woman next to her tense.

"Well, one doesn't want them undercooked," the woman pointed out, taking a morsel off the side plate as he offered it to her.

"*Hmm.*" Don narrowed his eyes at the contestants, chewing slowly. "Good flavour."

"Very good," the woman agreed, moving on to the next cake. "Now this one has some problems, I'm afraid. I think someone ran out of time."

Don sliced into it, revealing a pale, sticky centre. "Underbaked," he declared, and as the woman leaned over to examine the clumpy, slowly unfurling wedge he set on the plate he added, "Don't eat that one, Beryl. It'll bite back."

"Oh, you are awful," she said, but she didn't move to try the cake, and the two hosts, standing watching the judges with their hands clasped behind their backs, made sympathetic faces at the contestants.

"Never mind," the one in a short skirt said, their voice hearty. "I like a bit of fight in my food, me."

"It's half the fun!" the one in an overcoat and fascinator exclaimed, and they both laughed.

The woman on the stool next to Jade swallowed a sob, and Jade took her hand in one of her own as subtly as she could, squeezing gently. No one else moved, and the judges continued along the line of cakes, laying down their verdicts with a mix of bad jokes and knowing smiles. The bakers tried to laugh along where they could, but Jade could barely breathe for the tension thrumming through them all. It wasn't as though there was no chance of coming back from a bad technical challenge, of course, but if one had already had a bad signature bake, like the woman next to Jade (her name was Liz and she was a self-taught cook, that was how she described herself, frightfully practical and well-spoken and always wearing tasteful pearl earrings and well-cut clothes), things were fraught, to say the least.

"Last place is this one," Don announced, using both hands to indicate a particularly misshapen cake with broken edges and a burnt bottom. It was a hard gesture, brusque and final.

"That's mine," a bespectacled man with a twitch in his cheek said, raising his hand.

"Underbaked. Undermixed. You need to work on your presentation," Don said, delivering the verdict with casual brutality.

"The flavours were well-balanced, though," Beryl said.

"Better luck next time." She moved down the table and pointed at another cake. "Next is this one."

"Oh, that's me!" the oldest contestant said, pushing her glasses up her nose and waving. "Silly me, I think I put too much baking soda in."

"You *did*," Don said, with feeling. "I can still taste it, Myrtle. It'll be haunting me in my dreams. Or that might be you."

Myrtle flapped her hand at him. "Oh, *you.*"

Liz was fourth, and Jade felt her relax a little. Jade herself was third, which eased the tightness in her chest, not entirely, but enough for her to manage a breath that felt like more than a sip of air through a half-crushed straw. Third was fine, third kept her in the competition, third would do for today. But she needed to do better. One didn't win by coming third, after all. Third made it to the end, and that was something, that was *enough*, but enough didn't get the plate. She needed the plate.

The plate was everything.

THE NEXT DAY was wetter still, if that was possible, and a petulant wind had built up in the night. It set the trees sighing and shuddering, and rain whipped under the contestants' umbrellas as they walked through the attractive, rambling gardens and onto the sodden green where the tent crouched. It was rendered grubby by the dull light, and unsettlingly alive, the wind sending billows down its canvas sides like a beast twitching in its sleep. Liz walked next to Jade, adjusting her hair with nervous fingers. It was flawless, of course, and her blouse looked freshly steamed, but the shadows under her eyes weren't quite fully disguised with foundation, and the pale pink cardigan done tightly up over her chest made her look older than Jade suspected she might be.

"I hate caramel work," Liz said, her voice low as they walked the long route to the tent, chased by cameras.

"You've had time to practice the showstopper," Jade said. "You'll be fine."

"I don't even like *watching* caramel. It's very stressful."

Jade linked her arm though Liz's, smelling dusty perfume and toothpaste. "You're going to do just fine."

"I don't know," Liz whispered. "I just don't know."

AN HOUR LATER, Jade just didn't know either. The rain was coming down harder, drowning out what stilted conversation might've been attempted, and outside the tent the carefully staged chairs had blown over, rolling a couple of times before coming to rest. The hosts had resorted to writing cheery little notes on bits of card and holding them up to both cameras and contestants, and the wind tore at the seams of the tent, sneaking in the gaps and howling around the benches. Jade's meringue had started to slowly collapse in the humidity, and her sugar work was weeping. She gulped air as if she were out drowning in the downpour, wondering how much of her caramel would survive until judging.

"Hi Jade!" the skirt-clad host exclaimed, appearing in front of her bench. Jade jerked back, dropping an egg on the floor. "Oh, sorry! I want you to spill the tea, not the eggs!"

"No, no," she shouted back over the roar of the wind. "Can't make a meringue without breaking a few eggs!" She was grinning so hard she could feel her lips trying to split at the edges, tears prickling her eyes.

"Ha! Good one! How're you feeling? Confident? You did well yesterday!"

She could barely hear them over the rain on the canvas, but nodded enthusiastically anyway. "Yesterday was good! Today I just need to get the sugar work right and it'll be fine! I'm feeling really positive!" She could hear her own exclamation marks, as if they were sprouting above her head like alien antennae, and she hated them. But she was the bubbly one. She had to use all the exclamation marks, and giggle a lot, and be a bit cheeky and flirty. She didn't *feel* bubbly, not usually and definitely not now, but Abby, who had been two benches over, was the nervous, self-doubting one, so there couldn't be two. Jade wondered briefly if, since Abby had gone out last week, she could step into that role, and her gaze drifted to the outside table, which was still standing. She couldn't see the broken corner through the rain, or the stains on the wood, but she knew they were there. She'd seen them.

The host gave her two thumbs up and moved on, the cameras following them, and Jade rolled her shoulders, cracking her neck as she looked around the tent. Myrtle was opening a freezer to put her mousse in to cool, and Ed (the laddish, unexpectedly artistic one) called, "No, that's my freezer, love."

"Oh, *sorry*," Myrtle exclaimed, and retreated, walking slowly with her tray in both hands, as if it were full of jelly waiting to set rather than mousse. Her grey hair was firmly set in tight curls, defying the weather, and she toddled past Jade in her sensible shoes and support stockings. "Can't take me anywhere," she said, blue eyes twinkling.

Jade smiled politely, then turned her attention back to her showstopper. She still had three elements to complete, and she didn't have time to worry about Myrtle and her mousse. The clock was running down, and she wasn't going home because she finished late. Not a chance.

She didn't think about Myrtle after that, except to think it was lucky, when Ed was eliminated, that it hadn't been due to his mousse being disturbed in the freezer, but rather a drastic issue with his meringue, which he'd somehow managed to make with salt instead of sugar. It was inedible, and coupled with a poor showing the day before, it was his name the host in the overcoat called out, a tear trekking down their cheek and vanishing into their beard. Ed was hugged and back-patted, his sobs rising above the endless rain into something close to a wail. Jade didn't watch him go. She couldn't.

THE NEXT WEEK was bread week, the sun turning the tent into a greenhouse and setting her sweating uncomfortably, mopping the back of her neck with a piece of kitchen roll, her scalp itching under her headscarf. The heat threw her off, and her signature bake on day one (sweet cardamom rolls) bordered on over-proofed. That was better than poor Andy, though (the studious, scientifically-inclined one), whose oven tripped off. He didn't realise it until his plaited, boozy fruit buns had already been in for twenty minutes, slowly blooming into unrecognisable blobs. Something had spilled on the outlet, and he couldn't get it switched back on, his chest heaving with panicky breaths and little moans of fright escaping him.

Jade's rolls were all on one tray, so she let him use the second shelf in her oven, and Anette (the foreign one) did the same. Andy's rolls still ended up underbaked, but it was something. He bore the criticism stoically enough in the judging, but once the cameras were off he protested that he should be given some leeway. The crew (not the hosts or the judges, they were there to deliver support and verdicts respectively, not enforce rules) just said, somewhat apologetically, that it was his responsibility to check his equipment. Jade found her gaze drifting to the power points, but the outlet wasn't where Ed had been. Maybe the rain had got in.

On day two, as they raced to get their towering showstoppers of savoury doughs done, Andy's mixer broke. The Pyrex bowl shattered, the dough lashing out and sending shards exploding across his bench and into his assortment of waiting fillings. By the time he'd got new batches done he didn't have time to proof them long enough before baking. The structure was tight and hard, and Jade could see it when he arranged the shaped rolls and sticks inside his intricately woven basket of golden dough. He looked at the breads, shoulders slumped, then sank to the floor behind his bench with his back to the cabinets, elbows on his knees and his hands laced behind his head. Jade checked the cameras, then crept over to join him, dropping into a crouch by the cold oven.

"It's not that bad," she whispered, and he raised his head to meet her gaze.

"It is."

"You did well on the technical."

"But not on the signature. You know one out of three isn't enough." He looked across the room, to where Myrtle was frowning at her wonkily-shaped breadbasket, sprouting fougasse and breadsticks. "I should've had time."

"But your bowl—"

"I should've had time," he insisted. "Especially in this heat. They should've risen at least a bit, but they didn't at all." He scowled, gaze still on Myrtle. "It was her yeast."

"What?"

"She brought me some dough, to ask if I thought it was proofed, and knocked my yeast all over the floor. She gave me some of hers instead, but I don't think it was the same. It's barely risen at all."

Jade nodded, but didn't answer. Everyone always needed someone to blame. He *hadn't* had that much time, and he'd been rushing. Probably the water had been too hot when he added the yeast, and he hadn't waited to see if it frothed. Or he'd used too much salt, or his proportions had been off, or any number of things. Bread was a delicate beast, prone to being temperamental at the best of times. It was why everyone feared it, and why it had to be tackled with brutal precision. One had to let it know who was boss.

She put her hand on his arm. "Sorry," she said, and got up, straightening her floury apron. A little, ugly worm of satisfaction wound through her belly as she perched on her stool to wait. She felt bad for Andy, but she wouldn't be going out. Not this time.

AND THEN THEN WERE FIVE. Jade looked around the tent, her throat working and her mouth sticky. She was almost safe. *Almost*. She wanted the plate, of course, because the plate was the key to everything, but if she made the final three, she'd be safe, if nothing else. The competition was tight now, though.

Ahmed, with his quick, talented fingers and wild showstoppers.

Cassie, with her pretty summer dresses, Dr Martens, and quirky bakes.

Lewis, with his flawless, precise pastry work and half-glasses.

Jade herself, the bubbly one, the flavour queen.

And Myrtle, everyone's favourite grandmother, serving up one classic bake after another, never fancy, always a little clumsy, but also invariably *enough*. Maybe they wouldn't have been, if not for all those inevitable tent catastrophes, the dropped cakes and missed timers and forgotten ingredients, and the simple, human mistakes that Myrtle had so far avoided, but no one ever said winning didn't require its share of luck.

Two more bakes to go. Jade just had to survive two more bakes, and she'd be safe. She was starting to think that would be enough, that she didn't *need* the plate, but she still wanted it. Of course she did. Why else would she be here? She took a deep breath and pressed her hands against the worktop, the burns on her fingers throbbing. They hadn't had time to heal since the last bake day, and though the blisters had popped, her hand was still clumsy and swaddled in burn dressings.

It had been a silly accident, one of those *should've known better* ones. Myrtle had shuffled up to her with a brandy snap in one hand, begging her to taste it and see if it was burnt. Jade had been taking a batch of her own snaps out at the time and her grip had slipped, the tray escaping from her oven mitt and heading for the floor. She'd grabbed it with her bare hand, ignoring the sizzle of scorched flesh and the pain screeching into her nerve endings, saving the delicate, creeping tulles while Myrtle cried out in horror. The older woman had rushed her to the sink to get cold water on the injury, fussing and efficient all at the same time. Jade wasn't sure if it was annoying or soothing. A bit of both, she supposed. A mum thing, perhaps.

"Ready. Steady … *Bake!*" the hosts shouted, then did some strange sort of hoedown at the front of the tent. The judges looked on with indulgent smiles, Beryl with her lipstick staining the skin around her mouth, as if she'd been slurping on a luminous ice lolly. Jade shuddered, and glanced at the space when Andy's bench had been. There was still a touch of discolouration on the flooring.

But then was no time to think about Andy. The signature

bake was an ice cream sandwich, which was hardly on her list of favourite things, but she was the flavour queen, she could do this, and do it with a twist. Ice cream first, cream and sugar and eggs to make the custard base, with a little miso to give that depth of flavour. Cool it fast, then into the ice cream maker and lock it down before anything starts getting iffy. Then the cookies. Dark chocolate, roughly chopped to give big, toothsome chunks. A pinch of dried chilli, not too much, not enough to excite anything, just a suggestion. A lick of salt to hold it in place. The tent faded around her as she worked, the world becoming nothing more than sugar and flour and the heavy, sweet scent of browning butter.

"Jade," Myrtle whispered, and Jade looked up, disoriented. "Here." The older woman set a mug of tea on the worktop, then showed her a flask, tucked inside her apron pocket. "Leftover from my biscuits. I put a little tipple in for courage."

Jade blinked at the mug, then pointed at her headscarf. "I don't drink."

"Oh! Oh, no, of course not!" Myrtle grabbed for the mug. "Sorry, sorry— *Oh!*" Because in her haste she'd knocked it over, sending tea splashing across Jade's worktop.

Jade bit back on a curse, snatching up her tea towel and slapping it down to stem the tide.

"Oh, I'm *so* sorry!" Myrtle was trying to use the bottom of her apron to wipe the bench. "Let me clean it up—"

"It's fine, leave it," Jade said, trying to keep her voice level as she hurriedly mopped up the mess, waving the other woman away. "Really, Myrtle. Please."

"I didn't mean to offend you—"

"You haven't." Jade turned her attention back to her mixer, which was still beating the burnt butter and sugar. She stopped it, lifting the head and staring into the bowl.

She'd only gone and spilled the chilli powder somehow. She could see the red dust clinging to the side of the bowl, and that hadn't been there before. Did she have the jar in her hand when Myrtle came by? It was next to the mixer, top open, and she frowned at it. She *had* been about to add it, she supposed, and found a teaspoon to taste the batter. As soon as it touched her tongue she winced and spluttered. Inedible. She'd have to make it again. Her heart was going too fast as she whirled and dumped the bowl in the sink. She had time. She *had* to have time.

She did. It wasn't her best effort, her miso ice cream slapped on the barely cooled chilli-chocolate cookies at the last moment and all thoughts of decorating abandoned, but the flavours were good. Unlike Cassie, who'd somehow used lard instead of butter in the cookies, and whose ice cream seemed to have been made with soured milk. It tasted, Don declared, like old bacon and despair. Cassie couldn't explain how it had happened, and nor could anyone else.

Ahmed was star baker the next day. Cassie, shaken by the ice cream sandwich incident, was the opposite. She slid off the stool, her face twitching as she tried to give a bright smile for the cameras.

"It's been such a pleasure," she managed, her voice cracking. "I love everyone so much. We're all such good friends."

Lewis was already crying, and Jade could feel tears on her own cheeks as she hugged Cassie. "I'm sorry," she whispered to her. "I'm so sorry."

"Oh, no, it's been *wonderful*," Cassie said, loudly enough to be captured by the microphones, then breathed 'in Jade's ear, "*Watch her.*"

"What?" Jade pulled away, recoiling from both the warning and the possibility of being seen whispering. That wasn't allowed. There were consequences.

Cassie's voice rose again as she released Jade and shot a

look at Myrtle. "You all helped *so* much. You're all so wonderful. It's been *such* a good experience!" The tent darkened, the trees outside tossing as a sudden, wild wind rushed in, and heavy cloud robbed the summer day of light. The hosts stepped forward, smiles wide and sympathetic, and Cassie took a matching step back, her voice wobbly, her fragile poise abandoning her. "*Wait.* Can't I have another chance? I mean, the whole lard thing makes no sense. I don't know why there was lard on my bench. It wasn't on my list!"

"Come now, Cassie," Beryl said, taking one of her arms as the day grew even darker, fog boiling across the grass to swallow the trees, alive with chittering, directionless noise as it pulled the cloud down to meet it. "Only a poor worker blames their tools."

"No, please—"

"I'm disappointed," Don said, taking her other arm. "I expected better of you."

Cassie tried to pull away, but the judges' firm grip never faltered, their fingers sunk deep into her pale flesh. "No! No, *please!*"

The lights in the tent flickered, then came back stronger, making Jade squint. The world outside was lost to shadow, only a narrow margin of grass visible before the fog swallowed reality, and barely-glimpsed forms moved and shifted within it, fish in deep water. One of the hosts, wearing a tube top and a banana-themed headdress today, opened the door.

"We're going to miss you, Cassie! This hurts us more than it hurts you!"

"You go out, then!" she screamed at them, and Jade stared fixedly at the floor, tears dripping from the tip of her nose. She wiped them away as surreptitiously as she could, in case the cameras were watching, and didn't look up even when Cassie's scream went up an octave. Something growled and snarled, the sound rolling around the tent and coming from all directions at once. Jade still didn't look up when the door slammed shut, or when the screams lost definition, grew blurry and mushy, then finally stopped.

Only when Lewis hugged her, one-armed, did she risk a small peek around.

"She's gone," he whispered. "It's okay. They did it out of sight. That was nice."

They both glanced involuntarily at Andy's bench. Something dully white leered out of a gap in the flooring, and Jade pressed the back of a hand to her mouth. It looked like bone.

"Well done, bakers," the second host said, straightening their cow suit. "You're into the semi-finals! One more elimination to go!"

"I'm going to be sick," Jade said, her voice low and jagged.

"Not now," Lewis hissed, squeezing her a little more tightly. "The cameras are still on. Smile!"

Jade didn't think she could, not at first, and then Myrtle was there, fussing and petting her, patting her cheeks and cooing something unheard and meaningless. Jade found a frozen smile somewhere, one that lasted just long enough for her to press a hand to her chest and say how sad she was to see Cassie go, but how excited she was to be in the semi-final, and wasn't it *wonderful?*

Outside, the clouds rolled back and the sun got to burning off the final traces of the fog, painting the red spatters and scraps of white and purple debris in glossy colour. Faintly, through the last of the murk, she could see the judges wandering off to wherever they went when they weren't in the tent. Beryl still had something in one hand, gnawing on it absently.

Semi-finals. Imagine that.

THE TENT WAS SO thick with tension Jade thought she could smell the ghosts of past contestants rising in the hot air. She tried not to think about it, but found herself wondering how well the cleaning crew could really scrub things down, how much sank into the seams and joins of the flooring, or was soaked into the canvas. How much of what she was smelling was just her imagination and how much was the sticky heat of the day teasing traces from the tent like memories.

She caught Lewis's eye and he gave her a thumbs up, his expression fixed into something that was more grimace than grin. Ahmed kept staring at the space where Cassie's bench had been, and she wondered if he was seeing his own ghosts. Only Myrtle seemed not to be frozen by the loom of the penultimate bake, scuffling in her cavernous handbag for her asthma inhaler, and popping a couple of antacids, crunching them noisily. Jade took a deep breath. This was it. One final chance to get through. Everyone who made it to the final got to go home, and one would get the plate. *The* plate. She was *so close.* She just had to survive the next two days.

She cracked her fingers, straightened her apron, and smiled for the cameras. Three bakes. Two days. All to play for.

Ready.

Steady.

Bake.

It WAS a week for traditional bakes, and the signature was an interpretation of a Battenberg. Jade's green tea and jasmine cake was smooth, near-flawless, but so was everyone else's. Ahmed got a handshake. No one's marzipan was overworked. The sponges weren't underbaked, and none collapsed. The field was level.

Then, the technical challenge. Some strange, traditional bake Jade had never heard of, with a name she wasn't sure how to pronounce, and no instructions other than, *make the Ecclefechan*, which was singularly unhelpful. She thought, given the name and the dried fruit (which she hated working with. It hid all sorts of surprises), it might be like an Eccles cake, and started making a flaky, unsweetened pastry. But after a surreptitious glance at Myrtle humming around her bench and making what was clearly a sweet shortcrust, Jade decided Ecclefechan must be more like a mince pie. After that it was fairly straightforward. Dosing the dried fruit liberally with brandy subdued the more active ingredients and stopped the blinking, and rinsing the nuts with baking soda and water flushed out anything too toothy. Her mum's trick, and it always worked.

Her tarts had a touch of the dreaded soggy bottom, but Beryl declared them delectable, and even Don gave them a grudging nod. Only Myrtle's were rated higher, the pastry flawless and the filling perfectly balanced. Lewis had used too much brandy, making Beryl's eye twitch, although she did sneak a second bite, Jade noticed. Ahmed had gone the Eccles cake route and not sweetened the pastry, earning him last place. He bore it stoically, but his fingers tapped an anxious rhythm on his legs.

No one had missed the brandy step. No one had forgotten to pick over the nuts. There was nothing between them, and anything could happen in the showstopper.

One day to the final. One bake to go. They filed out of the tent into the long summer shadows, not talking.

All to play for.

THE SHOWSTOPPER WAS AN AFTERNOON TEA. Finger sandwiches, scones, pastry, a layered cake, biscuits, and mini cakes. It was a lot to do, and while there *was* time, there was nothing to spare. Jade set her folder on the worktop, open to the timetable she'd drawn up for herself. Bread first, and get it rising. She checked the mixer for debris, wiped the bowl out just in case there was something in there she couldn't see, and set the yeast to foaming. No shortcuts. Everything had to go *exactly* to plan.

She'd opted for fondant fancies for her mini cakes, and had just placed the sponge in the freezer for a fast cool down when she turned to see Myrtle leaning over Lewis's bench, cooing at the custard creams. He'd stamped them out in the shapes of ducks and chickens, to go with his *tea by the lake* theme, but as he was icing the chickens one of the ducks made a break for freedom. Jade darted forward and caught it before it tumbled off the bench, and as she did so she saw Myrtle drop an antacid into the cooling pot of strawberry jam. The contents boiled up like lava, glossy and red, sprouting whipping tentacles. Eyes snapped open in the seeds, rolling in every direction, and she started to say something. Myrtle straightened up, her gaze catching Jade's, and the younger woman paused, waiting for her to apologise, to exclaim over her clumsy fingers or absentmindedness, but she didn't. Instead she winked one twinkly blue eye and held up three fingers, the gesture hidden from both Lewis, who was corralling the other ducks, and the cameras. *Three*.

Three left, if Lewis went out.

They'd be safe.

And there'd be no proving anything, the antacid long devoured by the tentacles, which had coiled back on themselves, lurking under the glossy surface. In fact, *Jade* could be the one disqualified, for casting aspersions on the audience favourite. Or they both might be removed, leaving the two men to fight it out in the final. And neither of those options bore thinking about. She could still smell that charnel house stench seeping under the scent of baking bread and melting sugar.

"Thanks, Jade," Lewis said, holding his hand out for the duck she still had clutched in her hand. "I already broke my spare. Can't afford to lose another one."

Jade looked at the duck, which was trying to peck her, but its beak was too blunt too hurt. One only made that mistake once. The cameras were on them, Myrtle smiling in a way that showed too many teeth, and Jade looked at her own unattended bench. A lone eldritch shade that had broken out of one of the eggs when she was boiling them for the sand-wiches was inching across the worktop like a bloody cater-pillar. It must've clawed its way back up the sink, and she needed to stop it before it nested in the lemon drizzle batter. *Three.*

"Jade?"

The jam looked flawless. The tentacles wouldn't move until the scones were being assembled, and by then it'd be too late for Lewis to make more. And it wasn't even a *definite* fail, because there was always a risk of tentacles, no matter how careful one was. They could've come from anywhere.

She found a smile and handed the duck over. "The wings are small enough," she said, "But you've done the feet too well. Always risky, feet."

"Fair play," Lewis said, and went to redraw the feet on the rest of his biscuits, before any more got away on him. Myrtle's smile widened, and Jade didn't return it. She went back to her own bench, tasting blood and bone at the back of her throat as she caught the shade and bludgeoned it back down the sink with a wooden spoon.

Three.

Anyone could get tentacles.

It was still all to play for.

The *plate* was still to play for. The one that ensured you never had to do another contest again, not ever.

Three.

Ready.

Steady.

Bake.

3

COFFEE BREAK

*Look, I have nothing against coffee. I may be primarily a tea drinker, but coffee is an acceptable substitute at times. It's just ... well, coffee seems very **serious**, doesn't it?*

A little too intense.

*A little too ... **insistent** ...*

MONDAY.

So this happened today.

I mean, I think it happened. But you know, it *can't* have, right? I mean, I know, it's Monday, haha, Monday-itis, weekend regret, amirite – all that *stuff* that memes are made of. And to be fair, I was still a bit hungover from Sunday brunch, which had lasted about twelve hours and ended up with me taking Pete home in a wheelbarrow because not even the Uber would let him in.

I don't know where we got the wheelbarrow, come to think. Stace and Jay live in a flat.

I should probably take it back, but I don't remember

where I put it. Maybe Pete still has it. Hopefully he has my phone, too, because I've no idea where it is.

Anyway.

This thing that happened today – and yeah, I was still hungover. I think I'm still hungover *now*, and I've had about four bottles of Lucozade and three of the world's greasiest bacon butties.

So … hungover, in that *world's too bright and sharp and the angles are all wrong* way, like your brain being pickled has let you see the reality our beliefs are pegged on, and it's not that different, but it's not nice either. But I wasn't still drunk. The way my brain felt like it was shaking in my skull with every step assured me of that, as did the fact that Bri's laugh from across the office was like a drill straight into my cerebral cortex. So I clutched my Lucozade in one hand and my coffee in the other, and my first bacon butty of the day was sitting a bit uncertainly in my stomach, like it hadn't quite decided whether it liked the environs or not, and I went straight to my desk. I put on my headset, and I flicked the screen on, and a moment later I was talking to Mrs Joan Miller of Abergavenny about whether she'd like her next cruise to be out of Florida or Nice.

I don't remember what she decided, but she booked something, so I guess my patter is pretty much automatic these days.

But Joan wasn't what happened. What happened was that after Joan and I said our goodbyes (her telling me what a lovely young man I was and how I was very welcome to pop in for a cuppa next time I was in Abergavenny), I went to top up my coffee from the machine in the staffroom. It's one of those pod things, which kind of negates my effort in bringing my own to-go mug, but whatever. It makes better coffee than the ancient pot that used to sit stewing all day, smelling vaguely of oil and despair. I shoved a pod in and stuck my mug underneath, lining up two more pods ready to go. It was most definitely that sort of day.

And then the machine said in a smooth, featureless voice, "Error."

I stared at it. It had never said anything before, unless I counted it beeping hysterically that time when Steve had put the pod in backward and stood there jabbing the buttons in panic, trying to make it do *something*.

The machine looked fine. No flashing lights, no water indicator. I pinched the bridge of my nose and pushed the start button again.

"Error."

There was more emphasis this time, as if the machine was annoyed at me for not listening the first time, but that was definitely the hangover talking. I think. I took the pod out and checked it, but it seemed fine, so I put it back and tried again.

*"Error. Error. **Error.**"*

This time I switched it off at the wall and gave it the requisite thirty seconds, and while I did Jen came in.

"Is it playing up again?" she asked, clutching her mug to her chest. She's small everywhere – small face, small hands, small voice – and likes colour. Today she had neon green hair, a long red skirt, and a bright blue shirt. It made my hangover worse just looking at her.

"Seems to be," I said.

"Honestly, it's a nightmare," she said. "I don't even know where they got it from."

"Aldi centre aisle, knowing this place," I said, and we both laughed dutifully at my bad joke. She was right, though. There wasn't even a brand name on the thing, let alone a logo. Just smooth black plastic, and a little green light to say it was ready to go, or a red one to say it wasn't. I plugged it back in now, and the green light came on. I poked the button, and it spat coffee into my mug.

"Oh, well done," Jen said, as if I'd done something miraculous with it.

"Never fails," I said, and took my one meagre measure of coffee away with me. It felt a bit greedy to stand there feeding more pods in while she was waiting, and it wasn't like I couldn't go back. So I headed back to my desk, put my headset back on, and called Mrs Hannah Green in Donnington on Bain. She'd been through the French canals last year, and had expressed interest in one of the German cruises. She also thought I was a nice young man, and I swallowed my Lucozade burps and tried to be one.

Once Hannah had been convinced of the joys of cruising the Rhine, I headed back to the coffee machine. My one pod had been nowhere near enough to get me through a third call of the morning. I lined up my pods again, but I had barely shut the top of the machine before it said, "*Error.*"

"Oh, come on," I said, and tried pushing the button anyway.

"*Error. Wrong pod.*"

That was new. I opened the top and inspected the pod. Some store own-brand stuff, but it looked fine. And it wasn't like the machine could insist on some big-name stuff when it so clearly wasn't big-name itself. I picked one of the other pods and tried it instead.

"*Error.*" There was that irritated tone again. "*Try a different pod.*"

"I did," I said.

"*Try a different pod,*" the machine said as if contradicting me, and a new light lit up on the front. It was small and yellow and … I bent over to make sure I was seeing it right. It was a frowning emoji. I straightened up and stared at the machine. "*Try a different pod,*" it insisted.

I rubbed a hand over my face. I was too hungover for this. But I went to the store cupboard where we keep backup supplies and found a plastic bag full of unmarked pods. When I turned back to the machine, the emoji had changed. Don't tell me how I knew – I mean, the staffroom's small, but the store cupboard's at the opposite end of it to the coffee machine. I shouldn't have been able to see a detail that small. But I felt it. The machine was *smiling* at me. I stood there for a moment, considering just how bad a hangover I must have, then went and put a pod in the top of the machine.

"Good," it said, and the smiling emoji morphed into a grinning one. I shuddered, some whole-body rejection of my muddled mind, and hit the start button. The coffee spat into my mug, and the next two pods worked just fine. I put a couple of handfuls of the unmarked pods in the cupboard above the machine so they were easy to grab, then went back to my desk, already deciding that I was sticking with Lucozade for the rest of the day. I'd evidently had too much caffeine already.

The coffee was bloody good, though.

TUESDAY.

Okay, so all that stuff I wrote about the coffee machine yesterday? Total hungover drivel. I should've had more water and … I don't know, some vegetables or something, rather than Lucozade, coffee, and bacon butties.

Jen was in the staffroom with me today when I made a coffee, and it gave the little smiley face. I pointed it out to her, and she said it was a software update. Steve on reception told her – he'd had an email about it, with a link for the new coffee pods. Old ones won't work anymore, but on the flip side the new coffee is *so* good. Like, I had three cups today, when I'd normally only have one, and I noticed everyone was going back for more. Hope Steve's got that stuff on auto-reorder!

PS: Pete doesn't have my phone, so that's crap. And no one knows where the wheelbarrow came from, so I guess I own a wheelbarrow now ...

WEDNESDAY.

So today was really annoying. I mean, *really.* I'm still annoyed about it, and I'm just ... I don't know. My head hurts. I think I need a coffee. Or less coffee. Or something. It was like ... everyone I called was *so slow,* and they all wanted to *chat,* and one of them told me that they were very disappointed in me, because the last time we talked I was so nice, and I was just, *what,* I'm not *actually* your grandson or whatever, but of course I didn't say that, I just said my boss was rushing me, and she got all angry on my behalf and said she wanted to talk to them, and I had to say no, and—

Anyway. Work sucked, and everyone was hogging the damn coffee machine, so I had to go out and *buy* a coffee, and it was like water, I took it back for another shot, and I think they stiffed me with like a half scoop of coffee or whatever, and

Right, I'm back. I went to get some ibuprofen, because my head was killing me, and I feel a bit better now. Weird day, though. I managed to get a coffee in after work finished – I took it in my to-go mug, and there were a couple of other people doing the same. I think that machine makes it super-strong or something. It doesn't taste like it, but I'm getting stinking headaches after. I think I'm going to skip it tomorrow.

Thursday.

OH MY GOD I HATE STEVE SO MUCH. That dick didn't order any more coffee, or the delivery was delayed or *whatever,* I mean that's what he said, and that we were all drinking it too quick, like, *it's coffee,* of course we're drinking it, it's the only thing that makes working in this dump worth it. I wasn't even going to have any today, but after one phone call listening to some old biddy drone on about how the Caribbean was too hot and the Med was full of gigolos and Norway smelled of rotten fish and wasn't there a proper English cruise she could go on, I just *needed* a coffee.

Paula was in there jabbing the buttons, and Mike and James were there too, all staring at the machine and talking at once. Fifi had every cupboard open and Mike was trying every pod he could find in the top, and the machine had a sad, crying face emoji on it.

"What's going on?" I asked, clutching my mug so hard I could feel my knuckles creaking.

"We're *out,*" Fifi yelped, tipping old coffee pods over the table and searching through them frantically. "There's no coffee!"

"*Need coffee,*" the machine agreed. "*Need.*"

"How can there be no coffee?" I demanded. "We only got the new stock in on Monday."

"Because we *drink* it," James snapped, shaking his mug at me. I scowled.

"*We* don't! You drink Earl sodding Grey!"

"I can drink coffee if I want!"

"You said you don't even like it!" Fifi shouted, abandoning her search. "It's *your* fault!"

"What about you?" James shouted back. "You waft about with your bloody milkshakes!"

"*Frappes!* And at least that's coffee!"

"What's going on?" Steve had arrived at the door, his face tight and anxious. "Why're you all shouting?"

"*Coffee!*" we yelled, and he cringed as if we'd thrown something at him.

"*Need,*" the machine whispered, and when I glanced at it I thought for a moment it wasn't wearing a crying emoji at all, but the crying with laughing one my mum always uses.

"It's ordered!" Steve said, holding his hands out pleadingly. "It should've been here yesterday. I ordered it!"

"Sure you did," Fifi hissed. "Useless as tits on a bull, you are."

"Only got his job because Mummy's in corporate," Mike said, and raised a large mug. It had *This might not be coffee* on it, and Steve's eyes followed it as if half expecting it to come slamming down into his face. I half thought it would, too.

Then someone called from the reception, "Amazon delivery?" and we just about mowed Steve down in the rush to get to the box.

It was toilet paper, though. The sodding coffee never showed up and *my head.* It's been splitting all day. Feels like my brain's turning to soup.

Bloody *Steve.*

The office felt like my local on a match night. The air was so tight and stretched with fury that I could barely breathe, as if inhaling too much would scour my throat and airways, fill me with noxious, corrosive fumes that would turn me into a lit firework. My hands kept making fists without my being aware of it, and when Stella dropped a file she and Jen got into the sort of screaming match you expect at WWF.

Aled tried to break it up and they both turned on him, and I don't know what would've happened next if Steve hadn't come crashing in with two huge boxes of coffee pods. He dropped them on the table in the staffroom as we flooded in after him, pushing and shoving to be the first to reach the machine, half of us with our headsets still on, trailing wires and urgency.

My desk is one of the closest to the staffroom, and I was second to the machine, jabbing at it hungrily and elbowing Tej back when he tried to push in before I got my extra pods in. I only did two, though, because everyone was shouting at me to hurry up. I looked down at the machine as the smell of the coffee wafted to me, a shudder wracking about somewhere deep within my chest, and saw it grinning back at me. The emoji display, I mean. Not the machine itself. I think.

I let myself be pushed back out of the crush, cradling the mug close to my chest, and everywhere there were bared teeth and wide eyes and the faint scent of desperation.

I don't quite know what's happening.

Saturday.

I'm not hungover, which is something. I came home early last night. I was going to go out on the lash with a few of the lads, usual thing, you know, but the whole town seemed to have the same feeling as the staffroom yesterday. Like everyone was one missed coffee away from going all *Walking Dead* on the nearest barista. And speaking of them, I went down to the coffeeshop on the corner this morning, and there was no one there except a couple of old biddies drinking tea in a corner.

"What's going on?" I asked, while I waited for a double-shot mocha, because that was always my weekend treat. "Where is everyone?"

"Is new craze," the barista said, her accent heavy with the memory of an old, cold country. "Everyone crazy for weird coffee."

"What weird coffee?" I asked, thinking of the work machine. But that was just a *thing,* you know. Us getting all wound up. Too much work and caffeine, too little downtime.

She handed me my mug. "On the TikToks, you know? And the Instagrams."

"No – I lost my phone."

"Ah." She sounded vaguely approving. "All week they gives away the machines, and the pods. Everyone loves them. But is not enough. People fights over them, you know? Like the Black Friday." She snorted.

"Who's doing it? A supermarket or something?"

She shrugged. "I think is maker. I no use the social media. Is *kurva.*"

I didn't know what that meant, but I got the gist. And for some reason it wasn't the word that unsettled me. It was *maker* that did, even if I knew she just meant the manufacturer. But all I could think of was the machine at work, saying *need* with its laughing emoji.

And her coffee tasted crap. I chucked it in the bin and wondered if I knew anyone who might have a maker. And that very thought made me uneasy all over again.

I got a new phone finally. I kept forgetting all week.

SUNDAY.

My head hurts. It's raining. And I want a decent bloody coffee. I tried three other coffee places, and they're all a bloody rip-off. Spent a sodding fortune. And that machine –

the *Maker*, they're calling it, just that, no other name – really is all over the socials. Not just there, it's on the news too, even the big sites. *The Guardian*, the BBC. All with that sleek, blank black face and its smiling emoji. People are sharing tips on how to get pods, and loads are asking how they can get the machine themselves, since they don't have one yet. Everyone says you can't. They're not giving any more away, and there's not even a black market for the bloody things. The pleas from those without are oddly desperate.

*My mum has one and she won't let me use it. I **need** my own.*

Work has one but I'm meant to be on leave and can't someone help me?

I've got pods, I'll share if you let me use a machine.

My bloody neighbrs got one shes such a posh cow Im goin to take it she doesnt deserv—

Why does my head hurt *so much?*

I'm going to the pub.

Monday.

I am not still drunk.

I am not hungover.

This happened.

This happened.

So I went to work as normal. I walk, right – it's only like twenty minutes, so unless it's chucking it down it's fine. There was a bit of drizzle this morning, but the walk still sounded better than the bus. The pub was a bust last night. I had a few pints, even though there was barely anyone there. A few people came in asking for coffees, and old Tyne gave them an earful and kicked them out. It's not that sort of place. Anyway, the whole night felt a bit weird, and I didn't sleep well, so the drizzle was nice. It made me feel a bit more awake, and I was thinking about the coffee thing still. Not just the machines and pod drama I'd read yesterday, but also half looking forward to my first cup, and half thinking that there was something *off* about it, the way it had made my usual favourite coffee taste so crap. I was thinking it was some sort of new way to drive brand loyalty, some tinkering with the brew that made it sort of addictive or something, and that maybe I wouldn't have any today.

It was really quiet out. Like, *really* quiet. I started wondering if I'd screwed up my days and it was a public holiday or something. No cars roaring up and down the damp streets. No buses. Just a few electric vans purring about, sleek and black and vaguely unsettling, like sharks cruising a reef and sending all the little fish into hiding. No one else walking, either, and it wasn't a foul enough day for that. I mean, come on. It's England.

Then one of those black vans pulled up on the next block while I stood waiting to cross at the lights. No one got out, but the side door slid open, and my phone *bing*ed. I pulled it out of my pocket to check it, and as I did doors started flying open on offices and shops, and people came pushing and shoving out of the access doors to the apartments above, all heading for the van. One guy slammed into me, sending me stumbling off the kerb. I dropped my phone and caught myself before I could face-plant into the tarmac, scrambling back to safety with my heart pounding, then jumped back into the street to rescue my new phone. I inspected it anxiously, but there was only some scuffing on one corner. The message that had just *bing*ed in sat on the screen.

Shipment cnr Albert Rd & Green Way, it said, and there was a little coffee cup emoji and a grinning one. I stared at it, then looked up at the van. A mob surged around it, men in track pants and women in leggings and old ladies in dressing gowns all scrabbling to get to the door. As I watched a tall man with a big belly straining his black T-shirt shoved a little old lady out of his way. She stumbled, almost fell, then turned around and walloped him straight in the bits with her walking stick. He howled, doubling over as he clutched himself, then toppled to the ground like a felled tree. A woman in a fancy red dress stepped over him, trying to get ahead, and the little old lady hit her hard enough that I heard the *crack* from here.

"What the hell is going on?" I whispered, and looked at my phone. I didn't recognise the number. It was some wild marketing thing, right? But I still didn't get it, not until the first people sprinted past, clutching bags of coffee pods to their chests. I turned to watch a young guy with an impressive beard race down the street, and before he'd even reached the end of the block a couple of kids on e-scooters came tearing out of a delivery alley. One cut him off and the other hit him with a cricket bat, and the next minute they were racing off with the pods while he moaned and bellowed, clutching at his bleeding head.

That's when I should've gone home, of course. I see that now. But maybe because I'd been offline all week and hadn't seen it building, or maybe because I hadn't had a pod coffee since Friday, or maybe just because this is *Britain* for heaven's sake, we don't riot over *coffee* – tea maybe, but not *coffee* – I went into work.

LATER.

I had to stop writing for a bit there. I thought someone was at the door to my flat, but I think they were trying to get in next door. I smelled coffee there earlier. I still waited at the door with my heaviest saucepan raised like some frightened housewife in a soap opera, though. I wish I played cricket, so I'd have a bat, but it's so bloody boring. Once they'd gone I pulled the bookshelf in front of the door. It's a short, squat thing, cheap and nasty flatpack stuff, but the books are heavy enough. It'll slow people down, anyway.

So … work. Yeah. I was late by the time I made it to the building, because there had been three more of those vans along the way, and people seemed more and more rabid at each one. There were old men who'd pulled their military uniforms out of retirement and were trying to order everyone out of the way. Mums sending their kids in like half-size mobs. Dads pleading for someone to spare them just a couple of pods, please, how could they cope. Old women with completely merciless walker techniques. Teens charging in with the sort of single-minded determination normally reserved for concert queues. Posh retired sorts. Sharp-edged business types. I seemed to be the only one not charging for the vans, and by the time I'd skirted the second one I was starting to feel conspicuous. People seemed to be *noticing* me, and I'm pretty sure a gang made up of two teens in trainers and hoodies and a woman in a sleek suit and stilettos was stalking me, even though I had no pods.

Anyhow – our office building doesn't have anything as fancy as a reception desk downstairs. It's just up four floors to the one we share with a pet insurance company and a set of offices that have a sign saying simply *M&L Sons.* I always suspected they were debt collectors of some sort.

I took the stairs. There's a lift, but it always feels faintly claustrophobic, and I couldn't stand even the idea of it today.

The stairs were empty, just a few paper coffee cups rolling in my wake as I passed. My chest was tight by the time I reached our floor, and I had to swallow hard before I carefully eased the stairwell door open. I couldn't tell you what I thought might be waiting behind it, just that the morning had me strung tighter than the week's coffee before had.

There was no one in the hall. A few more empty cups littered the floor, but no one was jittering about the place in the grip of coffee mania, or whatever else I was scared of. I pushed through with a little more confidence, already telling myself that the scenes on the street outside had just been a slightly extreme sales and promo stunt. Black Friday type things, like the barista had said. I hurried to our office door, with its cruise ship and sunset logo stuck to the blank wood, and opened the door.

Or started to. The noise stopped me.

I've been in a fair few pubs when there's been brawls. Not in the punch-ups myself, mind – the last time I ended up in one of those I was fourteen or so. It's not my scene. But you might've gathered I don't exactly live in the best part of one of the better towns. Friday and Saturday nights feel like Roman arenas sometimes. Everyone's just waiting to see who's the gladiator and who's the lion. Plus, I grew up in a better place, but that only went as far as the town, not the home. So I know that noise. It's the hiss and growl of a hungry crowd, blood chemistry all stirred to hell with toxins and hormones and simple human fury, all the frustrations of life ready to be vomited out on some guy who spilled his beer on your trainers. It's raw and it's primal and it's unmistakable, especially when you've grown up with it.

Self-preservation is a hell of a thing. I didn't argue with the tune my instincts were singing. I did put my eye to the gap in the door though, and through it I could see Steve's reception desk, and beyond that the open plan office. Chairs were tipped over, computer monitors shattered on the floor. Ripped paper and snapped pens and the contents of drawers and bags and shelves were spilled everywhere, and as I watched, Aled sprinted across the office with his shirt torn half-off and his eyes wild, clutching a handful of pods to his chest. Jen raced after him, screaming, with a broom handle in one hand, and something roared, *"Need,"* in the background. The moan of my colleagues echoed it.

"Need!"

I shut the door very, very carefully and came home very, very carefully, dodging marauding groups of coffee hunters. Somewhere an alarm was going off, and a couple of blocks over someone was screaming, and the streets were still empty of cars. Even the black vans had gone, and when I crept back into my flat and checked my phone every social media channel was full of desperate pleas.

Where are the vans Im out Im out

Please someone must have some

Help our office is empty why are the shops all empty please my boss needed some he's freaking

I will do anything for a pod ANYTHING

IF SOMEONE DOESN'T GET ME SOME PODS IM GOING OFF

I drew the curtains. Filled every container I had with water. Checked how much food I had. Not much, really. Some pasta, some cans of beans, and a couple of sprouting potatoes.

And now here I am. Sitting on the floor and listening to more alarms going off. No sirens, though. There's not a lot of shouting outside – when there is, it's sudden and vicious and short-lived – screams for help and the merciless sounds of an attack, wordless and hungry. The radio stations are full of DJs pleading with listeners to send them pods. TV has nothing on but reruns.

And here I am.

Tuesday (a.m.).

I slept a bit, with the sofa pulled next to the bookcase.

Someone tried to get in at around four this morning, but it was just a half-hearted rattle of the handle. I think I'm alright for now. They only want one thing, and I don't have it. But eventually someone will come to check.

TUESDAY AFTERNOON.

The vans came past again this morning. I watched them, careful not to lift the curtain too far. More chaos. Still no cops, no ambulances, nothing. I tried calling 999 just for the hell of it, but it was disconnected. Not sure how that happens.

WEDNESDAY.

I think there were fewer vans today. The fighting seemed particularly vicious. The posts are dropping off on social media. What does that mean? Things are getting better?

THURSDAY.

Definitely fewer vans, but fewer people too. And the socials are down to people just posting one thing.

Need.

FRIDAY.

The power's out. I've been keeping the phone plugged in, guessing this could happen, but not sure how long I'll have it now. Not that it matters. There's no one to call. Power's out everywhere. And there was only one van today. About twenty people fighting to get to it, but they're all looking a bit weak and worse for wear, like a stag party at the end of a week in Magaluf. And the socials are the same.

Need.

SATURDAY.

Was thinking about the barista and her disdain for social media. I wonder if she's still out there, too?

No vans today.

SUNDAY.

How long does it take to starve to death? I've still got a bit of pasta left, and the water's stale but drinkable. But what about all the people fighting for their coffee? Do they even remember what eating is?

Still no vans.

MONDAY.

A week since ... well, not since it *started.* I guess that was two weeks ago, with the new machine. But a week since it all went pear-shaped. There's no power. No water. And the mobile internet's just gone down. What now?

TUESDAY.

Just ate the last of the pasta.

WEDNESDAY.

I haven't seen anyone on the streets for a while. Haven't heard anyone in the building, either. I'm thinking of going out. See if I can find some food. I haven't seen a van since Friday. Has it finished? What even *was* it?

THURSDAY.

I meant to go out yesterday, but I bottled it at the last minute. The noise of moving the sofa and the bookcase freaked me out, and I spent all afternoon crouched by the door with my trusty saucepan. Today I made it out onto the landing, but I could smell … things are bad. Things are *so bad.* How does this happen? Who *let* this happen? This *can't* be happening!

FRIDAY.

I have been out. Well, onto the landing. And I was right about the smell. The door on the flat opposite was ajar, and Mr Dejanee, who always wore these little sweater vests, like he was role-playing the Asian gent, was on the floor in his kitchen with his Maker … someone used it to kill him. I guess so they could take the pods, because there were none of them. There were cans and cans of soup in his cupboard, though, so I took some of them, and covered him up with a throw from the sofa. The Maker blinked and fizzed when I did, even though it was unplugged, and I fled back across the hall and into my own flat, leaving his door ajar. I can go back for more supplies if I need to.

I also found a bottle of whisky in Mrs Allan's flat. She wasn't there, but her Maker was, and it was still plugged in. Its smiley emoji lit up as I came in.

"*Need,*" it said cheerily, and I snatched the whisky from the little living room and ran again.

Do the machines know I'm here now?

SATURDAY.

I spent all night waiting for a black van to screech up outside and disgorge an attack force of Makers, like diminutive Daleks.

I *may* have had quite a bit of Mrs Allan's whisky.

SUNDAY (**A.M.**)

No vans, no Makers. No people, either. But I finished Mrs Allan's whisky and have a stinking hangover, and I'm going out. I can't take another day in here, hiding behind the curtains like a sodding vampire. *I'm going out.*

SUNDAY (**P.M.**)

The barista's alive. Her name's Zoya, and she almost brained me with a golf club when I sneaked into the cafe, looking for actual, normal coffee. It had been turned over, tables smashed, windows shattered, but all anyone was after was pods. I took a bottle of cold coffee (no longer *that* cold) from the ruins of the fridge, and turned around just in time to duck her swing.

"What the *hell*— Stop! *Stop!*" I yelped, cowering in front of her.

She called me something that was undoubtedly very insulting in Ukrainian, then looked at me more closely. "No phone man," she said, not lowering the club.

"Yes! That's me! And I don't – I haven't had the pods either!" Which wasn't *strictly* true, but it almost was.

"What you want?"

"I was looking for … anything," I said. "Anyone. I thought it was just me. My neighbour's dead."

"All are dead," she said, finally lowering the club. She kept her distance, eyeing me warily, and I was quite sure she'd have taken my head off with the thing if I'd made the wrong move. But all I did was stare at her.

"All?" I managed.

"Dead from other people, or dead here." She pointed at her head. "All is Maker, Maker, but there is no more, I think."

"But *how?* I mean, where did the Maker machines come from? And what was in the pods? And why? And—"

She cut me off with a lazy wave. "Does not matter. Wrong questions."

We looked at each other for a long moment, and I was aware that she was in heavy boots and a big jacket, with a bag on her back, while I stood there in my trainers and T-shirt, clutching my coffee.

"Um – are you leaving?"

"Better question." She almost smiled. "Soon city stinks. Is bad for the living."

I wasn't sure if she meant *for living in* or *for living people,* but both worked, and made sense. "Where are you going?"

She shrugged. "Somewhere with no people."

"Can I come?" I could hear the desperation in my voice as I said it, but I *had* to. The weight of the dead and rotting city was crushing me, and I hadn't even thought of it five minutes ago. Now I couldn't bear the idea of being left behind.

She examined me. "No passengers."

"I can … I can look after myself," I assured her. I had a feeling not as well as she could, but I'd survived, hadn't I?

She looked past the door at the grey sky, summer rolling toward us somewhere behind the clouds. "Get better shoes," she said. "And coat. Hurry."

I all but sprinted out of the cafe and back to my flat, not even paying attention to how the sound of my footfalls echoed against the walls of the silent street. I grabbed a cheap backpack I'd bought for a weekend walking in the Lakes with an ex and stuffed it with spare pants and socks and a couple of T-shirts, with my nearly dead phone and this notebook and a first aid kit from under the bathroom sink, then I was running back down the stairs again, half convinced she'd just waited for me to be out of sight before leaving.

But she was sitting at the cafe counter, eating a flapjack, when I stumbled back in the door. She got up and threw me a bar, then led the way out of the shattered cafe. I fell into step with her, and we walked straight down the centre of the road as we headed for the route out of town. Pigeons swung and cooed in the rubble of broken shops, and rats scuttled through the shadows, and at some point the sun came out.

We walked until it was dark, then holed up in a train station. There's no coffee here, but there are benches in the waiting room that are wide enough for dozing. Tomorrow we'll keep walking.

And after that, who knows? Who knows how far the Makers have spread, or what they've left in their wake? Who knows how long we can pass unnoticed?

But I guess we'll find out.

4

THE SHED

In the strange, stretched time of the pandemic, I lived in a small Yorkshire village, where I ran on fells that were burnt gold and breathless green in the summer, swallowed by ice and smooth snow in the winter, veiled by storm clouds and threaded with fine waterways, and burnished by cold, sharp sunrises. It was strange and beautiful and a world unto itself, remote from any other.

And in the garden, there was a shed ...

EVERYONE HAS A *THING*, EX-DCI CHARLIE MOSS THOUGHT, peering through her reading glasses at the needlepoint. Something they love. Something that amuses them. Something that feeds the soul and—

"*Dammit.*"

"Alright, love?" Percy asked, not looking up from his book. That was his *thing*. Books. The whole damn house was packed with them, and it was a fire hazard, if one was going to be honest about it.

"I've stabbed my thumb again," she said, holding the

offended digit out toward him. A fat glob of blood trembled on the ball of it.

He looked at it for a moment, then said, "Shouldn't you have a thimble or something?"

"I don't know." She dropped the whole thing – cloth and thread and vicious bloody needle – on the floor and sucked on her thumb briefly.

"Body armour?" Percy suggested.

"Probably," she agreed. "I don't think it's for me."

"No?" he said, going back to his book. "How surprising."

She glared at him, and he gave her a little sideways glance, the corners of his mouth twitching up.

"Crochet, knitting, needlepoint, and … what was the other thing?"

"Cross-stitch," she said. "But it's basically the same thing as the needlepoint. I think."

"You could try the garden again. It still hasn't recovered from when you took up vegetable growing."

"It takes so *long*," she said, slumping in her chair. "And it's so needlessly bloody complicated. Soil pH and companion planting and crop rotation and such rubbish."

"Planting the whole place out in April was probably not the best move," he said, turning a page. "Usually people wait until the frosts are done."

"It was warm!"

"It's Yorkshire," he pointed out. "And what about the bread making?"

"You can't tell me you actually think it's a good idea for me to try that again."

"Fair point," he admitted. She'd taken the batteries out of all the smoke alarms, since they were obviously just far too sensitive, but that hadn't stopped the neighbours calling the fire brigade. Not the best look for an ex-DCI.

"I can't just sit here," she said, getting up to glare out the living room window at the garden. It did look a bit rough. She probably should've started with a small patch, maybe between the wall and the shed where it was out of sight, rather than ripping up the whole lawn. That bit had been fun, though. She'd rented a machine with the delightful name of *rotavator,* and had thoroughly enjoyed tearing the whole place to pieces. It was the putting it all back again that had subsequently evaded her. She ran one hand down the window frame, frowning, and said, "This could do with some paint."

"*No,*" Percy said. "No DIY-ing. The spare bedroom still has no door."

"I'll fix it," she said, watching a rabbit emerge from the long shadows of a Yorkshire summer evening and hop toward the shed.

"I might just get someone in," Percy said.

"I need a *thing,*" Charlie said. The rabbit had stopped in front of the shed, its ears moving warily. "Why can't I have a thing?"

"You'll find it," Percy said, his voice firm. "Hopefully before you get gangrene or burn the house down, but … you know. You'll find it."

"I hope so," she started, and at that moment the shed door flew open. No, not the door – the entire front of the shed *unfolded,* and waving arms or tentacles or *something* shot out, wrapped around the rabbit, and jerked it inside. The shed folded back around it, and the garden was still again. Charlie stared at it, then carefully pressed on her stabbed thumb. "*Ow,*" she muttered, and kept staring at the shed.

"Char?" Percy said.

"What?" She had a feeling he'd said something else, but the *shed*—

"I said, have you thought more about the neighbourhood watch thing? Doing some talks and so on? There's been some thefts, you know. Lawnmowers and stuff. People would probably like a little guidance, and you never know – that might be your *thing*."

"No. Percy, have you noticed anything …" She trailed off. *Have you noticed the shed's suddenly gone carnivorous?* Percy had been his usual relaxed self through everything, including the near-house fire, but she knew he was getting worried about her persistent inability, two years after moving here, to just *stop*. To *enjoy a well-earned retirement*, whatever that meant.

"Noticed what?" he asked. "That your shirt's on inside out? Yes, I noticed this morning, but I thought maybe it was another sort of thing."

"No— Wait." She looked down at herself. Yes, her shirt *was* on inside out. She was going to have to be careful. Inside out shirts and … imagining things? That was what it had been, hadn't it? Of course it was. Sheds don't have tentacles, and sheds don't eat rabbits.

"What am I meant to have noticed?" Percy asked.

"Nothing," she said, giving the shed a last suspicious look then drawing the curtains on the fading day. "Nothing at all. I'm sorry."

He got up with a grunt of effort that made her heart give a sudden squeeze. When had he started making that noise? When had they *both* started making noises when they got up, or crouched down, or did *anything*? But then he was standing next to her, smiling as he took her hands in his.

"It's going to take time," he said. "Retirement's hard enough for anyone. And all you *ever* did was the job. Be patient. You'll find your thing."

She looked at their hands – all that faintly scaly skin and those pale brown spots, as if one started gradually turning into a lizard at the age of sixty, then lifted her gaze to meet his. "What if I don't?" she asked.

He shrugged. "Then we'd best increase our home insurance."

IT HAD BEEN a mistake to move out of Manchester, Charlie thought as she poked into the corners of the shed with a hoe. Why had they thought it was a good idea? At least in the city they'd known people, even if most of them were, admittedly, work colleagues. But there had been … She paused, watching a spider spinning frantically in the corner of the shed's window. *Stuff.* There had been stuff, all the endless ebb and flow of a city, museums and galleries and art shows and theatres, none of which they ever went to, but that wasn't the point, was it? The point was they could if they wanted to.

Here … well. There was a pub, where the conversations fell silent as soon as they walked in, and a fancy farm-style shop where she felt sure it cost her far more to shop than it did any of the *local* locals, and some strange place with a window full of crystals and dreamcatchers, the scent of incense washing out across the road from it with such strength that it made her sneeze from two doors away. And that was it, unless they wanted to drive somewhere. Which was *fine,* but it also wasn't very fine at all. She felt more observed and more *evaluated* than she had even when she'd been pushing for her promotion to DCI.

She leaned a little closer to the spider, inspecting the fine, resilient strands of its web, optimistic and fragile as morning promises. It definitely had a *thing.* She straightened up and cast a sharp look around the little shed again. It was an old wooden shack that had come with the house, gaps visible around the eaves and the old brown paint more peeled than intact. The door hung precariously from one rusted hinge, and was held shut with a stick stuck through a hasp. There was a shelf running around the inside at just about the right height to take someone's eye out, looking as if it'd collapse if the spider pulled on it too hard. The lawnmower sat in one corner, along with a clutch of rakes and hoes and various other garden tools she'd bought in her gardening phase. Some of them still had the tags on. A pile of old, cracked stone pots, left behind by the previous owner, nestled on the floor next to her own collection of empty plastic ones, and other than that, all the shed contained were spiders. Lots and lots of spiders.

She stepped back into the sunshine, out of the faintly damp scent of slowly rotting wood. There was nothing in there. No tentacles. No rabbit bones, sucked clean and shattered to release the marrow. Not that she'd really expected there to be, but … well, she had, a little. Or something that at least explained the tentacles, maybe a projector of some sort, rigged as a prank on the new residents in the village's midst. Although it would have to be a very clever one, given the rabbit.

But there should've been *something*. She'd seen it, and that had never let her down before. She saw what was there, plain and simple. She'd worked hard on that, over the years, to make sure she always saw what was in front of her, and not what she wanted to see, or expected to. That was how cases were fumbled, by letting one's head get in the way of reality.

So seeing carnivorous sheds was a troubling development. She wondered if she'd given herself blood poisoning from the needle stab, but that would've had to come on very quickly. Maybe her thread was toxic. She should give it up.

She sighed and looked around the garden, hands on hips and feet set wide and solid, a grey-haired woman with a whiff of authority ingrained in her skin. "Come on," she said. "What's all this about, then?"

She didn't expect an answer, of course – carnivorous

sheds were one thing, talking sheds something else entirely –
but a hedgehog snuffled out of the spiky-edged holly bushes,
making its way busily across the churned-up ground.

"Hello," she said to it. "What are you doing out?"

It didn't answer either – obviously, it was a *hedgehog* – but
it stopped and looked up at her with tiny bright eyes, and she
had to resist the urge to wave. Then it put its nose back to
the ground, stabbed forward, and snatched up a worm. She
could almost hear its squeak of joy as it gobbled it down.

"I'm glad someone likes the new garden," she said, and it
gave her another look, then trundled off again. "Watch out
for the shed," she called after it, and wondered if she should
call a hedgehog rescue. She was fairly sure they weren't
meant to be out in the day. But it certainly hadn't looked
poorly.

"Charlie?" Percy called, and she turned to see him leaning
in the doorway of the conservatory, tall and rumpled, the
sunlight rendering his hair thinner than she remembered.
"Do you want a toastie?"

"I was going to make a panzanella salad," she said.

"Yes. Last week. The tomatoes have started a new civilisation in the back of the veggie drawer, and they're sending out
advance forces to the cheese box, so I thought we'd get in
first."

"Hilarious."

"I try." He looked at the hoe she was still holding in one
hand and said, "Are you trying the veggie garden again?"

No, I'm checking to see if the shed's eaten anything recently,
she thought, but just said, "I thought I might."

"Good for you," he said, then added, "I've made you a
toastie anyway."

"Thanks," she said, and watched him vanish inside before
turning back to the shed. It looked at her blandly, and the
sunlight on the old, dirty glass in the one four-paned

window reflected strongly enough to make her squint. "Behave," she told it.

"There's a murder in the garden," Percy said, and Charlie blinked at him.

"What?"

"Crows," he said, nodding toward the wall that divided their property from the sheep-studded fields beyond. They were sitting on the patio, which had so far escaped Charlie's gardening efforts, and the birds were perched on the wall itself, watching them. They were oddly still and silent.

"There's only three," she said. "Does that really count as a murder?"

"I don't know," he said, taking a mouthful of beer.

"And how do you know they're crows? They might be ravens."

They watched the birds for a little longer, and the birds watched them back. One ruffled its feathers and gave a harsh, inquiring caw, and Charlie waved.

"Hi," she said.

Percy snorted. "You really do need to find your thing, don't you?"

"We have a hedgehog," she told him. "So maybe garden wildlife is my thing."

"Hedgehogs are nice," he said, and they went back to watching the birds.

The crows were still there when Charlie walked down to the garden with a bag of peanuts in one hand. She'd bought them for the bird feeder, but it had been an early casualty of the rotavator, so they'd been languishing in the utility ever since. She chose the corner furthest from the shed, ignoring the way the hair lifted on her arms as she turned her back on it, and scattered a handful of nuts on the ground.

"There you go," she said to the crows, who were still watching from the wall, then turned and retreated to the house. She needed to go and buy some cat food. The internet said hedgehogs liked cat food.

THE HEDGEHOG WAS BACK. Charlie stood at the window, chewing on the tender spot on her thumb where she'd stabbed it. It was near-dark, and she'd put the bowls on the edge of the patio, close enough to see and far enough from the shed … Well, far enough from the shed. But the silly bloody animal was evidently hoping for a repeat of its wormy treasure from earlier, because it was scuffling about in the broken earth, searching and sniffing, and it was never going to find the food at this rate.

"This way," she hissed at it. "Over *here.*"

Percy looked at her from where he was ensconced in his chair. "Char, are you watching this or not?" He'd put on some documentary about abandoned places, and she'd found herself wondering if any of them had tentacles.

"No," she said, her eyes on the shed. "You go ahead."

He didn't argue, just hit play again, and with the sound-track of a breathless presenter pointing out trees growing through the roof of an old shopping mall, she padded into the kitchen and pulled her wellies on.

The night was still when she stepped into it, windless and silent, and as she pulled the door shut behind her she had the sense she'd interrupted something, that the whole garden had the feeling of a private conversation cut short. She waited, her back to the door and one hand still on the handle, as if she might have to make a quick getaway. The far edge of the sky was still pale and carried a whisper of fading orange, and only a couple of stars were struggling out. The sheep kept up their inane yet somehow mournful calls, and somewhere she heard a motorbike.

Their house nestled into farmland on the outskirts of the village, no neighbours to overlook them, and she was oddly aware of the weight of the sky and the fields and the high, rich folds of the night creeping in to cover them, making her feel more like an intruder than ever. For a moment she considered just going back inside, not because she was afraid of the incoming dark, but because she was abruptly sure it wasn't made for her. It was made for wild things, for creatures living on the edge of humanity, and she had no right to take it from them.

Then the hedgehog gave a little squeal of delight and sprinted forward, pouncing on a worm that was barely a metre from the shed, and the garden trembled. She was quite sure of it, because she was watching carefully, and she saw the leaves on the scruffy apple trees shiver, and the leggy roses dipped and swayed, and the shed *leaned* toward the hedgehog in anticipation. Charlie abandoned the door and sprinted across the patio, almost tripping over a discarded plant pot, and the hedgehog jerked its head up in alarm. The shed bulged, and stars popped out across the sky in a sudden chorus of pale brilliance, as if the last of the day had dived for cover.

Charlie covered the ground in the same deceptively swift stride that had startled more than one bad sort in her career, her solid form not looking as if it was built for speed, but her wellies betrayed her. She stumbled on the broken earth of the garden as the shed exploded open, releasing a wild, writhing tangle of tentacles or arms or limbs or *something*, which snapped toward the hedgehog. It froze, half a worm still hanging out of its tiny mouth, and Charlie registered somewhere that she could see it so clearly because the tentacle things were glowing faintly with the captured light of distant suns, but she didn't think about it very much, because she was diving toward the hedgehog, arms outstretched.

She hit the ground on her belly and slid forward like a cricketer diving to catch a stray ball, and her hands hit the hedgehog just as the tentacles snapped over it. The hedgehog was flung across the garden, rolling into a ball as it went and tumbling into the shadows, and Charlie found her fingers tangled with something that burned with bone-shattering cold and felt like it could cut through her soul, insubstantial and almost desperately real all at once. Something screamed, high and on the edge of hearing, and the tentacles snapped away, folding back into the shed. The door slammed shut so hard she thought it might come off, and she lay there panting, staring at the thin, pale lines of luminescence lying across her knuckles.

The shed was definitely proving to be a bad development.

In the morning she drank her tea on the patio, watching the shed. It almost seemed to be watching her back from the flat glass of its window, and she wished that seemed more fanciful than it did. The crows had returned, standing guard on the wall again, and there was a strange, un-Yorkshire-like heat haze lying on the fields, stealing the blue of the sky.

"Charlie?" Percy asked, and she said, "Yes?" without looking away from the shed.

"How're your hands?"

She glanced at them. She'd told him she'd tripped and landed with her hands in a nettle, and it hadn't looked unlike it, raised bumps and welts on her fingers and wrapping around her wrist. She could still feel the chill, though, a deep ache in her knuckles that spoke of the spaces between the stars.

"Better," she said, and wondered if it *had* been a nettle, chill aside. It couldn't have been … it couldn't have been what she'd seen. She wondered vaguely if she should make an appointment with the GP, get evaluated for something. But there was a deeper, implacable part of her that was still listing observations in the same clear, cool voice it always had, and it knew what she'd seen. Because she always saw what was there. *Always.*

"Alright," he said. "I'm going to the library. I'll do a shop on the way home."

"Okay," she said, still watching the shed. The crows had come down off the wall and were picking around the garden with a jerky, high-stepping gait.

"Charlie?"

"*Hmm?*"

"Are you sure you're alright, love?"

She turned to look at him finally, at his knobbly knees showing under a pair of old khaki shorts, and his short-sleeved shirt with palm trees on it, and smiled at the faint air of confusion that lingered around him, even when he was quite sure of what he was doing, which was more often than most people gave him credit for. It had served him well, that air. The way people underestimated him.

"I'm absolutely fine," she said.

"Good." He watched her for a moment longer, then glanced at the garden. "That shed went downhill quick. Where did you get it, Poundland?"

She frowned. "It came with the house."

It was his turn to frown. "No. It wasn't here when we viewed the house, remember? I thought you'd ordered it for gardening or something. Got it installed."

"But it must have been," she said. "They wouldn't put a shed in the garden just as they sold up."

"That's why I thought you bought it," he said, and they both looked at the shed. It sat there, bland and a little saggy at the edges, as if caught out before its shed impression had quite taken. "Maybe it was a present from the estate agents," he offered, without much conviction.

"We got some sugared almonds," she said. "Not sure a shed is quite in their budget, even an old one."

"Well." He patted his pockets absently, checking on wallet and keys and reading glasses. "Never look a gift shed in the mouth. Call me if you need anything, love."

"Will do." She stood there with her cooling tea, listening to the front door close, and the car start up, then the front door open again, and the clatter of Percy getting his phone, then the door close once more and the car finally pull away. Only then did she set her mug on the table and walk into the garden, the crows watching her with cocked heads and glittering eyes.

"Morning," she said to them, and wondered if there was something special you were meant to say to crows, as with magpies. She couldn't think of anything, but then her mum hadn't had much time for such things. Her mum wouldn't have had much time for carnivorous sheds, either.

The crows watched her, not moving away, and she spotted something glittering in the dirt where the peanuts had been yesterday. She stepped toward it, and crouched to pick up a silver-painted ring with a fat pink plastic gem set into it. It looked like it had come out of one of those machines in an arcade, and she looked at the crows. They stared back, and she took the peanuts from her pocket, scattering a handful in front of her.

"Thanks," she said, then turned to the shed as the crows hopped closer, investigating the bounty. She grabbed the door and opened it before she could think too much about it, and glared in at the cobwebs and the lawnmower. "Well?" she demanded of it.

There was nothing, not even a shiver in the hair on the back of her neck, and she considered stepping in to poke around, but she'd already done that yesterday. Plus that thought *did* set her skin prickling, so she closed the door again and turned to look at the crows. They were watching her again, standing amid the peanuts.

"What?" she asked. "There's nothing there."

The crows looked at each other, then the smallest plucked a peanut up and ate it. That seemed to be a signal, because the other two started eating too, and she watched them for a bit before going to put the kettle on.

She was imagining things. Chasing hedgehogs in the night. Talking to crows. Falling in nettles. Retirement really didn't agree with her.

SHE SPENT the day attempting to right some of the destruction she'd wrought on the garden, primarily by setting up a bird feeder for the crows (the original one was bent and no good for bigger birds anyway, so she built one out of some old shelving from the cellar), and using some loose rocks the rotavator had excavated to create a place to set a large bowl of water, to serve as both bath and water supply. Then she moved stones from one part of the garden to another, arranging them into a border she could put a flower bed in, perhaps.

But mostly she watched for the hedgehog, and kept an eye on the shed out of the corner of her eye. The crows followed her, inspecting their new facilities and cawing at her in what she could only imagine was criticism of her handiwork, then digging in the loose dirt she left behind as she moved the stones.

Percy came back with pork pies and cheese for lunch, and set plates out on the patio table as she wandered over, dirt crusted into her knuckles and under her nails. The crows followed, perching on the low border of the patio to watch them.

"Good to see you making friends," he told her.

"They're better conversationalists than most," she said.

"There's been more thefts," he told her. "Mrs Singali at the library had her garden room broken into, and they took her digital radio."

"It's a right crime wave," she said, and went to wash her hands.

Charlie wasn't sure what woke her, only that she *was* awake, and seized with a sudden breathless urgency. She sat up and swung her legs out of bed, already reaching for her dressing gown, her senses prickling with the pressure of the night. Percy snored on quietly, and she slipped out of the bedroom, hurrying down the dark stairs with bare feet.

She didn't pause in the living room, just walked straight through to the conservatory and opened the door, letting herself out onto the patio. The bricks were cold and rough underfoot, and she took a couple of careful, steadying breaths, blinking into the darkness. The dawn was still a ways off, and the sky was smeared with stars, the moon out of sight, and the light pollution from the village and distant towns stained the sky at the edges.

And the shed was glowing at the seams.

She walked toward it, ignoring the bite of the broken ground on her bare feet, and looked for the hedgehog. There was no sign of it, but the crows were lined up on the wall, silhouettes of deeper, restless darkness. The shed shifted and groaned, spilling pale frosted light across the grass and letting loose little vapours that sparkled like eddies of frost. She watched it for a little while, her hands tucked in her pockets, one wrapped around the crappy ring the crows had given her. She couldn't remember moving it from her shorts pocket to her dressing gown one, but it was hardly the oddest thing she had going on today.

The shed door cracked open, just a little, and a tentacle sneaked out, patting the grass as if looking for something. The hedgehog, she imagined, or some hapless rabbit. The crows shuffled on the wall, and one croaked uneasily. She glanced at it and said, "I know. Creepy thing, isn't it?"

The tentacles paused and pointed at her, and she had that uneasy feeling of being *observed* again. She frowned at it, then looked at the empty hedgehog bowls on the edge of the patio, and the peanut-less bird feeding platform (it had taken on a lean, so she was going to have to fix its base more securely).

"No," she said to the tentacle. "You can't just go about eating poor wee hedgehogs and things."

It pointed at her for a little longer, then retreated into the shed. The door closed behind it, and the glow faded, and after a little while she went back to bed, unsure of what she was meant to do, but feeling vaguely cruel. Even sheds had to eat, she supposed. But not hedgehogs.

THE NEXT DAY she did a little Googling, then sent Percy out with a list. He came back and handed her more cat food, a dozen eggs, and a tub of raw beef without comment, and settled down with his book. He didn't open it, though, just watched her set the eggs to boil and start chopping the meat.

"Crows like it," she said.

"Of course," he replied.

"They can't just have peanuts all the time."

"Can't they?"

"I don't know," she admitted. "But it doesn't seem like a balanced diet."

"Well, we can't have unbalanced crows." He tapped his fingers on the book, then said, "The break-ins have been getting worse. Mrs Singali said her neighbour's cousin tried to confront them when they broke into his garage, and got bopped on the head."

Charlie made a sympathetic noise, checking her tablet. Raw meat was fine, apparently.

"Are you sure you don't want to do a bit of a talk for the village, love? Advise them on getting some decent locks, that sort of thing."

She looked at him. "No one needs to be told *that sort of thing*, Percy. They just need to go ahead and do it."

"It might be nice to help a little."

"I am," she said, and carried the plate outside.

The crows seemed to appreciate it, fighting over the eggs and gobbling the meat greedily, then eyeing her hopefully through the windows.

THAT NIGHT when she put cat food out for the hedgehog she also set a bowl of leftover shepherd's pie next the shed. The crows screeched and chattered at her, and the biggest, which had left an empty shotgun cartridge on the edge of the food platform among the peanuts and discarded eggshells, went and picked it up again, glaring at her.

"That's uncalled for," she told it. "Better shepherd's pie than you."

The crow eyed her for a moment, then put the cartridge down reluctantly.

"Thank you," she said, and picked it up, catching the whiff of old gunpowder. Behind her, the shed creaked in the long shadows of the evening, and she turned to it. The door crept open, and the bowl slid out, settling into the grass. It was spotlessly clean, and next to it a small daisy unfolded itself from the ground and glowed like a promise.

"Good shed," she said, and went to put the kettle on.

SHE DID the same thing the next night, and the next, and on, feeding the shed at the same time as the hedgehog, and ignoring the crows, who cawed at her and fluttered about the wall, or stalked her on the patio, trying to steal the food.

"Behave yourselves," she told them. "You've already had yours."

They brought her a thimble, which she thought was unnecessarily pointed, but she put it with the rest of the treasures anyway, which had taken up residence in a large bowl on the kitchen table. Old coins, and plastic hair clips, and shiny buttons, and pretty stones that still carried the echo of the river bottom on them. There was even a seashell, probably stolen from someone's windowsill.

One night she watched a rabbit hop past the front of the shed. The shed trembled, and she could almost feel it struggling with itself, but when she stepped out onto the patio it subsided, and the rabbit fled into the bushes. She watched it go, then topped up the hedgehog's bowls. There were currently a family of five living in the bushes, as far as she could tell. She'd built a little house for them out of more old shelving, and shored up the sagging bird feeder, and the garden was undergoing a quiet transformation. From that first daisy had come more, spreading out across the rough ground and soothing it into some semblance of order, a rumpled carpet of wildflowers that Charlie hadn't been able to find in any plant book. She'd even posted a couple of photos on some gardening forums, asking for help identifying them, and had been accused of using AI before being booted out of the groups. They were pretty, though, and at night they whispered and rustled and glowed with captured light.

There were also some things that looked like beans growing up the side of the shed, but she didn't fancy eating them. They moved when she wasn't looking.

Then came the night she woke with a start, alerted by some sound that was gone when she sat up. Percy sat up next to her.

"What was that?" he asked.

"You heard it too?"

"Yes – bloody *hell*." He stood up, grabbing his jumper. "I bet it's that damn lot that's been breaking in around the place."

"People are breaking in?" she asked, already pulling her dressing gown on and following him as he hurried to the stairs.

"Yes, I told you. They go for sheds and summerhouses, steal lawnmowers and stuff."

Charlie's heart was suddenly too fast, and the house too dark. "They're robbing *sheds?*"

Percy didn't answer as he ran for the patio doors, hitting the outdoor lights. They spilled across the table and chairs and the trussed sun umbrella, glittered on the dew coating the sleeping flowers, and didn't quite reach the shed, which lurked in darkness.

Charlie ran past Percy and down onto the soft long grass, ignoring him shouting to her to wait. The wildflowers licked her shins as she rushed to the shed, and a crow called on the wall. She glanced at it. It bobbed its head lightly, then flew at her. She flinched, thinking it might attack, but instead it landed on her shoulder, wobbling a little as she moved. She craned her head to peer at it, its sharp beak alarmingly close and its eyes reflecting the patio lights, then held her hand out. It dropped something in her palm before hefting itself away again. She shoved the prize in her dressing gown pocket, then looked up in time to see Percy reaching for the shed door.

"Don't—" she started, suddenly certain he'd open it onto a boiling mass of tentacles, and then what? Could she save him as she had the hedgehog? Or would it devour them both?

But Percy already had the door open, and he shone the torch inside, revealing nothing but the lawnmower and old pots. He looked back at her. "False alarm," he said. "It's all good."

"It is?"

"Either that or they thought our lawnmower wasn't worth stealing."

She gave an uneven sort of laugh, and followed him back to the house, her heart still feeling painful against her ribs. She didn't look at the crow's treasure until she got inside.

It was a man's signet ring, heavy and scratched, and still shimmering at the edges with fading traces of luminescence.

"The garden's looking good," Percy said the next morning. He stood with her at the edge of the patio, the wind plucking at his hair. It was cooler today, autumn whispering behind the skirts of summer and lending the scent of rain to the air.

"It is, isn't it?" Charlie said. The wildflowers were bright and tall in the grey day, and a previously unnoticed shrub was bursting with deep red flowers. She thought it was a shame she couldn't try vegetables. They'd grow well, but she didn't have any desire to eat anything that came from her garden. Not now.

"You seem to have found your thing."

"I suppose I have," she said, and leaned into him as he gave her a one-armed hug, her eyes on the shed.

"I'm glad it wasn't a break-in last night," he said. "Would've been awful if they'd done any damage after all your work."

"I don't think we need to worry about that," she said.

He smiled down at her. "Your reputation going to keep them all at bay?"

"Something like that," she said, and thought she'd have to bury the boot that was sitting by the shed, one of the beanstalks wrapped lovingly around it. It was the sort of thing that might get noticed.

And she didn't need anyone poking around the garden. One couldn't be responsible for the actions of strange sheds.

Even helpful ones.

5

NO TAKEBACKS

This tale is actually a very old one, resurrected and shaken off, polished up and told to sit nicely. It won't, but I did ask ...

And as to where this one came from, well. There really is a shop like June's in a village not far from where I used to live in Yorkshire, complete with an entire, red-lit room full of taxidermy, which I stumbled into by accident one day, and scrambled rapidly out of again. And while I didn't see a chest in there, it's exactly the sort of place that would have one ...

JUNE CLOSED THE GATES BEHIND FRIDAY'S LAST CUSTOMER AND slung the chain through the uprights, then squeezed the padlock shut. She was on the wrong side – the inside – but it was Halloween. She rather thought she wouldn't be home until the night was done.

She gave the gates a shake, making sure they couldn't open far enough to let in any stray animals or ravening children, and crossed the crowded yard with her shoulders hunched against an insistent, cold-fingered wind. She patted a large tin badger on the back as she passed, and straightened a scrap metal gull that was always tilting off its driftwood perch, then checked that the rolling doors to the back of the warehouse were locked. Not everything could fit inside, and the yard was packed with rusting farm implements and stacked pallets and old barrels and dubious garden art, and the vast wooden spools that came from the insides of rolls of power lines, all of it a little damp and grey in the early dusk of Halloween.

Satisfied everything was safe – or at least safe from people coming *in* – she strolled back to the front door and looked at the well-dressed skeletons standing on the little porch. The gingham dress on one was falling coquettishly off a bony shoulder, and the dog skeleton had slipped sideways as if exhausted by days of display. Some runaway leaves from the tree in the yard had become caught in the scarecrow's scant stuffing, bright against the creamy-white bone and pale straw. Pumpkins surrounded the little tableau, but it hadn't been cold enough to keep them fresh. They were collapsing in on themselves, orange grins turning to mouldy screams.

"Ew," June said, and let herself into the shop, locking the door behind her. She stood there for a moment with her back to it, listening to the silence. Faintly, a car passed on the road, but it could've been in another world entirely. In here was dusty, drifting quiet, full of old things and old memories and eternity. June took a deep breath, lifted her chin, and went to put the kettle on.

SHE PICKED her way through the shadowy, cavernous interior, clutching her tea and a packet of ginger crunch biscuits. It was, if possible, even more crowded in here than it was outside, the vast space sectioned off by shelving that didn't reach the ceiling and old wardrobes standing back-to-back, and islands of furniture collected in confused huddles as if unsure how they'd got there. A handful of traders rented pockets of stall space, from a jewellery-maker to an antiques restorer to a memorabilia collector, but mostly it was home to her own sprawling collection of … well, *stuff.* Hauls from estate clearances and flea market finds and things she'd bought or traded off customers. Dressmakers' mannequins and old travel trunks and '70s bar stools and mysterious bits of machinery and an entire room stacked with books in no semblance of order whatsoever.

There was also a dimly lit taxidermy room, a whole corner dedicated to lights and lamps made out of peculiar things, and racks of clothing that she gave the vague label of "vintage". It was a treasure trove. Or a scrapyard, if one listened to her friend Amy. June's own opinion varied depending on the day. It wasn't like she'd *set out* to own a scrapyard, but, well. Things happen.

She chose one of the sofas in the old-rather-than-vintage section of the shop to curl up in, smelling ancient spilled orange juice caught in the seams, and drank her tea with a book in one hand and the biscuits open on a replica Eames coffee table next to her. The silence filled her ears, and no matter how she tried not to listen, she couldn't help it. Even when the rain started, and the wind got up, still she listened, trying to concentrate on the words while she strained to hear something beyond the snarl of the weather.

She listened, and waited, and reminded herself that it couldn't be as bad as last year. Last year she hadn't been prepared. Not really. Last year had been her second Halloween, and she'd still thought (or hoped) that the first one, the one when she'd gone home, the one with the gates still locked the next morning, just as she'd left them, but with the … well, the *mess* …

Last year she'd still thought it had to be kids, or vandals, at least at the start.

She didn't think that now.

THE FIRST YEAR had been more confusing than horrifying. She'd called the police when she arrived at the warehouse the morning after Halloween, and hadn't *that* been fun. Packs of shapeless, white-suited intruders scouring her then-new (to her) warehouse, armed with cameras and markers and tablets, and leaving fingerprint dust and suspicion and *theories* ground into the floor behind them. They never found anything but a whole lot of blood that had, eventually, tested out as being maybe not human, maybe not even animal, but no one seemed in any rush to admit that.

The lab techs were very unhappy with the unidentified blood, although not as unhappy as the police. And as a certain meteorically successful, well-known and well-connected (if darkly regarded by certain less influential and predominantly female portions of the population) young businessman had vanished on his way back from a party in the area, June had had the delightful experience of being interviewed and fingerprinted and generally suspected at. She still had nightmares about answering the same question over and over.

Whose blood is it?

I don't know.

But whose?

I don't know!

WHOSE?

A good thing she'd gone to Amy's not-a-Halloween-party dinner that year, and stayed over, although it did mean that poor Amy had been dragged into the whole thing too. June had owed her a lot of wine-based lunches out after that.

The businessman was found a week later in the fells beyond town, still dressed in a Thor outfit, minus the foam hammer. He was very dead, from a heart attack rather than the expected hypothermia, and the official explanation was that he'd had rather too much to drink (this was confirmed by his blood alcohol levels) and had accidentally wandered out of town and got himself lost. June thought it was a rather exceptional effort to get oneself that spectacularly lost, and she'd also noticed a small paragraph toward the end of the article. It only appeared in the online edition of the paper, and it vanished not long after was published, but she had seen it.

A quantity of blood was discovered on the rocks below the ledge Sanders was found on. It has not been identified, and as the body had no visible injuries it may be unrelated.

June had read it twice, then walked into the storeroom and examined the trunk she'd never been able to open, the one she'd got at the house clearance that had turned her into the owner of a yard full of … *stuff*. The trunk was large, carved from old, smooth wood worn pale and lustrous by the years, and not particularly ornate. It could have held a tea set, or a few blankets, or nothing at all, although it had taken a lorry driver, June, her dad, and Amy to drag it in here. It was astonishingly heavy, and the lid refused to budge. Her dad had broken his best woodworking chisel on it before giving up.

So she had left it, sitting in the shadows, one more piece of clutter in a yard full of it. And she had barely thought about it until she'd come in to put the Halloween decorations away, after the police had gone and the fingerprint dust had been polished furiously from every surface. Now she couldn't stop thinking about the thing.

The house clearance had seemed like a great idea at the time. She had still had her pokey (if admittedly rather elegant) little shop in the centre of town when she went to the auction, enticed by the vague but interesting flyer that had come through her door two weeks earlier. It had promised everything from a homemade submarine to a collection of novelty teaspoons, but they weren't what she was interested in. Maybe if she'd had her yard then, she would've been. And then she wouldn't be sitting in a dark warehouse on Halloween, listening for the storeroom door.

But she'd had an antiques shop then, and she'd been interested in one listing only. *Dining table and eight chairs, early Victorian; one sofa, Regency; one chaise lounge, Victorian; various household accoutrements.* That was all the detail the auction house provided, plus some grainy photos that looked like they'd been taken in the poor lighting of a heavily curtained room. The starting price was low, and June hadn't really hoped she'd get it so cheaply. She'd bid on it anyway, her bank balance screaming red figures in the back of her mind. There had been a little competition, but not as much as she'd thought, and she won it right on the edge of her budget, staring at the auctioneer with something like disbelief as he announced, "Sold to the lady in the bobble hat," and moved on to the next lot.

She'd won. She'd won, and it was a bargain, even if it turned out that some restoration was needed. An absolute *bargain.*

And as far as the more valuable pieces were concerned, it really was. Even the rest of it had hardly been the *junk* Amy declared it to be when she came to help June unpack.

But there was also the trunk. She signed the purchase papers at a makeshift desk, her fingers stiff in the chill of the auction yard and her head still buzzing with the excitement of the win, and said to the small woman in the massive winter coat, "Where do I go to pick it up?"

The woman shook her head and said, "We'll deliver. That's part of the deal." She checked the papers and added, "You have to keep the trunk."

"What?"

The woman pointed at one of the pages June had just signed. "The trunk. There's one trunk you have to keep. You can't sell it."

June gave her a puzzled look, but she was mostly thinking about the delivery, and how much easier that would make things. No squeezing things into the back of her van, or hunting for someone to help her load and unload. "Sure," she said, and smiled at the woman.

"No takebacks."

"Um, no." She wondered vaguely if that was an auction saying of some sort as she wandered away to treat herself to a hot chocolate, sucking her finger where she'd cut it on the papers. As for the trunk, it wasn't like they could *force* her to keep it. It was hers to do with as she wanted now. And it hardly mattered. That dining set could make her business.

She wasn't so convinced with the wisdom of her purchase when the lorry pulled up outside her tiny shop, effectively blocking traffic through the entire one-way system in the village, and she discovered *various household accoutrements* actually meant *everything left in a six-bedroom country home by a reclusive collector with eclectic tastes and no heirs.* And she was legally bound to take it all – as well as pay a fine for blocking the road without prior authorisation. She called the local storage facility in a panic while the lorry driver went and parked in a lay-by outside town, telling her, "Overtime's on your tab, love."

The woman at the storage place said, rather apologetically, that they only had one unit free, and it was the smallest one, not much bigger than a garden shed. She suggested trying Skipton, but when June asked how much it would cost to store a lorry full of boxes and furniture the woman made an alarmed sound and said, "Hope you're loaded."

Which June absolutely was not. Her dad's garage was full of woodworking stuff, she had no garage, and the only person she could think of who might have room was Col, who said the roof to his barn had fallen in last winter and he hadn't been able to afford to fix it yet, but she could put anything she wanted in there if she didn't mind it getting wet, frozen, and chewed by rats. Which she supposed was better than paying a lorry driver to sit in a lay-by with it, but she also had to get it there over five miles of farm track, and that was met with an unequivocal *no* from the driver when she suggested it.

Defeated, she called the auction yard to beg them to take everything back, but the bored-sounding man who answered the phone just said, "You signed the papers. No takebacks," and hung up.

And that was when Amy, who'd stopped by with coffee and stayed for the drama, remembered the *For Rent* sign that had been hanging on the warehouse gates every time she drove past it for the last six months, and wondered aloud how much they'd be willing to take if June just stored a few things there until she could sell them. Which was how, a couple of months later (and just before Halloween), June found herself presiding over the best vintage marketplace in the Dales.

Or scrapyard, if you listened to Amy.

And three days *after* that first Halloween, after the finger-printing and the interviews and the cold eyes of the police, June had walked into the storeroom with a plastic skeleton cradled against her chest and found blood smearing the front of the trunk and the thin seam where the lid fitted, staining the pale wood in rusty shades. She stared at it for a long, confused moment, wondering how it had got there – and *when*, because the police had been in here as well as everywhere else – then she set the skeleton aside and poked the trunk with the toe of her trainer. Nothing happened, so she braced herself for the worst and tried the lid. It didn't budge, and the trunk merely sat there in dusty silence, its only decoration the words carved into the top: *No Takebacks*.

With no desire to repeat the whole interview-and-fingerprinting process, she carefully scrubbed the wood clean, catching a whiff of heather and high moors as she did so, then covered it up again, resolving to forget about it. Which might have worked, except for that one paragraph below the article on the news website. Still, she managed to ignore the trunk until she was sure the police were no longer casually stopping off at the food truck next to the yard for their lunch breaks, or looking for birthday presents among her taxidermy. It was spring before she co-opted three of the six stallholders to help her load the trunk into the back of her van, and she took it to the rubbish dump along with various boxes of scrap and recycling, and left it there.

It was returned by a large man in a high-vis jacket, who told her it was so valuable that she must've made a mistake, and resolutely refused to believe her protests to the contrary.

She tried selling it on eBay, but her ad was rejected for violating community standards, and it took a precious week before her account was approved again. It took Facebook almost a month to let her post on Marketplace again.

By now she was thoroughly sick of the thing, glowering at her from the back of the storeroom. She could feel it no matter where she was, like the heat from an unseen fire. Fire being something else she tried, but apparently the wood was impervious to it. A fine layer of soot, which merely served to accentuate the *No Takebacks* on the lid, was the only change after she'd persuaded Col to burn it with a bunch of his farm rubbish. He dubiously agreed to bury it for her, but a week later it was back in the shop.

"The sheep don't like it," he said apologetically, as they both stared at it, crouching in the back of his 4x4 like a dirt-caked toad.

"*I* don't like it," she said.

"Yeah, but I'm not relying on your lambs for an income. Dogs won't even go near the paddock it's in. I can't have it, June. Sorry."

So the trunk had gone back into the storeroom, and she'd covered it with a stack of old drop cloths and moving blankets, and tried to forget about it as the year ran inevitably down toward October. Maybe it had been nothing. Maybe the next Halloween would be different.

THE NEXT HALLOWEEN *had* been different, but not in the way June would have preferred. She had a feeling every Halloween would be different from the ones she had known, now.

And of course she'd tried to be rid of the damn thing again, after that second Halloween. *Of course* she had. Who wouldn't, after seeing … *that*.

She tried selling the trunk in the shop, on her website, on other people's websites. She went back to the auction yard. She even tried to find the house the trunk had come from, but the auction house's papers were apparently sealed better than MI6 files. Leaving the trunk by the side of the road with a *Free to a good home!* sign on it resulted in two people falling off their bikes when they swore it slid into their paths, plus a car crash and three dog fights.

Over the course of the summer, June chartered three different fishing boats to dump the trunk at sea, but every attempt was met with un-forecast storms, and the third boat sank at the dock while she and the crew were dragging the thing on board. She'd felt too guilty over that to try again, and had reluctantly returned home with the trunk on her mover's trolley. It was always lighter coming back, she noticed. Coming home.

No takebacks.

SHE'D FOLLOWED it last year, that second Halloween.

Not the trunk – *it.*

It had come out of the dark of the storeroom like a wraith, barely glancing at her where she peered around the office door. She'd watched it leave, passing through the front doors like they were curtains parting around it and resealing again. And while that was so utterly impossible she wondered if Amy had put something a little extra in her Halloween brownies, she knew she couldn't just let it go. Not after the blood and the police and the body on the fells. So she ran to open the gates and scramble into her car, glimpsing the creature already loping down the road with its legs long and insubstantial in the night. It looked around as she caught up to it, and she saw the emptiness of its eyes in her headlights.

It ran all the way to Harrogate with her following, the twisting roads dark and unpopulated, the high lands glittering with frost under the October moon. On the edge of town, with the Turkish Baths to one side and the Royal Hall to another, it stopped in the shadows of a tree on a little green, its head cocked, listening. Waiting.

June parked and waited too, wondering what she was

doing here, until the woman came around the corner in her black dress and zombie make-up. She was laughing at something on her phone, and the beast stepped forward. Other people had passed it, but no one had seen it. The woman did, though. She looked up, and her smile vanished. The phone dropped from her hand, and she took a step back.

"Oh no," she whispered. "Oh, not yet!" And then she ran. The beast loped after her, and June, who'd opened her car door to listen, slammed it and tried to start the engine, thinking she could chase after them, get between the creature and the woman, even run the thing down if she could.

The engine wouldn't start.

She threw the door open and ran, not sure what she could do but certain she couldn't let the woman just be run down like a fleeing rabbit. The chase was short-lived, though. A car came around the corner, going too fast for both the roads and the night. It hit the woman and the beast in one dreadful cacophony of squealing brakes, spinning across an intersection to fetch up against a lamppost on the other side. June stumbled to a stop, one hand pressed to her mouth as her stomach revolted, then she forced herself forward again, fumbling her phone out of her pocket. She thought better of it before she reached the woman, and shouted at a couple frozen on the pavement to call an ambulance. Being suspected of involvement in one death was bad enough. Two started to be a pattern.

The beast got up as she passed it, one leg hanging useless and blood painting its flanks. It struggled over to the woman crumpled on the tarmac, brushing past June. She flinched back, but the creature ignored her. It buried its muzzle in the woman's torso and tore something from her, releasing it like a luminescent soap bubble. There was a *ker-ching* sound as the bubble popped, condensing into nothing but a single bright spark before it was gone. The sound reminded June of an old-fashioned cash register, and she later read that the woman had gone from a shelf-stacker at Tesco's to the queen of a clothing empire with rather dubious (and deadly) work practices in far-flung countries, all in the space of three short but spectacularly successful years. No one could figure out how she'd managed it.

There hadn't been anything she could do after that. The beast staggered to the shelter of the bushes in the small green on the side of the road, and June backed away as more people arrived and the sirens started. She walked back to her own car, wondering if the beast was dead. Or if – and her steps quickened as she thought of it – if she could get back before it, would the trunk burn now? Could she be free of it? She had paraffin at the shop. If that didn't get it burning, nothing would.

She was almost to her car when she heard it whine, the sound small and lonely and forlorn, but she ignored it and tried the engine. It started first time, and she thought she heard another whine as she pulled away, but she couldn't have. Not with the windows closed.

AND NOW HERE SHE SAT, another year later, with the damn trunk still brooding in the storeroom, and it was almost midnight. She took another biscuit, then paused. There it was. A noise. Or the feeling of a noise, perhaps. It wasn't a sound like a footstep or a scrape of claws on stone. It was a sound felt in the deep frightened reaches of the animal mind, and June sat up, the quilt she'd pulled over her (handmade, probably in the seventies, in the most astonishing clash of colours) sliding to the floor. The lamp shed light over the coffee table, but the rest of the vast room was dark. Rain chattered on the roof, and wind snarled at its edges, and she could see her breath coiling in the dimness. Warehouses weren't known for their insulation.

She stood up and turned to face the darkness. "Alright," she said. "We need to talk."

The night regarded her.

"You're careless. You got hit by a *car*, for heaven's sake."

There was no response, just some shifting in the shadows.

"You fell off a cliff the first year. I mean, you're either careless or just plain clumsy."

Still nothing, although the silence seemed a little chastised.

"What if the police had seen you? Or, okay, they probably couldn't see you – but what if you'd trailed all that blood back here? *Again?*"

A form started to take shape in the darkness, nothing more than coalescing shadows and suggestion. Ears, long legs, a broad body. Teeth.

June crossed her arms. "If there's no takebacks, that means I'm responsible for you. And I can't do that if I end up in bloody prison, suspected of being a serial killer or something."

SHE HAD LEFT. Left the beast in the bushes and the woman on the road, and driven back to the shop, letting herself in the big gates and locking them behind her. She grabbed the paraffin from the shed out the back, and ran to the store-room, her heart loud and painful, jumping at every shifting shadow. She'd been prepared to burn the trunk where it stood, but it slid easily when she tried to move it, and she pushed it out into the yard as fast as she could manage, clattering down the three broad front steps and jumping back when the lid bounced briefly ajar then closed again. She pressed one hand to her chest as spots danced in front of her eyes, and peered around the yard anxiously. It wasn't here. It couldn't be. Its leg – two of its legs, she thought – had been badly hurt. It had been bleeding. It had been as fast as the car getting to Harrogate, but it couldn't get back so fast when it was injured. It'd take hours, if not days.

She splashed paraffin on the trunk, frowning at the carving picked out in the security lights.

No takebacks.

It had fallen off the cliff that first year, but had made it back to bleed all over her floor. It must've been horribly painful, dragging itself down the fells.

Maybe it healed really quickly, though. But no – it had still been bleeding when it got here, and still bleeding when it crawled into the trunk, which had to have been a day later at least, after the police had searched the place. It must've hidden somewhere, lying hurt and suffering in the dark, waiting. Maybe it needed the trunk to heal. Maybe it was some sort of cryochamber or something, where the creature hung in suspended animation while it recovered, and until it … did whatever it did again.

She set the paraffin tin aside and looked at the lighter in her hand. Where would it go, if the trunk was gone? Would it know, and just die out there, in the frost and the moonlight? Or creep all the long road back, still searching for safety?

It had *whined*. Just like Amble had, that time when she'd been fifteen and had come home to find the dog with his face swelled to twice its size. She'd run to a neighbour, and they'd managed to get him to the vet before his airways closed completely, but it had been a near thing. And his whine had never entirely left her, even if he'd gone back to trying to catch bees within a week.

No takebacks.

What if it suffered? Or was suffering now? She didn't

even know if it could feel pain, or was alive in any way she understood. But could she leave it out there, not knowing? June stared at the trunk for a long moment, then said a number of things regarding what the auction house could do, not for the first time. She thought about it, repeated a few of her favourites, and went to open the gates again.

She found the beast hobbling down the road halfway between home and Harrogate, one leg trailing and another bending in the wrong places. It seemed to be cut from darker pieces of the night, hulking yet insubstantial, and it looked at her with eyes that weren't quite eyes as she pulled up next to it.

She got out and opened the back passenger door. It tipped its head just slightly, one ear cocked. The other was torn.

"Get in," she said, and it whined, a small, questioning sound. She closed her eyes and shook her head, then stooped to pick it up, bracing for the weight of it. It had the same scent as the trunk, old wild land and magic as deep as the soil, and it might've *looked* insubstantial, but something in her back twinged as she hefted it up. She bundled it into the car, apologising as it whined again, and started to straighten up. It caught her hand in its teeth and she froze, bracing herself for the beast to go for her throat, or her face, or to tear away from her whatever it had taken from the woman in Harrogate. But it just held her hand delicately for a moment, then let go and licked her wrist. Its tongue felt like cold mud and she shuddered, backing away and shutting the door.

She drove back to the shop, dragged the trunk back to the storeroom, then stared at it for a moment. She didn't want to open the lid, in case ... well, in case it sucked her in. There was no point being coy about things when she'd just helped some sort of soul-stealing ghost dog escape the scene of its crime. So she made a nest of old moving blankets next to the trunk instead and carted the creature in from the car, setting it down amid the folds of cloth as gently as she could. Its legs were still sitting at ugly angles, and she'd got blood on her coat. The creature watched her with those strange eyes as she stepped back.

"We're going to talk about this," she said, and they stared at each other for a moment longer before she switched off the lights and stepped out of the room.

A rhythmic thumping started up in the darkness, drums or a heart or who knew what, and she slammed the door before she could see what nightmarish thing was rising out of the trunk or forming from the shadows. She locked the storeroom, ran across the warehouse, locked the front doors, and got herself on the other side of the gates as quickly as she possibly could. Then she locked those too, and went home to lock *those* doors, and to see if she still had some gin left from the summer. She felt she needed it.

It was only later that she remembered the sound Amble's tail used to make, whipping excitedly against the nearest piece of furniture. But that had been a *good* sound. Nothing like that … that *thing* could make a sound like that.

Any more than it could whine like a puppy.

And now here she stood, in the dimness of a new Halloween, when she should have burned the trunk last year and left the thing for dead in the night. It took a more solid form, its tail going wildly, and dropped to the elbows of its forelegs, tongue lolling and ears pricked.

"No injuries this year," she said. "It cost a bloody fortune to get the mess off the seats. What do you bleed? Permanent bloody ink? I had to tell the garage a tin of paint exploded in there."

The beast straightened up and took a step forward, head cocked. They regarded each other for a moment, then it pushed a chilly snout into her hands, tail wagging even more wildly. She shivered.

"Alright," she said. "No bleeding on things, and no takebacks."

The beast rolled to its back on the floor and offered her its belly. She wondered if monsters were really meant to like belly rubs. It seemed distinctly unterrifying.

She gave him – *it* – one anyway.

JUNE LIFTED her head and propped it up on one hand as Amy set a takeaway coffee on the counter in front of her. Warm cinnamon scents drifted from it.

"You look rough," Amy said. "Did you go to a better party than mine, then?"

"No, I just didn't sleep much," June said. "How was it?"

"*Ugh.* It sucked. I think I'm going to stop having them." Amy found a chair and pulled one up. "When I was a kid I thought dinner parties would be all fun and sophisticated, but I really just spend all my time trying to stop everyone getting drunk on red wine and arguing about politics."

June slurped coffee and made an appreciative noise. "Maybe you should go back to actual parties. Then everyone can get drunk on vodka and argue about their favourite movies."

Amy snorted. "What did you get up to, then?"

"I stayed here. Just until midnight or so, to make sure no one broke in. You know, after that first year."

"I wish you wouldn't do that. It worries me."

"It's safe enough."

"You'd be safer at home. I thought you got some security cameras, anyway."

"I did." She'd got them after the first Halloween, one

aimed at the gates and one covering the rest of the yard. There were none inside, so they wouldn't show her throwing a ball across the cluttered expanse of the warehouse, and the beast surging from wardrobe top to bedside table to armchair in pursuit. Or the moment its head turned in the middle of the chase, ball forgotten, and it trotted to the warehouse door, glancing back at her with its ears pricked. And while the cameras did show her opening the gates in the thin hour around midnight and going to her car, they didn't show the beast running long-legged into the night ahead of her. She wasn't sure if that made her feel better, because it would've been hard to explain, or worse, because that meant it was still just her and it and the trunk. *No takebacks.*

"Maybe next year you can start coming to my parties again," Amy said, and opened a paper bag, peering inside. "Scone or Chelsea bun?"

"Ooh, Chelsea bun, please."

Amy shared them out, twisting her scone and nodding in satisfaction at the jam and cream already sandwiched inside. "Good. I hate when they get all stingy on the jam." She took a bite, then waved at the entrance, talking around her mouthful. "You see the news?"

"Which bit?"

"Some crypto millionaire fell out of his window."

"Oh?"

"It was the top floor of Candle House. Middle of a Halloween party. He just started freaking out and threw himself right out a window in his Batman outfit." Amy took another bite of scone. "Landed in the canal, but from that height … Got to be drugs, right?"

"Right."

"Although there were some really dodgy rumours about him last year, too. It all sort of went away, but no one knew why." Amy made a face. "Maybe someone caught up to him."

"It's possible," June said, thinking of the sodden weight of the beast as she'd lifted it from the water at the next lock, well away from the flashing lights and hastily set up crime tape and shouts. The creature had whined as she laid it in the car, and licked her hand with its frozen tongue, and she wondered how many times she'd have to do this.

She'd taken the creature home rather than to the chill of the storeroom, staggering up her little front path under its weight. It seemed even heavier this year, and she wondered if it was the water. At least she'd taken the time to put a tarp on the back seat. She left the beast in front of the wood-burning stove, wrapped in her spare duvet. It'd be gone by morning, she imagined, lost for another year. It whimpered a little as she covered it up, and she wondered how hurt it was. Not that she could do anything about it – she wasn't quite sure what sort of vet one called for such things, but she was pretty certain it wasn't the local one who dealt with sheep and cows and the occasional elderly cat.

So she just left a bowl of water out, and some leftover sausages, since she wasn't exactly stocked up on ghost dog food, and watched the thing twitching and huffing by her fire. It must get lonely, stuck in a trunk all year. If that's where it actually was, and the trunk wasn't a portal or something. She hoped not. Having a portal to a place where things like this existed just hanging out in her storeroom was worse than having some sort of soul-collecting dog. She'd given the beast a final pat and tucked her old stuffed bear that lived on the sofa under the duvet with it. For the company.

"Bloody hell," Amy said suddenly. "Do you have a guard dog now?"

June followed her gaze to the large black dog padding long-legged through the cluttered yard, a tattered bear hanging from its mouth and its ears pricked with interest.

"That's Dorian," she said, and wondered if it was the

sausage or the bear that had been the culprit. Although she had a sneaking suspicion that naming him might've been a bad idea.

"You should put him on a leash," Amy said. "He looks like he's going to eat someone."

"Only if they deserve it," June said, and took a bite of Chelsea bun.

No takebacks.

THINGS THAT GO
BUMP IN THE NIGHT

Sometimes stories just fall out of my subconscious, and I have no idea where they came from. I don't ask, either. My subconscious is best left to its own devices. Things get weird in there …

"You do it," Bam said, nudging the hunched, scaled form next to her.

"Why me?" Gib asked. "I did it last time."

"Did not," the third member of the little group said. "*I* did, and got a shoe to the ear for my troubles, too. I'm not going first."

"Aw, go on, Moll," Gib said. "You're good at it, like."

"I am not," Moll said, punctuating the words with a slap to Gib's shoulder. "You take that back!"

"Good at being bad," Gib said, rubbing the spot Moll had hit. Even through his tough hide, the slap had been hard enough to hurt. A good thing Moll hadn't put their claws into it. Gib had seen shadows disembowelled by those claws. Moll really was very good at being bad, which made their reluctance to be the ringleader in these sorts of situations desperately trying. Then again, it was also the reason they were part of this little group. No one had ever accused the trio of being the worst of the worst. Best of the worst. Best at *being* worst. Worstest?

Gib sighed. He had a sneaking suspicion he was simply bad at being bad. His mum had suggested the other day that he might want to look into gargoyling like his uncle Fibble, but Gib was pretty sure no one was gargoyling anymore. There just weren't the buildings for it.

"Go on, Gib," Bam said. She was chewing on her tail, the long fringe giving her a rather attractive moustache. "Go on. Go on go on go on go—"

"Stop it!" Gib snapped. "Why are you even *here?* You got that internship in the cursed woods department. You should be haunting old cabins or leaving yeti footprints about the place or … or something." He wasn't quite sure what happened in cursed woods.

Bam was silent for a moment, then she lowered her tail and said, "I have hay fever."

"What?" Moll and Gib both stared at her.

"Hay fever. It's to do with the pollen. It's really hard to scare campers when you keep sneezing and can't breathe through your nose, and your fearsome screams come out more like *gnnnhhhh*."

Gib didn't know what to say. He looked at Moll in the hope the older beastie might have an idea, but Moll just scratched one ear and said, "But there's no hay in the woods."

"That's just the name. It's an allergy, is all."

"Like nettle stings?"

"I guess. But in my nose." Bam sniffed pointedly. "I was meant to be shapeshifter-ing around a campsite, being all ghoulish-like, but every time I sneezed I'd shift back into my normal shape, and one of the campers called me *cute*."

"*Ooh*," Gib and Moll said together, drawing back at the severity of such an accusation, and Bam nodded glumly.

"I mean, I'm totally cute—"

"Totally," Gib said, then realised he might have spoken a little too quickly. "I mean, in the way a hideous beast of the night realm is, obviously."

Moll shook their head and started plaiting their chest hair absently.

"Obviously," Bam said. "But *humans* aren't meant to think that. What's wrong with them?"

That drew an agreeing mumble from the other two. There *was* something wrong with humans. All the older beasties said it. Gib's mum had told him that when *she* was young, all one had to do was bump around in the night a bit, maybe do a little scratching in the walls or wear a long white dress and flee across some moors, and there'd be enough screaming and shrieking and sobbing to fuel the whole district for a month.

Now half the dens were using *electric* lights, stealing batteries and lanterns from humans just so they could see to polish their teeth, most had resorted to spooking cats to keep their energy levels up, and pretty much everyone was having to light fires to keep the elders warm despite the very real risk of scorched tails. It was that or acquire thermal underwear, and no one needed to see Great-Uncle Hut's five legs crammed into long johns made for two. Especially as there were other … appendages … that didn't seem to want to stay where they were put when a particularly gruesome beastie walked past.

They went back to staring at the scene in front of them.

"You do it," Bam said to Gib again.

"I don't want to. It's very discouraging when they just ignore you."

"*Ignore* you," Moll said. "Don't I wish. Got an eyeful of spray deodorant the other week. No one needs it."

Gib and Bam sucked air through their generous collections of teeth in the time-honoured tradition, expressing sympathy at the price paid for good work.

"Mind you, I smelled pretty good after. I mean, in a gross human way, of course." Moll looked at the plaits on their chest, frowning, and carefully undid them, messing the hair up again. "Not that I like that sort of thing."

Gib and Bam made agreeing noises, and after a moment Gib said, "One threw a jar at me once. It said it had nuts of some sort in it, but it was this weird brown paste. I …" He trailed off, then took a deep breath. His fellow fiends had been honest with him. He could tell them. "I ate it. It was … creamy. And sweet. And sort of stuck to my paws and my face and my tail, and mum shouted at me, because you know how risky human food is. Could get trapped and have to stay in their realm forever or something. But … but it was *so good.*" He didn't dare look at the others, but no one shouted *Traitor!* or rushed off to report him to the district supervisor, so eventually he looked up.

"I like marmalade," Bam whispered. "On squishy bread. Someone dropped one when they ran away on the campsite. Before I started sneezing. I wasn't going to eat it. I picked it up to throw it back, but then I *smelled* it …" She trailed off and gave a great sigh, redolent of graveyards and regret. "I just can't seem to get the hang of this."

"Wait till you're as old as me," Moll said, their ears drooping. "I should have my own district by now. I feel like I'm missing some sort of beastie gene. I get bored scratching and moaning and use their hair potions instead."

"You have great hair, though," Gib said. "Really healthy."

Moll looked down at themself. "I do, don't I? You have to

use both potions, see. Shampoo and conditioner, they're called."

"I like the shininess," Bam said. "I'd like mine to be shiny."

"And it smells of apples," Gib said, leaning over to sniff Moll's arm. "I wish I smelled of apples. Or had hair. I'm just scaly."

"You need moisturiser," Moll said. "It's a different sort of potion. For scaliness."

Gib stared at them. "Does moisturiser smell of apples?"

Moll hesitated, thinking. "Not usually. Coconuts, sometimes."

"I like coconuts," Bam said, and Gib immediately decided that he needed moisturiser that smelled of coconuts.

"Where do we find moisturiser? With coconuts?" he asked.

"A bathroom, probably," Moll said. "That's where they keep most of their potions."

"We should go to a bathroom," Bam said.

Gib *wanted* to agree, but he could already see his mum's drooping spines. "Is that a good place for scaring people, though? I've never heard of beasties in bathrooms, or hauntings in toilets or anything like that. It's usually attics and cellars."

Bam waved vaguely. "We're not getting far here, though, are we?"

"We haven't tried," Gib pointed out.

"Well, try, then," Bam snapped. "You're the one messing around. It's your turn to go first!"

Gib gave up. He *had* to go first, otherwise they'd just end up looking for shampoo and conditioner and moisturiser, and as much as he wanted to smell like coconuts, he had to at least *try*. Anything to be able to tell his mum he was *trying*.

"Alright," he said. "Stand back." And he shook out his six multi-jointed limbs, whipped his segmented tail menacingly, and dropped his belly low to the old wood floor. He scratched his way forward, his seven eyes glittering with threat and a guttural hiss rising from the back of his throat.

"Nice form," Moll said from behind him.

"Good tail action," Bam agreed.

Gib ignored them both, keeping his belly low as he slipped around a discarded sock that was bundled into a gunky ball, then paused by a bottle which still had some luminous liquid sloshing in the bottom of it. He tapped it, just enough to send it clattering out from under the bed and partway across the room.

Above him, the human shifted. "Socks? Is that you?" it asked.

Gib growled, making the noise harsh and deep, and scratched the floor again, dragging his talons across it with the whispering, deadly promise of razor blades.

"What're you doing?" the human asked. "Is there a mouse?"

Gib whipped his tail, setting the scales clattering against each other, the susurrus threatening as a rattlesnake.

"Yeah, yeah. Just don't leave the head in my shoe again. That sucked." The light clicked off, and Gib found himself hissing into the darkness. He stopped, sighed, and looked behind him.

"Good effort," Moll said. "I'd've been scared if it was me."

"No imagination," Bam said. "We can't work with no imagination. It's just not possible."

Gib knew they were right, but also … it wasn't *fair*. His mum always said how much fun it had been scaring people in the old days, but it was as if no one cared anymore. Even the beasties on the coveted kiddie-frightener teams were struggling. Humans were so scared of other humans that they had no fear left for beasties, and it wasn't *right*. How were beasties meant to fuel their homes? Their districts?

Themselves? How were they meant to keep their old beasties warm? How could they possibly do that without the humans' fear? The old, primal stuff? Didn't humans realise what they were *doing*, with all their wildly threatening, reality-filled lives? How could they be so *selfish?*

In the old days people had been generous with their fear. They'd even left out bowls of milk and bits of bread, or little offerings of herbs or coins or charms – whatever they could afford, just to keep the fright away, and that had been fuel in itself. Now most people didn't even notice the best sort of scares. Or if they did, they tried to film them on their phones, as if it was all some scheduled entertainment.

Gib stared out from under the bed at the grey shadows of the room beyond, the frustration and fury tasting like burnt sugar at the back of his throat, then abruptly scuttled out onto the heavy pile of the rug, his claws catching in the threads.

"Gib!" Bam hissed. "What're you *doing?*"

Gib ignored her, jumping gracefully from the rug to the bed, and scampered up the human's outstretched form to perch on its chest, glaring down at its face. Dimly, he was aware Moll and Bam were both hissing for him to stop it, to come back, not to get so close, not to *touch* the thing, but he was so *tired* of no one taking them seriously! This was how they lived, how they *survived*, and humans and their *self-centredness* were going to wipe out every single remaining beastie if they didn't do *something*. He reared up to his full height, flared all his scales out, and *hissed* in the human's face, accompanying it with a jab to the nose with one lengthy talon.

"Ow," the human mumbled, half opening its eyes.

Gib chattered his teeth, whipping his tail into a trembling frenzy.

"Fine," the human said, and before Gib could move, it had

wrapped an arm around him and tucked him into the soft folds of the covers, cuddling him close.

"You stink, Socks. What've you been eating?" the human asked, still sounding mostly asleep, then started snoring again.

Gib stared around in panic. The creature's heavy arm pinned him in place, and the sheets caught on the sharp edges of his scales, threatening to trap him like a fish in a net. He whimpered, twisting in the human's grip, and it made a soothing noise, scratching him under the chin. He considered it. Technically assault was against the rules, but the human started it. He opened his mouth, displaying teeth that were at least as impressive as his talons, and bit down.

"Bloody *hell*, Socks!"

Gib found himself unceremoniously ejected from the bed, tumbling across the floor in a distinctly undignified manner. He fetched up against a discarded trainer, looked at it, and promptly regurgitated half his dinner into the foot bit. In the bed, the human groaned.

"I'm sending you back to the bloody shelter, you little—"

Gib scuttled away as a pillow sailed toward the trainers, then looked around at Moll and Bam, who had emerged from under the bed and were sitting near the door, watching with interest. Moll beckoned to him, long fur swaying luxuriously, and Gib looked at the human again, then sighed. They may as well. He wasn't getting anywhere here.

THE BATHROOM WAS JUST down the hall, orange light from the street outside giving it an unearthly glow that Gib found quite reassuring. He put his paws on the edge of the tub and looked in at Moll, who was sorting through bottles.

"No apple," they said to Bam.

"Aw."

"There's rosemary and apricot, though," they added, popping the bottle's lid open and sniffing the contents. "I'm going to try it. Want some?"

"Sure," Bam said, and between the two of them they got the taps running, water splashing cheerily across the bottom of the tub. Gib clambered in cautiously, his ears back, and paddled through the swirling currents. It was very pleasant, the warmth on his scales and the whiff of fruit and the soft pale bubbles popping against his scales. Much nicer than the cold stream he usually bathed in.

Bam was sitting directly under the tap, spluttering in delight as the water plastered her fine dark hair to her body and bounced cheerily off her skull. Her drenching shrank her by half, and Gib had a momentary sense of loss, as if some vital part of her had been washed away.

Moll pointed at him. "Have a look by the sink for moisturiser."

"What does it look like?"

"It depends. A tub or a bottle, usually."

"Alright." Gib went to investigate, opening the first thing to hand. It smelled a little greasy and not like coconut at all, but he put some on his tail anyway, then moved on to a tube that reeked of mint. It was gritty, which seemed unhelpful unless he wanted to polish his scales, so he dropped it in the sink and stood up on his back four limbs to check the cupboard behind the mirror. It contained a treasure trove worthy of an alchemist, pots and tubes and bottles in all sorts of sizes and colours and materials. He stared at them, then shrugged and picked one at random. Nothing was shouting *very attractive coconut scent*, so he may as well try them all. He dribbled some pale oil onto his paws while behind him Moll pulled Bam out of the stream of water.

The older beastie tipped shampoo over her head generously, then added, "Close your eyes."

Rather belatedly, as it happened.

"*Ow!*" Bam yowled. "*Ow, it burns!*"

"Stop making a fuss," Moll said, upending the bottle over their own head. Bam was still screeching, and now Moll paused. "It is a bit strong," they admitted.

"*Ow ow ow!*" Bam wailed.

"*Ow,*" Moll agreed, dropping the bottle and slapping their paws to their eyes. "Oh, *ow!*"

Gib stared at them, his third pot of cream in his paws. This one smelled vaguely botanical, but the coconut was remaining elusive.

"How do I find the coconut?" he shouted at Moll over their screams. "Nothing says coconut!"

"Get the conditioner!" Moll shouted at Bam, ignoring Gib as they waved their paws blindly around the tub. "Maybe the conditioner will help!"

"*Coconut!*" Gib shouted. "*I want coconut!*"

"*Sod your coconuts!*" Bam bawled back, as her fumbling paws found a bottle and she waved it about wildly. "This is *poison!*"

Moll threw themself to the bottom of the bath, squirming toward the taps while bubbles and froth churned up around the two beasties, rising like the tide. "Make it stop! *Make it stop!*"

Gib threw the pot onto the floor, scattering cream everywhere, and leaped into the tub. He grabbed the shower head and had a moment's confusion while he tried to first find the taps under the still-rising foam, and then figure out how to redirect the water to the shower head. Finally his scrabbling paws discovered a lever, and he slammed it across, water blasting out of the shower head so violently he had to wrestle it into submission, almost toppling over backward. But finally he had it under control and he aimed it at Moll and Bam, pinning them with a heavy jet of water that sent the shampoo and conditioner sluicing off them and sudsing wildly out of the bath and up the walls. They both shrieked, partly in relief and partly in alarm, and as they did so the door to the bathroom flew open and the light came on.

The three beasties froze, two hairy and soaking wet, one scaled and covered in a generous application of every cream and lotion he'd found in the bathroom cabinet. The water kept running, drumming across the walls and sluicing across the floor now that Gib had rather lost concentration regarding where he was pointing it.

The human also froze. It wasn't looking directly at them, but rather at the phone in its hand. "What," it started, uncertainly, and tapped the mobile, still not looking past it. "What the hell are you? What've you done to my *bathroom?*"

"It's filming," Moll said, peering over the side of the tub with their hair rumpled into mohawks. "We can't let it film."

The human shifted its stance slightly, angling the phone toward Moll. "Did that thing *say* something? What *are* you?"

"Thing," Bam said, her eyebrows drawing down furiously. "*Thing?*"

"The light's too good," Moll said, giving Gib a wide-eyed look. "This close, the camera'll be able to see us. *Film* us."

"Damn right I'm filming," the human said. "This is the newest iPhone, too. *Super* clear. Bloody hell, this is going to go *so* viral! What *are* you? Some sort of genetically engineered cats or something?" The human paused suddenly, and finally lifted its gaze from the phone, looking around the bathroom. "Socks?"

Gib didn't exactly think. He was just so *annoyed.* So *frustrated.* Here this human was, faced with real, actual beasties of the sort that had haunted every human nightmare for millennia, and it was worried about *viruses?* And accusing them of being cats? Or eating cats? He looked at Bam, who was trying to make herself look fearsome, but mostly looked like a drowned mop; and at Moll, who was clutching their chest hair so hard they were going to pull it out, and then he simply turned and aimed the shower straight at the human.

Straight at the phone.

The human was still looking for the cat, and the blast of water took it unawares. It gave a strangled, spluttering shriek, and dropped the phone, which vanished into the wash of suds and water on the floor.

"Nooo!" the human shrieked, and dropped to its knees so hard all three beasties winced. It didn't seem to notice, though, just paddled wildly about, hands searching the foam for the phone. And as it did, Gib felt it. *It.* A wash of horror. It wasn't the same as fright, not really, but there was a familiar, twisting sickness to it, a swirl of disbelief and an aftertaste of terror, and his scales rose of their own accord, clattering with delight.

"Ooh," Bam said, scrambling onto the edge of the bath and shaking herself off, staring at the wailing, frantic human. "Oh, *Gib,* did you feel it?"

"Go," Moll said.

"But did you feel—"

"Go!" the older beastie ordered, their voice unaccustomedly sharp, and they went. There was no disobeying that tone. All three fled around the sprawling, sobbing human as it pawed its way across the floor, wailing as if it had lost a limb rather than some screen-thing. It was too panicked to even look at them as they passed, and Gib had never seen any of the creatures in such a state before.

It was almost enough to make a beastie feel moderately bad, but they didn't pause in their head-long dash for the security of the bed, just in case the phone was resurrected unharmed and the video restarted. Moll led the plunge into the shadows, into the soft spot where the world twisted into pockets full of lost dimensions, and they dived sleekly into the dim, familiar safety of home, unfolding around them like a faded bloom.

Only it wasn't so faded now. Or so dim. Or so cold.

They stopped on the threshold, hesitating, staring around. It *was* lighter. And the air wasn't freezing their wet, sudsy skins – or not as much as they might've expected. They looked at each other, no one wanting to be the first to say it, until Bam whispered, "It's different, isn't it?"

"Yes," Gib whispered back, as if to talk louder might scare off the change. "What did we do?"

No one answered at once, all waiting to see if the new warmth might desert them, the lighter edges to the world deepen to shadow again. They didn't, though, and finally Moll answered.

"We *scared* the human," they said, with something like awe. "I never thought of that. Of trying something new."

"It worked," Bam said, and clutched Gib's arm. "You made it work!"

Gib tried to understand it, but couldn't. The scratching under the bed and in the walls, they were *classics*. They were the very definition of scary. Everyone knew that. How was a *shower* scary? Was the human hydrophobic? "But how? *How* did it work?"

He and Bam both looked at Moll, who ran their talons through their damp hair carefully, working out some knots while they considered their answer.

"I think it was the phone," they said finally. "The phone being wet scared it."

"How?" Bam asked. "It's just one of those screen-things. It's not like we drowned its cat or something."

"I think," Gib started, then stopped again, holding a paw up so that no one talked over him while he tried to find the words. Eventually he continued. "Maybe humans can only experience the world through the phone," he said. "Did you see? It was looking at the screen rather than us. So maybe we blinded it."

Bam plucked at her tail. "That feels a bit harsh. Blinding it."

"I don't think we *blinded* it," Moll said. "Not really. It could still see. But when we took away its screen, it had to look at the world directly. Maybe *that's* scary."

The other two made doubtful noises, but didn't disagree. Gib thought it sounded very tenuous indeed – what sort of creature couldn't look at the world directly? But there was no denying the surge of fright that had washed around them in the bathroom. Or the creeping brightness in the district.

"Whatever it was, it worked," he said. "So what do we do now?"

"I suppose we try it on someone else," Moll said. "See if it works a second time. Test the hypothesis, like."

Bam sniffed her tail. "The same again? Perhaps we can find some apple this time?"

"And coconut," Gib said, and smiled a toothy, beastie smile, while a world away a human clutched their dripping phone to their chest and wished they'd taken out the insurance, and mourned the loss of the video full of beasties. Because if there was no video, nothing had happened. How could it have?

Nothing existed unless someone could post it online.

Not really.

7

THE NAETHANKYE
PRESERVATION SOCIETY

Despite the fact my dad was from Scotland, I had never actually visited until last year (other than going to Edinburgh once, but I'm not sure that counts). But once there, I fell completely in love with the isolated fishing villages and steep-sided hills above them, the cliffs and trails and crofts and castles. And, of course, the lochs.

So many lochs, hiding so many things ...

"ITEM NUMBER FORTY-THREE ON THE AGENDA," CAMILLE SAID, tapping her empty mug gently on the tabletop, less for the care of the stolid souvenir cup than that of the flimsy folding structure beneath it. Despite her caution, the spindly-legged table wobbled threateningly enough that her pen rolled away to lodge under the edge of a plateful of crumbling short-bread. The much-depleted association did own a gavel, but Camille was fairly sure its use would not only be excessive, given the size of the group these days, but would also contribute to the precariousness of the furniture when things inevitably got a little heated. Besides, she had a sneaking suspicion her predecessor had used it for flattening chicken breasts. Or she hoped they had. It retained a faint whiff of death and poultry that pounced on her every time she walked past the shelf where it lived, next to the Naethankye pebble in its padded case, and she didn't like to think of any other explanation.

"… *forty-three* …" Mike mumbled, scribbling frantically in his notebook. Camille had never been quite sure how he could write so much yet somehow still miss half the events of every meeting. It was a skill.

"The canal," Abigail said. She had her arms crossed over her flat chest, heavy-framed glasses pushed up into a thick tangle of hair. "We need to protect it."

"We need to clear it," Rob said, helping himself to another hefty wedge of tea loaf. "Drain it, dredge it, whatever."

"No," Abigail and Jeff said together.

"Think of the wildlife," Jeff said, tapping one luminously purple nail on the table.

"I am," Rob replied. "That's why we need to get on this as soon as possible." He looked at Camille. "I'm right. You know I am."

She retrieved her pen, rolling it between her fingers and trying to ignore Mike's frantic scribbling. He was sweating, drops standing out on his forehead and rolling gently down his nose to splatter on the page.

She clicked the pen a couple of times. "*Hmm.* Well, it can't continue as it is."

"… *dredge* …" Mike whispered, not looking up.

"We can't drain it," Jeff said. "It'll destroy the whole ecosystem."

"Oh, and it's not being destroyed already?" Rob demanded.

Abigail leaned forward, sliding her hands across the table and making it lurch. She ignored the sloshing of the half-empty mugs (printed with the Loch Naethankye logo and rejected from the souvenir shop because the ink had smeared into alarming forms), and looked at Camille rather than Rob. "We just have to keep people away from it for a bit. It'll sort itself out, surely."

"That seems a little optimistic," Camille said.

"Well, it got itself *in*."

"She's right," Jeff said, adjusting his hair. It was particularly glossy today, and Camille wondered what shampoo he used. Something too expensive for her tastes, no doubt. "We should at least give it a chance," he added. "Not just rush in with something as drastic as dredging."

"And how d'you propose to keep people away, then?" Rob asked. "Every muppet and their damn dog walks along the canal, *all* the time. It's a bloody highway of Lycra and whatever oodle everyone's got at the moment. Labradoodle? Cavoodle? Zippy-bippy-boodle?"

"We've got the authority to shut the path and waterway down," Jeff said. "We can cordon it off, say it's an environmental hazard. I mean, it is, in a way."

Abigail nodded so enthusiastically her glasses slipped onto her nose. She pushed them back up into her hair. "Exactly. We can say there's been a … a bloom of toxic algae. The village council won't object." She said it as a statement, but still kept her gaze on Camille as she spoke, eyebrows raised.

Camille didn't answer straight away, still rolling the pen in her fingers. The little back room of the hall was warm, the shelves lining one wall jumbled with cans and jars and coils of old rope, bits of driftwood and lost umbrellas and nets used for scooping rubbish out of the water. A tattered leather sofa nestled under the window, and an armchair with a comfortably sagging seat was wedged into a corner by the shelves. A solid old coffee table sat between them, scarred with mug rings and spills and age. Cosy, but no good for meetings unless at least one of them sat on the floor, which is why they squeezed the folding table and a clutter of matching chairs into the limited floor space every time. It hardly befitted the gravity of the situation, but it did the job.

"People won't listen," Rob said. "People never listen. And we can't risk that."

Into the silence that followed, Mike whispered, "... *spring* ..."

"Any other action is going to be *so* major," Jeff said. "Not just for the environment, but generally. I mean, dredging? Draining? Do we even have the budget for that?"

"We used to," Rob muttered. "Bloody tight—" He cut himself off with a shake of the head. "Anyway. Fair point. *Do* we have the funds, Cammie?"

Camille grimaced. Rob was right, they *used* to have the budget. But memories were short and those of politicians, even volunteer ones, even more so, and each successive council election seemed to result in the association being carved a little thinner. To be fair, they hadn't needed all that much for years. Decades. *Multiple* decades. It had been quiet, and a good thing too, considering how membership had dropped off, leaving just the five of them, the stone, and some half-hearted traditions. But that was all the more reason they should be granted the funds they needed when they needed them. "I might have to knock on a few doors with my hand out," she said aloud.

"Shameful," Rob said, taking a large bite of tea loaf. "*Shameful.*"

"So's what you're doing to that cake," Abigail said, grinning. "You know it's vegan?"

Rob made a rude gesture at her with no heat behind it, and took another, larger bite.

"Well?" Jeff asked. "I've got to get back to work. What's the decision?"

Camille tapped her fingers together, her eyes straying to the framed photos on the walls, the rise and slow decline of the Naethankye Preservation League captured first in stiff black and white, all heavy moustaches and huge skirts, through sepia kilts and waders, and into washed-out, bare-foot colour. The League had been going long before the advent of photography, of course, had been *needed* from long before, and the steady shrinking of numbers filled her with a sneaking unease and undefined shame, as if the whole thing were her fault, even if she'd actually *added* Jeff after she'd been made chair. Five members still hardly constituted growth, though, and she had to admit to a certain relief that all the photos were digital now. She hadn't bothered to print any out for years.

"*... funds ...*"

"It's going to take some time to get the dredging organ-ised," Camille said. "Let's cordon it off in the meantime. If it looks like that might do the trick, we can skip more extreme measures."

"I'll take a bet on whether we lose a dog or a kid first," Rob said. "Who's with me?"

Jeff got up, taking his high-vis jacket from the back of the chair. "I'll get some barriers and caution tape from work. I can be set up before the end of the day."

"I'll make some signs," Abigail said. "Are we going with algae bloom?"

"Yes, let's do that," Camille said. "Jeff, call us when you've got everything and we'll meet down there."

"Will do."

Camille tapped the mug lightly on the table again. "Meeting adjourned." She didn't move as Abigail, Jeff, and Rob got up, folding their chairs and wedging them behind the sofa. Jeff hurried out first, pulling his jacket on over a rather nice cardigan and low-cut top. It should've looked ridiculous over his heavy trousers and work boots, but somehow it didn't. Nothing ever looked ridiculous on Jeff, and Camille wondered sometimes if he had fae blood in him. Surely no human could have cheekbones like that. Abigail followed him, already on her phone, long skirts swirling around her, and Rob looked at Camille.

"You want help tidying up?"

"I can manage," she said. "You'll be late for work."

He nodded, but didn't move for the door. "You know the cordons won't be enough."

"It depends what it is."

"Well, that fishing club from Inverness are never coming back. And we still don't know who those trainers we found floating about belonged to."

Camille rubbed the back of her neck. "I know," she said. "But those two have a point. Zero tolerance is a rather outdated approach."

"They'll have us setting up a petting zoo for flesh-eating conger eels next."

She frowned. "Aren't all conger eels carnivores?"

"My point exactly."

"Well, I don't think it's conger eels, and you know the council seems to have rather sidelined us. All the money's going to trying to attract more tourists. So it may take me some time to make them see sense, and we may as well use that time to try something new."

"I'm betting it's a dog first," Rob said. "Hope it's a yappy one." He turned and headed out, a solid, red-faced man with a permanent scowl that didn't reach his eyes.

The room fell silent in his wake, until Mike whispered, "... *bloom* ..."

Camille looked at him. "What do you think?"

He didn't answer, his grey head bent over his notepad, the pen digging into the paper. "… *meet* …"

Camille left him to his scribbling and went to wash up the mugs.

CAMILLE CAME BACK from washing the dishes to discover Mike had finally finished his notes and slipped out of the room without saying goodbye. That was quite usual for him, so it was impossible to tell if he was happy with their plan of action or not. Not that it mattered. They didn't have an awful lot of choice right at the moment. She locked the door and headed for the canal, not waiting to hear anything from the others. As chair of the League she was paid a rudimentary retainer, and that combined with some varied freelance work around the village meant she didn't have a job she needed to be at right now. Or not one more important than this, anyway, and for all she was willing to *try* not destroying the whole canal to deal with one pesky invader, she did share Rob's doubts that this could be handled so easily.

The path to the canal was well-worn and well-kept, but not signposted. The tourists all came for the lake anyway, and whenever some newcomer got fancy ideas in their head and demanded, over the objections of the more established members of the community, that footpath signs were put up, they disappeared again rather swiftly. The signs, not the newcomers. Mostly, anyway. The locals needed their space to breathe, particularly over the summer season, and there was no reason to encourage tourists to wander. They were best kept to the ice cream vans and souvenir stalls of the lakefront, where they could wander about aimlessly and exclaim over the fudge selection and the way the mountains heaved out of the water, encircling the loch greedily and barely leaving enough room for the clustered, whitewashed buildings of Naethankye at its edge.

The day was a little gloomy and overcast, the trees already stripped of their leaves by the encroaching winter, everything feeling damp and trapped between the hostile wilderness of slopes and streams. Even so, Camille encountered two women jogging bouncily back toward the lake, neon shoes flashing in the dull light, as well as a young man wobbling along on a bicycle, a small girl perched on a seat behind him and an even smaller one swaddled in a blanket and stuck somewhat unceremoniously in a basket on the handlebars. They were all wearing helmets, even the tiny child, and the little girl on the back sang tunelessly as they passed.

"*... and the monsters shouted jump, and the baby took a big old—*"

"Charlotte, *enough*," the man said. "Can't we sing itsy-bitsy spider or something?"

"Only if it's the one about the spiders that eat your brains," the little girl said, and then they were gone down the path, no doubt bound for a spot of duck-feeding at the loch's edge, or a diversion to the playground, which had reached a hundred twenty-three days without incident. Camille expected that wouldn't last much longer. Clear one faery ring from under the slide, and up pops a portal below the swings. It used to be a full-time job, someone checking every morning, but as with everything else there had been downsizing. Now she only went around when she knew there was a problem. She didn't *want* any kiddies caught up in a dimensional web, obviously, but one also needed to be fairly compensated for one's efforts. She couldn't be carrying out pre-emptive checks for free. She had a mortgage to pay and salamanders to feed, just like everybody else.

The canal came into view around a turn in the path, the

threadbare trees peering anxiously at their reflections in the still green water. A towpath ran down both sides, and the lock that led to the lake was closed, fat retaining walls stained with moisture and algae. There were locks all along the extensive, wandering length of the canal, stepping it gently down from their lake to a wider waterway that led to the distant sea. And that was the problem, she was sure of it. The sea was distant, but not unreachable. It was still strange that something had made its way so far upriver, but it certainly wasn't impossible, and she had no other explanation for what was happening.

She strolled down the towpath, hands in the pockets of her jacket and her scarf pulled snugly up to her chin, eyes on the water. It gave nothing away, no hint of the treachery beneath the surface, and she could almost have fooled herself into thinking there was nothing to be seen at all, until a scream broke the day's calm, drifting around the bend of the canal ahead of her. The scream was accompanied by the frantic yapping of a small dog, some impressive swearing, and finally a shriek of rage that turned her stroll into a jog.

Camille rounded the bend to find waves spreading across the canal, jagged and urgent, and a woman in a pink jacket clutching a small, dripping, and ferociously snarling dog in one arm, brandishing a cane in the other.

"*You get back here!*" she screamed at the water. "*You get back here and face me like a person!*"

The waves subsided into ripples, and nothing surfaced to answer her challenge. The woman leaned over the bank and jabbed the cane ineffectually at the canal, her hair dishevelled and a rain hat threatening to slip off her head.

"*Coward!*"

"Is everything alright, Nina?" Camille asked, and the woman straightened up, glaring at her.

"You," she said, shaking the cane at Camille, then back at the water. "What d'you call this?"

"A canal?"

"*It almost ate Mr Mo!*"

Camille, who had once been nipped by Mr Mo for the temerity of plucking him out of a nest of flower imps, made as sympathetic a noise as she could manage. "We're coming up with a plan."

"I have a plan for you. Get the damn thing out!"

"It's not that easy. Environmental considerations and all that."

"Bollocks," Nina said, with a forcefulness that suggested she would've had a stronger choice of words if not for the delicate ears of Mr Mo. "What about consideration for the village?"

"I agree. But here we are. And it's not doing any harm. Well, not much, anyway."

"It will."

Camille agreed, but she made a doubtful noise anyway. One had to keep up a certain public face, after all. "Most of us are fairly used to looking out for ourselves. I don't think anyone's really going to be taken by surprise."

Nina sniffed. "Wait till one of your precious tourists get taken. *Then* you'll have to do something."

"*Not* my tourists," Camille said, the public face slipping rather rapidly.

The older woman lowered her cane. "I know. Are you still struggling with funding?"

"All the budget's going on spot-the-monster tours, and no one cares about what's happening behind the brochure."

"It does seem a bit off, that."

"A bit? Planting bloody footprints on the beach and shadows on the sonar, just to keep the tourists coming, rather than looking after Naethankye?"

"True. They should be more worried about risks to help-less little old ladies and their innocent dogs," Nina said without a trace of irony, despite the fact Camille could clearly see the blade extending out of the side of the cane and running its full length, like an overgrown chef's knife. Nina examined the dog, who was panting and trembling with equal degrees of enthusiasm. "I need to go and get Mr Mo dried off. He's in shock."

Camille nodded and watched Nina stride off, her stockings creasing above her sensible shoes, then looked at the canal. "Picked the wrong one there, didn't you?"

The water gave back a sullen sort of agreement, and she was quite sure she was being watched, even if nothing showed itself. She tapped her fingers on her legs, thinking about it, then turned and strolled toward the lake-end lock. There was a house there, all old thick stone and deep-silled windows, a remnant of when the canal had been busy with trade and the lock keeper had been on call at all times. In summer the cottage was overgrown with climbing roses, its window boxes and compact garden a riot of blooms that drew in all the bees (and also hid a well-stocked if not entirely *safe* herb garden), but now it was as dull as the surrounding woods, slowly sinking into hibernation.

Camille let herself in the front door, the lock house still warm with the morning's fire, and went to the freezer. A little digging rewarded her with a chicken carcass she'd been saving for some unplanned Sunday dinner, and she took it with her as she went back outside, climbing to the lock gate, where she had a little vantage point of the canal. The water was opaque and blank, the ripples long since died away, plus a light rain had started and was pocking the surface, making it even more impossible to see into the depths.

"Come on, then," she muttered, and flung the chicken into

the middle of the water. The ducks had rather sensibly made themselves scarce, she noticed.

The chicken landed with a splash, vanishing below the surface then bobbing back up, rolling over gently, fat and pale. Nothing happened for a moment, and she waited. She needed to know what they were dealing with. The best description she'd had so far was also the least reliable, coming as it was from a gentleman called Davy, who admitted he might've had a tipple or two before staggering home along the canal. The landlord of the local pub (not the picturesque tourist one, the one two streets back with a permanently broken window and Australian beer posters for decor) had confirmed it had been more than one or two, casting Davy's recollections in a dubious light. According to him, the canal had been invaded by Cthulhu themself, but Camille doubted that. A small backwater in a remote Scottish glen was hardly going to be ground zero for the return of the Great Old Ones. More likely it was a confused kelpling, or—

"Hello," she said softly. Something was happening, a swirl of movement, a deepening or lightening of the water, as if the currents had come to life. There then gone again, and she waited, the rain ticking softly on the shoulders of her jacket and dampening her hair.

Then, without warning, the water exploded into a boiling froth and a whirlpool opened below the chicken. It vanished, sucked down faster than Camille could devour a decent eclair, and the water bubbled back up again, leaving the surface disturbed but empty.

She watched for a little longer, but nothing else happened. She hadn't got a good enough look to be sure of what it was, and she'd just lost her Sunday dinner. Or *a* Sunday dinner, since admittedly she couldn't remember how long ago she'd bought it, and had really had no plans for it even at the time. But still. It was the principle, and expenses weren't going to cover it, either. She sighed and went back inside to have a cuppa. So much for that.

THE DAY DID NOT IMPROVE. She armed herself with a large cup of tea and a box of Jaffa Cakes, and methodically tried calling every member of the Naethankye village council and tourism board, which were one and the same. Her calls were either not answered, or the answers were various versions of *we'll raise it in next month's meeting*, or, in the case of the treasurer, she was told that as they were heading into the slow season any new projects would have to wait until summer, when they had more funds available. Camille didn't bother pointing out that they'd have *less* funds then, due to a winter without much tourist income, or that a mysterious and clearly hungry entity in the canal was hardly a *project*.

The point wasn't the funds, after all. The point was that no one cared what happened outside the loch. The loch and its tourists were everything, and nothing moved so slowly as a village council run by local businesses, all trying to keep everyone's pockets lined, particularly their own. This was no different to every other request, for new bus shelters or footpath repairs or patches in the library roof. Behind the perfect shopfronts along the lakefront, the picturesque, cobbled lanes and cute wooden benches were potholes that swallowed bikes, and leaking water pipes that caused sinkholes, and rubbish collections that only ran once a month at the best of times.

So, no. She wasn't surprised at the refusal. But to make matters worse, Jeff called to tell her his boss would neither let him requisition cordons and barriers, nor leave early.

"I'm so sorry," he said. "And I don't understand it. This is important!"

"That's alright," Camille said. "I think you'll get your preference of leaving whatever it is undisturbed. No one wants to give us any funding to do anything."

There was a pause, then Jeff said, "I mean, I'm happy about that, but I thought we had authority to do this sort of thing. That's what the town records say. The Naethankye Preservation League can demand whatever's needed to get the job done."

"Things change," Camille said, hearing the weariness in her own voice. "People forget."

"But what do we do, then? We can't just leave it there. All I wanted to do was make sure it wasn't hurt. I didn't mean it should *stay*. It really might try to eat someone."

"We'll come up with a solution."

"Really?"

"Sure. And in the meantime we can still hang Abigail's signs. Give people a head's up."

Only she found out, fairly quickly after hanging up, that Abigail hadn't been able to print the signs, because she usually used the printer at the local tour office where she worked. But they had suddenly decided she was using too much paper and ink, and causing too much wear and tear to the printer, even when she offered to pay, so that was that.

Camille called Rob to tell him everything was off, then spent the afternoon monitoring the canal. She managed to warn off one elderly man walking an outrageously fluffy white dog when the water started to swirl softly, a trail of bubbles following the pair along the bank. The walker retreated rapidly, dragging his snarling dog and shouting that he didn't know what they were paying her for if she couldn't keep on top of such things. Camille just nodded. There was no point arguing. Although, she did consider that maybe she should've just let whatever was in the canal grab the dog. She might've got a glimpse of it that way.

She was just pouring herself a rather morose glass of whisky when someone knocked on the door. It was dark already, the rain and cloud ushering in the night even earlier than the time of year demanded, and she opened the door warily, one hand on the ash staff she kept above the boot rack.

Mike looked at her from under a large umbrella, his thin face pinched with cold.

"Oh, *sorry,*" she said. "I forgot to call you. It's all off. Can't so much as get barriers to block the path."

He looked at her for a moment longer, then held a bag up. It was a big canvas tote printed with the logo of the local supermarket, slick with dripping rainwater, unremarkable and uninteresting.

She looked from him to it, then back again. "What?"

He cleared his throat a couple of times, and she stepped back.

"Come in."

He shook his head, and turned back into the night, looking around expectantly. A heavyset figure loomed up, a sou'wester jammed down over his ears.

"Evening," Rob said.

"Evening," Camille said.

"Ready?" he asked.

"For what? And why are you dragging poor Mike out in this weather?"

"*… forgot …*"

"I didn't drag him. He dragged me."

They both looked at Mike, who pulled the sleeve of his coat back to check his watch. He frowned, peering back toward the canal, then nodded. A pair of small torch beams bobbed toward them through the murk, and Camille took her coat from the hook by the door and pulled it on, lifting the hood over her head and swapping her slippers for wellies.

"Do you have a plan, Mike?" she asked, wishing she had time to change into her waterproof trousers. She wasn't sure alien-print pyjama bottoms were really suitable for monster hunting, but if no one was coming in she could hardly run upstairs and fuss with her wardrobe.

Mike didn't answer, just turned and walked around the house, heading for the lock gate. Camille and Rob followed, exchanging dubious glances.

Jeff and Abigail caught up with them as they stood at the edge of the lock, staring into the canal. The outside light from Camille's house glimmered on the rain-rumpled surface of the water, turning it into fractured, captured scraps of luminescence, while beyond its reach the dark laid claim to the rest of the waterway. Mike set the bag down and waited, his arms dangling at his sides.

The rest of the little group waited too, Abigail swamped in a large, waterproof purple poncho that reached her knees, and Jeff in a flat cap and something that looked rather like a trench coat. No one spoke, and the sound of the rain swallowed the world.

They stood there long enough for the outside lights to click off on the timer, leaving just the ones from the living room and kitchen filtering out, barely enough to illuminate the windowsills. Jeff started to switch his torch back on, and Camille stopped him with one hand. She wasn't sure if Mike *knew* anything, or if he was just guessing, but she was willing to trust him. He'd sat in on more meetings than just hers, older ones and stranger ones, and for all that his notetaking could stand to be a little more effective, there was nothing wrong with his hearing.

They waited there in the darkness, the rain plastering

Camille's pyjamas to her legs, cold and clammy. She was definitely regretting not changing, and was just wondering if her faith in Mike had been misplaced in this case when a bloom of light swirled across the dark water, spectral and diffuse.

"*Ooh*," Abigail whispered, and Mike opened the bag. Camille was expecting bait, but instead he produced large, handheld spotlights, handing them out without comment. Then he looked at Camille, waiting.

She examined the light, then looked back at the water. The glow was still there, pulsing and coiling, outlining something vast yet fluid, impossible to parse into shape or sense. It wasn't a kelpie or a sprite, that was certain. "Mike?"

He handed her his phone, open on what seemed to be a wildlife-for-kids type page. Rob leaned over her shoulder as she read aloud, "*Squid are attracted to light, and fishermen in the Mediterranean will often use nets on the surface in combination with the boat's lights to catch—*" She looked at Mike. "I don't think that's really an option, love. No net, for a start."

"A *net?*" Rob said. "You're lucky it hasn't tried to eat your house, Cammie, given the size of it."

"We can't catch it," Abigail said. "There's not enough of us. And where would we put it?"

"Plus how would we get it back to the sea to release it?" Jeff asked, pointing at the glowing water. "We'd need a tanker for that thing."

Camille had been watching Mike while the others talked, and he sighed slightly, looking at the sky, then pointed, first toward the lake, then downstream, along the canal to where the next lock waited a few miles on.

"*… light …*"

"We lead it," she said, and he nodded just slightly. She looked along the canal, then back at him. "It's a long way to the sea."

He didn't respond for a moment, then raised one hand, rubbing his thumb and first two fingers together in the age-old *money-money-money* sign.

"If we walk it out it won't cost that much," Rob said. "It's bloody miles, though."

"I have to work tomorrow," Abigail said. "Perhaps we can take shifts?"

Mike took his phone from Camille and replaced it with something else. A mug, not unlike the souvenir one she'd used in the meeting. Almost identical, in fact, one of those print on demand type things. The Naethankye Loch one had a picture of the lake monster on it, wearing a tam o'shanter at a jaunty angle. This one didn't, and she looked at it for a long time while the rain trickled down inside her wellies and the other three argued about how they'd deal with boats, and foot traffic on the canal path, and how many nights it would take to lead the glowing creature out through all the locks, because it was hardly going to be possible during the day.

She opened her mouth to say something, then stopped, thinking of the retired gavel and the dodged phone calls and the tatty back room they had to use, when once the whole hall had belonged to them, to the Naethankye Preservation League. The whole *town*. Back when they'd been respected, honoured for the work they did. They'd *mattered*, and now they were nothing more than a quirky, fading local tradition, barely indulged, their very reason for being become nothing but a legend and a T-shirt logo.

"… *shifts* …"

Yes. Everything shifted. Everything changed. And everyone forgot all the *other* work that was needed, even if the monster was nothing more than bones in the unmeasurable depths of the lake. Because the other work didn't bring in the tourists, so no one even cared about it.

She nodded, just slightly, and walked to the lock controls.

They were manual, a massive hand crank that boaters could climb ashore and work themselves, negating the need for a lock keeper. She braced herself and threw her weight against it, struggling to get the mechanism moving.

"Cammie?" Rob asked. "What're you doing?"

Behind her, a spotlight went on, turning the night stark and making her squint, even with her back to it.

"*Cammie.*" Rob grabbed her shoulder, pulling her away. "That's *into* the lake."

She looked up at him, then straightened, the brand on her wrist burning, the one all the chairs acquired when they took the position. The one that marked them for life as the authority on the lake, as the one charged with its survival and protection. There was no enchantment to it, no magic, but it burned anyway, as if to remind her of her responsibilities. "Yes," she said simply, and pointed at the handle. "Open it."

"What?" Abigail asked, her eyes wide and her mouth a twist of fright. "We're letting it into the *lake?* It's trying to eat people in the *canal!* Imagine what it'll do in the lake!"

Camille nodded. "This lake has always had a creature. It *needs* one. We need to take advantage of this." Beyond Mike, the water was rippling, the creature gathering itself to advance on the lights.

"You can't! We're meant to protect the town, not set monsters on it!"

Camille found herself smiling, against the rain and the night and the slowly building sound of disturbed water. "It's not the town we protect."

"It *is*," Abigail insisted. "We're the Naethankye Preservation League!"

Rob spoke before Camille did. "The lake was here first, and the creature in it. The one called the Naethankye. *That's* what we protect."

"And all else that comes besides," Camille said.

"But … but shouldn't we vote on it, at least?" Abigail asked. "We don't know what this is going to do!"

"No," Camille agreed. "But we lost Naethankye decades ago, and the town has been dying ever since. This is our chance to bring it back."

They stared at each other, the moment full of rain and doubt and the slow creaking of the lock handle, shivering with the weight of the creature investigating the walls.

"Camille," Jeff called, his voice high and tight. "It's here."

She reached for the handle, but Rob got there first, hefting it into motion. "Get to the other gate," he said. "It's not going to like being trapped in the lock itself. Hurry!"

"Come on," Camille said to Abigail, and they ran for the other end of the lock. They barely made it before the doors to the canal popped open, pulled from the outside by something vast and furious, Mike running to join them with the light. Jeff already had his switched off, replacing Rob at the handle, turning it as fast as he could to close the way back. Abigail and Mike kept their lights on the water, the surface reflecting the beams back and making it impossible to see into the depths, but there was *something*. It was in the currents and the ripples, in the rise and fall of the water as it splashed against the walls. Camille watched the gate into the canal ease closed, agonisingly slowly, still two metres open, then one and a half, then one, closing further and further until suddenly the water within rose into a thrashing fury.

"It knows it's caught!" Rob yelled. "Get that gate open! *Get it open!*"

The water exploded upward, and even as Camille grabbed the handle she glimpsed tentacles writhing within the sudden surf, great curling things strung with phosphoresce and fury, the entire lock filled to the brim with otherworldly hunger. Abigail pushed her out of the way, cranking the handle frantically, and the gate to the lake started to ease open, water pouring into the gap from the higher level on the far side.

"*Hurry!*" Rob yelled, as the creature twined itself upward, growing like a waterspout, full of threat and promise. Abigail cranked harder, and Camille turned her spotlight on the beast, tracing its vast limbs up into the rain-soaked night, wonder and terror momentarily freezing her in place. It wasn't fleeing into the lake, wasn't fighting to get back to the canal. It wasn't *scared.* It towered over them, and she felt its regard, felt its *want.*

She'd got it wrong. This wasn't an accident. This wasn't simply some dumb and hungry beast, strayed out of its usual hunting grounds and trapped, confused and lost. If it had been that, there would've been no runners or dog-walkers coming back from the canal at all. No, it had been searching. Waiting, even. Waiting for recognition, waiting for its ceremony of welcoming, waiting to be *known.*

Rob had taken over from Abigail, as if he could open the gates any faster, and the young woman had her face covered with both hands, like a child hiding from ghosts. Jeff was running along the bank to join them, and Mike nodded at Camille.

"... *decide* ..." he said, so softly she only saw his lips move amid the shouting and splashing and steady rain. She nodded, and looked back at the beast. At the monster.

"Welcome," she said, raising her tattooed hand, and flourished it toward the lake like a particularly flamboyant salesperson showing off their latest wares. "We, the Naethankye Preservation Society, preserve the unknown against all threats, human and otherwise. Enter, and be safe."

The creature rose still higher, cut from night and water and legend, then simply collapsed through the still half-closed lock gates, funnelling through them like it was no more substantial than the water itself. It shot away into the freezing depths of the loch with its colours running like a meteor shower.

A stillness descended, broken only by the swirl of disturbed water and the patter of rain on their jackets, then Abigail said in a near whisper, "Is it gone?"

"Yes," Rob said, voice jagged with exertion. "Straight into the loch." There wasn't quite judgement in his voice, but it was close. That was fair. There would be a cost, after all. Camille hoped they didn't lose too many tourists next summer. At least the creature would have the winter to get accustomed to its new home, before the tour boats started plying the waters and the paddle boarders popped up like spores. They always lost a *few* anyway. The water was colder and deeper than people expected.

"Drink?" she asked, as Jeff started winding the gate closed again.

"*Yes,*" Rob said.

"I want to go home," Abigail said, the words wobbly at the edges, then hurried off without waiting for an answer.

Camille looked at Jeff.

"Oh, I'm still in," he said. "I signed up for bonkers, and you've really delivered. I thought for a while there we were going to be doing nothing but selling lucky charms and Nessie knockoffs to the tourists for tea money."

Mike patted him on the shoulder, and took the mug from Camille, handing it to him instead.

Jeff turned it toward the light. The logo was inexpertly drawn, but clear enough, all coiling tentacles and one large, glaring eye. Around it in a circle was printed, *Cult of the Kraken.*

"We're a cult now?" he asked.

"We always were," Camille said. "Kind of have to be, to

keep the Naethankye legend going for so long when everyone thinks we're just ripping off Loch Ness."

"I did wonder about that."

"We had a creature," Rob said. "Properly, I mean. Loch bloody Ness nicked the idea and ran with it, and next thing everyone thought *we* were the fakes. Then she … well, she stopped appearing, and it's been downhill ever since."

"They just had better PR," Camille said, and nodded at her house. "Come on. I've still got some Jaffa Cakes left."

"Kraken, though," Rob said, following her as she headed down the path toward the warm lights. "Is anyone going to believe that? In a *freshwater* loch?"

"I have *so* many TikTok followers," Jeff said. "We'll make it work."

Camille let her visitors file past her into the house, pausing to look back at the blank, grey expanse of the loch stretching into the night, the mountains hidden by darkness and cloud, everything damp and strange and alien, and hoped he was right.

Cult of the Kraken. It had a nice ring to it.

And one had to move with the times. A *League* was desperately old-fashioned, after all.

She slipped inside, closing the night out and going to find some dry trousers, while in the dark, still waters of Loch Naethankye something leviathan turned, slow and strange and content.

For now, anyway.

8

A SUMMONING OF ROSES

Did you know you can buy ouija board scratching mats for your cat? I do now.

And that gave me an idea ...

IT WAS RICHLY DARK, AND DECIDEDLY COOL.

Not *cold*, not shivering-your-skin-off chilly, and certainly not toes-blackening-in-the-frost freezing, but cool enough that little ghosts of breath emerged when anyone warm-blooded spoke, writing drifting conversations in the air. It was just the right amount of cold, in other words, a coolness that spoke of deepening nights and shortening days, longer shadows and more profound slumbers, of the world turning in on itself as the year ran down its days.

The dark, now. That was something else. There was nothing *moderate* about the dark, nothing uncommitted. It was *sumptuous,* an all-encompassing, luxuriant dark, the dark of a big cat's pelt as it prowled midnight rainforests, or the vast depths of a shark's eye in the endless stretches of the oceans. It was long velvet curtains and aged wine in sealed barrels, buried cellars and locked attics and the secret ways of the earth.

Not that it was impenetrable, of course. The dark never was. It merely awaited the light, languidly self-assured and insouciant. The light would come to it, after all. Why go to the effort of finding the light itself?

It had the air of a sultry, shirtless Dr Ian Malcolm in that respect.

So there *was* light in that irresistible darkness, enough to illuminate the endless, vast columns of tree trunks, drawn in shades of green and grey, lifting to the unseen canopy and shrouded in wandering wisps of mist. The ground wasn't frozen, soft with leaf mulch and warm earth, silencing the passage of the throngs that slipped through the curious night, winding their own paths between the trees, their destination unspoken but fixed.

And what a throng it was. Clawed and hoofed, winged and toothed, scaled and horned and tailed, in possession of excessive amounts of limbs or none at all, angular and hard or amorphous and blobby, and all ranges of hairy and fluffy and feathered in between. They hopped and shuffled and growled and groaned their way through the infinite march of the looming forest, some with giant eyes that swallowed the dark, others lighting their way with flaming torches or floating green orbs of swamp gas, casting the night in ghoulish shades and reflecting on multi-pupiled eyes and glossy scales, and causing at least one dark-dweller to yelp, "*Oi!* Get that out me face before I feeds it to ya!"

"Sod off, cyclops," someone else yelled back, and elsewhere came a screech of outrage as a tail was trodden on, while further off someone wailed that they'd stepped in something nasty, which only sent a ripple of amusement through the crowd.

And cutting through it all, and making *everyone* flinch, were the frazzling beams of LED headlights, directed from some unknown source. The beams somehow splintered on every leaf, stone, tooth, and scale, so managing to attack the eye from half a dozen directions at once. It was impressively fiendish.

"Outdone themselves this year," Nessa commented, squinting against the glare. A yip and a crash from further up the path suggested someone had been dazzled enough to walk into a tree or trip over a rock, and a cheer of raucous laughter washed around them.

"Bit garish," Gabe said. "Bloody obnoxious, in fact."

"Sort of the point, isn't it?"

"I suppose," he said. "Just … we've never had headlights before." He raised a hand to shield himself from a sudden assault of light from the left. The LEDs were roving about at will, impossible to anticipate or track. "It seems a bit tacky, is all."

"They're not tacky," Hanna said. "They're modern."

"They're *human*," Gabe pointed out.

Hanna huffed, and flounced a couple of tentacles. "You old-timers don't get it. We need to *evolve*. Can't be running about with candelabras and storm lanterns these days."

"Nothing wrong with a good candelabra," Gabe muttered, and stretched, his spine crackling alarmingly. *Old-timers.* How were they still using these expressions? That's what *he* would've called the oldies when he was as bright-toothed and scaly-tailed as Hanna. All their modern attitudes, all the talk of *evolving* and *embracing progress*, yet not a scrap of imagination. Some youngster had pulled the old bleeding wall trick last year, and acted like it was their own damn invention. How *trite*.

"I quite like the shininess," Nessa said, and held up one hand. The white glare of the LEDs shattered and dripped off her long talons, rendering them even more fearsome than usual. She'd always had good talons, Nessa. Timmy did too, but in all the wrong places, and was currently slowing them up because he had to stop every few paces to clear the dead leaves off his claws. Pootsie, meanwhile, was off to the side making dramatic choking noises due to the mulch gumming up her suckers. Worse still was Bob, whose night vision had been somewhat fried by the light show. They'd walked into half a dozen trees before Nessa took pity on them and gave them a piggy-back. She was in human form, and therefore unlikely to impale them on a stray spine, quill, or random orifice.

"*Shininess*," Gabe grumbled, and kicked a startled pebble, which promptly tried to bite his foot. Joke was on it, though, as Gabe was wearing his favourite steel-capped cowboy boots. The pebble wailed in frustration, and the little group forged on through the not-actually-very-dark-at-all forest.

LEDs. Bah.

Given the disorientating lights, and Timmy and Pootsie's leaf issues, and Nessa still carting a whimpering Bob, it took longer than usual to reach the Gathering. They certainly weren't the only ones having issues, though, and at one point Gabe had to detour to help drag a handful of frantic, winged strays away from the lights. The exact source was still impossible to pinpoint, but the very boggy patches of standing water that reflected it were apparently just as irresistible to those that way inclined. Tricky to extricate themselves from, too, especially if any of the bog's residents were close by and feeling peckish.

Eventually, though, everyone – or nearly everyone, there had been a couple of casualties between the lights, the bogs, and the usual squabbles – was gathered in the clearing, a brutal, blighted gap in the heavy pelt of trees and undergrowth. The ground was twisted and cursed, a tarry mess of shattered stone and oozing swamp, like an infected socket left in the wake of a pulled tooth.

Gabe gave a satisfied sigh. The image always calmed him. He liked pulling teeth.

The crowd packed themselves between (and into) the trees that circled the edge of the clearing, everyone pushing and shoving to get a good spot. Not that there was any knowing where the best spot was, of course. One was as likely to be plucked from the back of the crowd as the front. The atmosphere was distinctly festive, competing tunes tumbling from fiddles and harmonicas and accordions, as well as the dolorous tones of an organ. Imps shoved their way through the gathering, or ran along its edge, lugging bottles of Hvalur beer and scorpion wine and salmon vodka, or jugs of Yorsh and Karsk and curdled cement mixer cocktails. Still more were doing a brisk trade in hot dogs and roadkill and intestines on sticks, and winged imps swung in with green smoothies and raw eggs and uncooked fish for the more health conscious.

Gabe took a jug of flaming sambuca from an imp, flicking it a foil-wrapped chocolate coin in payment. It looked at the coin, then at him, and made an *and?* gesture. Gabe grumbled, and found another coin in the pocket of his waistcoat.

The imp squeezed both coins between scaly fingers, then said, "They better not be melted."

Gabe held the jug up. "This better be brand name."

"Like you know the difference," the imp said, and scuttled off with its coins before Gabe could aim a kick at it.

"Twice the price it used to be," he complained to Timmy, who had finally caught up, dead leaves still sprouting between his toes. "And green juice? That was one of our best inventions. But it wasn't meant to be for *us*."

Timmy took the jug from Gabe and had a swig. "Someone's selling tofu cottage cheese ice cream, too. What's wrong with some good scorched entrails?"

"We're not all monsters," Hanna said, and the other two looked at her. She scowled. "I mean, we *are*, but that doesn't mean we have to eat dead things."

"But why wouldn't we?" Timmy asked, taking a hot dog from a passing vendor and flinging them a packet of Fisherman's Friends in exchange.

"It's cruel."

No one said anything for a moment, just stared at her blankly, then Nessa clipped Hanna around the ear.

"*Ow!*"

"Stop talking tosh," Nessa said, and put Bob down. "You alright?"

"No," they said disconsolately. "All I can see is stars. Can you point me in the right direction if I get a call?"

"Of course," Nessa said, petting the other's horny head gently with one long-fingered hand. Like Gabe, she was old school enough to take pleasure in wearing a human form, and she did go in for very pleasing forms, as far as that went, with thick dark hair and generous curves. The younger generation seemed to prefer retaining their own forms at all times. They said it was dishonest to shape-shift, but they were *demons*. It seemed to Gabe that it was more dishonest to *not* be dishonest, but he'd tried having that conversation with a young scrap called Nap'sj'n-f-it at one point, and he still wasn't sure which one of them had won, if either. It was like talking to a completely different species.

Now Hanna looked inclined to argue further about the merits (or lack thereof) of eating dead things, but when she started talking Nessa growled, and clicked her talons in a pointed manner. Hanna settled for muttering mutinously and slurping her green juice.

Nessa abandoned Bob, her compassion evidently exhausted, and crossed her arms, tapping those murderous talons against her smooth, bare skin.

"What d'you think?" she asked Gabe. "Better than last year?"

"Doubt it," Timmy said, around a mouthful of hot dog. "Why would it be? We've been in decline *forever.*"

"Don't be dramatic," Pootsie said. "Decades, maybe."

"Centuries," Timmy said, and grabbed a clam juice cocktail from an imp.

"He's right," Gabe said. "Nothing good's happened since we kicked off the Industrial Revolution and got the pollution really pumping."

"Rubbish," Nessa said, waving to an imp who was carting around a luminously yellow sports drink cocktail that looked like the end product of some serious dehydration. "Remember all those boy bands and pop princesses in the early noughties? We signed more musical contracts at the end of the nineties than even in the sixties. And what about all the souls being flogged after the financial crisis in 2008? It was *amazing.*"

"Oh, sure, if you're into contracts," Timmy said. "But I haven't done a decent possession since 1793."

"Possessions are boring," Nessa said, and Timmy placed one segmented claw on his thorax.

"*Sacrilege.*"

"Possessions are *cruel,*" Hanna put in, and Nessa put one hand on the young demon's face and pushed her away. Hanna hissed, but didn't bite. Gabe doubted anyone would bite Nessa, unless it had been previously agreed upon, probably in writing.

"I prefer wreaking vengeance," Pootsie said. "Love a nice

bit of vengeance, me. Haven't had a good, bloody rampage for a while though. Last year my summoner just wanted me to make sure someone else's cake didn't rise, so they could win some sodding village fête. Hardly vengeful, is it?"

"I hope I'm not called up by a teenager again," Timmy said. "Last time their friends all said I was AI. *Bad* AI."

The others made sympathetic noises, and Gabe said, "That's still better than the one who summoned me to be a prom date. A prom date! And he wouldn't even let me do a Carrie. He just wanted to make his ex jealous. They ended up getting back together, and when I went to spike the punch some human had already done it. The best I managed was setting off the sprinklers."

Nessa took a gulp of her drink, shuddered, and said, "You can't just do what they tell you. No wonder you're having no fun."

"We can't just do what we want, either," Timmy pointed out. "They do command us."

"Rubbish. I was summoned to help someone win the lottery, but they didn't specify which one, so I won them a lifetime supply of chicken feed. They live in an apartment, and I made sure the company can't ever stop sending it." She cackled. "They're *drowning* in the stuff. So much fun!"

Hanna had crept back, and now she said, "That's not even evil. That's just petty."

Nessa hissed at her. "Tell that to the silly human still trying to figure out how to make chicken food lasagne. Anyway, I did other stuff while I was up there."

"Like what?" Gabe asked. Nessa's exploits always cheered him up. She was a *proper* demon.

"You know. Stuff." She grabbed a scorched, flattened possum and munched on it, and he'd almost have thought she was avoiding answering, if that wasn't impossible. This was *Nessa*.

Gabe looked at the portal, trembling in the centre of the clearing. Of course humans could call up demons any time, but Halloween was always the clearest connection, as well as being the time of year when the most accidental summonings happened, what with people using ouija board tablecloths and decorating with random pentagrams and so on. Accidental summonings were the best, too. One might only get twenty-four hours before being bounced home, but those were twenty-four hours of not being bound to anyone, free to cause whatever mischief came to mind. A lot of chaos could be caused in twenty-four hours by an enterprising demon.

"No tech bros, either," Timmy muttered. "They're *so* boring. Oh, make me a crypto. Oh, build me a platform. Oh, magic me a space rocket. None of them think of anything *interesting*. I'll take a teenager again over that. But a proper disaffected one, with a decent imagination and a burning desire to tear up the world. Don't get enough of them these days."

"Too much stuff online," Gabe said. "They never think to turn to the nether when things get tough. They go to bloody Reddit instead."

"No ambition," Nessa agreed, and they all stared at the portal, watching it begin to twitch and pulse as the hour drew near. "I want a would-be witch. Inexperienced. Easy to guide. Preferably in unrequited love."

Pootsie made an approving sound. "I want an influencer who can't quite break through to the big leagues. Deeply jealous of their rivals, and spectacularly insecure."

"Single, almost-successful businessman," Gabe decided. "Lots to prove. Watches Andrew Tate and calls himself an alpha. You can do a lot with that."

"Watches Andrew Tate?" Hanna piped up. "You're not going to get a soul out of them, then."

"Eh, true," Gabe said, as the others muttered agreement. "*Thinking* about watching him, maybe."

"*Ooh*, that's good," Nessa said.

"I want a PETA activist," Hanna declared. "Or an anarchist. Someone up for decent productive mischief, anyway. We can bring down the institutions of mass murder. Or a government, I don't mind."

The others all sighed, except for Bob, who was sitting morosely on the ground with their wings over their eyes.

Pootsie nudged them with one hoof. "Bobsicles? What about you?"

Bob shifted a wing enough that they could squint at the others. "I just don't want a cat."

There was a pause, then Nessa said, "What?"

"That's what happened last year."

"*How?*" Gabe demanded. "I mean, sure, they run the humans, but they're *cats.* They don't do anything but hiss at us and bite our tails."

"Some bloody idiot made a cat scratching thingy shaped like an ouija board. Damn creature summoned me, and I spent the entire sodding year letting it outside, then back in half a minute later, then back out again. Plus it made me transform into a heated bed when I wasn't beating up the neighbourhood dogs or opening cans of food. Oh, and putting breakable stuff on the edges of tables for it to knock off." They sighed deeply. "And I think I'm allergic, too."

"*Huh*," Nessa said, after they'd all considered it. "I thought they'd be more evil."

"Hairy, mostly."

They waited, slurping their drinks and chewing on bones, and considering the vagaries of cats.

THE PORTAL SURGED, flashing with twisting currents of deeper, more impenetrable darkness, and Gabe readied himself. There were far more demons than there were summonses these days, and one was so rarely called by name. That meant every call was up for grabs, and one had to be quick to answer. All around the circle, the demons shuffled for position, ready for the explosion of messages billowing into the depths, just waiting to be claimed.

A bell rang out, high and clear, and the crowd surged forward in a fury of wings and horns and shiny suits. Someone whooped as they latched onto the first call and vanished, but more bells were ringing now, sparking twisting, open channels in the abyss, snaking and snapping through the clearing and into the trees. Gabe elbowed two smaller demons out of the way, employed his steel-capped boots on another, dived past a four-armed, three-headed giant, and grabbed the thread of a summons. It lashed around him like the snatching legs of a kraken then retreated, dragging him with it, and he spun into the void, shouting in triumph. His body flashed and twisted, fracturing and reforming as he traversed dimensions, screaming in glorious agony until he emerged into a shadowed, dimly lit room, lit by flickering candles and the blue glow of a screen. Silence clamped down around him, accompanied by the strange, sticky scents of the upper world. The sharp chill of his own retreated.

Gabe took a moment to catch his breath, rolling his shoulders deliciously and breathing in the cloying and somehow *rounded* air of earth as he straightened up from his crouch and combed his fingers through his pale hair, settling it into place. A robed figure regarded him, unspeaking, their face hidden in the shadows of a hood and their hands hanging loose at their sides.

"You rang?" Gabe said, his voice deep and smooth as he spread his arms, fingers smoking gently.

"Oh, *bollocks*," the hooded figure said, a squeak on the edges of the words. "What the hell … where did you come from? Who are you?"

Gabe tipped his head. "You performed a ritual of summoning. What did you expect, a chameleon?"

"A what?"

Gabe examined the room, frowning faintly. He was inside the expected circle, standing amid a pile of what appeared to be twigs and stones, with a blank-faced mobile phone jammed in the middle. Candles were set at the points of the star that filled the circle, and the lines had been executed with … "Are those rose petals?" He sniffed. "And *scented candles?*"

"Um, yes," his summoner said. Gabe could see now that the hooded robe was fluffy, and had green frogs printed on it. "This was meant to be a cleansing ritual. To help me be … I don't know. Better, I guess. So rose seemed nice?"

Gabe pointed at the star. "You didn't think this was slightly less cleansing ritual, slightly more raise hell?"

"I don't know. I'm mostly into historical romance, to be honest." They waved at the twigs under Gabe's feet. "Sage, see? And some crystals and stuff."

Gabe raised his eyebrows, and they looked at each other for a moment before the summoner admitted, "I did think the sulphur smell was a bit off."

"So you don't want me to wreak vengeance on your enemies? Win you a fortune? Claim the heart of your beloved?" Gabe looked at the robe again. "Maybe update your wardrobe?"

The summoner barked, a flat, unhappy sound that might've been a laugh. "If only it was that easy."

"It is. You just tell me what to do, and I'll make it happen."

He grimaced. "The wardrobe might take a bit of willingness on your part, though."

"No, it won't work. None of it will. It's *me*. That's why I was doing the cleansing ritual. *I'm* the enemy." They pressed both hands to the top of the head, as if afraid it might be about to explode off. That'd be fun, at least for Gabe. "I mean, who else would mess up this bad? Try to create a nice vibe and raise a sodding demon instead? I mean … sorry, is that rude? You are a demon, right?"

"Right."

The summoner nodded, and pulled the hood back, revealing a soft-cheeked face framed by long dark hair. Their eyes were rimmed with red. "Hey, maybe this isn't so bad. Can you, like, possess me or something?"

Gabe stared at them blankly. "Why would you want that? Possession will trap your soul in a corner of your vessel, screaming in incomprehensible pain and horror as I do terrible things in your name, with your hands. It'll drive you to cosmic insanity, if you even survive it."

The summoner shrugged, an exhausted little motion. "It still sounds better than this."

"Than what?"

There was silence for a moment, then the snivelling little human pointed at Gabe's feet. He looked down, and spotted the mobile phone, the screen dark. He stooped to pick it up, expecting it to radiate the usual sort of desperation and desire that hung around the devices like an oil slick, staining everything it touched. That was another cause of the decline in summonings, of course. Humans barely even needed demons anymore.

That wasn't what he felt, though. The device dripped with prickly viciousness and petty hate, misdirected rage and confusion, all shot through with stabs of fear and squirming insecurity, none of which belonged to the summoner. The summoner gave off nothing more than ground-down despair.

Gabe licked the phone with a little hum of pleasure. *So much delightful nastiness!* "Oh, I could just eat them all up," he said, mostly to himself, then looked at the summoner. "Why don't you want me to wreak some vengeance? You've got your enemies on speed dial, by the feel of it."

The human shrugged and slumped slowly to their knees, as if their legs had simply given up. "There's no point. There'll always be more."

"You're very defeatist," Gabe said, wrinkling his nose. "What on earth were you doing summoning me if you weren't going to do anything?"

"I told you! I didn't *mean* to." Their voice was jagged, and they wiped their nose hurriedly, but Gabe could still smell the saltiness of their tears. "Go on. Just possess me, or kill me, or whatever. Someone else'll do it anyway, if you don't."

"Can't," Gabe said, licking the phone again. "You summoned me, so I can't hurt you."

The human tilted sideways and collapsed, banging the side of their head hard enough against the floor that Gabe winced. From downstairs, someone yelled, "Shut *up!*"

"I can't even get a demon to kill me," the human whimpered, curling into a ball, the movement brushing the rose petals out of place, setting a ripple into the ether as the barrier broke. "Everyone's right. I really am a waste of space. I wish I'd never been born."

Gabe moved a couple of scented candles away from the creature's robe, which was now clearly a dressing gown. It looked highly flammable, and while that might be entertaining, the thought gave him the same uncomfortable feeling as seeing Bob struggling in the lights, or hearing Hanna talk about *productive mischief*, whatever that was meant to be when it was at home. Some young demon rubbish like green juice and vegetarianism. Mischief was mischief. That's what they were here for. Havoc and mayhem, not *productivity*. Humans did make it bloody hard to get up to anything truly troublesome, though. They were always a step ahead these days.

He stepped out of the broken circle and crossed to the room's one small window, looking out at a dull backyard, the grass deep green and fiercely trimmed, the flower beds tightly curtailed. There was nothing of interest out there, and he licked the phone again as he turned back. The room itself was pale and bland, as lacking in character as the backyard, with a sort of performative neatness to it. The only signs of character were the frog dressing gown and the twigs in the middle of the floor.

The summoner kept crying, quiet and contained, the sobs of someone used to ensuring they weren't overheard. Gabe leaned against the windowsill, regarding the door. The lock had been removed, and he wondered if that was for the miserable creature's safety, or against it. The quality of the sobs gave him the answer, though. He tapped the phone against his lips, thinking. So much tastiness here. So much *vindictiveness*, in the phone and in the air of the house. So much … *unallowed* in the sorry little human. Unpermitted.

And oh, he did love the impermissible. That, at least, humans would never take away. They *loved* not permitting things. He straightened up.

"Come on."

The human looked up at him, eyes streaming. "What? Are you going to possess me after all?"

"No. It's Halloween. We're going to *party*, baby." Gabe did a few lewd dance moves that made the human blink. That seemed reasonable. He was an impressive mover, after all.

"I can't," the human said finally. "I'm not allowed."

Gabe grinned, wolfish and seductive, and leaned down,

his eyes bright as he extended one well-manicured hand. "You've got a demon now, little human. Let's see anyone stop you."

"I *can't*." The summoner looked fearfully at the door.

Gabe grabbed the human's arm and lifted them easily to their feet. "Get changed. I'm not going out with you in a bloody dressing gown. I've got standards."

"But—"

"*Go,*" he hissed, the word shaking the room and setting the person downstairs shouting again.

"Oh, *no*. Oh, you shouldn't've—"

Gabe's grin widened, showing far too many teeth as he pressed his face so close to the human he could've kissed them. "Oh, *yes*. This is when the fun starts. *Get changed*."

The summoner squeaked, and bolted for the closet. Gabe turned back to the window. He was here. He may as well have some fun. A little corruption could go a long way to making a demon happy, and if there were some advantageous side effects for the corrupted, well. That wasn't his problem. It wasn't some ridiculous *productive mischief*. It was just mischief, as befitted a senior demon.

"Are you sure you can't hurt me?" the summoner asked, struggling into – oh, devils devour the silly thing – a *unicorn onesie*.

"I'm sure," Gabe lied. He wasn't being soft, either, like Hanna and her cohorts. It wasn't like that. It was just that humans tortured themselves and each other so well. Took all the fun out of it.

He was doing this for *him*, for the sake of proper demonic activity, not for the sorry kid peering through the unicorn's mouth with wide, anxious eyes.

If it helped them, he reminded himself, that was *entirely* beside the point.

"You look terrible," he said, and the human giggled.

"Thanks."

"Ugh. *Humans.* Wash your face and meet me outside." He swept out of the room in time to meet the shouting human from downstairs stomping toward him, stinking of vicious little acts of cruelty, the sort that never leave scars, or even bruises, not on the outside, anyway. But they cut deep enough to shatter the soul, and became beacons to those who'd leave more, a wounded fish spilling blood in the water. A demon could only *dream* of being so brutal.

Gabe wasn't in his human shape when he met that human.

The result was *delicious*.

"Come along, little unicorn," he shouted up the stairs a few minutes later, licking his lips with a forked tongue. He belched, and stooped to polish his boot tips. "I want to *party!*"

"But Mum—"

"Gone trick or treating. Don't make me drag you out. *Move!*"

"Oh no," the human muttered, but ran down the stairs and followed the demon out into the wild dark of All Hollow's Eve, rife with glorious darkness and gleeful magic and the shivering, dubious promise of mischief in all its dangerous, troublesome, *delightful* forms.

Because what would Halloween be without mischief?

And a little demonic troublemaking, just to keep the tradition alive.

9

FIBONACCI'S WORMERY

*I am not a science-y person, but I love the concept of it. How lucky are we to live in an age where so many things are being discovered and explored and theorised, and where we're free to learn about it in any way we desire? This is amazing. This is **magic.***

*And when I say magic, I mean it. So much of magic, over all of history, has simply been science we didn't understand yet. So I never see science as being antithetical to magic. It **is** magic, marvellous and breathtaking and full of mystery.*

Although I freely admit I tend to play fast and loose with both magic and science in my stories.

And this one is no exception …

"No, Fibs, *stop*," Hugo said, grabbing the cat around the middle and lifting her off the table.

She hung from his hands, looking up at him with reproachful green eyes. She was mostly tabby, with an admirable application of eyeliner, and had a swathe of white down her belly and legs, as if she'd slid through wet paint.

Knowing her, Hugo thought a little gloomily, she probably had. He'd been under the impression cats were *easy*, but he'd rapidly discovered it was a full-time job just to stop Fibs launching herself out the windows of his third-floor flat whenever she spotted a passing pigeon.

"If I'd known you were going to be this much trouble, I'd've left you in the box," he told her.

"*Mmmaow?*" Fibs's eyes widened slightly. She was technically called Fibonacci, but he'd decided on that before realising how many times a day he'd be yelling the name due to her sneaking out the door and stalking the neighbour's dog; putting her paw in his tea; inexplicably vanishing in the confines of the one-bed flat that also served as his workshop; or – as now – sticking her nose in the middle of his work. *Fibs* was much easier to shout.

He sighed and hugged her, scratching her head gently. "No, I don't mean it. But if you've got cat hair in the wiring again, I'll shave you."

"*Mrrr!*" She pressed her paws into his chest, straining away, and he set her on the floor.

"Go and do cat things." He waved at the unused cat tree in the corner, and the very well-used bookshelves, where Fibs had made herself little nooks and crannies by the simple expedient of pushing to the ground any books she disapproved of. He'd discovered she was highly averse to calculus, Lovecraft, and Tolkien, but quantum physics and Philip K. Dick seemed to meet her approval.

Fibs trotted off, tail waving gently, and he went back to the box in front of him. It looked like nothing more than a simple storage bin, rectangular and tall with rounded corners, somewhat like a shoebox stood on its end. It was made of plastic, which Hugo was dissatisfied with, but he didn't have the money to splash out on an insulated metal version yet. He needed to prove the concept before he could start asking people for money. Crowdfunding wasn't as generous as all that.

The tub was roughly half-full with a mucky and somewhat whiffy mix of old teabags, apple peels, eggshells, and sundry other food scraps, and here and there the glossy coils of worms broke the surface momentarily then disappeared again, scaled-down monsters in the depths. The lid, which Hugo was currently fiddling with, featured some thick charcoal filters, connections to mild heating elements in the sides, and a variety of small sensors connected to a transmitter.

He turned to his laptop, tapping through the app, where it should be reporting back the internal temperature of the bin (optimised for healthy worms and rapid composting), how much longer before the filters needed changing (to keep the wormery whiff-free for apartment use), and a counter indicating how many litres of landfill had been avoided through the bin's use. Currently everything was reading the same: *1.61,* which meant nothing.

"Pants," he muttered, and blew hopefully on the sensors. Nothing. He unplugged the charger (for the next version he wanted solar power for the heating elements, but he needed to prove the design worked first) and left it unplugged while he went to make a cup of tea. That usually fixed things.

It did not fix things, and on top of that the compost was stinking the whole apartment out by the time Hugo wedged the lid back on. Fibs was registering her objections by pushing his entire Pratchett collection off the shelf one by one, ignoring his entreaties to leave them alone. He set the wormery outside the kitchen window, wedging it behind the little metal railings he'd set up to stop it falling to the street below, then looked at the cat as she jumped up to inspect his work, her mouth dropping open and her ears going back.

"I know," he said. "Can't go on like that. No one wants their kitchen smelling like a rotting swamp."

"*Mmmr?*" She patted the lid with one paw, but it was firmly clipped down, and with the railing in place there was no way for her to knock the bin over or push it off the sill. He'd only made that mistake once, and it had been both expensive for him to replace, and very nearly disastrous for the postie passing below.

"That's got you," he said to her. "Want a treat instead?"

"*Mmmr!*"

She ran out of the little flat's open kitchen to jump back into the bookshelves, emerging a moment later with something shiny in her mouth. She carried it onto the sofa, looking expectantly from him to the jar of cat treats on the cluttered coffee table, and he followed her, stopping to pick up the fallen books on the way. Maybe he should put some railings on the bookshelves, too.

On the sofa, he took a small handful of treats from the jar and offered them to Fibs, who set her gift in his hand then took one of the biscuits delicately. He frowned at what she'd given him: a glossy, iridescent oval the size of an acorn. He was just wondering if she'd stolen it from next door when it sprouted legs, the sharp tips digging into his palm. He yelped, jerking back instinctively and shaking the thing off, scattering the treats everywhere as he did so. The creature took flight, wings whirring busily as it shot toward the open kitchen window.

"What the *hell?*"

The luminous beetle vanished into the grey day without offering an explanation, and Fibs ignored both it and him, scrounging among the cushions for the dropped biscuits. Hugo sighed and went to wash his hands. No one told you about this sort of thing when you picked a kitten up out of a half-crushed box behind some bins. Damn animals should come with warning labels.

HE WOKE in the thin hours of the morning to clattering in the next room. He rolled over, tipping his phone toward him, and groaned when he saw the time. Just after three a.m.

"Fibs," he called. "What're you up to?"

There was no reply from the main room, just another clatter, and he sat up, swinging his legs off the side of the bed and rubbing both hands over his face.

Another clatter, this time rather louder, and the unmistakable sound of a mug being flung off the worktop to crash to the laminate flooring.

"*Fibs!*" Hugo hurried through the door barefoot, fumbling the overhead light on. "What're you *doing?*"

He was answered by a screech from the kitchen area to his left, and he jumped. That was a whole new sound. Was she hurt?

"Fibs?"

A very small mewl answered him, but from his right, and he swung toward it. Two white paws and a pink nose poked out from under the sofa, and Fibs stared up at him, wide-eyed. He blinked at her, then looked back at the kitchen. If it wasn't her, then …

He took a careful step forward, and the screech came again. It sounded more like nails scraping across metal than a cry now.

"Hello?" he said, then immediately felt ridiculous. The kitchen was tiny. There was nowhere for anyone to hide.

"*Mrrr?*"

Hugo looked down at Fibs as she leaned against his leg, staring up at him, and he picked her up. There was a speck of blood on her snout, and he examined her with a frown. "What've you got in here?"

"*Mrrr.*" She looked past him at the kitchen, and he tucked her into the crook of one arm, feeling obscurely safer.

They approached the sink cautiously, to the accompaniment of a couple more screeches, a little quieter than before, and Hugo stopped an arm's length away. He still couldn't see anything, and Fibs was leaning away from him with her ears twitching, eyes wide and expectant. He picked up a folder from the breakfast bar, which was hardly an impressive weapon, but it was something.

"Ready?" he asked Fibs, and she looked up at him, then back at the sink, showing no inclination to get down. Hugo raised the folder with as much threat as he could muster, and stepped up to the bench, peering down into the faintly tea-stained stainless bowl.

He wasn't quite sure what he'd expected, but it was not a large, purple-blue crab with startlingly large orange claws. It took another run at the side of the sink as his shadow fell on it, legs screeching on the metal as it struggled to climb out.

"What …?"

"*Mmmaow!*"

Hugo lowered the folder and looked at Fibs, who'd leaned back against him, her tail twitching. "Is that what got your nose?"

She didn't answer, glaring at the crab. Hugo tried pushing it off the side of the sink with the folder, worried it might climb out, and the crab grabbed the flimsy plastic in one claw, almost wrenching it away.

"Hey!" He struggled for a moment to reclaim his property, then abandoned it to the crab. "*Fine.*" The folder slid into the sink, covering the creature, and he and Fibs looked at each other again. "I'm going to have to catch it, aren't I?" he said.

"Can't have it getting out and dying behind the fridge or something."

"*Mrrr.*"

Hugo put Fibs down on the breakfast bar, then armed himself with a saucepan and a pair of tongs. He was still trying to find the lid when Fibs yowled, and he jolted upright to see the crab had used the folder as a ramp to climb out of the sink. It was scuttling sideways toward Fibs, who had her tail bushed out and one paw raised, ears back.

"*Leave it!*" Hugo tried to grab the crab with the tongs, but the soft plastic simply slid off the creature's hard shell. It snapped at them irritably, then resumed its charge toward Fibs, who seemed to have forgotten she could jump to the floor to get away, and simply backed all the way to the edge, yowling again. Hugo had another couple of goes with the tongs, then as the crab made a final dash toward the cat, he hurriedly upended the saucepan over it, trapping the creature in place. The kitchen was still for a moment, then an irritated scratching started inside the pot. It didn't move, though, and Hugo dropped the tongs into the sink, puffing air out over his lip.

Fibs approached the saucepan and sniffed it warily, then looked at him with wide eyes. "*Mrrr?*"

"You can't eat it." Or he supposed she could, but then he'd have to kill it, and how was he meant to do that? He looked around the kitchen, as if an answer might be lurking among the mugs on the draining board, then blinked and looked back at the pot. It was a *crab.* In his third-floor apartment. He'd been too busy trying to work out how to deal with it to wonder where the bloody thing came from. Upstairs? An escaped dinner, fallen from their window box and into his? He doubted it. Upstairs was home to a slightly frantic woman with three kids under six. He doubted they were cooking live crabs. A pet? Did people have pet crabs? He rubbed one hand over his face. He supposed it was possible, and he'd best not go around killing the thing until he know where it came from.

It was a good excuse, anyway. He went to find the saucepan lid, before Fibs knocked the whole thing off the bar and they were right back where they started.

Hugo set the saucepan on the counter of the exotic pet store, trying not to look at the large scorpion in the tank just to his left. He felt like the thing was glaring at him.

The shop worker looked at the pot, then at him, her eyebrows raised. She had short, pink hair and an assortment of piercings, and a chameleon was sitting on her shoulder, seemingly unsure whether to keep to the khaki of her uniform shirt or try for the luminous tones of her hair. "Selling soup?" she asked him.

"I found this," he said, taking the lid off.

She peered inside with a wariness which suggested she wasn't unaccustomed to people turning up with potentially bite-y cargo. She nodded. "Rainbow Land Crab. Nice specimen."

"Do you want it?"

"We don't buy creatures," she said. "No knowing how healthy it is, or what parasites it's carrying. We're a pet shop, not a trading site."

"I don't want to sell it. It turned up in my kitchen last night, and it doesn't belong to anyone in my building." Hugo had knocked on all the doors first thing, even downstairs, in case the crab had scaled the wall, but no one had claimed it. Upstairs had screamed and slammed the door in his face when he'd taken the lid off the pot (although the kids had all been clamouring to keep it), and next door had yelled they'd report him for harbouring vermin. He wasn't sure crabs were really classed as vermin, but he didn't want to harbour it either way.

The woman lowered a pen into the pot, and the crab seized it, brandishing it like it was challenging them to a duel. *"Huh.* Seems to be pretty healthy. You want the pot back?"

"Yes," Hugo said, a little indignantly.

"Alright. Give me a moment." She picked the pot up and wandered along a display of empty tanks on the wall, finally choosing one to tip the crab into. It kept hold of the pen. "I'll get him set up properly later."

"Do they just ... occur in the wild around here?" Hugo asked, although *in the wild* was pushing things for a Leeds council flat, and she gave him an amused look.

"No. Someone dumped him. Thanks for bringing him in." She handed the pot back, the chameleon goggling at him, and Hugo walked back out into the day, trying to feel relieved.

He just really wished he knew where the damn thing had come from in the first place. *Dumping him* was unfortunately far too common for far too many pets, as Fibs proved. But it still seemed unlikely that would lead to the crab climbing three storeys to get to his kitchen.

Hugo opened the door to his flat with a box of cat food in the pot under one arm, and stepped into a scene of utter carnage. He froze, staring at the room that encompassed his living area, his little kitchen, and his workspace, all of it very compact and somewhat cluttered, but also always tidy. Not now, though.

The table where he worked had been swept clean, scraps of paper and notebooks and pens strewn across the floor, along with his laptop, which was upside down on the laminate. The back cushions of the sofa were pulled out of place, one simply facedown, the other marooned in the middle of the coffee table. The bookshelves looked as if someone had been sweeping armloads off them at random, and the mixing bowl that usually held fruit on the breakfast bar had been thrown halfway across the room, bananas and apples and mandarins torn to pieces and mushed into the floor and furniture. Mugs, plates and cutlery had tumbled from the draining board to the floor, and for one confused moment he was certain he'd been broken into.

But the door had still been locked, and the only window open was the kitchen one, the wormery still sitting in its railings, the lid lying on the windowsill next to it.

"Fibs?" Hugo said, hearing the bewilderment in his own voice. She wouldn't have done this, would she? *Could* she, even? The books and the table, maybe, but surely not the crushed fruit?

There was no answering mew, and he called her again, a little louder, but she still didn't appear. The bedroom door was mostly closed, which was odd. He usually left it open. He took a hesitant step toward it, wondering again if he'd been broken into, and shifted his grip on the pot, just in case.

"Fibs?" He nudged the bedroom door open, his shoulders tight with tension and his arm aching from carting the saucepan around. "Fibs, are you in here?"

The bedroom was empty, but the covers were rucked up, and his pillows had been flung to the floor. Hugo frowned, then very cautiously crouched down to peer under the bed. Nothing but dust bunnies and a forgotten sock.

"*Mrrr?*"

Hugo turned and spotted Fibs peering out from under the sofa, much as she had the night before. "What've you done?" he asked her, still with that same tone of bewilderment.

"*Mrrr!*" She seemed faintly indignant, but she didn't come out.

He went into the kitchen, picking his way around a devastated banana and an apple that looked very much as if a bigger cat than Fibs had been taking enormous bites out of it. He looked around uneasily, wondering if he'd missed another crab. There didn't seem to be anything lurking though, and he sighed, setting the pot down.

"If you don't like the new cat food, you could just not eat it, rather than trashing the place."

"*Mrrr.*" She still didn't emerge from under the sofa, and he started picking up the bruised fruit. He wasn't even going to fit all this in the wormery bin.

THE TRIP to the pet shop and the apartment clean-up took most of the day, and by the time Hugo sat down with the wormery it was almost dinner. He'd put the lid back on without checking inside earlier, and now he peered dubiously at the contents. The smell hadn't improved, and inside everything was churned up, not with the gentle movements of worms, but more as if someone had been digging in it. He sighed, and looked at Fibs, who was siting on the edge of the table with her tail curled over her toes. She stared back at him with wide green eyes.

"Have you been at this?" he asked her, and her whiskers twitched as her ears went back, giving her the look of a maiden aunt who's just been asked if she wants to go skinny-dipping in the Thames. "You do use a litter box," he pointed out, but she maintained her horrified look.

The compost suddenly heaved upward, and he jumped, almost knocking the bin over. The sticky mass of decomposing food matter had formed a mound in the centre, far too large to be worm-sized, and Hugo drew back, trying to keep an eye on what was happening without being at risk of … of *something*. He didn't know what. It was a tub of fruit scraps that had been sitting on the windowsill, not the floor of some tropical rainforest. Did he think he was going to be attacked by the bloody worms or something?

A shiny head emerged from the muck, and he found himself staring at the snout of … well, it was definitely *something*, just as he'd feared. It was either the biggest worm he'd ever seen, or— The critter's tongue flicked at the air, and Hugo grabbed the lid and jammed it back on hastily.

"It's a *snake*," he said to Fibs, whose eyes widened still further. "How's there a *snake* in my wormery?"

She jumped off the table and crawled back under the sofa.

"Thanks," he called after her. "Great help." He checked the time. The pet shop would be shut. He'd need to take it tomorrow.

He went to find some gaffer tape to secure the lid. He wasn't having a repeat of last night. Or today, although that seemed unlikely to be down to the snake.

GIVEN the trashed flat and the spontaneously appearing snakes and crabs, Hugo was surprised he slept at all that night. But he must have, because he was definitely dozing when the door to the wardrobe swung open with a gentle creak.

He sat straight upright, heart leaping into double-time. "*Fibs?*"

"*Mrrr?*" The answer came from his pillow, and he put one hand on the cat, reassured by her warmth as he peered around. The curtains didn't cut all the light from outside, and the bedroom was dim but outlined clearly in deep shades of grey.

The wardrobe door creaked again, easing open and not falling back, as if someone was holding it from the inside. Hugo stared at it, his heart going so fast now that black spots swam across his vision.

"*Mrrr,*" Fibs protested, wriggling, and he realised he was holding her too tightly.

"Sorry," he whispered, lifting his hand without looking away from the wardrobe. The door still hadn't swung closed, but nothing had emerged, either. Hugo couldn't decide whether he was best to go for the light and hope he blinded the attacker, or to pretend he was still sleeping and count on the element of surprise. Sleeping upright, admittedly, but maybe whoever it was would think he was sleepwalking. Or sleep-sitting, whatever.

He hadn't checked the wardrobe earlier. Of course he hadn't. There hadn't been any indication anyone had actually broken in, and it wasn't like a crab was going to open the wardrobe door and scuttle in. Or a snake. He took a shaky breath, licking his lips, and reached slowly toward the bedside light.

He froze as the door creaked again, and a … a *limb* came out, too oddly shaped in the low light for him to make out what it could be. A large paw, perhaps? It wasn't a snake or a crab, so that was something. Hugo stayed where he was, hand in midair, unable to look away from the thing creeping out of his wardrobe. It had paused for a moment, then started moving again, a dark triangle emerging like a small sail. Hugo frowned, abruptly more curious than scared. What *was* it?

The triangle kept coming, the door easing wider as the bulk of the creature followed, and Hugo had the sudden impression that what was coming out was *vast,* as if he were seeing just a fraction of whatever it was, the wardrobe abruptly become an entirely other reality, where the world's familiar dimensions no longer applied. He reached out for Fibs again, but as soon as he touched her she yowled and bolted off the bed, heading for the door.

"Fibs!" he shouted, suddenly terrified she'd be snatched up and thrust into the void inside the wardrobe. As she shot across the floor, the creature, rather than retreating, exploded into the room, the triangle resolving into a great, leathery wing that was rapidly joined by its pair. The beast leaped into the air, its wingspan seeming to take up every scrap of space, then it collided with the overhead light and wheeled clumsily onto the bed. Hugo shrieked as one wing caught the side of his face and he got a whiff of rotting fruit and hot breath. He tried to launch himself up and tumbled to the floor instead, legs still tangled in the bedding, while the creature plunged into the curtains behind him and brought the rod down with it as it crashed back to the bed. Hugo gave up on finding his feet and scrambled out the door on all fours, slamming it behind him the moment he was out. The crashing of picture frames coming off the walls and the bedside lamp bouncing to the floor filtered out to him, and he leaned against the door to make sure it stayed closed, panting.

But nothing tried to break out, and the room quietened, and finally his heart slowed enough that he could breathe again. He pressed one hand to his chest and said in a wobbly voice, "Fibs?"

"*Mmmaow?*" She was back under the sofa, and he wondered if he could join her. It seemed by far the safest place here.

THE WOMAN with the pink hair arrived on his doorstep before nine that morning, with a large cage in one hand and a noose-type thing on the end of a pole in the other. She looked him up and down as he answered the door, still barefoot and in his pyjamas. He hadn't dared go into the bedroom to look for any clothes.

"Morning," she said.

"Hi," he said, wishing he'd asked her name when he called earlier. She hadn't offered it, and he'd been too panicked to ask, and now it seemed weird to do so. So he just stepped back to let her in, adding, "Thanks for coming."

"Call it professional curiosity," she said. "I'm not animal control, you know."

"I did try the RSPCA. They said they needed to know exactly what they were dealing with, and I'm not going in there to look."

"You've really no idea what it is?"

Hugo very much wanted to say, *It might be a dragon,* but the woman was looking at him with a half smile on her face that suggested she was finding him far too entertaining already, and he didn't want to lose what slim shreds of dignity he had left. "It was dark."

"How did it get in?"

He shrugged helplessly. "I left the kitchen window open?"

She nodded. "And the snake?"

"It's in my wormery." He pointed at the bin, still sitting outside the window, and she frowned slightly.

"That's not the right size for a wormery. They need more space."

"It's experimental. I'm creating one that anyone can have, no matter the size of their home. It's got full connectivity to ensure ideal conditions, with a super-intuitive app, and—"

"Alright, alright. That's still too small, though." She

walked into the kitchen and lifted the bin in from the windowsill, examining the tape.

"I didn't want the snake to get out," Hugo said. "I have a cat."

She gave him a look that said *how boring* without her needing to use the words, and peeled the tape off. Hugo looked for Fibs, but she was up in the bookshelves, which seemed like good judgement.

"*Huh,*" the woman said, staring into the wormery.

"*Huh?* What does that mean? It is dangerous?"

"There's nothing in here."

"*What?*"

She took a spoon from the draining rack and stirred the contents of the tub carefully. "Nothing. Did you mean it's a compost bin?"

"No, it's a *wormery.*" He joined her in the kitchen, peering into the tub. The contents had gone down by at least half, and it had lost much of its damp, sticky look, as if it had dried off overnight. "That's not possible." He took the container from her and shook it, but nothing emerged.

"Right," the woman said, giving him a flat, unfriendly look. "I'm leaving."

"You can't! There's still a … a *thing* in my bedroom!" Hugo was horrified to find his voice squeaking at the edges.

"I'm not going into some strange bloke's room when he's got me out here under false pretences."

"I didn't … I'm not … there *was* a snake," Hugo protested. "And there *is* something in my bedroom! Honest!"

"Sure." She picked up her stick, stepping away from him. "I'll take your sodding head off if you try to stop me leaving."

Hugo waved both hands frantically, trying to demonstrate just how harmless he was. "*Please!* I'll go into the bedroom first. I'll show you. Just … just don't let it get me, alright?"

She hesitated, and he rushed to the bedroom door.

"Please? I'm scared it's going to eat my cat." *Or me.*

She examined him, her face still hard, then sighed. "*Fine. Just in case there really is something in there, because you are not equipped to handle it.*"

"Thank you," Hugo said, not even bothering to be insulted. She was right, after all. "Thank you *so much.*"

"Whatever. But stay in front of me, or I'll break both your arms."

"Got it." Hugo took a deep breath, and slowly eased the bedroom door open, his chest tight and his hand shaking on the handle. There was nothing immediately visible, just the bed and curtains in turmoil, and he tiptoed to the wardrobe, pointing at it urgently. "It came out of there."

"Open it."

He really wanted to refuse, but he couldn't, or she'd leave, so he got himself behind the door and opened it slowly, too nervous to so much as peek around the edge to see if there was anything rushing out. The woman peered inside, and poked around with her stick, then looked at him.

"I should report you to the police," she said.

"What?" He stepped around the door, discovering the inside of the wardrobe empty except for his clothes, half of them pulled off the hanger and puddled on the bottom. He frowned, then pointed at them – or, rather, what was *on* them. "Look! My cat didn't do that."

The woman craned her neck to look, then prodded him with the stick to push him away so she could get a little closer to the door. "*Huh,*" she said, examining the deposits the creature had left behind. "You're right."

"See! Can you tell what it was?"

She hesitated. "I know what it *looks* like, but it can't be."

"I had a crab in my kitchen and a vanishing snake in my wormery. I'm not sure *can't* is working here."

She frowned, looking around the room. "These windows are closed?"

"Yes."

She pointed the stick at him. "Move and I kneecap you."

"Not moving." He put both hands up and stepped right back against the wall as she crouched down to look under the bed.

"*Huh,*" she said again, and Hugo swallowed hard.

"Is it there?"

The woman looked up at him, her face tight and hard. "Are you a sodding animal smuggler?" She sounded more outraged than she had when she'd thought he was trying to trap her.

"*No!* I swear, I have *no idea* what's happening!"

She lay down on her belly, and used the stick to poke something under the bed. Hugo swallowed a whimper as the sound of scratching claws drifted out.

"Hello, lovely," she said, in a much warmer tone than Hugo had thought she was capable of. "Aren't you a beauty?"

More scratching, and Hugo's knees felt horribly weak. He wasn't going to collapse in front of her. That would be *beyond* embarrassing.

The woman lunged forward suddenly, and the scratching became frantic, a hiss of alarm filling the room. Fibs yowled from next door, and Hugo shouted, "It's alright! Everything's okay!" He wasn't at all sure it *was* okay, as the woman had half-vanished under the bed, and a vast dark wing lashed out from under the side he was standing on, making him swallow a scream. An orangey-brown, furry body followed, then another wing, clawed tips working across the floor like giant, webbed hands, and Hugo grabbed his dressing gown without thinking, flinging it over the creature. It collapsed to the floor with a startled grunt, and the woman backed out from under the bed.

"Nice one," she said with something close to approval, and grabbed the cage, opening the top. She bundled up the creature in the folds of cloth and deposited the whole thing in the crate, then secured the top again. "There you go, my beauty." She looked at Hugo. "You can pick your dressing gown up later."

"No need," he said weakly, one hand pressed to his chest. "What *is* it?"

"Fruit bat," she said.

"That's not a bat! It's *huge!*"

"It's not a local bat," she corrected him. "Must've escaped from somewhere."

"But how did it get in my bedroom?"

She shrugged. "Your kitchen window was open, you said."

He thought about it. "I suppose. But what about the crab? And the snake? Do they eat crabs and snakes? Did it bring them in?"

"Fruit. Bat," the woman said, enunciating clearly.

Hugo scowled at her. "Well, I don't know. Doesn't mean they *just* eat fruit, does it?"

"Well, they don't eat crabs." She examined him, and her expression softened just slightly. "Probably a bird dropped it." She seemed to be ignoring the snake.

"Oh." He rubbed the back of his head, looking at the floor. "I should've thought of that."

"Amazing how often people say that sort of thing." She picked up the crate and left, crooning to the bat as she went, and Hugo looked at the wardrobe for a moment, then collected his clothes from the bottom. They needed a soak and a good wash. Or possibly an incinerator.

It was almost lunchtime when Hugo finally put the wormery on the table and took the lid off with a sigh. "Where—" he started, talking more to Fibs than to the missing worms, then stopped.

It was full of sand.

Not simply dry earth, as if it had become even more dehydrated in the absence of its inhabitants, but *sand.* Golden, silken sand, fresh from the dunes above a tropical beach, or the vast stretches of a distant desert. No apple peelings or springs of old lettuce decorated it. It was flawless.

Hugo very carefully replaced the lid, and looked at Fibs, who put her head to one side.

"*What* is going on?" he asked her.

"*Mrrr.*"

He narrowed his eyes. "Where did that beetle come from? The pretty one?"

"*Mrrr.*"

The window had been open to the wormery on the sill when the crab appeared, and the bat as well. But that made no *sense.* The bat was huge, and what the hell was the crab doing in the wormery? What were *either* of them doing in it? Then again, where had the snake gone, and the worms, and why was there sand in it now? He lifted the lid to take another peek inside, but nothing had changed.

"Do I need a day off?" he asked Fibs, and she just tipped her head again. "Am I having a mental break?"

She didn't reply to that, so evidently he wasn't so far gone he really thought he was having a conversation with a cat. He got up, took a rubbish bag from under the sink, and picked up the wormery.

"Enough of this," he said, took the lid off, and tipped the contents of the bin into the bag, the sand rushing out with the sound of an outgoing tide. Something else came out with it, landing with a solid *thunk,* and Hugo flinched, almost dropping the tub and imagining a scorpion like the one in the shop, or a tarantula, or another snake. The sand stopped, and he set the bin on the floor, peering into the bag. Nothing moved, but something did gleam dully up at him. He hesitated, then went to get the tongs, just in case it was some sort of posh scorpion, pretty as the beetle had been. It didn't move away from the tongs, though, and he fished the object out, looking at Fibs. She'd jumped to the floor and come to investigate matters, sniffing the edge of the tub curiously.

"What's this, then?" he asked, and gingerly set the object on the table. It still gleamed, and he blew the last of the sand off it, revealing dull, richly graven gold curled around a deep red gem, alight with rich colour in the glow of his work lamp. "*Huh,*" he said, feeling like he was channelling the woman from the shop, and picked the thing up. It was heavy, too heavy to be painted plastic. And that colour … Hugo had seen artefacts in museums before with colour like that. New gold didn't have it, more tempered and refined. Very old stuff did, though. *Very* old.

He went back to the bag, sifting through the sand with the tongs, but there was nothing else there. "What's going on, Fibs?" he asked her. "It's a *wormery.* It's not a … a sodding teleportation device. Is it a trick? Someone pranking me or something?" Not that he knew anyone who would, and who smuggles a fruit bat in for a prank, anyway?

She didn't reply, just put her front paws on the edge of the bin, then before he could grab her she'd dived headfirst into it. He started to laugh, thinking she'd be stuck with her hindquarters sticking out, or the whole thing would fall over, but instead she simply kept going, giving a startled *mmmaow?* as her legs and tail followed her into the suddenly bottomless wormery.

"*Fibs!*" Hugo didn't stop to think, didn't hesitate. He just grabbed her tail, because the rest of her was gone, and there was no bloody way the wormery was going to just *take* his cat, gold amulet or not. For one moment he thought he'd missed, even though he could feel the soft fur of her tail against his palm, because there was no weight to her at all, then suddenly the room was very distant, and the smooth confines of the tub's sides rushed up to greet him, and he was plunging after her with a startled cry that sounded very much like hers had.

The darkness was violently all-encompassing, pressing the breath from his lungs and the very memory of sound from his ears, stars and galaxies spinning in his vision, leaving him bewildered as to whether he was passing out or having a stroke or *what* was happening, because he hadn't just fallen into a *countertop bin*. He tried to gasp for breath, but there was no air to be found, and he pulled Fibs toward him by the tail, silently apologising for the rude treatment, then clutched her to his chest. They were tumbling, or spinning, or entirely still while the universe swirled around them, alive or dead or neither, and he buried his face in the cat's soft fur and felt her purring with something like wonder, galaxies reflected in her green eyes.

Then quite abruptly there *was* air, and he gasped in a stuttering breath, chest heaving. He found himself standing, and collapsed to his knees, expecting the smack of the laminate flooring. Instead the ground gave softly beneath him, cool and shifting, and he squeezed his eyes shut, holding to Fibs's steady, rumbling purrs and gently dusty scent. He stayed like that, waiting for pain or nothingness or nausea to take over, but finally, when the world had steadied around his harsh breath and the calm presence of the cat, and nothing had attacked them and they didn't seem in danger of falling into some other rent in reality, he opened one eye, peering around cautiously.

The sky was a dark dome stitched with stars, luminous

and delicate and casually eternal all at once, the constellations wild and unfamiliar and full of the drifting arms of galaxies. Below it vast dunes swept up in peaks and waves, hills and valleys and graceful, rippled contours, a freeze-framed ocean of sand. There were no lights but the stars, no buildings or cars, no blinking satellites or planes passing overhead, no whisper of sound, no life to be seen but him and Fibs, who looked up at him and said, "*Mrrr?*"

"I don't think we're in Leeds anymore," he said, surprised to find his voice wasn't that wobbly. She pushed at his chest, and he let her jump to the sand, looking around with her ears twitching gently. He got up, and turned in a slow circle. "What the hell, Fibs? What *is* this?"

"*Mrrr,*" she said, and set off resolutely across the shifting dunes, her paws light and silent, a shadow in the vast desert beneath distant, drifting star systems.

Hugo took another look around, but there was no wormery waiting to take them back, no helpful *this way home* sign, no landmarks at all.

"Right," he said, for no reason other than to say something. He clicked the tongs, which he'd still somehow held onto, and followed the cat.

It wasn't like there was much else he could do.

COMMUNITY WORK

Lovely people, this story comes with a content warning. There is mention of self-harm and suicide, although only in the sense of one character's concern for another. But I wanted you to know, and there are 21 other stories to read if you would rather skip this one. Please look after yourself above all things.

MACK POKED THE KETTLE WITH ONE FINGER, THE KNUCKLE bunched and twisted with arthritis. The kettle didn't respond, and he sighed, straightening up and looking around the little shed. Jim was snoring unevenly in the old armchair Mack's wife had thrown out of the house ten years ago (which just showed how much life was still left in it. And the rips on the arms and back only gave it character anyway). Pete was peering through his glasses at his phone, where he'd be watching either tractor racing or tractor demos, or possibly a new tractor launch video. The man had a passion, and Mack supposed it was harmless enough, but it did make conversation a little wearing. Pete was even wearing a woollen hat with a tractor brand emblazoned across the side, pulled down to his blossoming ears.

"The kettle's broken," Mack said.

Jim grunted, shifted a bit in his chair, and went back to snoring.

"Eh?" Pete said, without looking up.

"The kettle. It's broken."

"They don't make them like they used to," Pete observed, his eyes still on his screen.

Mack rubbed his hands together, the knuckles painful even in the heat put out by the little wood burner in the corner of the shed. *They don't,* he thought, swallowing a sigh. Or things simply ran down before you expected. After all, he'd flattered himself that he was rather well-built, back in the day. Clare had certainly thought so. But now his hands seemed to be trying to twist themselves into unfamiliar structures, and his eyebrows had inexplicably sprouted all the extra hair that should've been on his head (although at least he still *had* hair, unlike Jim, who'd been bald since he was forty), he had to get up to pee twice every night, and everything inexplicably hurt, everywhere, all the time.

"I'll see if there's a spare in the house," he said.

"Right enough," Pete replied.

Jim just kept snoring, and Mack shrugged into his jacket, doing it up gingerly, then let himself out of the shed and into the winter-kissed garden, the night's frost still gilding bare branches and hardy leaves in the shade. The sky was so pale as to be only the memory of blue, and the smoke from the wood burner hung in the air like a whispered secret.

Mack trudged up the path to the conservatory and let himself in, calling out as he did, "Love? Do we 'have a spare kettle? The one in the shed's given up the ghost."

There was no reply, the house still and silent, smelling faintly of the toast he'd burnt that morning. Photos of children and grandchildren and half-remembered holidays peered down at him from the walls, and he kicked his boots off, padding across the floor in thick socks to the kitchen.

"Clare?"

Still nothing. She must be at the shops, but Mack was seized with the sudden, terrifying conviction that she was *gone*, whisked away by something unseen, leaving him mired amid floral furniture and memories, drowning in loss. He hurried through the house, checking the bedroom, the bathroom, even the spare bedrooms, a weak grey panic rising in his chest, then finally thought to look out at the drive in front of the old bungalow. The car was gone. Of course. She was at the shops, or doing a shift down at the RSPCA shop. Or at the library. Or having a coffee with some friends. It'd be on the calendar, and he should've thought to check before panicking.

"Silly old man," he said to his reflection in the hall mirror, then stood there for a moment wondering what to do. He couldn't just take the kettle from the kitchen. What if Clare came back? She'd want a cuppa. He supposed he could take it, make the teas, then bring it straight back, but that seemed like an awful hassle. He went to check the calendar, but although it said, *Clare library*, it didn't say for how long, and he couldn't remember what her usual times were, so he found his mobile phone where he'd left it on the worktop this morning (hearing his oldest daughter saying, "*Dad*. What use is it having a phone if you don't keep it on you? Honestly!"), and called Clare.

She answered quickly, her voice low. "Hello, love. Everything alright?"

"Yes. How's the library?"

"Busy. It's school holidays. I'd forgotten."

"Oh. Me too."

They were both quiet for a moment, considering when

such things had been monumental affairs, then Clare said, "Did you need something?"

"I … yes. The kettle in the shed broke. Do we have a spare?"

She was silent again, then said, "Do you know, I think we do. We bought one on holiday that time, remember? When the B&B one looked like someone had been boiling hamsters in it?"

Mack laughed softly. He did remember. Clare had always loved little, unplanned getaways. He'd come home from work on a Friday afternoon to find the girls beside themselves with excitement, bags already stacked in the hall, a cool box of food ready to be loaded into the car. And Clare would've found a campground in the middle of a forest, or some tatty seaside hotel with salt on the windows and gently peeling wallpaper, or a creaking mobile home with a door that didn't shut properly, leaking cold air and the bleating of sheep around the edges. It was never fancy, but it was always an adventure. And once the girls had grown and left, they'd ventured into hotels and B&Bs instead of tents and mobile homes, but some of the best trips Mack could remember were the ones where they'd been constantly wet, and cold, and eating soggy sandwiches out of foil.

"We should take another trip," he said.

"Maybe," Clare said. "I think I put the kettle in the loft."

"Oh. I'll take a look."

"Make sure you get one of the boys to spot you on the ladder," she said, and he heard something like a sob rising behind her. "And don't go into the trunk. I have to go."

The line went dead, and Mack looked at his phone for a moment, then put it back on the worktop. He peered into the hall at the loft hatch. He didn't need anyone to spot him. He wasn't *that* old.

Ten minutes later, trying to navigate his way off the drop-down ladder and onto the relative safety of the loft's boarded floor, he reluctantly admitted to himself that he possibly *was* that old. But it was bit late now, especially considering his phone was still in the kitchen. He probably should have put it in his pocket, in case he got stuck up here. Although surely Pete would notice he wasn't back and come looking for him at some point?

"If the tractor videos ever run out," he mumbled, and with a final heave got himself settled safely on the loft boards. He peered around the low, cramped space, lit reluctantly by one bare bulb. Stacked boxes were labelled with things like *Xmas decs* or *beach toys* or simply *misc,* which seemed unhelpful. He pulled the nearest *misc* box to him and opened the top, discovering a jumble of bubble wrap and bits of foam, with no treasures cushioned in it. Packing materials, he supposed, although they hadn't moved for forty years and had no intentions of moving now. Or he didn't think they did.

He tried a second *misc* box, but that seemed to be a lot of half-finished craft projects – knitting needles and wool and bits of stitching type things, flowerpots half-painted and foam balls with googly eyes stuck to them. He remembered Clare trying all these things, now. When she'd first retired, she hadn't seemed to be able to find anything to settle into. She'd joined pottery classes and book clubs, cooking courses and stained-glass workshops, and even the Women's Institute very briefly. She'd tried gardening, and keeping bees, and bird-spotting, then one day had just packed everything up and signed up to volunteer anywhere that would take her.

Mack hadn't been surprised. She'd never been the sort to sit at home, no matter how interesting the hobbies. He *was* a bit surprised she hadn't seemed to want to do as many trips, though. He missed them a little, himself, but mostly he was happy with his shed, and doing some woodwork, and once a week wandering down to the Man Shed in town and teaching younger men how to build things or repair them, rather than just throwing them out and starting again. Everyone was too quick to do that these days.

He folded the top over on the second *misc* box and looked around the attic. There was a large trunk pushed up against the end wall. A proper, honest-to-goodness trunk, with smooth, worn wood strips and metal fastenings, and a beautifully shaped, domed top that made him want to run his hands over it to feel the grain. He didn't remember seeing it before, but Clare couldn't have got it up here on her own. Why did they have a trunk anyway? And what had she said? Look in the trunk? Or *don't* look in the trunk?

He couldn't quite remember which it had been, and it seemed odd of her to mention it. There were no boxes marked *kettle*, and no cheap, off-brand ones hanging about loose among the old hiking boots and disused suitcases and bin bags of old coats, spilling out like shed skins. He'd look in the trunk. She must've said to. *Must* have.

Mack shuffled down the length of the loft, bent over to avoid hitting his head on the beams (that was the other annoying thing about getting old, he thought. Where once a bump was just a bump, barely a bruise, now it seemed to result in the weary skin just giving up in panic, and a completely disproportionate amount of bleeding as a result). He eased himself to the floor in front of the trunk, since crouching was asking far too much of his hips and knees. It was just as lovely close up, even with the light half-blocked by his own shadow and some gentle scuffs and small stains showing up under closer inspection. They merely told stories for those who could read them. He ran a hand over the wood, and it was warm to the touch, that deep, glorious marriage of good grain and good workmanship. He leaned down enough to sniff it, and even as old as it must be – and he was sure it was, no one made things like this these days, and there was no way to wear wood like that artificially – he could smell the memory of deep forest and distant sun in it. Wood had its own magic like that, he thought as he undid the hasp. It remembered.

He wasn't entirely sure what he expected to find when he opened the trunk. Old photos, perhaps, or diaries. A wedding dress, even if they'd been married in Gretna Green, him in a jacket with ice cream on the collar and Clare in a summer dress a touch too short for the disapproving cleaning woman who'd served as their witness. But it was that sort of trunk. It should hold treasure of some sort.

Instead it held a small pile of clothes he didn't immediately recognise, a shapeless beige coat and what looked like some pleated khaki trousers and pastel cardigans. He frowned at them, moving them to one side. They were women's clothes, but Clare would never wear that sort of thing. She told him once that if she ever developed a passion for blouses he was to put her in a secure facility immediately, as she'd evidently lost her marbles. She wore summer dresses and jeans and men's shirts and black jumpers with low fronts, and always had. These weren't hers.

Beneath the clothes he found Clare's old medical bag, the one she'd used all through school, and for her first ten years as a GP, until Mack had finally made enough money to buy her a new leather one for Christmas. That one still held all the household medical supplies in the top of the airing cupboard. He smiled at the old bag, and opened the top to see what she'd stashed inside it. The smile faded as he peered at the contents. Syringes. Lots of them. Syringes and vials and some blister packs of tablets, and he took some out, taking his glasses off his forehead and settling them on his nose as he turned toward the light.

The vials read *phenobarbital*, and the tablets *Rohypnol,* and he stared at them for a long time, then checked the bag again.

There were at least a dozen vials, and four blister packs of the Rohypnol. That was the date rape drug, he knew that. A sedative – a strong one. And he wasn't *sure* what phenobarbital was, but it certainly wasn't aspirin. It wasn't the sort of thing you just had on hand, in case of emergencies. He had an idea, in fact, that the only emergency it was used in was if an animal was in pain and needed to be put down quickly. He sat there in the dim-lit loft, the trunk no longer beautiful, and thought of Clare and how hard retirement had been, and how many things she'd tried and given up on when she never gave up on *anything*, and how she didn't want to go on trips or for days out anymore, and wondered how much else he'd missed, ensconced in his shed. Suddenly the kettle seemed so very, very, *desperately* unimportant.

MACK TOOK the vials and tablets downstairs with him, and stood in the kitchen, mired in confusion. One couldn't just throw such things in the bin, he knew that. They had to be disposed of properly, and normally he'd ask Clare how one went about it, but he could hardly do that with her secret stash. Eventually he put them in a bin bag, bundling them up tightly, then took the kettle from the kitchen and went back to the shed, barely noticing the softening lines of the garden as the day wore on toward lunchtime.

Jim was still snoring. Pete was still watching tractor videos. Mack was seized by the sudden urge to yell at them both, to tell them to wake up and *pay attention*, just like he hadn't been doing. To halt the easy slide into complacency and indifference, to realise that just because work had stopped didn't mean *life* did. But instead he put the kettle on and stashed the bag in the bottom of his toolbox, then stood there staring at the pieces of wood he was meant to be turning into a hedgehog shelter, his hands hanging stiff and useless at his sides, just like the rest of him.

He could barely contain his impatience as he waited for the clock to edge close enough to midday that he could shake Jim awake and shoo them both out into the garden.

"You're in a rush today," Pete said, putting his phone in his jacket pocket. "What's wrong with you?"

"I'm meeting Clare for lunch," Mack said. "I don't want to be late."

Jim yawned hugely. "See you tomorrow?"

"Not tomorrow," Mack said. "We might go away for a few days."

"Fancy. Where to?"

"The seaside," Mack said, because it was the first place he thought of.

"Right enough," Pete said. "Watch out for mermaids." He chortled to himself as he headed across the lawn, Jim ambling after him, two big, slope-shouldered men, becoming oddly homogenous as age dulled their edges.

Mack took the kettle back up to the kitchen then headed straight out the door, hurrying to the bus stop. It was quick enough to get into town, the buses frequent, but he was still impatient, rocking on his heels and craning his neck to peer down the road, almost forcing the bus door open when it finally pulled up.

"Easy there," the driver said, as he fumbled in his pocket for his pass. "Don't do yourself a mischief, rushing like that."

Mack just gave her a tight smile and sat down in the nearest seat, willing every light to be green, every road to be clear, every car to give way to them rather than trying to push ahead. And it sort of worked, the lunchtime traffic light and the bus driver making good time. It still seemed an interminable wait before he could hurry down the bus's steps, almost slipping on the last one, and turn toward the public library, checking the time as he went. She should still be there. They'd go out, and have a nice lunch, and then he'd just … *ask*. Ask how her days were shaped now, how she was managing life beyond work, how she was *feeling*, and mean it. *Listen.* All the things he should have been doing and was so suddenly horrified to realise he evidently wasn't.

He pushed through the door of the big building and went straight to the desk, where a young man with a wilderness of curly black hair was scanning books in. "Is Clare here?" he asked.

The librarian blinked up at him. "Hi. Um … Clare the volunteer?"

"Yes. I'm sorry. Hello. She's my wife."

"You must be Mack," the librarian said, and extended a long-fingered hand across the desk.

Mack shook it, making himself smile and swallowing a scream of impatience. "Yes. Is she here? It's quite urgent."

"She's not in today."

Mack pressed a hand to his chest, which was suddenly too tight. "She didn't come in?"

"It's Wednesday," the young man said, as if that explained everything. He must have seen the confusion on Mack's face, because he added, "She does Tuesday mornings and Friday afternoons. Not Wednesdays."

Mack didn't answer, thinking of the calendar. Maybe he hadn't looked at it properly, but he was sure every Wednesday morning was pencilled in with *Clare library*. But maybe not. Maybe it was the RSPCA shop instead. "Oh," he said aloud. "My mistake. Thanks." He turned and headed back to the door, raising a hand at the young man's farewell, and on the street outside he hesitated, then took his phone from his pocket. He dialled Clare's number and put it to his ear, waiting.

It rang twice, three times, four, and his heart was doing terrible swoops when she answered.

"Yes, love? I'm a bit busy."

"Clare? Where are you?"

"At the library," she said, and he thought his heart might stop entirely. For one moment he wondered if there was more than one library in town, but he knew there wasn't. He swallowed hard, hearing her saying from an echoing distance, "Mack? Are you still there?"

"Yes," he managed. "I was going to meet you for lunch."

"Oh, no. It's far too busy. Let's do it another time."

He nodded jerkily, then realised she couldn't see him. "Yes, okay," he said. "I'll see you later."

"I might be a bit late. I'll pick something up for dinner on the way."

"Alright," he said, as if his world wasn't collapsing around him. "Love you."

"You too," she said, then she was gone, and he sat down heavily on the library step, the phone spilling from his hand. A young woman with a hard face and too much make-up picked it up and held it out to him.

"You alright, mate?" she asked, holding a cigarette away so the smoke didn't drift over him. "You look a bit rough, like."

He looked up. "I think my wife's lying to me," he said, as if she could help.

She nodded, taking a drag on the cigarette. Her fingernails were very long and painted in stripes. "Everyone lies," she said, and waved his phone at him. "Bet you lie to her, too."

He took the phone, thinking about it. "Not about big things."

"Whatever. Sure you don't need an ambulance or something?"

"No," he said, then as she started to turn away he said, "Do you know how to track a phone?"

She turned back, looking him up and down. "Not sure I want to help some bloke who's planning to chase down his wife."

"Please. I found …" He took a breath, wondering why he was talking to this complete stranger about it, with her drawn-on eyebrows and heavy lashes. "I think she might … hurt herself."

The young woman scratched her cheek and he was momentarily alarmed for her, in case she stabbed herself in the eye with one of those fearsome nails. "Should go to the cops, then."

"I'm not sure, though. And she'd be so upset at me if I made a fuss over nothing."

She sighed. "It's not the movies, mate. You can't just *track a phone.*"

"Oh." He tried not to let the loss show on his face, but nothing seemed to be working right, and the young woman sighed again.

"You got one of those Find My Phone things on your computer at home? Anyone set that up for you?"

"I …" *don't know,* he started to say, then realised he *did* know. Clare had set it up for both of them, although he knew it was really for him because he kept forgetting his phone in random places, often on silent so that they couldn't even call it to find it, but she'd set up hers as well. *Just in case,* she'd said, and Mack got up abruptly, then swayed with the sudden movement.

The young woman grabbed his arm to steady him. "Easy. That a yes, then?"

"Yes," he said. "Thank you. Thank you so much."

"Whatever," she said, but she stayed with him until he got

on the bus, her perfume too strong and fighting with the cigarette smoke, making him dizzy.

It was a good plan, but by the time Mack got home and fired the computer up, and remembered what the website was, and got logged in, and figured out how it worked, he discovered the little dot that was Clare's phone was all the way over in Leeds. He stared at it. Had she gone shopping? Was that all this was? But why would she lie about it? And why would she go to *Leeds*? She always said she hated going into the city. Although, she wasn't in the city centre. She was off in the suburbs somewhere, so it couldn't be shopping. Was she visiting someone? But they didn't know anyone there. He didn't think.

Mack sat for a while, trying to imagine who his wife might be visiting in the leafy green streets of Alwoodley. Someone she'd met volunteering, maybe? A new friend? A new … He tried to push the thought down before it could take too much form, but there was no stopping it. She'd had all that trouble adjusting, then suddenly she'd been *happy*, as if she'd finally found something that fitted her. He'd thought it was the volunteering, but what if it wasn't? What if all those Wednesdays (*and don't forget the other days*, his treacherous mind added. *Who knows how many of those RSPCA notes on the calendar are **really** for the RSPCA?*) were spent elsewhere? With someone in Alwoodley, for example? Someone who listened when her husband didn't? Someone who asked *questions* her husband didn't? Someone who had convinced her she didn't need the stash in the trunk? Which, of course, he would be crushingly grateful for, if that was the case, but …

He couldn't think like this. Not about Clare. He was being

ridiculous, and he knew it. But still he kept the computer open on the Find My Phone site, and when the dot started to move he followed it until it pulled into the drive, his stomach sick with apprehension. Only when he heard her coming in the door did he suddenly realise he still had the webpage open, and hurriedly shut it down, pulling up a page on holiday apartments in Blackpool instead.

"Hello, love," Clare said, setting a bag from the local Indian on the table. "I got you korma."

"Great," Mack said. "How was your day?"

"Long. One of the other volunteers didn't come in, so I stayed on." She took her coat off, and he found himself inspecting her, as if she might give herself away through a mis-buttoned shirt or smudged make-up. But she looked just the same as always, in faded jeans and a black jumper, and when she kissed his cheek all he could smell was the familiar scent of her soap and perfume. "Did you find the kettle?"

"The …? No. I'll get one in town tomorrow."

She frowned. "I could've sworn we still had one. Do you want to have another look now?"

He managed a smile. "Do you think it was a guy look?"

"You said it, not me." She smiled back at him. "Come on. Let's do it now, then we can have dinner."

Clare found the kettle straightaway, and after she'd finished teasing him he said, "Where did that trunk come from? It's very good workmanship."

"Oh, I picked it up somewhere," she said vaguely. "You didn't go into it, did you?"

"You said not to."

"Good. I still need my secrets." And she winked at him, but he couldn't bring himself to smile back. Not this time.

THE NEXT WEEKS WERE *FRAUGHT*. That was the only word Mack could think of to describe them. Clare refused to go away to the seaside, and he had to admit that Blackpool in January was hardly that appealing. But she insisted it was due to having so much work on, with other volunteers being out sick, and Mack soon discovered that Wednesday wasn't the only false entry on the calendar. Monday wasn't book club either, not unless book club was now being held in Alwoodley. After the first week he borrowed Jim's car, telling him theirs was in for repairs, and followed Clare.

He expected to see her going into some man's flashy house, the long decades of their marriage suddenly cast aside by the upheaval of retirement and aging and the confusion that accompanied both. But to his astonishment, she parked their car in Leeds, then collected one of those rent-by-the-hour city cars and drove off toward Alwoodley. There, she sat in the car outside a large house behind high gates. She didn't get out, and no one got in, and at the end of the day she drove back, swapped the car, and returned home with him following as well as he could, and trying to remember all the things about tailing someone he'd looked up on the internet.

Clare did the same thing every Monday and Wednesday, never parking in the same place, sometimes not staying as long, sometimes barely stopping, and Mack found himself more and more intrigued. She always came home and told him some anecdote about the library or the book club, and he wondered if they were real, saved from another day, or simple fabrications.

After the second week she asked him again if he'd been into the trunk, and again he said no. He awoke a couple of nights later to the bed empty, and when he pulled the curtains aside to peer into the garden he saw the light on in the shed. The next day the drugs were gone, but Clare said nothing. Neither did he. She wasn't acting like someone who was suicidal, and she wasn't meeting anyone else, so he doubted she was going to bump him off to get him out of the way (his current internet habits were giving him some rather suspicious ideas).

The next time she went out and he followed, in a car he'd found through a Facebook private car hire site (which was a strange idea but also rather convenient), she went into the house. She was wearing the unfamiliar khaki slacks, and a shirt with the logo of a cleaning company on it, with a scarf pulled up over her nose and her hair hidden under a cap. She didn't look up at the camera on the gate, and she already had rubber gloves on, for all the world as if she was about to start scrubbing toilets. When she left again, only a couple of hours later, she did so calmly, without any rush at all, and Mack was left more bewildered than ever. She was sneaking out to *clean houses?* Was she robbing them? Researching how the other half lived? What sort of hobby was this?

The news told him the next day, the paper left out on the table where Clare had been looking at it.

Lawyer accused of abuse dead from suspected overdose.

The address wasn't given, but Mack recognised the house in the photo.

Clare didn't go to Leeds that week, just told Mack she had the Wednesday off from the library. Did he want to go for lunch? He did, and as they sat in the pub, sharing a ploughman's and drinking (a pint of ale for Mack, a half of cider for Clare), he wondered how one said to one's wife, *did you murder that man?*

HE NEVER WORKED out how to ask the question, and the next few weeks were quiet. Then suddenly more volunteers had dropped out, and Clare was doing full days again. Mack didn't follow her this time, just tracked her phone, and eventually found the paper on the table again, open to the story. He didn't know if it was a warning, or her way of telling him what she was doing with the contents of the trunk. He supposed the latter. He had to.

Overdose suspected in deaths of accused child pornographers.

He stopped tracking her phone after that, and suggested she take the software off it. She didn't need it, after all, since she never lost the thing. He also mentioned the Facebook car rentals. How it could all be done in cash, with no one noting your card details or looking at your licence. If you found the right person, of course.

Local businessman dead of suspected overdose after being let off rape charges on technicality.

Local woman suspected of dog-fighting ring overdoses.

Death of serial abuser ruled an overdose.

"We should take some trips," Mack said.

"Oh?" Clare asked.

"We don't want things getting too predictable," he said, tapping the date on the latest article. "You know. Falling into cycles. Becoming patterns."

Clare didn't answer for a long moment, drying a mug slowly as she stared through the kitchen window into the garden. Spring was flushing the world with colour, if not warmth.

"True. We mustn't become predictable," she said. "Just because we're old. There's no excuse."

"There's not," he agreed, getting up and putting his arms around her. "We've got so many years ahead of us yet. We should keep them exciting."

She rested her head on his shoulder for a moment. "Would you like to do some community work with me?"

"I think I'm better behind the scenes," he said. "Logistics, as it were."

She looked up at him and smiled, and it was the same smile as she'd had when she wore the summer dress that had been too short for the cleaning lady's comfort, but which Mack had always thought was the most wonderful piece of clothing he'd ever seen. "A good marriage is always about teamwork," she said.

"And never getting too complacent."

BLACKPOOL DATE-RAPIST OVERDOSES ON ROHYPNOL.

SCARBOROUGH ABUSER *dead of suspected overdose.*

HARROGATE: *Perpetrator of elder abuse found dead, overdose suspected.*

THE WITCHING HOUR

*Sometimes a story just appears, offering no explanation for itself. It simply **is**.*

It's a day-trip to an unknown town, the signs on the notice-board mysteriously specific. It's an overheard scrap of conversation, or the glimpse of a back garden spotted from a passing train, peppered with improbable bird houses.

It's illogical and bewildering, and raises more questions than it answers, but there's a joy in the not-knowing, in the sketched, unseen shape of the larger world beyond the story's borders.

For me, anyway. And I hope you enjoy it too.

"*Double, double, toil and trouble.*"

The women's voices rose in the night, one strong and full of ferocious energy, one a little mumbly, and the third somewhat hoarse, as if the chanter had been smoking a pack a day for the last few decades.

"*Fire burn and cauldron bubble—*" The chant was interrupted by the third woman breaking into a hacking cough, then spitting into the flames. They flared purple and green, and the second woman gave an admiring *ooh*.

The first woman, who stood a little taller than the other two, long thick hair flowing over her shoulders in a glossy mass that reflected the light of the fire, scowled and said with admirable firmness, "*Fillet of a fenny snake—*"

"I couldnae get one," the second woman remarked, rather more clearly than she'd been chanting. "The pet shop won't sell me any more sneks. So's I got eel."

The first woman put her hands on her hips. "*Eel?* Maisie, that is *not* the same."

"S'kind of the same," Maisie said, and took off a well-patched, once-pointy hat that looked like it had been sat on so many times it had forgotten what it should look like.

"*It's not.*"

"They's both like wiggly," Maisie said, demonstrating by flapping one arm about in a manner that was quite unlike either an eel or a snake.

"Goddess help us," the first woman sighed, and ran a hand over her generous locks. The fire cast her face in flattering angles but seemed disinclined to do the same with the two other women, who may have been older or may have simply looked that way.

"*Goddess,*" the third woman said, and spat into the flames again. They went with blue and pink sparks this time, and she nodded approvingly. "Who's this goddess you keep on about, Ann?"

"*Alethea.*"

"I thought your name were Annabeth," Maisie said, settling her hat back on her head and pulling it firmly down to her ears. "I'm sure it were."

"It were," the third woman said. "Only she's fancy now."

"I have taken a name more suited to the feminine goddess I am," Alethea/Ann/Annabeth said, adjusting her robes. They were very well-cut, and featured delicate embellishments on the hem. She'd done those herself, silvery cross-stitch and beads.

"*Goddess.*" The word dripped scorn, and was accompanied with another spit into the fire, but the flames barely flickered this time.

"We all carry a goddess within us, Kitty."

Kitty, who looked less like a kitty – or a goddess – and more like she might have had a few scraps with one or both entities and not necessarily come off best, found a pipe among the folds of her robes and said, "Bollocks."

"Where do we carry this goddess, then?" Maisie asked, looking down at herself and smoothing her robes over her belly. She'd had to take the hem up, and they still dragged on the ground. "Only I thought it were water retention, like."

Alethea took a deep breath, looking up at the stars smudged across the sky in deep burning swathes, glittering with hints of purples and greens and pinks. The tops of the trees were deeper slices of darkness, framing the clearing, and, it seemed, the entire world. All was silent beyond, only the muted grumble of the fire and a hungry sucking as Kitty tried to get her pipe going. Alethea shot her a sideways glance, and said, "It's metaphorical, Maze. It means that we are all, at heart, goddesses. We merely need to embrace our essential divinity to tap into the deep power of the feminine."

"Oh." Maisie thought about it. "So, meta-whatever – is that like a new tampon, then?"

Kitty snorted laughter, sending puffs of smoke out of her nostrils like a small, scruffy dragon. They formed intricate coils in the air, then sped off toward the trees. "Seems more likely than any *goddesses* hanging about. So does that mean you were praying to yourself then, Ann, with your *goddess help us*? Or cursing with your own name?"

"It's merely a form of speech," Alethea said, then

shrugged. "But why wouldn't I pray to myself? What power could be higher than our own sense of the divine?"

Kitty pointed with the stem of her pipe at the sky above the trees, where a shadow was drawing across the stars, less cloud than *presence*. "That, for a start."

Alethea looked at it, and nodded. "Come on. Let's get back to it."

They took their positions around the fire and the big cauldron suspended from a frame above it, the liquid inside dark and glooping softly, releasing scents of rosemary and damp earth and sweet, sharp fury. They didn't hold hands, and there was no dancing. Just three women in mismatched robes standing with their palms and heads raised to the night sky, Kitty with her pipe clamped between her teeth, making her words indistinct.

"*In the cauldron boil and bake,*" they started, and the fire shivered to attention, the flames licking around the pot sparking and flaring in strange colours that were greens and purples and blues, yet not.

"*Eye of newt and toe of frog,*" they intoned, Alethea's voice rising warm and strong, carrying them all. She did have a knack for this sort of thing, Kitty thought. The showy bits, like.

"*Wool of bat and hair of the dog—*"

"*Maisie!*" Alethea dropped her hands to her sides and glared at the shorter woman. "*Hair of the dog?* Really?"

"I've got a stinking hangover," Maisie said. "It's our Sue's cider. She had a tasting day yesterday, and I'm not over it yet."

Kitty cackled, and the fire danced in admiration. She had a good, hoarse, dirty cackle, which was at least partly down to the pipe. "Did you no' take some remedy?"

"Sure, but maybe not enough." Maisie rubbed her belly again. "Or maybe it's the goddess kicking off."

"This goddess is going to kick off soon," Alethea muttered, glancing at the darkening in the sky. She pulled back the sleeve of her robe to reveal a smartwatch. "It's almost the witching hour. How are you *still* hungover?"

"It were a big tasting."

"That's a contradiction in terms. And anyway, aren't you supposed to spit it out when you're tasting?"

Maisie looked horrified. "I'd never! Sue would turn me into a potato."

"Only if you spat it *on* her, I reckon," Kitty said, taking the opportunity to re-light her pipe. "She's not much for the charms these days, other than the cider."

"I think she made those charms too strong and all," Maisie said. "I woke up in the airing cupboard with a traffic cone, three chickens, and a small rose bush."

"A rose bush?" Alethea started, then shook her head. "No, never mind. Can we just focus? We've got *minutes* left till the witching hour, and you know we have to be done by then. Start again from *wool of bat.*"

"Was bloody hard to get, that," Kitty observed. "Seamus didn't want shaving again. Think his tummy's a bit cold."

Maisie made a sympathetic noise, and Alethea pressed both hands to her forehead.

"Can we just *start?*"

"Oh, sure. Just saying."

"I really wish you wouldn't."

"Covens are meant to be social, you know," Kitty said. "It's not all cursing and spiting."

Alethea pointed at her watch. "Can we discuss this later? Please?"

Kitty huffed, but took her pipe out of her mouth and lifted her head to the sky. A shiver of anticipation ran through the clearing, trembling the long grass and setting the sleeping flowers swaying.

"Wool of bat and tongue of dog,
Adder's fork and blind-worm's sting—"
"I—" Maisie started, and Alethea cut her off.

"I swear to the Goddess, Maisie, if you're interrupting to tell me you used a plastic fork from the chippie and some mosquito venom *I will put you in the bloody cauldron.*" She glared at the other woman, who considered it, then nodded.

"Fair do's," Maisie said, then added quickly, "But it were like a chicken wishbone, because it's sort of a fork, right, and some of that bee venom serum stuff. Right pricey it were, too."

Alethea squeezed her eyes shut, took a breath, then started again.

"Lizard's leg and howlet's wing—"
Kitty stopped chanting and started to say something, and Alethea snatched up a bottle of alcopop from beside the fire and threw it at her. The sort-of-goddess had excellent aim, but Kitty was quicker. She grabbed the bottle before it could hit her and opened the top, releasing a whiff of bubble gum and taking a gulp as she went back to the chant.

"—For a charm of powerful trouble,
Like a hell-broth boil and bubble."
The shiver hadn't faded away, even with the interruption. Instead it grew and swelled, rolling between the trees, setting the branches quivering. The vibration of them seeped into the air, setting it singing in a high, strange hum, the noise that one hears in deep and utter silence, the sound of existence, the whisper of a soul, a sliver of the universe twisted into form.

"Double, double, toil and trouble;
Fire burn and cauldron bubble."
The reverberation of that strange sound wasn't felt as a physical thing by the women. It didn't shake the earth beneath their bare feet, or sway them where they stood. But

it crept in anyway, raising the hair on their arms, and setting the fillings in Maisie's teeth tingling with acid, and crackling like static electricity in Kitty's knee replacement, and sparking on the tips of Alethea's hair. They shuddered and delighted in it, raising their arms and voices higher to a sky roiling with that strange cloud.

It was no longer a dark presence, and less obscured the stars than fed them, transforming them into delicate scarves of variegated purple and green that draped and danced and twisted across the sky, luminous and vibrant. Two counties over, a small man with a thermos mug and an expensive smartphone captured what he insisted were midsummer northern light in the south of England, and was promptly laughed out of all the natural world photography forums he frequented. He took revenge by using his shots to win two creative photography competitions before the next summer.

"Cool it with a baboon's blood,

Then the charm is firm and good."

Alethea stepped forward and threw the contents of a small jar into the cauldron. The brew erupted, foaming and frothing in rabid fury. The clouds trembled, the colours intensifying until the women had to shield their eyes, and the clearing flooded with multihued light that painted the trees and the flowers and the tangled grass in luminescence. The fire roared as the cauldron boiled over, setting the flames flaring ravenously upward, and for a moment the light was so intense Kitty had to close her eyes. She could see the blood vessels chasing themselves across the inside of her eyelids, as if she was staring into the sun. Then the light was gone, not fading or melting away, simply gone as if it had never been.

For a moment the night was still, the silence so intense it packed the ears with the cotton-wool sense of an after blast, then somewhere an owl posed its endless question, and further off a motorbike revved on a distant road, and closer a dog started barking in delayed alarm.

Kitty coughed, took another swig of alcopop, and stuck her pipe back in her mouth. The fire had gone out, swallowed by the charm and the overflowing cauldron, and she fumbled for her lighter.

Flat white light popped into being as Alethea switched her phone torch on, and shone it at the other two women. Maisie flinched.

"That's awful bright, An— Alethea. Don't we have the lantern?'

"Well, I need to be able to see to light the bloody lantern," Alethea said, and crouched down by her bags. A moment later she set a plastic camping light next to the ruins of the fire, its gentle yellow LEDs illuminating the cauldron lying on its side a couple of metres away. There was a large hole in its base.

"Bloody hell," Kitty said, in between enthusiastic puffs on her pipe. "Another sodding cauldron shot. This never used to happen."

"They don't make them like they used to," Maisie agreed, padding over to take a closer look at the cauldron. It was steaming slightly, and bits of its base were still crumbling softly away.

"It would help if people got the ingredients they're supposed to," Alethea said.

"Oh, aye. And that were proper baboon's blood, were it?" Kitty asked.

Alethea checked her watch. "We just got done in time."

"What were it?" Kitty demanded, taking a swing of alcopop. She grimaced. "This is *dire,* this is."

"I like 'em," Maisie said. "Makes me feel like a teen again."

"We didn't have these when we were teens. It were ale down the tavern or naught. Not"— she inspected the label, peering at it in the low light—"Blue sodding Paradise something or other."

"It's the idea of it, though," Maisie insisted. "Young things make me feel young."

"There are better young things for that," Alethea observed, adjusting her robe over her breasts. It really had a very complementary cut.

Kitty shook her head and handed Maisie the bottle. "You have it. I brought some wine. Nice pinot noir from that flash shop." She looked back at Alethea. "Then we wait out the witching hour, and meantime our resident goddess can tell us what she used instead of baboon blood."

Alethea sighed and took a thermos flask and a plastic glass from a strappy backpack. She poured herself a large measure of something that had the sharp whiff of botanicals, then went to sit on one of the handy logs they'd dragged up for that purpose. "*Fine.* My contact at the zoo got fired—"

"For stealing vials of baboon blood?" Kitty asked.

"No. I mean, we only need it once a year. But apparently he was secretly renting the chimps out for tea parties and there was an *incident.*"

"*Ooh,*" Maisie said. "I'd quite fancy that. A chimp tea party. Like those old ads on the TV."

"It was nothing like that," Alethea said. "It seems chimps don't much like tea parties."

Kitty waved impatiently. "So what did you use?"

Alethea shifted uncomfortably. "I did *try* to get some, but what with it being so close to witching hour—"

Kitty blew smoke at her, and she coughed, waving it away irritably.

"Okay, okay. Port."

"Port?" Maisie asked. "Like, wine?"

"Well, *fortified* wine."

Kitty cackled. "Oh, no wonder the bum blew off the cauldron, then. We weren't even in the same *postcode* as the ingredients."

Alethea sighed. "I know." She looked down at her hands, clasped around the plastic glass of gin and tonic (with just a twist of lemon, because being in the woods was no reason to slum it). "I hope it works."

"It will," Kitty said comfortably. "Don't it always?"

"Yes, but we have less of the right ingredients every year," Alethea pointed out. "How's it even the right spell anymore?"

"What happens if it don't work?" Maisie asked. "What happens if the witching hour passes and we haven't done the spell right?"

Kitty shrugged. "I imagine we walk back down the hill and get on with our lives. Or crumble to dust. One of the two."

"We did it in time," Maisie said, and looked at the other two anxiously. "*As starts the hour, so ends the charm, and the witch's life is bound from harm.* We did that, right?"

"We tried," Alethea said.

Maisie drained her alcopop and took another from her bag. "I *like* being a witch."

Kitty tapped her pipe out and started refilling it. "I like being alive, more's the point. I'm not even sure how long it's been now, but I don't fancy the alternative so much."

"We did all we could," Alethea said. "We can't help that ingredients are getting scarce."

"I should have tried harder to get a fenny snake," Maisie said. "There must be other pet shops."

"It's all a state of mind, anyway," Kitty said. "It's not about the charm, or the ingredients, or even the hour. It's here." She tapped her head.

Alethea shook her own head. "It's not," she said. "It's *here.*" And she tapped her chest. "You don't think it, you feel it. And we'll feel when we lose the magic, too."

"Well, I'll certainly feel if I crumble to dust," Maisie said, mostly to herself.

"Mayhap it's both," Kitty said after a moment. "Belief is head and heart, right?"

Alethea raised her glass. Kitty clunked her bottle of wine against it, and took a gulp straight from the neck.

And then they waited.

Waited for the witching hour to pass, the one hour each year when witches are no longer witches, the one hour that legend holds witches are most dangerous, because the witches created those legends, and know that the opposite is true.

Waited to see if the charm had worked, or if it even mattered. Because magic was a powerful thing, but the will was more powerful still.

Or maybe, in the end, they were no different.

One just had to believe to know magic.

And to have a good supply of cauldrons.

THE FOURTH FLOOR

*This is one of the very rare instances where I can point to some-thing and say, **this**. This is where the story came from. Because I did move into a new apartment recently. And I did have a very confusing encounter with a new neighbour.*

For the rest, however ...

MOVING INTO A NEW APARTMENT'S ALWAYS AN ADJUSTMENT. An exploration, if you will. Figuring out where everything fits. Forgetting where the cutlery drawer is for the first couple of weeks. Walking into the wall on the way to the loo in the middle of the night, because the door's not where you think it should be. Starting awake because next door's or downstairs' snoring chorus is loud enough it feels like they're in the room with you. Discovering which of your own doors slam and which squeak, and how loudly.

Your stuff expands slowly into the new space, creeping across surfaces and making homes in cupboards, fitting and not fitting in unpredictable and frustrating ways, every space *just* the wrong shape. Moving the sofa and the table half a dozen times before deciding where you want it, which is likely exactly where the last tenant had it, because there's only so much room in a 40-square-metre apartment.

Then, of course, there's the neighbourhood to explore. Finding the nearest supermarket or corner shop, and figuring out how much you can carry back if you walk, and if that seems sensible or more likely to end in a tangle with a car, a dog, or a mugger. Plus if it's even worth it, or if all you'll find on the shelves is some short-dated milk and half a mouldy cabbage.

There's just all these *things*, you know? It's not simply packing up your old place and unpacking at the new one, sorting out power and water and all that. I mean, obviously that's the main stuff, but then there's this endless litany of tiny discoveries and adjustments and complications that never make it onto a moving day to-do list.

Things like where the bins are, and when they're emptied, and if anyone cleans them or if you need a hazmat suit and breathing apparatus to approach, plus possibly a cricket bat to fend off rats or seagulls. Where the letterboxes are, and whether delivery drivers will bother finding them, or just drive past and send you a "no one was home" notification when you've been waiting in for eight hours. If anyone cleans the common areas, or if there's a rota, which will inevitably be enforced by some terrifyingly bored and over-involved individual in a buttoned-up cardigan and severe glasses.

There's always one of those, by the way, whether the cleaning's an issue or not. Always a self-appointed guardian eyeing your balcony for rogue plants, or your mat for care-lessly collected dirt. There's always a busybody, just as there's always a chatterer who tries to corner you in the entrance hall. And, of course, there is always, *always* a weird neighbour.

You know the ones I mean. The cat lady, the train collector, the guy who dives into his apartment at the slightest sign of movement and whom no one's ever really seen. The nocturnal rubbish-collector, the midnight opera lover, the one whose balcony's stuffed with garden gnomes and metal butterflies and an endless chorus of wind chimes.

It's basically law. Every apartment block needs one weird neighbour, and if you're not sure who yours is, well. Check your wind chimes and get back to me.

IT USUALLY TAKES a few weeks or a month to figure out the neighbour dynamics, to work out who's harmlessly weird or *avoid at all costs* chatty, as opposed to who's just working night shifts or being a welcoming, good-neighbour sort.

But I think I got a head start on things this morning.

I was in the lift, on my way down to the garage, where a combination of the overflow of my stuff plus a bewildering assortment of ornaments, lidless pots, and half-burned candles I'd cleared out of the apartment were taking up the space where my car should be.

The lift shuffled down one floor then stopped, and I backed up against the wall, hoping there wasn't going to be more than one person getting in. It had been uncomfortably intimate in here with the letting agent when I viewed the place, carefully avoiding eye contact and trying not to wheeze from his overpowering cologne.

Thankfully, when the door opened it revealed just one woman with well-set grey hair, a quilted bag tucked under her arm. She stepped in, her legs solid and tan under the sort of khaki walking shorts women of a certain age always seem to favour, and she smiled broadly at me as the door slid shut again.

"You're new," she said, poking 0 for the ground floor. Handy. At least I didn't have to make small talk while we both meandered into the garage.

"Just moved in," I said brightly, putting on my *I promise I'm harmless and make no excess noise* new neighbour grin.

"That apartment on the second floor," she said, nodding approvingly. "Good. It's been empty for ages."

Second? *She'd* got on at the second. "Third," I said.

"Second," she repeated, in a tone that brooked no argument.

"You live on the second?" I suggested, and she gave me a suspicious look, like she thought I might try stalking her.

"I live on the fourth. The one with the big balcony. You're just under me."

"On the third," I agreed.

"The *second*," she said, enunciating carefully, and the door opened on the ground floor. She looked at me expectantly, unmoving, and after a moment I got out, giving her a nod and a smile. I wasn't sure what else to do.

I took the stairs the rest of the way down, and by the time I stepped into the garage she was gone, if that was even where she'd been headed.

It was a fairly harmless sort of weird, at least.

Although in some small part of my mind I must've half expected there'd be no button for the third floor when I got back in the lift with the last of my boxes, because I was oddly relieved to see it still existed. It glowed the same deep red as the display when I hit it (why red? Hardly comforting, is it?), and the lift pootled smoothly upward without interruption.

When the door opened I peered out a little cautiously, as if Ms Fourth Floor might be lying in wait to accuse me of being in the wrong place, but there was just the empty corridor, mats neatly aligned outside each of the three red doors, just as it had been when I left. I dragged my boxes into the hall while the lift complained and tried to close the door on my leg with rather more enthusiasm than seemed safe, then finally snapped closed triumphantly when I stepped out.

I hefted my stuff to the end of the hall and let myself into the quiet of the new apartment, that same relief seeping into my bones as I spotted my books on the shelves, my running shoes capsized by the mat. Funny how things get into your head.

I DIDN'T THINK about the woman again for a few days. I was too busy pulling my life out of boxes, shifting things from one place to another then back again, nesting into the space and making it home for however long it'd last this time. I discovered the person next door ran the washing machine every other night at ten p.m., and the one at the end of the hall had a dog which barked periodically, with no pattern I could discern.

They were tolerable things – the washing machine late enough to be annoying, but not loud enough to keep me awake. The dog's erratic barking made me vaguely anxious at first, in case it was me disturbing it, but it's not like I keep strange hours. It'd adjust or it wouldn't. For myself, I ran the dishwasher in the afternoon and kept the TV low. I hadn't been there long enough to make myself a nuisance. I hoped.

So things were okay. More than okay, in fact. The apartment was comfortable, warm and sunny, the garage convenient, the local shops free from mouldy cabbages and the bins free of rats. It was easy to feel settled, to begin to shape my days to their new surroundings. I stopped walking into the wall on the way to the loo, and started opening the cutlery drawer first try.

And then it started.

The noises from upstairs.

I thought it was another washing machine at first, or maybe a particularly loud dishwasher. Gurgling and splashing noises, at any rate, groans and knocks, all at two in the morning and loud enough to drag me out of sleep. I drifted into consciousness with a sense of grudging inevitability and lay there staring up at the ceiling, lost in the dimness of the shuttered room. The churning noises continued, just a tiny bit too loud to be ignored, and I started doing that thing of counting how much sleep I'd get if I fell asleep now … and now … and now …

But sleep wasn't forthcoming, so eventually I got up, made a cup of tea, and watched rubbish on YouTube. It was better than lying there fretting.

It was quiet again for a few days after that, and I'd just about decided it was a one-off, a timer set wrong on some appliance, when I woke again to rushing water and dull thudding, a migraine come to life in the ceiling. It was four a.m. this time, and it sounded less mechanical, more *organic*, as if someone was having a swampy hoedown up there.

I listened to it for a while, trying to make sense of it, to find rhythm or patterns, but it was too late or too early or I was too tired. And, fine. It was the weekend. Maybe my confused upstairs neighbour (assuming she *was* upstairs and not downstairs) was having some sort of wild after-pub party.

I found some earplugs left over from a plane trip, burrowed back into the pillows, and resolutely ignored the muffled beat of what *could* have been a multitude of feet. She really must have a bloody big balcony up there. And a thriving social life, but then anyone had one of those when compared to me.

ANOTHER FEW DAYS OF QUIET, and then I woke with my heart seizing in my chest, a hot fear-sweat already rising on my shoulders. I all but threw myself out of bed, halfway to the door before I realised the ceiling wasn't falling in on me.

I fumbled the overhead light on, still panting, and saw the shade wobbling in its fitting to the rhythm of a heavy beat that reverberated down through the walls and into my feet. I huffed air, half relieved it wasn't an earthquake, half miffed that I was going to have to Do Something. There's being a tolerant neighbour and there's being walked all over – or stomped all over.

With a groan, I kicked into a pair of trainers, grabbed my hoody, and stumbled out into the hall, surprised none of my neighbours were out there with me. The party must've been directly above me.

I took the stairs, my feet loud on the concrete treads but any echoes muffled in the cramped space. At the top I pulled open the door onto a dark and silent hall. It only had two apartment doors, not the three of my floor, so evidently the balconies weren't the only thing bigger up here.

I marched to the end of the hall, where a door that matched mine stood, raised my hand to knock, then paused. It was silent up here. No music behind the door, no voices lifted in delight, and definitely no wild stomping. I looked over my shoulder, to the door at the other end of the hall. Surely they'd have been out here if it had been that loud?

But it *had* been that loud. I could feel the sweat cooling on my shoulders, and the lingering shudders of fright in my legs. I stood there for a moment longer, my hand still poised to knock, but I couldn't hear anything. Pipes? Could it have been some weird plumbing thing, air caught and clattering in a blockage? That was a thing, apparently, although I wasn't sure whether I'd read it or heard it. Bloody unhealthy pipes if that was the case.

I dropped my hand and stood there for a little longer, like a guest unsure they'd got the right date for a party. Everything stayed silent, the building slumbering around me, and eventually I retreated. I didn't want to be That Neighbour. No one wants to be That Neighbour.

THE NEXT DAY I made banana bread, wrapped it lightly in foil, and retraced my steps up to the fourth floor. It was mid-afternoon, a civilised sort of time, and I knocked briskly on the door of my upstairs neighbour. Oddly, the hall up here seemed less well-kept than my own, the walls scarred with scuffs and scratches, and the floor tiles chipped in random patterns, as if someone had been dropping heavy things about the place. A damp, dank smell drifted from somewhere, and I wondered about pipes again. In the daylight it seemed more likely than a four a.m. line dancing competition.

I knocked a second time, and thought I heard movement behind the door, as if someone was lurking, spying through the peephole at me, but there was still no answer, so I took my bread and retreated. I knocked on the door next to mine instead, and a small woman in giant glasses answered so quickly I stumbled back a step. She evidently *had* been watching me.

"Hello," she said, eyeing the cake. A ginger cat with a deeply disgruntled expression glared up at me from next to her.

"Hi," I said. "I've just moved in next door."

"Not just. It's been seventeen days."

"Oh. Right." There didn't seem to be anything I could say to that. "Um … is there any trouble with the plumbing in the building, d'you know?"

"You can't flush cat litter," she said immediately.

"I don't have a cat."

"Even so."

Neither of us spoke for a moment, then I offered her the cake. It seemed rude not to.

She took it, inspected it, then handed it back with much the same expression as the cat. "We don't like bananas."

"Good to know." We stared at each other for a bit longer, her, me, and the grumpy ginger feline, then I nodded and fumbled with my own door, dropping the keys twice before I could get it open. She and the damn cat watched me the whole time, and when I squinted out the peephole from the safety of the other side they were still standing there. Great. This place was apparently overrun with weird neighbours.

That evening I slipped out and headed up to the fourth floor again, itching at the thought of my nosey next-door neighbour and her cat peeking out to watch me pass (I couldn't help imagining Ginger had his own, feline-height peephole). The stairwell was locked at the top, which seemed like both a fire hazard and a personal affront, as if they were intent on keeping out the riffraff from the lower floors. I scowled at the door, then turned and went home again, leaving a trail of baked banana scent behind me.

I had a fat slice of the bread for dinner, raising my mug of tea to the ceiling as I ate. They'd had their chance at it.

"I tried," I said, but the ceiling remained silent other than one ominous creak.

I guess you've spotted the flaw in my approach here. If the door to the stairs was locked, why not use the lift? I mean, *obviously*. But I was sick of chasing weird neighbours, and didn't want to become the annoying one, plus the cake really did smell damn good. So somehow I just didn't think of it, and by the time I did I'd already carved into the loaf.

Half-eaten baked goods hardly seemed designed to take the sting out of a noise complaint.

So I resolved to wait and see what happened next. I was probably making a fuss out of nothing, after all.

WHAT HAPPENED NEXT WAS APPARENTLY a full-scale mosh pit kicking off above me on a Friday night. Or early Saturday morning, to be precise.

And sure, it was the weekend, but I swear a brand-new crack ran across the ceiling as I bolted for the door. I didn't even bother with shoes, just ran for the stairwell, taking them two at a time and just about dislocating my shoulder when I tried to pull the locked door at the top open. I swore, raced back downstairs, and jabbed the lift button furiously until the door dinged open with something close to reluctance. I stumbled in, avoiding my reflection in the mirrored wall, and slapped the button for the fourth floor.

The door was agonisingly slow to close, and I slapped the button again, half a dozen times. The lift thought about it, then headed down with a certain stately deliberation.

"*No,*" I snapped, as if the lift was a recalcitrant dog who'd widdled on the rug, and that had about as much effect as you might expect.

We kept trundling downward, and I patted my frazzled hair into place as well as I could, assuming I was about to be joined by another nocturnal resident. There wasn't anything I could do about my current outfit of pyjama trousers with a rip in one leg and an old T-shirt with bleach stains on it, but hopefully my hair wouldn't cause anyone to panic.

The lift stopped on the second floor and the door slid open on a completely dark hall. The air that crept in was chilly, and I pulled a little further back from the threshold, as if afraid something might materialise in the shadows and grab me. Nothing did, and I poked the fourth floor button again, a nasty unease drifting in my belly. I didn't like that dark. It wasn't as empty as one might like.

The door closed and the lift set off with rather more enthusiasm this time, before delivering me back to my own floor with an air of satisfaction.

"No, you crappy thing," I muttered, and tapped the fourth floor button irritably. "Come *on*."

The lift's door shut once again, and once again we lurched away in the wrong direction, while I complained and poked every button I could. We ended up down in the garage, where the lift gave a rather terminal wheeze. The door slid open and all the lights inside went out, turning me into a ghost in the mirror. I tried a button tentatively, but nothing happened. Not even a flicker of illumination around it. I sighed and got out, trudging to the stairs. At least the lights out here were working.

I climbed back to the third floor and got all the way to my door before I realised my keys were still on its inside.

I SPENT the rest of the night sitting morosely on my doormat, moving whenever the hall's motion activated lights went out, and occasionally wandering downstairs to see if it was light out yet. That seemed to take far longer that was reasonable, but eventually I thought it was late enough to knock on the cat lady's door.

She popped out instantly, and I wondered if she'd slept in the same position as me, only on the right side of her door, lucky thing. It was either that or she simply stood behind it all the time, the royal guard of the apartment block.

"Yes?" she said.

I tried for a smile, my face feeling stretched and unnatural. "I'm locked out. Could you maybe call a locksmith?"

She examined me, the disgruntled cat leaning around her with an expression which suggested he'd thrown up hairballs better looking than me. Fair enough. I felt about as bad as that. But the woman said, "Alright," then closed the door again.

I hoped she was quick about it. I was going to pee on her mat if I had to sit out here much longer.

Luckily, she *was* quick. I was back inside my apartment within an hour, 150 euros lighter. Not that I cared by that point. I handed over my card, shut the door behind the locksmith, and just about ran for the loo. Then I crawled into bed and slept for a couple of hours before getting up again and calling the building's management.

"I need to make a complaint," I told the disinterested man who answered.

"Do you, though?"

"What?"

"Do you need to? Or do you just want to?"

"I need to if I don't want my ceiling falling in," I snapped.

"Alright, alright. Some people are all about the drama, is all."

I stared blankly at the wall, took a breath, then said, "It's the apartment directly above me. They keep playing music, or dancing, or—"

"Above you?" he asked, interrupting me with that same bored tone.

"Yes—"

"You're apartment 3C, right?"

"Yes—"

"There's no one above you."

"Well, their terrace then—"

"Drama," the man said, sounding like he was throwing his

hands up, or rolling his eyes, or both. "Find someone else to tell tales to, can't you? Or at least make it more believable. Bloody hell." He hung up, still muttering, and no one answered when I called back.

I stayed where I was for a little, looking doubtfully up at the ceiling, then went out onto the balcony. I leaned out, peering up to try to see the terrace above, but the angle was all wrong, or it was stepped back or something. I couldn't see anything past my own overhang. But there clearly was a fourth floor. I'd been up there.

The combination of sleep deprivation and irritation was evidently getting to me, because I trotted down the stairs, out of the building, and along the road until I could look back and get a clear view of the whole residence. The whole residence and its one-two-three-four, *four, clearly four* floors.

Or not clearly, but definitely.

Sort of.

I pinched my forehead, squeezing my eyes closed then opening them again. I really hadn't had much sleep. I could see the building just fine, but when I looked up at the top of it, everything got oddly indistinct. I tried rubbing my eyes, but it made no difference. I had the strangest idea I was seeing the top floor through clear but choppy water, the image fractured and unreliable.

"It's there, though," I said, startling a woman walking past with a Scottie dog in a plaid coat. "Excuse me," I said, and pointed at the building. "How my floors does that have?"

"I carry mace," she said, and hurried off, dragging the well-dressed dog behind her.

"It's four," I said. "Definitely four."

I went back in, taking the stairs all the way up, counting the floors as I passed. One. Two. Three. Four, and the door still didn't open. I put my ear to it, almost hesitantly, but heard nothing except the whisper of my own breath, uncomfortably jagged.

"Definitely four," I whispered again.

THAT NIGHT it sounded like a stampede, buffalo charging over hard-packed ground. I think. It's not something I've heard outside of a nature documentary, but my whole bedroom shuddered in just the way one might imagine it would, if a herd of buffalo raced over the top of it.

I ran upstairs (with the keys clutched in my hand this time) and didn't even try the door. I just hammered my fist on it, yelling as I did. "Hey! *Hey!* Shut up in there, can't you? *Shut up!*"

No one answered – I hadn't really expected them to – and a moment later I was running down the stairs again, down and down and round and round, out onto the street and back to my vantage point, craning my neck as I searched for the lights of the party.

There were none.

The lights in my own apartment spilled gently onto the balcony, not affording a view inside from this angle, but filtering comfortably out into the night. Above that ...

Above that was nothing.

No, not nothing. Worse than that.

Something.

In the night and the dark, the fourth floor swam into focus, but it wasn't any sort of focus I understood. It was *too* clear, too sharp, cast in lines that made no sense. They drew shapes out of the emptiness that made my eye twitch, and that was nothing compared to what my brain was doing as it struggled to comprehend what I was seeing.

That place – because it was no more a fourth floor than it

was an apartment – that *place* was made up of angles and planes that couldn't exist, things that shifted and connected and concertinaed and collapsed, inverted mountains and towering cities and fractured, looming voids, and I understood with sudden, perfect conviction that no one had been tap dancing above my ceiling, or partying down in the wee small hours. Instead dimensions had been colliding, physics turning inside out and reality crumbling, doing terrible things to my plaster.

"Maybe not four," I whispered, and my head gave a warning throb.

I WOULD'VE SLEPT in the car, likely after driving a couple of towns or preferably countries away, but I'd left the keys inside along with my phone. So, reluctantly, I crept back in and up the stairs, tiptoeing as if I might bring the brutally alien, broken world of the fourth floor crashing down on me if I made the slightest noise. For all I knew, I might.

The cat lady's door popped open as I padded toward my own, sending me scuttling sideways into the far wall like an alarmed crab, and she regarded me with bright, inquisitive eyes while the cat gave me that patented feline stare of superiority.

"It's late," she observed.

"There's something wrong with the fourth floor," I replied. "Like, really wrong."

She looked up, and I did too, waiting to see those weird angles intruding into the corners of the corridor, crumpling our reality to reveal something mind-breakingly beautiful and brutal under its skin, but there were only a couple of stray cobwebs.

"It looks alright," she said.

"It's not. It's not even *there.*"

She shrugged, and the cat yawned, exposing worn yellow teeth & a pink tongue. "It'll come back."

"*What?*"

"It'll come back when it's ready," she clarified, as if that made it any better.

I blinked at her. "There is a *hole* in the *world* where the fourth floor should be."

"Don't be so dramatic. It's more of a tear. A little one."

"*That doesn't help.*"

She sighed. "It's handy."

"*How?*"

She considered it, then said, "No pigeons. I don't like pigeons. And it keeps the rent down."

I slumped against the wall, abruptly exhausted. "I'm not bloody surprised it does. What *is* it?"

"A bit of a blip."

"A blip."

The cat huffed, something far too much like laughter, and narrowed orange eyes at me.

"Yes. A blip. A tear in dimensions." She waved vaguely. "It comes and goes."

I wondered if *I* was having a blip, coming and going a bit myself, but the wall was cool on my shoulder, and my thumb still smarted where I'd caught the nail assembling shelves the other day, so it felt pretty real. "Are we safe? What if it spreads?"

She gave that some thought, frowning under her huge glasses. "It never has before. The second floor gets a bit muddled sometimes, but third and first are always okay. Prime numbers, you know."

I didn't know, but I wasn't going to ask, either. I wiped my mouth. "Where do they go? The fourth and the second?"

Neither the woman nor the cat answered straight away.

We just looked at each other for a long time, then finally she said, "I like carrot cake."

Once again I found myself without an answer, so I just nodded, a polite, neighbourly nod, and lurched to my door, fumbling my way inside. I was desperately cold, as if the chill of unknown dimensions was seeping through the floor. Or ceiling.

A blip. And here I'd been worried about rubbish collection and washing machines. I pulled a blanket off the sofa and took it under the table with me, where I sat for the rest of the night with the rapidly shrinking banana bread.

To be fair, I didn't like pigeons either. And the rent was admirably cheap. I could agree with that.

The neighbours were *really* weird, though.

But then, weren't they everywhere?

13

EDUCATION ISN'T FOR EVERYONE

This odd little tale arrived from nowhere I can quite identify. Violet just appeared, small and mousy and overlooked, so I followed her to see what happened.

I'd say I'm hoping she didn't notice me, but I have an idea she most certainly did ...

IT HAD TO BE PERFECT. THAT WASN'T A CONCEIT. IT WAS A necessity.

Violet pressed another handful of ferns into place, using dead and dying leaves that were already brown and curled at the edges. The sort of leaves one would *expect* to find lying about on the muddy floor of the woods. Cate, with her high-tech thermals and her knife lashed to her thigh like that woman in the old movies, with her constellations tattooed on her forearms and her high-tensile rope stitched into her trousers – which she'd shown Violet the other day, boasting about how she was getting around the rules – Cate had used fresh leaves.

Violet knew. She'd seen, had watched from where she'd curled herself into the fork of a tree, as still and silent as the owlet tucked into a gap in the trunk nearby. She'd sat there so long the owlet had toddled out and investigated her coat, checking the pockets for snacks. But there were none. Those were against the rules, too.

Violet had waited until she knew Cate would have moved on, no longer lingering in the cover of the trees but looking for a place to hole up for the night. That was part of the Exam, knowing how your opponents moved. Violet knew Cate didn't like the dark. That was why the other girl had hurried with the trap, turned it into something a bunny would've been hard-pressed to miss.

Violet liked the dark. Her night vision was good – all the carrots, her mum told her. Eat *all* the carrots, and she'd see in the dark better than anyone! Violet thought her mum put too much stock in the power of an orange vegetable. She thought it was down to all the practise. All the blindfolds in the forest, and the lost days in the mines, and the caverns—

No, she didn't think about the caverns. But she did think the reason she was so good in the dark was mostly to do with the fact it simply didn't scare her. It felt like a cocoon, a security blanket knitted just for her, swaddling her in its comforting, impenetrable folds, small and silent and invisible.

It was like that – fully dark – when she came down from the tree, the owlet carefully deposited back into its nest. It would be barely a mouthful, and she wasn't that hungry yet. Thin light filtered through the trees, trickling from the stars and the thin, petulant moon, painting the world in shades of dimness. It was just enough to see by, if one was patient and careful and understood how to read the varying textures of the night. Violet was all these things, and it didn't take her long to disassemble Cate's trap. She would have left it in place – she knew where it was, so it was no threat to her, and such things could be used strategically – but Cate had used some fishing line. That would come in handy. Bringing in line was against the rules, of course, but everyone knew the rules were there to be circumvented. That was part of the Exam, too.

Violet played a different Exam, though. She didn't circumvent the rules. She would stand there stolidly while the adjudicators patted her down, digging thin cruel fingers into her deep, empty pockets and running them around her sides, sometimes pinching rudely at the round swell of her belly and the soft expanses of her thighs. She didn't flinch. She merely waited, and eventually she would be handed back her knife (a folding one with a wooden handle that had been her aunt's) and her shoes (cheap things of worn leather, hand-me-downs of hand-me-downs, the soles replaced so many times yet still wearing thin), and then the adjudicators would say, with some puzzlement, "All clear."

They'd move on to the next girl, bending over them, cowing them with their grown-ness, their very existence, and finding sweets tucked into hidden pockets, or matches rolled into the tops of socks, or thin rope stitched carefully into a jacket collar. Always something, and once one thing was found, the adjudicators would usually move on. So maybe someone kept their razor, or their water purifying straw, or their compass, even if they lost something else.

And always someone would lean to someone else – never to Violet, not to Violet with her stockiness and her silence and her plain brown cardigan pulled over her brown tartan skirt, and her dad's old anorak swamping her almost to her knees in faded, stained blue, and her glasses always sliding down her nose. No, no one ever leaned to her, but one of the girls with her plait lashed by a band that would prove to be wire, her cheeks painted with flashes of pink in the cold, would lean to another, each of them so slim and muscled as to be reflections of one another, although maybe the other's hair would be in a bun, rehydration packets rolled within it, and she would whisper, "Does she have *nothing?*"

The words would be a mix of sympathy and glee and horror, and Violet would stare dully out across the field that marked the start of the Exam, the empty green field with its tall border wall formed of thick, horned hedges, and she would ignore them all.

Finally, when the inspections were done and the adjudicators were satisfied they'd done their duty (with perhaps a little less thoroughness to those girls whose parents had bigger houses or bigger bank balances), the gun would go. There was no ceremony, no audience to cheer them on, no countdown, just the adjudicator's brief, "All clear," then the Mistress's sharp, ringing tones.

"Right, girls. The Exams begin. You are year fives, therefore you have five days to prove you deserve your place at the school. Go forth and win."

Then there would be the snap of the gun, and all the lean, strong girls would sprint out across the grass, scattering as they made for spots where they'd identified weaknesses in the green walls, gaps that could be forced through. There were no teams, although sometimes girls would pair up to help each other get started. Not often, though. Being too close to another competitor could lead to an "accident", a knife to the calf instead of the branches, a knee to the jaw, an elbow to the eye – or a sharpened stick. Enough to slow someone, and maybe even enough to put them out of the Exam before it even began. Places were limited. Classes shrank every year at the Academy. They had to. The world couldn't support too many people getting Educated. Just look what had happened last time.

Violet never ran. She would walk sedately across the

grass, watching the girls ahead of her, until they'd all vanished through the wall. Only then would she choose the biggest gap they'd left behind to slip through, the hard work already done. Smarter didn't mean faster. She'd learned that, in the caverns and the darkness and with the blindfolds.

Now it was the third night, the halfway mark of the competition. Cate was still in play, but she was getting hungry. Not hungry enough to quit, but hungry enough to make mistakes. Harriet was out here somewhere too, quieter and more careful than Cate, and Violet had seen signs of others. They didn't bother her. No one noticed the dumpy brown girl in her dumpy brown clothes. Why would they? She was the smallest threat ever, until she walked up to the stage, pushing her glasses up her nose, and took her place with the rest who had survived the days without tapping out with dehydration, or poisoning from bad water or misidentified mushrooms, or injuries that were never quite explained.

Every year the other girls had been surprised when Violet made it through, but she knew that was changing. It had to. For five years she had survived against the odds. There were fewer places every year, and last year two girls had been disqualified because they were declared to have smuggled equipment past the adjudicators. Of course, they *had.* Violet couldn't be caught that way, but she was aware there were other ways to be taken down, just like there were other ways through the fence than alone.

She gathered up the line from Cate's trap and slipped deeper into the woods, a mousy shadow, poking at the ground ahead as she went and listening for ambush. She didn't think it would happen this year. Next year, perhaps. The following year, definitely. Ten years of schooling, the lucky ones got. From six to sixteen, and then if you were *very* lucky you went into the Higher Education Exams. They – They with a capital T – said it was fairer than the old ways, when it had been down to how good you were at remembering things and how much money your family had as to what sort of Education you got.

Violet didn't know if it *was* fairer, especially given how the adjudicators went about things, but her dad had got almost all the way to year six, and her aunt … her aunt had got through every year of a Higher Education. Violet supposed that wouldn't have happened without the Exams, because the only money she had ever seen had been what her aunt brought home after she got an Educated Job. Plus she knew her aunt was very bad at remembering things, like how the Wars had started, because she'd asked her once, when she'd been reading an old book that her aunt had been given after her final Exam. Her aunt had just shrugged and said, "I can look that up, Vivi. I can't look up how to set a snare when I'm out there in the dark." And she'd gone back to showing Violet how to tell which frog was edible and which would set you hallucinating for three days.

A crack hissed through the woods, a call to attention, and Violet stopped. It had been a branch pushed a little too far out of the way as something pressed against it. It was too sharp and clear for a stick that had been stepped on. She sank to the ground, her anorak pooling around her. Out there, it had been that sad old man blue. In here, in the thick night, turned inside out, it was dull greys and greens and browns, blending with her skirt and muddied legs and long mousy brown plaits to become nothing more than a little patch of undergrowth.

"*Shhh*," someone hissed.

"You *shhh*," another muttered. "She's not here."

"Well, she's not *now*, with you crashing around like a tractor."

"It was *one branch*."

"It's enough. I mean, have you even seen her since we've been in here?"

"No." There was a faint noise, someone clicking their tongue against the roof of their mouth in annoyance, and Violet recognised it. Paula, with her waterproof boots and rip-proof leggings and her long blonde hair wrapped in a scarf that could be used as a fishing net – and, judging by last year's Exam, as a strangulation device.

If Paula was here, that meant Beth was the other voice, and Dani couldn't be far away. They were cousins, and had run every Exam together, protecting each other and ensuring they got through to the next year. There had been a surprising uptick in injuries since they'd entered Education. And the deaths had been rather more physical than usual. More frequent, too.

"It's no good," Paula said. "We've still got two nights. We'll regroup."

"Fine," Beth said. "I hate creeping around in the dark anyway."

They made very little noise as they moved away, but Violet heard them go anyway. And she waited, her legs cramping from her crouch and a branch tickling her neck irritatingly, and her throat dry with thirst.

The thin hostile moon vanished, and the stars burned brighter, and drifted above the trees, and Violet waited. The cold crept up her legs and sank teeth into her bones, and some small insect buzzed hungrily in her ear, and still she waited.

The stars were gone and the sky was pale when she heard a smallest of movements off to her left, and she very care-fully, creakingly, turned her head in that direction without moving her body at all. She caught a flash of mud-smeared leggings as someone stole slowly through the undergrowth, and she nodded to herself. Only after they were gone did she stand and carefully stretch, then creep out, searching for water and to see if her snare had caught her some breakfast. She should be safe for now. They'd try another spot later, and she'd have to be careful. They were noticing her, and that was risky.

SHE HAD CREATED a food store for herself in the hollow of a rotting tree, down by the stale, stinking water of the old duck pond. It buzzed with insects, its bottom clogged with ancient algae and weeds. This whole place had been some sort of garden once, belonging to the building that housed the school. It had been a house in the before times, and people had lived in it, a family with other people to work for them and presumably build duck ponds.

There were no ducks in the pond now, and the old statue that rose from the centre was cleaved off at its belly. Violet wished there were ducks. But they were loud, plus she'd have to light a fire, because she doubted duck meat was good to eat raw. She didn't even like eating the frogs raw, but it was safe, and a fire was too risky. Keeping her strength up was important, though. Her dad was very clear on that.

She crouched at the base of the tree, leaning over the water, and slurped at its green murk through a filter made from material torn from her skirt. It wasn't perfect, and the water still tasted of dead fish and mulchy leaves, but it got the worst out. No one liked coming down here. The insects bit, and there were rumours something lived in the pond itself, some distorted remnant of the past, twisted by the destruction that had changed everything, but not killed by it.

Violet doubted that was the case, but she repeated the rumours anyway. It gave her some safety.

Or it had.

It was the sudden silence of the birds that warned her. The insects still droned on, but a giltern squawked, and a parrot-headed magpie shrilled its alarmed cry. Violet didn't hesitate, simply slipped into the pond water and retreated behind a growth of rushes, her feet tangling in the hard limbs of the water lilies and her hands buried in the accumulated silt of the bottom.

Mary emerged from the trees, moving slowly, and hesitated on the edge of the pond, checking both ways. After a moment she relaxed, and looked back. She nodded, and Pat slipped out to join her, her hair caked with mud.

"She here?" Pat asked, her voice low.

"No," Mary said, and walked straight to the tree. To *Violet's* tree. "Look – she's got a stash. A hedgesquirrel and half a dozen frogs."

"Are they safe to eat?" Pat asked.

"Sure. She knows all this stuff."

Pat grabbed a frog. "I'm *starving.*"

"Yeah, but we'll just take a couple, okay? Leave the rest."

"But—" Pat started, and Mary cut her off.

"No. I couldn't have got through the first couple of years without her. She taught me loads."

"She's creepy."

"I know, but still." Mary handed Pat another frog, then took two herself. "This'll be enough. Come on." She turned and headed away, and after a little while Violet surfaced, blinking at the dull daylight, not unlike a frog herself.

SHE WAS STILL in the pond, collecting more frogs to top up her supplies and tucking them into the pockets of her jacket for safe-keeping when Pat stepped out of the trees again. Violet froze, willing herself to melt into the background, but there was no hiding. She was too late. She hadn't been paying enough attention.

"You!" Beth said, pointing somewhat imperiously at Violet where she stood on the side of the pond. "You've got food!"

"I've got frogs," Violet mumbled.

"And a hedgesquirrel," Pat said. "Mary showed me. She didn't want me to take it all, though. Thinks they're friends or something."

There was no sign of Mary herself, Violet noticed, pushing her glasses up her nose. She stayed where she was, unmoving, and watched Beth, Paula and Dani approach, Pat trailing behind them with a grin on her face. Paula had her scarf loose at her side, and Beth bounced a folding knife in her hand. It was a little like Violet's, but the blade looked longer.

"Where's the stash?" Dani asked Pat, and she pointed to the tree. Dani went to investigate while Paula and Beth still watched Violet.

"Looks slippery in there," Paula said. "You want to be careful."

"I am," Violet said.

"There's not much here," Dani called. "A couple of frogs and a hedge thingy. Won't go far."

"What else've you got?" Beth asked.

"Nothing," Violet said, letting a little note of alarm creep into her voice.

"Show me your pockets." Paula took a step forward. She'd hit her growth spurt before anyone, and she towered over Violet, who gave a hiccough and took a frog out of her pocket, offering it to the bigger girl. "That's more like it. Give me the whole jacket. Come on."

"But it's cold," Violet said. "I'll freeze."

"Not my problem." Paula swung her scarf gently. *Give me the jacket.*"

Violet struggled out of it and handed it over. "My knife—"

"You won't need it," Paula said, and Violet spun around and launched herself across the pond on all fours, taking great leaping lunges, not bothering to try and run over the tangled, slippery bottom, just surging through the water in bounds. Paula shouted and tried to follow, but the weeds and lilies snatched at her feet, sending her crashing into the water, swearing and thrashing. The others were shouting, too, and Violet knew they'd be fighting through mud and the rushes on the shoreline, trying to intercept her on the far side. The reeds were thick and sharp, though, and drew blood at the touch. Or they did if you ran in upright, and she heard yelps of pain as her pursuers did just that.

Violet slipped out of the pond, still on her hands and knees, keeping her head down and squinting behind the protection of her glasses as she scuttled right into the heart of the rushes. Only when it became so thick she could barely push forward did she stop, dropping to her belly with her heart pounding. The ground was wet and sludgy, and a black, double-headed snake flicked its tongues at her. She flicked hers back, and it stared at her for a moment, then headed on its way.

She waited. She was good at waiting.

She smelled the fire only half an hour or so later. They must've been very hungry indeed.

Soon after that she smelled cooking frogs, and her stomach grumbled hungrily. She dug her fingers into the muck and uncovered a few snails, checking their shells for the tell-tale markings before apologising quietly and smashing them between her palms, plucking the flesh out.

It wasn't much, but it was something, chewy and stagnant-tasting and enough to keep her going. That was what everyone got wrong, she thought. They thought the hunger was *too much*, like it was that which would break them. And sure, when they hit the ten-day Exam, the hunger would be a bigger problem. But five days was fine. Five days meant all she really needed was water and a little nibble now and then to keep the worst at bay.

She watched the sun casting shadows through the reeds as the day moved on, and she waited.

Mary was crouched by the fire when Violet emerged from the reeds the same way she'd gone in, sliding over the edge of the pond and back into the murky water like some oversized, mud-encrusted amphibian. She paddled to the far shore, picking her way onto drier land and squeezing her clothes out while Mary watched silently. There was no sign of the other four girls.

"Where did they go?" Violet asked, picking her jacket up and shaking it out. She found a frog lingering in one pocket, and she let it hop away.

"Wandering in their own little dreams," Mary said. "Beth was still together enough to try to head for the graduating field, but I don't think she'll make it. How long does it last?"

"Three days." Violet offered the other girl a snail, and she shook her head. "It's safe, Mary. I wouldn't do it to you."

"For now," Mary said, and stood up. "What happens next year?"

"We do the same."

"Someone's going to realise."

"Maybe," Violet said. "But then we'll think of something else."

"And the final year? What then?"

"By then it'll be just you and me," Violet said, and smiled. It was a small and very sweet smile, but Mary shivered, hard enough that Violet could see it.

That was okay.

That was as it should be.

After all, Education isn't for everyone.

14

DECK THE HALLS

As a child of the South Pacific, I was always fascinated by the idea of a dark, cold Christmas, the night held back by lights and pines. This was fed in large part by the beautiful Moominvalley Midwinter *by Tove Jansson, in which Moomintroll, encountering the idea of Christmas for the first time, concludes it must be some terrifying beast come to devour us all.*

And given how many festive creatures are rather toothy, I think he wasn't far wrong ...

A LIST OF FESTIVE BEASTIES

I WAS NOT, UNFORTUNATELY, ABLE TO INCLUDE ALL THE beasties I came across when hunting out rather unfriendly festive entities, but these are the ones I did use, in no particular order. I have, as ever, played rather free and easy with appearances and attributes, so I apologise if I've ruined anyone's favourites. I shall blame it on writer's licence and the vagaries of my subconscious ...

· · ·

Odin: The father of all gods in Norse mythology, he was often described as a bearded old man wearing a hat and a cloak. He also liked riding his eight-legged horse Sleipnir across the midwinter night's sky, delivering gifts to those down below, and this, combined with the Nordic midwinter celebrations of Yule, means he's sometimes associated with Santa and the season. Plus he would absolutely not miss a party.

Saturn: Saturnalia is the Roman festival dedicated to the god Saturn, and runs from December 17–23. Celebrations involved role reversals, gift-giving, and plenty of revelry (plus some sacrifices, depending on what account one reads).

Grýla: In Icelandic folklore, Grýla is a ravenous, bad-tempered ogre or troll who haunts the mountains, and every Christmas she hunts down naughty children to drag off and throw into her stew pot. She's also mother to the Yule Lads and mistress(ish) of the Yule Cat.

The Yule Lads: Grýla's thirteen sons take turns to visit Icelandic children in the nights leading up to Christmas, bringing mischief in the form of slamming doors, licking spoons, eating the yoghurt, stealing sausages, and … other stuff. Lock up your sheep.

Jólakötturinn (The Yule Cat): Grýla's feline companion is also out causing trouble at Christmas. He checks to make sure children are wearing new clothes, and if not, he eats them. Because that seems reasonable.

Tomten: A fickle little beast in Scandinavian folklore, Tomten can be a helpful caretaker and household protector, but if you don't give him treats he'll fly into a rage. He might settle for driving you mad with his tricks, but if he bites you, it's game over.

Krampus: We all know Krampus. Saint Nicholas's sidekick, he gets to beat the naughty children, then shove them in his sack and steal them off. He might snack on them later, or take them to hell. Either way, clean your rooms, kids.

Frau Perchta: So if you've been good in Austria and Bavaria, Frau Perchta might give you a little treat. If you haven't, she'll disembowel you and fill the cavity with straw. Which is kind of an overreaction, in my mind, but don't tell her I said that.

Mari Lwyd: In Wales, on New Year's Eve, if you want to keep an undead horse and her zombie groupies out of your house, you have to have a battle of wits with her. In rhyme. Which … I think I'd end up with a zombie house if I had to do it.

Père Fouettard: The lovely Père and his wife liked to butcher wealthy children in France, Belgium, and Switzerland, and would salt the body parts in barrels. Saint Nicholas was not best pleased, and his solution was to make Père immortal, and allow him to dole out punishment to naughty children. Like he did when he was alive.

Hans Trapp: After making some very dodgy deals with the devil to become rich, Hans took to roaming the French countryside dressed as a scarecrow, hunting children to cook over an open fire. Now he turns up at Christmas, going door to door looking for more tasty snacks.

Straggele: Frau Perchta has a whole entourage of Straggele, who share the feasts people leave out for her, and give her a hand with all that disembowelling. It's hard work single-handed.

Kallikantzari: In Greece, Bulgaria, Serbia, and Turkey, the all-male Kallikantzari spend all year underground, working on bringing about the apocalypse (so basically a pack of supervillains). At Christmas, though, they come to the surface to cause trouble, and are described as having horns, being covered in black fur, and being … ah … *well-endowed.*

Belsnickel: A scruffy, filthy little monster, he turns up a couple of weeks before Christmas in some areas of Germany, with pockets full of cake and a whip in one hand. For balance, I guess.

Deck the Halls

"No," Greta said, pointing a finger at the group in front of her. The nail was gnawed so short that the skin around it had been rendered raw and inflamed, but that was only to be expected at this time of year. It was Christmas, after all, and bitten nails, insomnia, and a certain creeping dread were seasonal necessities.

"But," one of the group started, and she raised her finger, turning the pointing *you* into a *stop*. She didn't know what the speaker's name was, and, if she were honest, all thirteen of the creatures in front of her were entirely interchangeable as far as she was concerned, even if they weren't identical. She had no intentions of learning to tell them apart, preferring to regard them as a single entity, a multicellular organism formed from a hodgepodge of little trolls in misbuttoned, badly darned cardigans, all equipped with big beards, worn-down boots, and knitted hats pulled down to their impressive eyebrows.

"One day each," Greta said, and looked at the elf next to her. "Whose day is it today?"

"Bowel Licker," the elf said, examining her clipboard. Her name was Dina, and her nails were, like the rest of her, immaculate, but *she* didn't have to deal with the organisation-level stuff, did she? She just had to tick the damn things off on her tablet and call it good.

"Bowel Licker?" Greta said, suddenly realising what she'd heard. The trolls tittered.

"*Bowl*," Dina said. "Like cake bowls."

"Oh."

"Don't be gross," one of the trolls said. "It's species-ist."

Greta scowled at him. "One of you's a sheep fancier."

"*Sheep Cote Clod*, thanks very much," a gnome in mucky wellies said.

"Just a fancy name for it, though, innit?" another with a greasy beard put in.

"Shut it, Sausage Wiper." Sheep Fancier shoved his brother, who shoved him back harder, sending him crashing into a third who was dressed all in shades of black and grey, with night-vision goggles on his head.

"Sausage *Swiper*, and them's breakfast sausages!" the greasy-bearded gnome snapped.

"Sure they are," the goth gnome said.

"Not sheep, though, is it? Or cow teats!"

"That's for the milk," another with a pale beard said. "And I take it from the buckets. It's not *weird*."

"That's not what I saw," a gnome with three pairs of binoculars around his neck said, and the milk-drinker threw a sodden scarf covered in questionable stains at him.

Greta grimaced, and clapped her hands together to get their attention. "I don't *care*," she said. "But you get one night each, remember? Those are the rules. So you can't go out scoffing yoghurt and stealing meat and peeking in windows all at the same time."

"Only tonight?" Bowl Licker whined. "But I'm late starting."

"You best get on then, hadn't you?" She pointed across the hall, which bore more than a passing resemblance to the arrival hall of a small local airport, with a coffee cart in one corner and double doors at both ends. One set were wooden, heavy and old-fashioned, with intricate carving on the frame. The others, facing them across the length of the hall, were heavy glass sliding doors, with a red light shining from a box set above the frame. An empty platform was visible through the glass, grey and misted with drifting snow.

The hall between the doors was crowded with desks, elves typing desperately at workstations, or scuffling through printouts, or gulping hot drinks with their eyes on the giant display screens that looked down from the walls. Rather than arrivals or departures, a rolling count of children's names washed across them, picked out in gold, silver, and bronze. A few years ago it had been decided that green for good and red for naughty was too limiting, and a sliding scale had been introduced, where gold was tops, bronze was unacceptable, and silver was somewhere in between. Greta would really have liked to know what slobbering, brain-frozen middle management snow-ghast had come up with that. It was now much harder to tell at a glance the difference between gold and bronze, plus bloody *everyone* was fighting over which silver tier kids should get visits to scare them good – sorry, *gold* – and which were better served bribes as rewards for not being bronze. The new system was at least 60 percent responsible for her gnawed nails.

Although, Christmas. There was always something.

"But I only got to steal like twenty sausages on my night," Swiper wailed. "And three of them were vegetarian, so it shouldn't even count!"

"Get out or I'll tell your mum," Greta said.

"She won't care," a gnome with mysterious stains on his cardigan said, waving a meat hook at her. "She *likes* our mischief."

"Says we're charming," Sheepy agreed.

"Best boys," a very short gnome put in.

"There are rules," Greta said. "And you know what? I've got better things to do than listen to you whine. It's Christmas Eve, so I'm calling it. You're done, the lot of you. Get your act together for next year, or I'll start blocking your shuttle passes."

"Aw," Bowl started, and Greta took a bell from her pocket. It was small and somewhat tacky, a metallic silver that had rubbed off in places to reveal the white plastic beneath. Daubs of red suggested it might've had some decorative touches at some point – or that it had been dropped in something a little unpleasant. A scrap of ribbon, looking oddly as if something had been chewing on it, was threaded though the top, and a bit of cotton wool stuck out of the bottom, silencing its clapper.

"Don't make me use it," she said, and the Yule Lads looked at her for a moment, then at each other.

Finally Meat Hook shrugged. "Whatever," he said, and turned away, leading the other twelve to the wooden doors and pulling them open onto the velvet darkness of the winter night. They trailed out, the second to last gnome throwing the door violently shut behind him, making one elf scream and another drop her coffee. The last gnome staggered back from the slammed door, still sucking absently on a spoon, then opened it again and wandered out into the cold.

Greta watched them go, then put the bell back in the pocket of her waistcoat. Her suit was a sombre grey, finely pinstriped, and her only nod to the day was a glittering silver bracelet with tiny Yule trees hanging from it. Dina, who had opted for a similarly tailored outfit, but in deeply festive reds and golds, offered her a thermal mug. The lid was off to allow room for a frothy mountain of whipped cream, liberally sprinkled with crushed candy canes.

"What is *that?*" Greta demanded.

"Peppermint hot chocolate?" the elf offered.

"Do I look like I need peppermint hot chocolate?" Greta demanded, and jabbed a finger at her own face. "Do I look like peppermint hot chocolate is going to help me?"

"You've had six double espressos in the last hour," Dina said. "We don't want a repeat of last year, do we? You were so rude to Tomten he bit you. It's just a good thing you're not human."

Greta patted her hair, feeling all the little curls and loops that were escaping, betraying her careful dressing. "All I said was I'd put a muzzle on him if he munched on any more naugh— Bronze kids. You can't just go around biting people these days. The paperwork gives me migraines."

"Sure, but the venom had you hallucinating so badly you were out of commission all through New Year's Eve. I was left holding the baubles when Frau Perchta went rogue and started riding Mari Lwyd down the Champs-Élysées, disembowelling everyone who looked at her funny. The Straggele tore four gendarmes to pieces before we got things under any sort of control. I'm not paid enough for that."

Greta took the hot chocolate reluctantly. "Is Mari alright?"

"No, she's been sulking all year and kicking anyone who gets close enough. She didn't get a single rhyme battle in, because she doesn't speak French, plus anyone she tried to challenge got themselves chopped up by Perchta and her pack. We only got hold of that old witch because she was looting the gardens in Versailles for straw to replace people's organs with, and there's not much of that to be had in Paris these days. The cover-up was a *nightmare,* and I'm not doing it again just because you're in caffeine overload."

Greta sighed. Dina had handled it all perfectly, of course, as she did everything from an elf having a panic attack over a broken cookie to Krampus "forgetting" he wasn't actually meant to steal any kids off to hell. But she didn't blame the elf for not wanting to step into her own role. Every year she decided to quit, and every year she ended up back here anyway, watching the minutes count down from Christmas Eve to Christmas Day, and hoping Odin didn't decide to check in on Yule, or at least not until the work was done. Debauchery needed to work on a timetable, after all. She took a sip of hot chocolate, and winced. It was very sweet, intensely pepperminty, and … "Is there schnapps in here?"

"The Kallikantzari are the next dispatch."

"Oh, hell." Greta gulped the spiked hot chocolate as the wooden double doors banged open, unleashing a swirl of snow and frozen air that snarled around the bent legs of the new-comers. Legs, and … other things.

"Woo-hoo!" the largest of the Kallikantzari shouted, and shook himself off, scattering snow off his dark, silky pelt and setting things flopping about the place. A young elf on a tea run dropped his tray of mugs, eyes wide as he stared at the goblins. They cheered, and one jumped out of the pack to give a suggestive wiggle in the young elf's direction. He abandoned the broken mugs and fled, his ears so red they looked ready to catch alight.

"Greta baby!" the lead goblin shouted, and strode forward with his arms outstretched. "Give us a cuddle, gorgeous."

Greta held her hand out to Dina, palm up, and the elf slapped a large pair of metal kitchen shears into it. Greta flicked the catch off and worked the handles a few times, the shears making some satisfyingly fierce snipping noises. The Kallikantzari pack's attention went straight to the blades.

"Easy," the lead one said, while a few of his fellows covered their more delicate areas protectively with their hairy paws. "We're just being friendly."

"This is a place of business," Greta said.

"Aw, come on. We've been underground all year. This is our one chance for a little fun." He put one big foot up on a nearby desk casually, knee wide, and the elf sat at the computer pushed her chair back so fast it tipped over, spilling her to the ground with a squeal. "Easy, sweetheart," the lead Kallikantzari said. "No need to throw yourself at my feet. There's plenty to go around." He gave everything a little jiggle, and Dina gagged audibly, then turned it into a cough.

"Stop it," Greta snapped at the goblin. "I'll cut you down to half a day if you don't respect my staff."

"Aw, want me all for yourself?" he asked, running his

fingers through the thick hair on his chest, fangs shining with just-polished vigour.

Greta did not. She wasn't against horns and hair on principle, although her tastes usually ran a little more to scales and claws, but this wasn't about personal preferences. It was Christmas Eve, and that meant she had no time to even think about what she might or might not want. "You have festive mischief to get on with," she said. "You don't have time for this."

"Oh, we always have time for this," the leader said, grinning at the other Kallikantzari. A cheer of agreement came back, accompanied by more wiggling and some pointed hip thrusts. From the thirsty look glazing the eyes of a few of them, Greta was starting to fear for the potted Christmas trees.

"I'm telling you, you don't," she said, and pointed to the giant countdown clock above the glass departure doors. "Move it. Remember your jobs. A little mischief, a sprinkling of chaos. No shagging inflatable reindeer."

"What about real ones?" a smaller Kallikantzari asked hopefully from the back, and a large one with a heavy coat of silver-shot hair clipped him around the ear. "*Ow! What?*"

"You think a reindeer wants you groping it?" the older goblin asked.

"I can *ask*."

"You better," the other said, and faced front again, giving Greta a sharp nod that was only slightly undermined by the wink he delivered at the same time.

She went for another swig of her hot chocolate, found the mug empty, and waved it at the assembled goblins irritably. "Well? What're you waiting for? Go!"

"I'll be thinking of you all the way," the leader said, still grinning, and waved toward the departure doors. "Let's rock this Eve, boys!"

A cheer went up, and the Kallikantzari charged forward in a wash of flowing fur and gleaming horns and dangling bits, the older goblin giving Greta another wink and miming a phone next to his ear as he ran past, all muscular thighs and big arms and broad shoulders. She turned to watch the light above the doors go green and the panels slide obediently open at a tap on Dina's tablet, the goblins still whooping and cheering, chest-bumping and fist-pumping as they barrelled through. Dina tapped her tablet again and the door slid closed, cutting off both the noise and the arctic blast that had all the elves grabbing coats from the backs of their chairs and cramming hats over their pointy ears. The Kallikantzari could be seen through the glass, first carrying on their roughhousing, then slowly stopping, looking around and stomping bare feet, clapping their hands on their arms and starting to shiver visibly as they waited.

"Dina," Greta said.

"Oops," the elf said innocently, and checked her tablet. A moment later – long enough that the goblins were hunching their shoulders and fluffing up their fur, but not long enough that they started banging on the doors – a sleek silver carriage swept into the platform, its sides formed of tinted windows as deeply dark as the Arctic night. A door popped open, and the Kallikantzari shoved and wrestled each other as they piled in. It snapped shut behind them, and the shuttle pulled out at a speed that sent a storm of snow swirling around the doors, obscuring the platform from view.

Greta exhaled slowly, and jumped at a gurgle of liquid close to hand. Dina steadied her boss's thermal mug, added a little more schnapps, then beckoned to the young elf who'd dropped his tray. He rushed over with a new load of drinks, his ears still luminously red, and Dina took a hot chocolate, tipping it on top of the liquor.

"You want cream?" she asked, and the young elf took half a step toward the coffee cart.

"No," Greta said, taking a hearty swig of hot chocolate. She looked at the young elf. "Monty, right? You okay?"

"I broke the mugs," he whispered.

"Never mind. Happens to the best of us."

"Greta threw a monitor at the big one's head once," Dina said, scrolling though her tablet. "And kicked another in the tender bits."

Monty stared at Greta, swallowing visibly.

"Those were two separate occasions," Greta protested.

"Same Christmas Eve, though."

Greta shrugged. "They deserved it."

"That's true," Dina said, and looked at the wooden door. "We should have … ah, yes. Tweedle-munch and Tweedle-chew."

The doors swung open on two very human-looking men, one tall and curved at the shoulders, his belly incongruously large under a yellowing white singlet and brown braces, his green trousers smeared with uneasy stains. The other man was squat and round, a ball held up on spindly legs, sporting bushy sideburns and filthy nails. He wore a blue shirt done up to the neck, the top button biting into the soft flesh viciously. The pair marched in measured, synchronised steps up to Greta and Dina while the room fell silent. No one spoke. No keyboards clattered. No one so much as rolled their chair to a different position. Everyone simply watched, as if to move might be to attract the pair's attention, and that would be something terrible.

"Père Fouettard, Hans Trapp," Greta said.

The men's gazes were directed at her, but they didn't seem to quite land, as if staring at something just beyond or just before her, in a slightly different time or space or version of reality. They didn't speak, and she curled her fingers around the bell, squeezing it until the edges dug painfully into her skin.

She cleared her throat, then managed, "Your shuttle," with a gesture at the departure doors. The silvery carriage was already in place, Dina's finger hovering over the tablet while she did her best not to look at the men.

The pair didn't answer, just ground into motion again and marched out to the platform. As the doors slid shut behind them and they were thankfully lost behind a screen of shifting snow, the room whispered back into life. No one mentioned the two men, no one looked to see where they'd gone, or muttered their names in imprecation or curse. Even those who dealt with monsters had creatures who haunted their nightmares, and Père Fouettard and Hans Trapp were the worst of them.

They had been human, once. And while Grýla, mother of the Yule Lads, might hunt children for her stew pot, and Belsnickel be desperate to beat them with his switch, and Krampus haunt the shadows, waiting to drag them off for snacks – or to hell, depending on his mood – those were creatures born of smoke and story. They were baked from the dreaming bones of the world, breathed into being by belief, so *other* from humans that their hunger seemed no different to that of a tiger, instinctive and inevitable.

Humans who ate children, though … they were a different breed. A different *kind*. Père and Hans had been cursed by Santa to chase their hunger for all eternity, which Greta was unsure about. She couldn't tell if it was punishment or reward, really, and with Santa it was always hard to tell, strange old monster that he was. But she did know that no children were at risk from the pair tonight. Not where the shuttle would be taking them. She and Dina made sure of it.

The snow was still racing in blinding whirlwinds in the wake of the shuttle when the wooden doors banged open again and a squat, burly creature in red overalls charged in, a vast ginger beard and long hair overflowing from under his matching hat and turning him into a mobile hairball with bared teeth and staring yellow eyes. He stopped just inside the door, gaze rolling one way then the other, and Dina grabbed a candy cane off the nearest desk and flung it at him. He snatched it out of the air effortlessly and shoved it in his mouth, crunching noisily.

"On you go." Greta pointed at the departure doors. "Good Tomten! Good boy!"

Tomten hissed, fangs long and discoloured, and the bite scars on her forearm throbbed in alarm. She took a plate of sugar cookies from a waiting, anxious elf, and flung one like a frisbee toward Tomten. He caught it and crammed it into his mouth, humming with pleasure.

"Come on, come on." Greta laid a trail of cookies across the floor to the departure doors, keeping a wary eye on the biter as she did so. Dina opened the doors with a tap on the tablet, and Greta flung the last cookie onto the platform, then stepped back smartly as Tomten scampered forward, gobbling the cookies as he ran. He vanished onto the platform, and Greta let out a breath, rubbing her arm.

"Done," she started, but even as she spoke one of the elves screamed, leaping to her feet and sending her chair flying backward.

"*Watch out!*" Dina shouted, and Greta spun around, expecting to see Tomten rushing back in with his snaggly fangs bared, the treats deemed not good enough, or her insults of the year before still rankling him to fury. Instead she was bowled over before even setting eyes on her attacker, sprawling to the floor and dropping her mug, the last of the hot chocolate splashing across the tiles. Heavy feet in hobnailed boots skidded through the mess, and she pushed herself up to see Dina step in front of Père Fouettard and Hans Trapp.

"Stop!" the elf shouted. "You're not authorised to be back yet!"

Père grabbed her tablet, trying to wrest it away. Dina fought back, teeth bared, as Greta rolled to her feet and ran to help, but not fast enough. Hans slapped Dina across the face, so hard she let go of the tablet and staggered back, almost falling. Père snarled in silent triumph, jabbing the screen with one nicotine-stained finger.

"Drop it!" Greta shouted, and lunged for the tablet. Hans caught her from behind before she could reach Père, hooking her around the waist with muscular arms, his belly pressed against her almost obscenely.

Monty, the young elf, ran forward with a tea tray brandished like a shield. Père evaded it and punched him almost casually, and as the elf collapsed, the monster added a kick that sent him sliding away across the floor. Half a dozen other elves charged into the attack, waving wastepaper baskets and staplers and mugs, and Tomten came bounding in through the open glass doors, snarling and snapping.

The elves scattered again with shrieks of alarm, and Dina threw herself at Père, leaping on his back and trying to link her arms around his neck. Greta stomped on Hans's foot, but his heavy boots protected his toes too well, and his grip didn't so much as shift. She twisted and writhed, trying to fight her way free, while Tomten scampered across the hall and set elves scattering as he scoffed cookies and mince pies, oranges and fruit cake and energy drinks and unshelled nuts.

Père gave a final heave and threw Dina off, and she slammed into the floor with a pained yelp, curling into herself and clutching her arm.

"*Dina!*" Greta shouted, and two skinny, panicky elves

rushed forward, armed with desk chairs. One smacked Hans hard enough to make him stagger, and he let go of Greta with one hand to fend the attack off, still as alarmingly silent as ever. Greta tried to throw herself out of his grip, and he dug his fingers into her ribs so deeply she felt the flesh tear under his filthy nails, squeezing the breath out of her. She gave up on trying to get free and pawed at her pockets instead. The bell was hot under her fingertips, and she fumbled to remove the cottonwool one-handed while Hans tightened his one-armed grip on her still further. His breath heaved in her ear as he pushed the elves away, setting her skin crawling.

Père gave a sudden, almost audible grunt as he realised why Greta had stopped struggling, and he grabbed her wrist with his free hand, all but crushing it. She bit back a scream, fighting to hold onto the bell, but Père ground the bones of her wrist together so painfully she lost her grip. The bell tumbled to the ground, still muted, and spun silently across the floor, Greta watching it go helplessly. It rolled straight to Monty, who was still struggling to sit up, one hand pressed to his bleeding mouth.

"Ring it!" Greta screamed. *"Ring it!"*

Père was already charging the young elf, and Monty shrieked, but snatched up the bell and whipped the cotton-wool away, scrambling to his feet and trying to break into a run before the monster reached him. He didn't make it, Père grabbing the back of his festive jumper and reaching for the bell, and Monty flung it as hard as he could across the room. The bell tumbled gracefully away, and as it did so it *ding-ding-ding*ed gently, a sweet, high sound that collected on the edges of the world, rolling from one side of reality to the other, shivering at the corners of the universe as if the stars were singing from the unseen sky. Père threw Monty to the ground and turned back to the tablet. He tapped it frantically, and a shuttle hissed into the platform fast enough to set the walls shaking.

Hans pushed Greta away, and he and Père glanced at each other, then ran for the platform.

"Stop them!" Monty shouted, struggling to his feet. "We can't let them get away! They could go *anywhere!*"

Greta didn't answer. She could see the red display on the front of the shuttle. *Market* it said, and it didn't matter which one. It was Christmas Eve. Every market would be teeming with kids sitting for photos with fake Santas, eating candied nuts and drinking hot chocolate, having tantrums over toy stalls and begging for candy canes, children beyond count, small and smart and wild, scented with sugar and promise and magic. The pair were heading to their own winter wonderland, an unsuspecting hunting ground of those who'd been protected from legends for generations. But even so she simply watched as the doors of the shuttle slid open then shut again behind the once-men.

"Why aren't we *stopping* them?" Monty demanded. He started for the open platform doors, and Greta grabbed his arm as he passed, wincing. Something had cracked horribly in one wrist when Père twisted it, and the other felt like a horse had stood on it. The young elf looked at her hand, then up at her. "But," he started, and the shuttle shuddered. They all looked at it. It rocked alarmingly, the dark windows giving away nothing, but they could hear, very faintly through the soundproofing, some rather ominous thuds.

"The bell," Monty whispered, no longer trying to pull away. "What does the bell do?"

Greta stepped back from the open platform doors, pulling the elf with her, and went to crouch next to Dina. No one spoke. The shuttle rocked a few more times, then stilled. Snow curled and chased across the deserted station, the night pressing in heavily beyond the lights, everything drawn in shades of winter grey other than the ominous red of the shuttle's display, which had changed from *Market* to *Error*.

Then the shuttle doors slid open. They stood empty for a long, icy moment, then a scrawny black cat ambled into view, licking his chops. He jumped to the platform and strolled to the hall doors, ears back against the wind. The glass doors slid shut as soon as he was inside, and still no one moved or spoke. Monty started to say something, and Greta tightened her grip on his arm, silencing him and ignoring the pain in her wrist as the cat's gaze slid towards her. The creature's eyes were wrought from silver and old ice, the pupils slices of endless abyss, and the snow rested on his coat like a dusting of starlight, refusing to melt.

"Jólakötturinn," Greta said, bowing her head. All around the hall elves knelt, avoiding eye contact with the Yule Cat, waiting. From under her lashes Greta watched the creature yawn, revealing bloodstained teeth and a void resting velvet in his heart, and she hoped desperately that they hadn't traded one set of deaths for another. It had been the right choice, of course, to stop the hungry pair's escape, but death by cat seemed unfair, even if the cat in question was Jólakötturinn, and therefore less cat than simply *cat-shaped*.

The moment stretched until she could hear it breaking at the edges, and the Yule Cat took one prowling step forward, his eyes fixed on her, then the platform doors slid open again. Heeled boots clicked in, and a tall woman in a glittering silver dress stooped to pick up the cat, holding him at arm's length in front of her, where he dangled docilely, ears back. Her pale eyes matched his, and they stared at each other, the wind carrying the snow inside to dust the dark skin of her bare shoulders and pull her translucent hair into tangled curls. She smiled suddenly, revealing pointed teeth.

"Kisu," she said, gentle reproach in her voice. "You didn't leave me any."

The cat yawned again, then burped loudly enough that it echoed around the hall.

"Disgusting creature," the woman said, and tucked the cat into the crook of her arm. She barely glanced at the huddled crowd in the hall, just turned and walked out into the snow, her back straight and her head high. "You're welcome," she called, as the doors slid shut behind her. The snow twisted into a blizzard, and when it cleared the platform was empty of cat, woman, and shuttle.

Greta let Monty go, and he staggered upright, walking in a wide-eyed circle as she looked at Dina. "Alright?" Greta asked.

"Something broke," Dina said, inspecting her arm, which was hanging at a strange angle.

"You've not done that arm before," Greta said.

"No, that's new," Dina agreed. "You?"

"Same wrist," Greta said, holding her hand up, and Dina shook her head.

"You'd think it'd be stronger, the amount of times you've broken that one," she said, and Greta made an agreeable noise.

"What is *wrong* with you?" Monty asked, his voice a whispered scream. "What happened to those men? Who was that woman? And what was the deal with the *cat?*"

"Everyone thinks Krampus is the one to worry about," Dina said. "But he's basically a celebrity these days, and he *loves* it. Shoving kids in sacks is a publicity no-no when you're a seasonal icon, so other than when he gets into the Killepitsch and winds up all punchy about the good old days, he mostly just boozes it up with all the fake Krampuses and does a lot of karaoke. Which is torture, by the way, and if he ever invites you along, say no."

"What?" Monty said. "I don't—"

"Grýla, on the other hand," Greta said. "Everyone forgets about Grýla."

Dina nodded. "Mother of the Yule Lads, mistress of the Yule Cat."

"As much as anyone can be mistress of any cat. Especially *that* cat."

"True. But she has real power, in the night and the ice and the silence."

They were quiet for a while, as the elves helped each other off the floor and started righting chairs and picking up fallen papers, then Monty said, "I thought Grýla was a troll, or an ogre. Not …" He waved vaguely at the doors, in a manner that indicated some admirable curves.

"She's whatever she wants to be," Greta said, looking around. "*Tomten*. Where the hell did that little biter go? Do we still have eyes on everyone?"

Dina grabbed her tablet with her good hand. "Dammit – someone get me a new tablet! The screen's shot, and who the hell knows what Odin's up to by now."

"Shagging someone, probably," Greta said dismissively. "Where's Saturn, more to the point?"

"Here!" an elf shouted, righting her monitor and pointing at it. "Got him. Pub in Ireland."

"Bloody hell – is he on the whiskey? We need feet on the ground if he's on the whiskey. There were three sacrifices and a load of unhappy maidens last time." Greta spotted Tomten finally, lying on his back and being fed mince pies while a slight, elderly elf rubbed his belly. "*Janine!* Stop messing about. He needs to get on the shuttle, *now!*"

Janine waved dismissively, but got up and led Tomten off, passing him a pie every few steps. He and Greta hissed at each other as he passed, then she checked the clock. "Twelve hours, people! Under twelve hours to Christmas!"

Monty turned in a slow circle, taking in the room. Chairs overturned and snow melted on the floor, candy canes and cookies crushed underfoot and Christmas trees spilling potting mix and broken baubles, drinks puddled on floors and desks and chairs, mugs and glasses shattered in exclamations of fright. "Christmas?" he said, his voice wobbly. "We almost *died!*"

Dina patted his shoulder with her good hand as an elf hurriedly rigged a sling and a splint for her broken one. "It's only your first year. You'll get used to it."

"*To almost dying?*"

"Don't be so dramatic," Greta said, holding her wrists out to be wrapped in ice packs. "Worse comes to worst, we call the cat again."

"That it? That's your plan? You *call the cat?*"

"Only as a last resort," she said, trying not to shiver as she felt the weight of those silver eyes again. It wasn't the first time she'd looked into them, much as she wished it was. She saw them in her sleep sometimes, and she was never sure if that meant Jólakötturinn was seeing her back. She worried it might, but that was Christmas. Sometimes the only choices were desperate ones, and one did what one had to do. She checked the clock again. "Dina, we should be getting returners from early time zones soon."

"On it." She took a new tablet from a strained-looking elf and scrolled through it. "First incoming in––"

She was cut off by the swoop of the shuttle, and they looked up as the glass doors flew open. A large-bellied man with a platypus under one arm strode into the hall, bare-chested over red shorts and flip-flops, sunglasses perched in his white hair. He brought with him a whiff of sunscreen and salt, plus a large tray of sausages and shrimp in his free hand. He slung it on the nearest desk, still sizzling, put the platypus down next to it, much to the alarm of the elf whose desk it was, and took an open bottle of beer from the pocket of his shorts.

"Ho-ho-ho, mates," he bellowed, and swigged the beer as he headed out the wooden doors, a quartet of displeased kangaroos hopping after him. One of the splinter Santas, given life by cute cards and vague belief, roaming across the world in the hours before Christmas Day kicked in, bringing back bloody shrimp and platypuses. Greta had argued that, as reflections of Santa, they shouldn't be her department, but no. The North Pole had a very narrow view of what they accepted as their responsibility, and as far as she could tell it was one sleigh and a small selection of snobby reindeer, while here she was juggling gods, monsters, and marsupials. Also far too many traffic cones and the odd confused drinking buddy when one of the Santas got stuck into the beers. There had even been a basket of chickens once.

"Schnapps," Greta said, snapping her fingers at Monty, and he fled. She looked at Dina. "Is he coming back?"

"No idea," she said, and handed Greta a bottle from inside her coat. "Christmas isn't for everyone."

"Found Odin," another elf called. "He's in Hamburg."

"Don't—" Greta shouted, but she was too late, and the screens flicked to the Yule god. Him, and a whole collection of other people, and possibly some not-people, too. She tipped her head sideways, then winced and looked away. She didn't have time to worry about Odin, and he looked to be entertained enough not to be getting up to too much trouble. They still had twelve hours left before the North Pole took over. Plenty of time for the old gods to spread their chaos.

Christmas wasn't for everyone, true. But Christmas Eve? That was only for the very brave. She took a swig of schnapps. And often the well-lubricated.

Because there was always bloody something.

15

DREADFULLY SORRY

*Okay, yes, I am aware I have a surprising amount of very weird apocalypses (apocalypsi?) going on in this collection. But, to be fair, I think there were a fair few in the last one. Which is not to say I'm fixated on the end of the world. Just that my subconscious throws up some really strange possibilities when I **do** think about it, and I'm not going to examine things beyond that ...*

THE BUILD UP HAD BEEN INTENSE. BEYOND INTENSE – IT HAD been drenched in the sort of claustrophobic horror that struck the street prophets speechless, because it appeared they might actually be right. Something was coming, and while it wasn't the coming they'd been waiting for, it promised end times all the same.

Bunkers were suddenly doing a roaring trade, not that there was time to build them before it arrived. But as it looked like there wasn't going to be any use for money by this time next month, why not buy bunkers? Half-built or half-arsed or both, it had to be better than nothing. Bunkers, and water purifiers, and stacks upon stacks of canned goods and carefully sealed bags of flour and sugar, and medications and bandages and survival rations. If you could afford it, of course. And could fight your way through the hordes at the supermarkets, or scour the far reaches of the internet for the few places still delivering.

The ones who could *really* afford it were already out of here, wherever *here* happened to be for them. London and New York and Brussels and everywhere else abandoned to the care of those in a lower tax bracket, the one per cent loading up their fancy floating blocks of flats and heading offshore, as if the end times might simply bypass the Bahamas or French Polynesia or the Maldives, deeming them too exclusive to be annihilated.

Regular people took off out of the cities too, up into the hills or out to the deserts, looking for empty places to stake their claim. That was a tricky thing these days, though. We were a crowded planet, and if *everyone* ran out of the cities, there just wasn't that much free land. Not in most places. But people tried it anyway, and went burrowing into old mines, or tourist-trap caverns – or, in the case of those who'd spent their free time exploring strange places, into forgotten hides left over from old wars, or the sort of caves where you imagined prehistoric beasts still lurked. Some of them knew what they were doing. Some of them just thought they did. Plenty of people died before the end even came, died in fights over the ownership of diggers while they tried to build their DIY bunkers, or died in the bunkers themselves when they left out little details like structural supports or an air supply.

Some people were frantic with the fragile hope of any kind of survival, buoyed by a blinding belief that money could buy a different reality, or driven by an unearned conviction that they were the Chosen Ones who would prevail when society collapsed, due to their unending diet of

Bear Grylls documentaries and a loyalty card from Survivalists-R-Us. Others took it as a golden ticket to party into Armageddon, and why not? If you don't think survival will even be an option, why not get as drunk and high as you can, so when it comes it's just one really bad trip?

The rest of us just got on, you know? Someone had to stock the supermarket shelves so the mums and dads could brawl over who got the last bag of organic wholegrain flour. Someone had to rehydrate the young couples who'd been living off the grid with unfiltered water and #SurviveTheEnd utility belts when they were found delirious in some farmer's water trough. Someone had to clear the stolen, drained SUVs off the road and ferry the families back to the nearest train station with a reminder that yes, the red light means empty, and public transport won't kill you just this once, but road rage just might. Someone had to collect the abandoned pets, and check on vulnerable people who'd been deserted in much the same manner – left in an unlocked house with a couple of full food bowls and a promise their loved ones were just popping out to the store.

It could make you angry. It *did* make you angry, or if it didn't you were probably one of the poorly equipped survivalists or family-dumpers yourself, but there wasn't much point to anger. So we just carried on. And I guess that carrying on – never mind the *keep calm* bit, we were all way past that and living in a constant state of near-hysteria, where even a rerun of *Everybody Loves Raymond* seemed like the funniest thing we'd ever seen – I guess it stopped us thinking so much. Stopped us looking up and trying to see that first glint of the oncoming end.

THE TELESCOPE HAD SEEN it first. The one that was meant to see the beginning of our universe discovered the end of our world instead. One moment there was nothing but the terrifying, crushing beauty of the void peering back at us, and the next it was just *there*, sleek and undeniable, glittering with the reflected light of a thousand dying suns and birthing galaxies, its colours changing as it advanced mercilessly, inexorably, toward us.

Obviously it didn't just trundle in our direction with the stolid determination of our own ships. If that had been the case, we'd have had time to cycle through a few panicked generations and probably done ourselves away through a brisk nuclear war over the resources we suddenly had no time to use, or runaway climate change (because nothing discourages half-hearted efforts at saving oneself more than the knowledge that there's nothing to save oneself *for*). No, the thing *stuttered*, like the gimmicky yet horrifying movement of movie monsters, and each stutter carried it tens or hundreds of light years closer.

At first no one was sure what the glint in the telescope's eye was exactly, and astonished, gleeful astronomers were rushing about the place making proud statements to the press about how they'd discovered an entirely new celestial body. But within a couple of weeks, the glee gave way to foreboding. Because the shape was too regular, the movement too purposeful. And those *stutters* … Nothing moved that way. Nothing we knew about. Nothing *natural*.

Cue the doomsday cults getting *really* excited, the churches getting overrun, and a whole lot of people who'd been regarded very dubiously by their peers emerging from their basements and saying *I told you so.*

Aliens were real.

Obviously all the governments of the world had been preparing for this. There were big folders of protocol laid out in minute detail, and plans for what world leaders were to do, and who was in charge, and all the rest. But human nature being what it is, the boring bureaucrats who pointed this out were shouted down, and instead a handful of world leaders (who did *not* represent the world as a whole, even if they pretended they did) declared they'd try to blow the thing up.

Because nothing says *Welcome, intelligent beings* like flinging incendiary devices at them without so much as a *can you take your shoes off at the door.*

So here's this alien technology that can shutter-jump across the universe like a kid skipping stones across a pond, and all these Big Manly World Leaders (who, to be fair, weren't all men, but the feeling was there) take control of a bunch of nuclear warheads that were ticking away in the skies and take some potshots at it.

Yeah, the nuclear warheads were already in orbit, because of course they were. Turns out we weren't always told the truth about the new satellites popping up all over the place. All we thought was, great, TikTok live from Everest base-camp! Endless true crime podcasts in the Scottish Highlands! Oh, and Google Maps isn't going to lead a busload of school kids on a field trip up a one-way street to a nudist camp again. So it's for a good cause.

We probably should have asked what the nudist camp story was distracting us from.

We should have asked what *a lot* of things were distracting us from.

On the plus side, the alien ship – which by this stage serious people were telling us was the size of a small village or an out of town mega-mall – didn't just reach out and vaporise us with some fancy alien weaponry when the Big Manly World Leaders launched their attack. The ship, in fact, didn't even seem to notice. The nukes splatted out harmlessly before they got anywhere near it, making little blips in the video footage like flies dying in one of those blue light zappers. The serious people told us there was likely some sort of forcefield that protected the ship from running into meteorites while blipping its way across the universe, and which would be more than strong enough to deal with nukes. There was a hint of *obviously* in their delivery, and I'm ninety-nine percent certain one of them rolled their eyes while the camera was on their colleague.

The Big Manly World Leaders then declared they would launch specialised rockets to intercept the alien ship, with the intention of forming a physical barrier the ship couldn't cross. The serious people didn't give their opinion on this, or not on network news, anyway. All over the internet, though, were a lot of equally serious yet anonymous articles pointing out that our rockets were smaller than meteorites, so …

Anyway, we needn't have worried. It became very clear, shortly after the launch of this elite strike force, that a handful of Big Manly World Leaders and a larger assortment of much richer and more powerful people, some of whom were household names and others no one had ever heard of, were in charge of the rockets. Not in order to intercept the aliens, of course.

There followed a panicked scramble by the remaining slightly less rich and powerful (some of them abandoning their yachts and survival ranches, which were swiftly claimed by their staff), and within a couple of days rockets were being launched from Cape Canaveral and Baikonur and Wenchang and random places where no one had even known there *were* launch sites. For a couple of weeks it became perfectly normal to see a streak of light as a vessel left the atmosphere not far away, and there were at least five collisions that saw bits of rocket rain back down to earth.

I'd guess the world lost ninety percent of its wealth over

the space of a fortnight, and I can't say anyone missed them. There was some schadenfreude when it was reported by the serious people, who had re-emerged now no one was bothering to keep them quiet, that a number of the rockets seemed to have overstated their capabilities and were drifting helplessly away from the stations that had been hastily erected by those first escapees. There was a *lot* of schadenfreude when the owner of a microchip company got a video link working and begged someone to send a cleaner and a maintenance person out, since the toilets were already blocked and the caviar jars had popped in zero gravity and were gunking up the air filters.

After that we all lost a certain amount of interest, other than checking in on the socials every day. Evidently it had turned into a bit of a posh, elderly, Lord of the Flies–type situation, with factions forming between world leaders and tech entrepreneurs, all of them competing for control of the one station. I don't think many of us much cared. The serious people told us the ship was still coming, and that meant light entertainment like watching the leader of the free world having a slapping fight with a nuclear arms magnate was kind of low on the urgency list.

THEN CAME the day that the serious people had warned us about. The day the village-sized ship would reach us. We still had access to cameras on the satellites, and we still had power in most places. Civilisation had not broken down completely in the absence of expensive leadership. Sure, things were a bit rough in places, but for every rogue police force or feral army division or bonkers wannabe militia who thought all their Christmases had come at once and had set out to prove just how bad humanity could be, there was a ramshackle yet irresistible force of the same working in the opposite direction, rallying the hopeless, looking after the sick or wounded, collecting the lost and scared and forgotten of every species, protecting food sources and securing water supplies. Humans were the worst and the best in equal measure, and all the end of the world showed us was that nothing changes. Some people were always going to be kind, and some were always going to be cruel. And some were going to be so bloody rich that they thought they were above it all, and ended up in a fight to the death on a spaceship stinking of rotting caviar and blocked space-loos instead. I mean, honestly, give me the incoming aliens any day. At least I can give my cat a final hug before I go, and he can bite my face, the little thug.

But back to the day. *The* day. The day when it was all going to end. I guess I expected a vast shadow to fall over us as the alien ship descended, flattening cities and levelling mountains as it claimed our world for its own. Or maybe we were so unimportant as to be beneath its notice, and it would simply brush us out of the way as it passed, sending us spinning like a top out of orbit and into the far reaches of the universe, the seas icing over and the trees and hills and earth shattering to crystals as we went. Maybe it'd blast us out of existence for our cheek in trying to do the same to it. I mean, fair's fair. Maybe we'd be taken prisoner, used for food or labour or displayed in alien zoos. Anything was possible. The serious people had been peppering the ship with radio messages and morse code and light signals and anything else they could think of, trying to portray us as refined, civilised, intelligent creatures who were absolutely ready to embrace our fellow universe-dwellers, but there hadn't been so much as an acknowledgment. I think the nukes had probably got us off on the wrong foot.

I went down to the beach to watch. Everyone had their

phones out, and someone had set up a projector on the side of the toilet block, which would've been a great idea if it wasn't three in the afternoon on a summer's day, and so bright it was pretty much impossible to make any detail out. I supposed it'd be handy if we were all still here once it got dark. There were half a dozen barbies on the go, the smell of sausages and lamb chops drifting among the trees, and kids were running up and down the pale sand between the water and the grassy foreshore. It wasn't crowded – everyone had their own ideas of how they were going to spend the end of the world, and not all of them wanted it to be here.

I did, though. Henry – my cat – padded alongside me like the little weirdo he is as I walked to the water's edge. There was no wind, and the sun baked off the sand and the water, making me squint even behind sunglasses. Further down the beach I could see the burned shells of half a dozen houses that hadn't survived the early riots, but otherwise it was all old couples wandering along hand in hand, and groups sitting under the trees with coolers of beer, and even a few people out on paddle boards. But almost everyone had a phone in their hand.

I walked into the sea and sat down on the gentle slope of sand, the water washing around my legs and my phone held clear. Henry climbed onto my shoulder and balanced there, complaining in little mewls about my hair being in his way. I ignored him, watching the live footage. It was early morning somewhere off the coast of north Africa, cutting between a feed from the satellites as they watched the ship descend, and the video running from telescopes all over the world. Slowly they cut out as the vessel dropped lower and lower, no longer stuttering. It reflected the world, but in reverse, so when seen from above it was wild blue ocean and long white sand beaches, and seen from below it was high blue sky and the telltale trade wind streaks of the clouds. People had gathered on the distant beach to watch, and mobile uploads started appearing as people streamed what they were seeing. No one spoke, and around me I heard the beach fall silent, other than the kids and a couple of dogs barking as they played.

The vessel closed on the beach, coming to a stop just offshore, its belly all but touching the clear waters. The reflections of fish darted and jumped in the footage taken from above by someone's drone.

A woman stepped forward, her hair in fine dark braids and her back very straight, and waded into the water up to her shins. The ship loomed above her, the shape of a clam, or a walnut shell.

"Hello?" she offered, first in her own dialect, then in French, then in English.

The ship didn't answer, and she moved slightly, as if to glance behind her, then lifted her chin and walked forward another couple of steps, her multicoloured skirt swirling in the water like the wings of a nudibranch. She reached out, and someone shouted behind her, in alarm or warning. She still didn't look around, just laid her hand lightly on the hull of the ship. There was a general *wasn't me* move backward from the crowd, and the ship shivered. The woman shivered too, and in some small side window on the feed a very excited serious person was demanding to know what she was experiencing, but the woman wasn't looking at a phone, or anyone else at all. She dropped her hand and stepped back. The ship rose very slightly, and a tiny port opened in its side, right next to the woman. Someone screamed, and a ripple of unease passed through the crowd. I felt it reflected in the groups on my own beach, but I kept my eyes fixed on the phone. Even Henry chewing on my hair couldn't distract me.

A small metal arm extended from the port, with a piece of folded paper clasped in a claw. The woman hesitated, then took hold of the paper gingerly. The claw let go, the arm retracted, and then the ship rose like a malformed bubble, drifting away.

"*What?*" the serious person was screaming on the video. "*What does it say?* **What does it say?**"

People on the shore in the video were shouting the same question, but the woman just stood there and watched the alien ship leave, not moving until it had risen so high that none of the footage from the beach captured it anymore, although the satellite feeds showed it moving sedately out of the atmosphere and clear of the orbiting space junk and warring autocrats before skipping off again in that unsettling, stuttering movement.

But finally she turned back, raising her hands for silence. Around the world, every person who'd been able to find power and signal leaned forward. My nose was almost touching the screen as I watched her unfold the paper. She opened her mouth, shut it again, and frowned.

"*What is it?*" the serious person screeched.

The woman cleared her throat, and read out in warm, accented English, "Dreadfully sorry. Wrong number. Do excuse us."

AND THAT WAS how the world almost ended. We never knew who the right number was, or what it might have meant if it had been us. But some things changed. It's hard to forget, when the end came, who chose to be kind and who was cruel, and these things matter.

Plus rescuing the drifting spaceship full of arguing, nuke-enthusiast rich people just kept slipping down the to-do list somehow.

And that made a surprising difference.

16

HOW USEFUL

I have no explanation for this story, other than the fact it crawled out of my subconscious fully-formed, as such things are wont to do, and I didn't want to just leave it wandering about shedding everywhere, so I wrote it down.

Because, in the end, that's what writers do. We take all the mess in our head, give it a polish, and hand it over in the hopes you'll find it entertaining, if nothing else.

And likely happy that it's not living in your head ...

THE EGG ARRIVED IN THE USUAL WAY, VIA THE SUPERMARKET delivery, which the driver offloaded from green crates at the front door in a jumble of cans and a clutter of fresh goods. At least it wasn't all crammed into a few overloaded totes, like used to happen when Nora still went to the supermarket on the bus. The amount of times she'd staggered in the door to find the bread squashed under the baked beans, or the eggs cracked and seeping across everything else, was unthinkable. Such a *waste*. And her shoulders were always so painful from lugging it all, the handles creating welts across her fingers, because no matter how hard she tried, the bags were always just that touch too heavy. Of course, she could've got one of those little fabric shopping trolleys, but that felt like such an insult. Such an *old* thing to do, toddling down the road with it wheeling faithfully after her, all but shouting, *look at the little old lady off to get her groceries!* Ugh.

No, the delivery was much better, even if she had to carry everything inside piecemeal while the driver pretended not to be impatient, because they didn't supply bags (and that was a good thing, the lack of plastic bags, a very good thing indeed, but also wildly inconvenient at times). She did miss the gentle excitement of treasure hunting in the almost-out-of-date section of the fridge, though, or the simple fascination of lingering in front of the deli counter, examining the soft lines and blurred edges of imported cheeses with their exotic names and shiny labels, the glossy bellies of olives and the mysterious, multicoloured promise of tapenades and pestos and pickles.

Sometimes the deli workers would give her little samples, quite as if she could afford to buy any of it, like she was some housewife throwing dinner parties in an extravagant sweep of plates and silverware, all gleaming in the candlelight. She liked the fish counter too, the glittering flanks of fish emerging from the ice, the green growth of parsley blooms and the seaside whiff of salt and decay. Yes. She did miss that.

Of course, that had been when she used to go to the fancy supermarkets. She never bought much in them, maybe a fat, golden bread roll, or a small tub of fancy yoghurt to justify her presence, but she always liked to look at what they had, a tourist in a different world. She didn't go anymore, though, not to any of the shops, the bus rendered hostile and ominous with its tricky steps and scowling passengers. She'd only fallen the once, but it had taken months for her knee to heal up fully, and an ugly stiffness lingered when it was cold.

And it wasn't that she was scared of it happening again, not really, but there had been the young woman – barely more than a girl, really, at least to Nora's eyes – who had laughed when she'd fallen, the sound flat and ugly, and the young men who'd just stared at her, with her bag of tomatoes spilling across the bus floor and the oranges bouncing out onto the street, as if she were no more real than the clips on their phones. Two older women had rushed to help her up (older than the young people, but not as old as her) and the pity in their eyes had been worse than the laughter. She'd had her daughter show her how to set up online shopping after that, at first just for while she was unable to walk far, but then it had simply stuck. It was easier, especially if it was raining, or cold. It just made sense.

"Hello," she said to the young man offering her a tablet to sign. He wasn't *so* young, she supposed, his hair ceding ground to his forehead, but at some point almost everyone had started to seem young. "You're new. It's usually Charlotte."

"She's off," he said with a shrug, making no move to help her take the groceries indoors. Charlotte always did, even though Nora knew it wasn't part of the service, or possibly even allowed.

She picked up a can of shop brand baked beans and frowned at them. She hadn't expected a delivery today, not even this week, and she wondered how she'd made that mistake. Ticked the wrong box somewhere, presumably. At least there wasn't a lot, just milk and eggs and a handful of pantry staples. "On holiday, is she?"

"S'pose." He looked from her to the bags. "Everything alright here?"

"I'm sure it's fine," she said, and made a show of checking everything. "What's your name?"

"Martin. If it's all good, can you sign?" He offered her the tablet again, looking over her at the house.

Nora sighed inwardly. These young people, with their impatience. Not that Charlotte was any older, she didn't think. Not enough to make a difference, anyway. So maybe it was all down to personality. She straightened up, wincing at a twinge in her back, and took the tablet. The pen – or stylus, or whatever they called it – was hard to grip in her arthritic hands, designed for more flexible fingers, but she scrawled a signature as well as she could and handed it back.

"Cheers," Martin said, and jogged down the steps of the little terraced house to where a muddy white van was idling at the kerb, rain spotting the windscreen.

THERE WAS a can of cat food in with the muddle of soup and beans, and Nora held it for a moment, staring at the happy tabby on the label. A month, and she still couldn't bear to stop buying it. She swallowed against an unreasonable tightness in her throat and closed the door, cutting the world off. Next time. Next time she'd remember to take it off the list. The delivery had taken her by surprise, was all. She needed to be more careful with all those little checkboxes.

She examined the eggs before she put them in the cupboard, more by habit than for any other reason. The box wasn't wet or stained, but it was always reassuring to see the round brown domes of the eggs looking smoothly back at her. She didn't see anything amiss at first, tapping a gnarled finger over one then the other. "One-two-three—" She stopped, frowning, and took her finger back to egg two, resting the smooth pad of her fingertip on it. Was it …

warm? She touched the other five eggs, moving more slowly now, then returned once more to the odd one out. It *was* warmer, she was sure of it. None of them should've been warm, coming from the air conditioned supermarket into the refrigerated van, and through the winter streets to her door. How *odd*.

She picked the egg up, cupping it in one palm, the loose band of her old wedding ring (worn on her other hand for forty years now, because she had always liked it, and one didn't need to dispose of the parts of marriage one liked along with the parts one didn't) tapping softy against the shell. It made a dull noise, muted and soft, and she felt inexplicably guilty, as if she might wake the egg's slumbering occupant.

She stood there in the kitchen for a little, frowning at the window and feeling the warmth of the egg in her hand, and it occurred to her that she'd seen something on the news, one of those little feel-good filler pieces, about people hatching supermarket duck eggs. Maybe that's what this was. A stray duck egg. Or maybe the same thing could happen with chicken eggs. Either way, she could hardly turn it into lunch. She was struck by the simple joy of having a living thing in the house again, unidentified though it might be, and she kept it cradled in her hand while she found a woolly hat her grandson had left behind, fashioning it into a nest. She set it on the windowsill above the radiator, where the heat could drift around it, and went to finish putting away the groceries, humming to herself softy.

An egg! Fancy that.

THE EGG RESTED by the radiator until that evening, when Nora took her dinner (tinned tomato soup and one piece of brown toast, spread with margarine and cut in half to make two triangles, with a glass of squash) through to the living room. She ate her dinner on a tray, in front of the TV, and tonight she brought the egg in with her, setting it on her lap. With the living room door shut and the heating on low (one could hardly have it on high, not with bills the way they were, even if the chill sneaked in around the windows and nipped at her bones) it was almost cosy, and she fancied the egg was warming her as much as she was it.

She petted it absently as she ate, just as she might have Holly, although the egg was lighter and lacked the cat's rusty purrs. It was still company, though, in an odd, undefined way, and she wondered what it was about humans that made it so important to care for something, even if it were no more than a plant or an errant egg. As if to care for something other than oneself was the very essence of what it was to be human. She wondered if the girl who had laughed when she fell had anything to care for. She thought perhaps not, because how could one be so careless with others if one cared for anything at all?

"Don't you worry yourself," she said to the egg, petting it gently while on the screen the news panned over fractured building and crumbling streets, filled with rubble and woe. "You're safe here."

She almost thought she felt it shift in response, something rolling over gently in its sleep, and she smiled, taking a final bite of toast. Probably there was nothing there, and she was being a silly old woman, mourning her cat and telling herself stories about eggs.

But maybe she wasn't. And one could never turn one's back on hope.

For the next few days, Nora kept the egg warm. If she wasn't holding it on her lap while she read, or knitted, or watched TV, she nestled it in its hat on top of a hot water bottle, and tried to chase the winter sunlight for warm patches, remembering how Holly would move from window to window as the day wore on. The egg seemed to be growing, the skin becoming leathery and faintly pliable, and Nora was convinced it really was moving, usually when she was looking the other way. She thought she would see a shadow in it too, when she held it up to the light. Not enough for her to tell what was inside, but she supposed she wouldn't know the difference between a duck or a chicken anyway, all bundled up in there. So she just kept it warm, and talked to it softly, and when her daughter called she told her about the egg.

"An egg, Mum?" Jayne asked. "From the supermarket?"

"It was on the news," Nora said. "People have hatched duck eggs from supermarket ones."

"Okay, but you buy chicken eggs."

"So maybe it's a chicken." Nora slid her fingertips over the egg, feeling the texture of its surface. It wasn't a chicken. It was already too big.

"Are you feeling alright, Mum? I know it's been hard, losing Holly."

"I'm fine, dear."

"Have you thought more about the home?"

"Yes," Nora said, looking at the brochure tucked under the TV guide. She wasn't lying. She had, and all it had done was convince her she'd hate it. She was fine here, with her shopping deliveries and patchy heating and tiny patio out the back for the summer. The stairs were getting tricky, but she could always move her bed downstairs into the living room. It would be fine.

"Some company would be good," Jayne said.

"I don't need company." She had an egg now.

Jayne sighed, a breathy sound that crackled across the phone. "I don't like it, Mum. What if you fall again?"

"That's why I don't take the bus anymore."

"That's not the point."

Nora made an agreeable noise as the egg shifted beneath her hand. She was sure it was the egg, not her. She checked it, but there were no cracks she could see. Not yet.

"I'll come by next week," Jayne said. "We'll have lunch."

"Alright, love," Nora said, and they made their goodbyes. Nora stayed sitting on the sofa, looking at the egg and soothing it with gentle hands. She knew what lunch would entail. It was always the same. A bite to eat at a garden centre cafe, set to Jayne's persistent, loving nagging about moving into some assisted living facility that they'd then simply *happen* to drive past on the way home, and possibly detour into, "just for a look, since we're here." It made Nora so indescribably tired that she wondered if she should just give up and let herself be packed away. But would they let her keep her egg? Probably not, she imagined. Eccentricity was hardly encouraged in such places. One needed more money to be able to be eccentric.

Nora thought the egg would have hatched by the time her lunch with Jayne came around, but it was still whole, unsettlingly heavy in her hands, and had swollen so much she needed both to support it. It had darkened too, making her fearful it had gone bad, but it was still warm, and at night, when she cradled it in her lap in front of the TV or rested it on the spare pillow in her bed, she felt it shift and shudder. She couldn't imagine what might be in it. Certainly not a chicken or a duck, unless it intended to come out fully grown. She'd looked up ostrich eggs on the tablet Jayne had given her, but they were pale and chalky, rather than the deep blue-grey her egg was developing. She'd looked at reptile eggs too, but they were nowhere near as big, not even saltwater crocodiles. And, of course, she doubted the local supermarket would be stocking either ostrich eggs or crocodile ones.

She was just putting a final dusting of powder on her nose when the doorbell rang, and she hurried downstairs, careful on the frayed carpet runner. She barely noticed the twinge in her knee, and she wondered vaguely if the heat from the egg had been helping, or if it was merely the fact she had something else to think of now.

"Mum?" Jayne called from the kitchen, and Nora burst into the room, smiling at her daughter with her skinny jeans and smart jacket and bracelets clanking on her wrists, and the threads of grey artfully disguised in her streaked hair, but still squeezing Nora's heart.

"Hello, dear," Nora said, and kissed Jayne on the cheek, her daughter barely taller than her, even in her heeled boots. She'd always bordered on *fragile*, Jayne, in build if not in disposition. "You're looking well."

Jayne gave her a critical look, then cocked an eyebrow and said, "So do you."

Nora straightened the front of her jumper, and zipped her jacket over it. "Thank you. I'm feeling rather well, to be honest. How's Sadie?"

"Good," Jayne said, wandering around the kitchen as Nora sat to pull her insulated boots on. The day was chilly. "Busy. She sends her love."

"She's always busy. She'll burn herself out," Nora said. "When did you two last take a holiday?"

"It's hard, with Jacob," Jayne said. She'd stopped in front

of the egg snuggled into its hat, stretching the limits of the wool. "What the hell is this?"

"I could look after Jacob," Nora said, and joined her daughter. "That's my egg."

"But it's huge! That's not a chicken egg!"

"I know. It keeps growing." They peered at it together, then Nora picked it up, offering it to Jayne. "Here. Feel it."

Jayne touched it gingerly, then made a face. "It's warm. Creepy."

"It's always warm," Nora said, and put the egg gently into her bag.

"What're you doing? You're not bringing it!"

"Of course I am. What if it hatches when I'm out?" What an awful thought, some little creature emerging into an empty, friendless world. Nora wouldn't have it.

"It can't be a real egg, mum. Where did you get it, really?"

"I told you. The supermarket delivery."

"No," Jayne said, and Nora wasn't sure if her daughter was protesting the fact it had come from the shop, or its simple existence.

She ignored the protest either way, closing her bag firmly around the egg, speaking before Jayne could say anything else. "Shall we go?"

"Sure," Jayne said, sounding fairly bemused. Worse, she sounded *indulgent*.

Nora bit down on a flash of anger, adjusting the collar of her jacket. "After you," she said, waving at the door, and Jayne led the way out, bouncing her car key in one hand. Nora locked the door after them and checked her bag. The egg seemed comfortable, and she stroked it gently. "It's going to be okay," she whispered, and it shivered under her touch.

Lunch was fine.

Jayne was fine.

Sadie was fine, even though she never came with Jayne to visit Nora, not since the little to-do when Nora had heard about the man at Sadie's work, the one who'd been sending her nasty photos. Nora had only been trying to help, but one had to be careful, she supposed. Sadie was a sporty sort, muscular and taller than Jayne and Nora, stronger on the outside but not so much under the surface. She hadn't lived through what they'd had to (until Nora had fixed things), and that delicacy showed sometimes.

Jacob was fine too, although he never came with Jayne either, or on his own. Nora didn't offer to look after him again, as much as she'd like to. No fourteen-year-old boy wanted to stay with his gran in a pokey old terraced house, especially not when his other set of grandparents had a sprawling country house with a heated pool and a tennis court. Nora was just pleased to hear he had a good football coach now. The last one had been … problematic.

Jayne pushed a brochure across the table as they lingered over their tea, the predicted garden centre cafe full of soft conversation and grey heads nodding over plates of cake. "Sadie's aunt's looking at this one. It's got kitchen gardens."

"I've never had a garden."

"Wouldn't it be nice to?"

Nora made a small sound that could've meant anything. She had never wanted a garden. She could barely keep her peace lily alive, and the thought of being responsible for a whole garden of fussy plants was rather horrifying. They were much more difficult than children or cats, although they did have their uses. She'd spent a certain amount of time in public ones over the years. Aloud, she said, "If Sadie's aunt can afford it, I can't."

"We'd work it out, Mum. You know that."

Nora's bag was hanging on the back of her chair, and she reached one hand into it surreptitiously. The egg seemed hotter, shifting under her touch like desert sands.

Jayne sighed. "Mum. leave the bloody egg alone. Seriously, what pound shop did you get that from?"

"I told you. The supermarket delivery."

"Fine, don't tell me. But I hope you're not ordering junk off dodgy websites. You have to stick to the ones I told you about. You'll get ripped off. It happens *all the time.*"

"Yes, dear," Nora said, and pulled her bag onto her lap. "I'm tired now. Can we go?" She wasn't really, but she *was* tired of fending off brochures and explaining her egg, so it was close enough.

"Of course." Jayne got up, hurrying around to help Nora put her coat on. "Do you need anything at the shop before we go home?"

"No," Nora said, letting herself be bundled into her coat like a child. "I've still got plenty from this week's delivery."

Jayne frowned. "This week? But you got the egg in last week's one, didn't you? I thought you were doing every other week."

"I do, usually. I must've made a muddle of the bookings. More bananas than I know what to do with now!"

Jayne gave a little laugh, one that didn't cover the fact that *muddled the deliveries* was sure to be going on the *Mum's Dotty* list along with *trying to hatch an egg.* But she just said, "Oh, well. As long as you're alright."

"I am," Nora assured her, and followed her docilely to the car, smelling the crisp green scent of potted plants and damp earth. She held her bag close, and the egg shifted, the movement clear even through the old leather, and she whispered, "*Shhh.*"

"What?"

"Nothing."

Jayne nodded, looking at her phone, already distracted by the tasks of the day and the demands of life, and the whole vast world beyond that of her mother in her outdated boots and dull jacket, and her grey, lank hair that needed styling. How strange it was to find oneself so unnecessary, Nora thought. So excess to requirements, just waiting to be packed off into a home, out of sight and out of mind, preserved for one's own good. She wondered if it was a little like the days when children were sent off to public school not for the pricey education, but so they could neither be seen nor heard, nor worried about at all. Her situation wasn't such an awful one, she supposed. No one had withdrawn love from her, after all. Merely their attention, which wasn't so bad.

At home in the kitchen, she set her bag on the table and offered Jayne a tea, but her daughter just hugged her and gave her that concerned look again. "You'd tell me if anything was wrong, wouldn't you, Mum?"

"Of course. Just as *you'd* tell me if you were having any problems, wouldn't you?"

"Yes." The answer was quick, but not quite truthful, and Nora sighed inwardly. She only ever *helped*. She never *interfered*. It wasn't her style. But she didn't push the point, and Jayne glanced at Nora's bag and shook her head. "Good luck with your egg."

"Thanks." Nora waited in the doorway, watching Jayne climb back into her car, and waved until she pulled away. Only then did she close the door and return to the kitchen, taking the egg out of her bag and holding it up to the grey light coming through the window. It gave her nothing back, bland and unremarkable except in size, and after a moment she sighed and put it on the table in its swaddling of woollen hat, giving it a brisk pat. "I'll get your hot water bottle in just a moment."

She went upstairs to change into her joggers and a fleece,

discarding her town clothes, and was just hanging her jacket up when a noise from downstairs made her pause. It sounded like the door – had Jayne come back? But Jayne always rang the bell first, a polite little gesture that Nora always appreciated. She stood there, a hanger in one hand and her jacket in the other, her mouth slack with sudden alarm. Had she locked the door? *Had* she? But it was broad daylight. No one would just walk in now, would they? *Would* they?

Another noise, feet soft on the old carpet, and she looked for her phone. It wasn't here. It must still be downstairs. Why was it downstairs? Jayne always told her to keep it on her, in case she fell again.

The stairs groaned under someone's weight, and Nora blinked, dropping the jacket and hanger. *The egg*. She moved fast, her heart stuttering. Someone was in her house. What if they touched her egg? What if they *took* it? She grabbed the lamp from the bedside table, pulling the plug out of the wall, and ducked behind the door just as the floorboard at the top of the stairs creaked. She raised the lamp, arms shaking, and someone stepped into the bedroom. She brought the lamp down as hard as she could, driving it into the intruder's face, because everyone thought a quick bop on the head instantly knocked someone out, but in her experience all it did was infuriate them. Heads were harder than that. Noses weren't, though, and they *hurt*.

The intruder cried out, staggering backward, and Nora rushed them, raising the lamp again. It was a man, hoody pulled up (another good reason not to go for the head), and he fended her off, shouting something unpleasant as he retreated towards the stairs. She hurled the lamp at him, and it spun off one of his outstretched hands then tumbled to the floor.

"That's got you," he snarled, lunging forward again, but

Nora had kept hold of the cable. She pulled, hard, and the lamp slithered under the man's feet. He tripped on it, stumbling sideways, and tried to recover, but his foot caught the lamp again and he staggered into the banister. He could have saved himself, grabbing for the old wood, but Nora was already charging him, teeth bared in fury. She hit him in the belly with both arms outstretched, and he was already off balance. He tipped backward with a howl of horror, vanishing over the banister and into the stairwell. He landed with the crack of a broken tread, and Nora thought she heard another crack too, low and ominous, then all was silent.

She stayed when she was for a moment, her heart going too fast and her vision filled with swirling spots.

"Oh dear," she whispered. "Oh, *dear.*"

She wasn't sure how long she stood there, her fingers painfully tight as they clutched her jumper, but she thought it would've been even longer if movement below hadn't startled her.

Was he still alive? Surely not. He hadn't made a sound since he'd landed, not since that nasty *crack*, and she knew about final sounds. Some things were unmistakeable. Was there more than one of them? Why hadn't the other come rushing up to attack her, then? She hesitated a little longer, frozen with indecision, then took a slow step forward, leaning on the wobbly banister to peer into the stairwell.

The man was sprawled at the bottom of the stairs, staring up at her, but there was no life behind his eyes. Even if she'd been unsure about that, his neck was at an angle so extreme it seemed cartoonish. He wasn't making any noises, not now, not ever again.

Something else was, though, and it looked up at her with round dark eyes, the pupil star-shaped and luminously green. Skinny shoulders hunched over a potbelly and knobbly legs, and heavy wings twitched and flexed, all in shades of stony grey, while a thick, muscular tail curled on the carpet behind it, sleek as a lizard's. She held its gaze, her chest too tight as she wondered at some distant level if she might be having a stroke, or a heart attack, and hallucinations along with it.

Then the creature grinned, pointing a bony finger at her. "Okay," it said, voice guttural, and she spotted the woollen hat on its head.

She blinked. "You're not an ostrich," she said, hearing the inanity of the statement but unable to stop herself. "Or a crocodile."

"Okay," the creature agreed, and looked at the broken body of the man. "Okay, okay, okay." It grabbed the intruder's arm and towed him away, scuffling down the hall to the kitchen. The man's face regarded Nora as he vanished, and she tipped her head to one side, recognising him. It was the delivery driver, the one with the muddled delivery. The one who'd replaced Charlotte, and who hadn't helped her carry her groceries in.

"Oh," she said, and wondered what to do now. Calling the police would be problematic, even though it had been self-defence. Calling Jayne would be even worse. She'd be so *upset,* as if Nora had done it on purpose, which she hadn't. And then there was Sadie. Sadie with her cool lawyer's eyes and quick sharp mind and *sensitivity* despite it all. Sadie who'd poked around in old news stories after the incident with the unpleasant man at her work, and suddenly stopped visiting, or bringing Jacob by. As if Nora wouldn't protect her grandson with her every breath. As if she hadn't already, what with the football coach and his greedy eyes and *extracurricular* interests. And that had been an accident too, or mostly. Just like Jayne's boyfriend, back before Sadie, and the teacher with the hungry mouth, and— Well, none of it mattered. It was all just coincidence, really, but the police got a bit funny about such things. She was going to have to come up with a plan, was all, since not driving did make things a little difficult.

And all of that was quite besides the fact she seemed to have some sort of monster in the house, if a rather more pleasant one than others she'd dealt with. She wasn't at all sure what to do about that, but she supposed she just had to get on and handle it. That was what one did, after all.

She walked slowly down the stairs, becoming aware of a gentle humming drifting from behind the closed door to the kitchen. She hesitated when she reached it, goosebumps springing up on her arms, and wished she'd thought to put her fleece on, but she had been rather distracted. She took a deep breath and pushed the door open slowly, seeing first the little table with the scattered remnants of an eggshell on it, constricted down to the exact same size as the one she'd had for dinner the night before. Her gaze drifted to the rug on the floor, slightly rumpled, and a man's shoe, keeled over on its side like a wrecked car.

And, next to it, the creature was sitting on the floor with its spindly legs splayed in front of it, leaning back against the cabinets as it used both hands to force something into its mouth. It looked at her, eyes squinted with effort, swallowed hard a couple of times, then let out a resounding burp that seemed like it rattled the panes of the windows.

"Manners," Nora said automatically, and it licked its broad lips with a pointed tongue.

"Okay," it said docilely, then tipped its head on one side in a strange reflection of Nora's own movement from earlier. Then it leaped up, making her jump, and scuttled on all fours to the coat hooks by the door, belly swaying. It stood up on its hindquarters to snag her old quilted coat, the one she used to take the bins out, and carried it to her, holding it out in one heavy paw, vicious talons delicate on the old cloth.

"Okay," it said to her encouragingly, and she took the coat, slipping it on without taking her eyes off the creature.

"Thank you," she said, and it made a sound that was remarkably like a purr, leaning its warm flank against her leg. She hesitated, then petted its head gingerly. It was like touching stone warmed by the sun, smooth and ungiving and full of mysterious life.

"Okay," it said, and burped again.

"Okay," she repeated, looking at the shoe. Just the shoe. No mess, no fuss. Just a shoe. How easy. How unexpected.

How *very* unexpected, and how very *useful*.

She grinned suddenly, wolfish in the dull light of the old kitchen, thinking of sly football coaches and rude bus passengers, of condescending bank tellers and impatient shop workers and men, *so many* men who didn't understand that not everything was theirs to take. Thinking of broken ground and secret hiding places, and how *everything* got harder as one aged, but how the rage never decreased. There were just *so many* things to be angry about, after all, and so many things one simply needed to protect one's family from, because no one else was going to do it.

She petted the creature again, and it bared its teeth at her, eyes half closed in delight and a shred of cloth caught on one jagged canine.

Oh, how *useful*.

How very, very useful indeed.

17

SPOILSPORT

I do not like sports.

I mean, I don't hate them. Just don't ask me to participate in, watch, or otherwise be involved in them. As with many things in life, I am very happy for other people to enjoy them, but I will sit this one out, thanks.

But despite that, nothing in this story is autobiographical. Not saying I might not have thought about it, mind ...

EVENTUALLY, ONE DAY, IF ONE SIMPLY KEEPS TRYING, A LONG shot has to pay off.

It *has* to. It's not *impossible*. That's why they're long shots, not no-shots. Something to do with sports, probably, Griff thought. He'd never been good with sports. It was one of those things that everyone just *got*, but he never did.

At school, in those terrible, enforced sessions of mandated humiliation and sweatiness, he'd see the ball and think, *right, it's going to bounce **there**, so I can catch it **here**,* and put himself hopefully in position, arms out like a supplicant. Only it would bounce entirely differently, and he'd miss, and trip over his own feet, or run into one of his team members, or he *would* grab it, but it'd be one of the games where you're not meant to touch the ball with your hands, and the least he could hope for would be a lot of raucous laughter and some snide insults. That was if he avoided the more physical consequences, of course.

His experience of team sports as a whole was that they were awful and illogical and *pointless,* and the rules were unnecessarily complicated. It was just a damn *ball.* A bit of rubber or foam or what have you, and there was all this mythology and ritual and tradition and stinking *masculinity* wrapped up in it.

So no, he didn't like ball sports, and he didn't much like swimming, because pools were fetid breeding grounds for fungal diseases, contaminated with shed hair and skin cells, and urine barely concealed by the stinging funk of chlorine. And that was before one even contemplated the horror of communal changing rooms. Griff had no issues with naked-ness as a concept, but school swimming classes weren't exactly the respectful environs of a life drawing class. It was all shouting and towel-snapping and *horseplay*, which made it sound wholesome and outdoorsy and playful, when in actual fact it was nothing more than the strong snarling at the weak, leaving scars that would last a lifetime.

Then there was running. He was alright at running. He didn't *enjoy* it – he couldn't imagine how anyone could enjoy huffing along with their lungs screaming and their legs aching, sweat collecting in unpleasant sticky patches and clothes clinging to every bump and angle of their body, all the chafing and jarring and panting, and the inevitable sham-bling wit shouting, "'Urry up, they're catching you!" and laughing like they should be on *Live at the Apollo*. But at least running didn't have rules. Or not unless you entered a race, and the fact that anyone would willingly do that left him with serious doubts regarding the human species as a whole.

No, he didn't enjoy running, but he *could* run. And running was useful. You never knew when you might need to run.

Like now, for instance.

GRIFF BOLTED ACROSS THE BROKEN, weed-riddled ground of the empty lot. Well, *bolted* was generous. He was certainly aiming for a bolt, but he could tell from his dragging legs and gasping breath that it was a lot more like a lumber.

A fast lumber, though. As fast as the rain-drenched, dim-lit dark would allow. He just hoped it was fast enough.

He checked his watch, the dark, glossy face filled with a timer that was counting down rapidly. *Thirty-five seconds.*

He reached the far side of the lot, grabbed a panel in the solid metal fence, and worked it carefully out of alignment. *Thirty seconds.*

The base of the panel was firmly embedded in concrete anchors, but the top was loose, the clip that locked it to the next broken, allowing him to pull it apart just enough to squeeze through the gap. The edges were sharp on his fingers, and it pinched him in a sensitive spot as he wriggled past, making him wince.

Then he was into the empty construction plot on the far side of the fence, abandoned along with the lot that bordered it six months ago when the developer ran out of money. The portable offices and earthmoving equipment had all been relocated two months later, as had any CCTV cameras. Griff might not be good at running, or ball sports, but he was good at finding things out.

Twenty-five seconds.

Griff trotted across the muddy morass of the construction site, a small, slope-shouldered man with hair that had started thinning in his teens (he blamed the stress of school sports for that).

Twenty seconds.

He reached the gates to the site, made of the same thin metal sheeting as the fence. He took a little dentist's mirror on a stick out of his pocket and slipped it through the gap, checking each way on the road outside.

Fifteen seconds.

No one in either direction. It was almost two a.m., of course. There *shouldn't* be anyone out there, but the human element was always the trickiest. It liked to do things like *ball sports.*

Ten seconds.

Griff let himself through the gates, deliberately knocking some clumpy dirt onto the pavement beyond, a scruffy little welcome mat.

Five seconds.

He replaced the already-cut padlock on the chains, where it would look locked to the average person, but would be an open invitation to the un-average – the bored teen in search of adventure, the lost looking for shelter and privacy. In a day, maybe two, there'd be so many fingerprints on the lock and fence that his gloved smudges would be lost beneath them, and his footprints would be buried under those of other intruders, or simply the rain, which was forecast to continue for the next four days at least. He'd checked.

The timer dinged, and he walked calmly down the street toward the park and the long stroll home. Somewhere, on the edge of hearing, a siren started up, but it was so distant

Griff only heard it because he was listening for it. And of course, there was no guarantee it was the one he was expecting. He couldn't tell exactly where it came from, after all.

But he rather thought he knew.

GRIFF TURNED up to work the next day in neatly pressed khaki trousers, his shirt (pale blue today, with very small, barely discernible flamingos all over it. Loud shirts were tacky, but shirts with a little fun were good for morale. Perhaps even good for students' morale, but he was mostly thinking of his own) daringly open at the top button, and his corduroy jacket already feeling a little warm. It was unpleasantly humid, the rain suffocating the day and trapping the unexpected heat to the land, one of those strange early autumn days that still confused everyone, and that the buildings weren't built to cope with. At least he only had morning classes, and could hide in his office for the rest of the day in front of the fan while he marked papers.

He was interrupted midway through an explanation of how the Black Death had contributed to the breakdown of the feudal system of agriculture – a particular passion of his, as he rather liked the early methods of farming. Or the theory of them, at least. He was quite sure that he would not have wanted to be involved in the practicalities of threshing or anything like it. It sounded sticky and sweaty, and even less rewarding than teaching.

The interruption came in the form of a quick, almost apologetic knock at the classroom door, which was followed by Agnes, the administrator, putting her head around it.

"Mr Heaton?" she said, for the benefit of the students. "You're needed in the office."

"Oh," he said, and looked at the bored faces of the

teenagers in front of him. One or two were asleep with their heads on their desks, probably dreaming of ball sports. "Three paragraphs on the rise of enclosure and its impact. If you finish before I get back, there's no homework."

That sent everyone scrabbling about for pens and notepads, and he followed Agnes out into the hall. "What is it?"

"I don't know exactly," she said, twisting her fingers together. They were long and thin, a piano player's fingers. "But the police want to talk to you."

"The *police? Me?* What do they want?"

"They didn't say." She turned to lead the way down the hall, her fingers wrestling each other ceaselessly. "Oh, Griff – I hope there hasn't been a *complaint.*" She whispered the word, looking around anxiously as she did so, as if someone might jump out of a classroom and berate her for it.

"As in … *no*. No, I'm sure," Griff said. "Certainly not about me!"

"Oh, no, not you! But what if they're interviewing us, gathering evidence and so on?"

"On whom?" Griff asked, as they approached the office. He could see the blurred forms of two people standing behind the frosted glass of the door. "None of us would … you know. And I've never seen anything at all untoward. Have you?"

"No," Agnes admitted, and straightened the front of her blouse. "But one never knows, does one?"

"I suppose not," Griff agreed, although he couldn't imagine a single person on staff who might be guilty of even looking at a pupil the wrong way. Other than Mrs Timmons, of course, but she was so far past retirement age everyone had stopped asking about it, and her version of looking at children the wrong way was a furious glare while she waved a wooden spoon and explained in great detail how discipline had worked in her day. Which was not the correct way to do things, of course, and the head had been forced to have words with her on numerous occasions, but even the most difficult of students seemed to regard Mrs Timmons with a certain amount of affectionate wonder, like a museum piece come to life, and there had never been so much as a complaint about the spoon.

The police turned expectantly toward Griff as he opened the door into the administrator's office. They weren't wearing uniforms, but they were unmistakably police anyway. It was something in the way they looked at people.

"Mr Griffith Heaton?" the woman asked.

"That's me," he said.

"DI Sonia Denny," she said. "This is DS Andy Forshaw."

"Mr Heaton," the DS said gravely. He was disconcertingly tall, with a large belly and an even larger chest, making the DI look tiny next to him. She was short and rounded, but Griff had the sense of her being rounded the way a Rottweiler was, not a bunny.

"How can I help?" he asked.

DI Denny looked at Agnes. "Can we use your office for a minute?"

"Oh! Oh, of course. Can I … would you like a coffee or something?"

"No, thank you. We won't be long."

"Right." Agnes backed out the door, pulling it closed behind her, leaving Griff and the two detectives looking at each other.

"Seat?" Griff offered, pointing at the chairs pulled up to the desk.

"Right you are," the DS said, and sat down in one of the guest chairs, resting one ankle on the opposite knee. The DI went around to the other side of the desk and sat down in Agnes's big chair, waving Griff into the one next to DS

Forshaw. Griff sat down carefully, shaking out the legs of his trousers to keep the crease, aware the detective sergeant was watching him with a certain amusement. The DI regarded him silently, her face calm and still, and he gave her a small, expectant smile, lacing his fingers together in his lap.

"Nice shirt," the DS said, pointing at Griff with the end of a pencil. He'd taken a notebook from somewhere and it was resting on his knee. "My mum's right into flamingos. She'd love that."

"Thank you," Griff said. "I like your, um …" He looked the other man up and down hopefully, but even his socks were somewhat boring.

Forshaw laughed. "You're alright. We don't get to show too much individuality in our sartorial choices, do we, Sonia?"

The DI gave a small smile. "Not really."

"I mean, it's for the best," the DS said. "Can't have the coppers swanning around in miniskirts and tank tops, can we?"

"You'll just have to keep your miniskirts for the weekend, Andy," the DI said.

Forshaw chuckled, then looked back at Griff. "You like your job, then?"

"Um … yes?" He was still distracted by the miniskirts, and it seemed like an odd segue. He supposed it was to make him feel off balance, and it rather worked.

"Get to express yourself a bit and all that." The DS waved at Griff's shirt again.

"Yes, I suppose so. I'm sorry, but what—"

"Do you have creative outlets?" Forshaw enunciated the words clearly, as if he wasn't quite sure of them.

Griff frowned. "I don't really understand what this is all about."

"Do you paint?" DI Denny asked. "Write? Sculpt?"

"I like those colouring books," Griff said. "The complicated ones, with all the little detail?" Both officers made impressed sounds, as if he'd declared he sculpted metal with chainsaws or something. "There's never enough time, though."

"No, there never is," the DI agreed. "Gardening?"

"No, I live in a flat. I'm sorry, but what's this about? My class is going to riot if I don't get back soon."

The inspector looked at Forshaw. "What's this all about then, Andy? Shall we tell him?"

The DS flicked back through his notebook, stopping on a page full of cramped, surprisingly neat handwriting. "This is one of them long shots, really, Mr Heaton, but you wouldn't happen to know anything about the swimming pool over in Shipley being filled with tadpoles back in the spring?"

"*Tadpoles?* Why … *How* would anyone even do that?"

"Our question exactly," DI Denny said. "It was closed for pre-summer maintenance, and by the time they found them the whole lot had hatched. Or changed, or whatever they do. Bloody frogs everywhere. It was a right mess."

"Really? What about the chlorine? Wouldn't that kill the tadpoles?"

"You'd think. But the chlorine was right down because of not being open," Forshaw said. "So you don't know anything about that?"

"No, of course not." Griff adjusted his cuffs. "I don't much like creepy crawlies and that sort of thing."

"Ah. So you wouldn't know about the cockroach infestation in the tennis club a bit after, then?"

Griff made a little gagging noise, and pressed a hand to his chest. "Absolutely *not.*"

"How about moles?"

"What about them?"

"Mole colony in the cricket pitch in early summer," DI

Denny said. "*Very* persistent, and kept recurring. Ended up with the pitch being completely unusable for the whole season."

"Well, that's dreadful for the teams, of course," Griff said. "But I really don't see why you're asking me about it. I don't have anything to do with sports. Not at all. They just don't interest me."

DI Denny clasped her hands on the desk. "The thing is, Mr Heaton, that all the sports clubs in the local area seem to be having a rather rough time of late. And sports is a community, even when they're *different* sports. All the clubs have been very sympathetic toward each other, while also being relieved it didn't happen to them. But because everyone talks, the darts league mentioned someone was trying to get them pushed out of their usual pub due to them using potentially lethal projectiles."

"Oh dear," Griff said.

"And the bowls club has had weekly noise complaints this summer, which is the period over which all these events have taken place."

"How terrible for them."

DS Forshaw nodded. "You said you didn't have a garden, Mr Heaton?"

"That's right."

"Any reason why you've got eight 44-gallon drums of grass food in a storage unit in Keighley, then?"

Griff just sat there for a moment, a tic jumping in his cheek. "I don't know what you're talking about."

"Rented under a different name, obviously," DI Denny said. "But wouldn't you know it, the security guard is a member of the darts team. They all knew it was you complaining, everyone in the pub did. And he saw you move the drums in. As a security guard, he has the right to check on the contents of a unit to see if it's dangerous."

Griff licked his lips. "So? It's grass food. It's not dangerous."

"No, but the eight 44-gallon drums of weedkiller the local football club just tipped all over their pitch, thinking it was grass food, seems like an astonishing coincidence." She leaned back again. "And I rather think we'll find that the bar codes on the drums in your storage unit will match the ones that the club bought."

Griff looked down at his hands, counting his breath. *Inhale. Hold. Exhale. Hold. Again. Again.* The moment lengthened, and he could hear rain on the windows, and a truck backing up somewhere outside. The office smelled of stale floral perfume and reheated tuna pasta, and he took one long breath then looked up at the inspector. "I'm so sorry," he said. "I just … I hate sports *so much.*"

The DI raised her eyebrows. "You're confessing?" She managed to keep her voice level, but there was surprise lurking in the corners of the words.

Griff gave a helpless little shrug. "You've got me. And I think I probably need help. Unresolved anger issues after all the bullying I was subject to in P.E. in school, most likely. And then I went and became a *teacher.*" He dropped his face into his hands, choking on the words as a sob forced its way out. "What is *wrong* with me?"

There was silence, other than DI Denny clearing her throat a little uncomfortably.

Finally Forshaw said, "Right, then. We best get you down to the station for a proper statement."

"Of course." Griff looked up, and a tear ran down his nose. "Oh, dear. I'm sorry. I don't mean to make a scene."

The DS clapped him on the shoulder. "Never mind, Mr Heaton. We'll get you through this. Shall we go?"

"If we must."

GRIFF KNEW the rumours would be flying around the school (where he'd been firmly advised to take an extended sabbatical), and the town. Maybe even the whole county. Knew there'd be a nickname, knew that someone would dig out old school photos of him in his sports gear, all knees and elbows and unhappiness. Knew that every person he talked to would have a little snicker behind their words. The man who hated sports so much he had to try and ruin it for everyone, but had got his comeuppance. Serves him right, mad old sod, they'd say, or words to that effect. Who didn't like *sports?* Must be something wrong with him. He'd become an object of ridicule and pity, and it wasn't going to fade any time soon, if at all.

And that was fine.

That was perfect.

As he sat outside the courtroom waiting for his hearing to begin, his lawyer – a rather budget-friendly one he'd found online, who had smudges on her glasses and a run in her tights – tipped her phone toward him. "Look at this," she said. "Still not a single lead in those robberies."

"What robberies?" Griff asked, and she gave him a disbelieving look. He shrugged. "I've been somewhat busy."

"Sure. Right. A bunch of pawnbrokers got ripped off over the summer. Not the big names, more those nasty little places that push people into off-the-book loans they can't afford, then collect with great enthusiasm."

"Oh, dear," Griff said.

"I wouldn't feel too sorry for them. A couple of shops got into a right mess when the amount of money they were claiming had been stolen didn't tally with their books, so, you know. Hardly upstanding citizens themselves."

"I'm sure they'll find the culprits. The police really are very good."

"Nah," the lawyer said. "Twelve robberies, one after the other, before anyone even realised it was a pattern? Multiple places in one night? Not a scrap of evidence? Got to be pros. They'll be long gone. Speaking of …" She poked at the file on her lap. "You're going to get some community service, probably maintaining the cricket pitch and cleaning the pool, just to rub your nose in it. Be done in a year, though. What'll you do after that? Stay here?"

"Oh, no," Griff said. "I don't think I could bear it. It's so embarrassing."

"Fair enough." She got up as the court officer beckoned them in. "I'm sure you'll think of something. Smart man like yourself."

"A fresh start," he said. "That's what I need."

"Good call. Chin up and all that."

And Griff followed her into the courtroom, to be sentenced to his community service. Because anyone who was running around sabotaging sports clubs was a little weird, but ultimately harmless. Not very bright, of course, with the evidence so poorly hidden, and definitely not any kind of career criminal, the way he'd been so happy to confess, and had even asked for court-mandated therapy sessions to be part of his sentence. Just one more confused human with hangups and issues that had boiled over into misguided action, and was now drowning in the consequences.

No one like that would be capable of planning a *real* crime, even if some of the purchases he might've been seen making – bolt cutters and masks and cans of spray paint, corrosive substances and lubricants and a variety of interesting tools – could *potentially* be useful for more than just sabotaging sports clubs. He'd been so easy to catch, after all, had drawn so much attention to himself. He was clearly a terrible criminal, and terrible criminals always mess things up.

Terrible criminals, in the minds of both police and large, angry loan collectors, weren't capable of good crimes.

That would be an impossibly long shot.

18

AN OTHER DAY

I've worked in various kitchens over the years, from cafes in Yorkshire to boats in the Caribbean to resorts in Greece. All differently equipped, all catering to different needs, all entirely unlike the other.

But all entirely alike, too, in the sense of being somehow out of step, adrift and apart from the world, out of time and place.

Which means this story makes perfect sense to me. In a weird, kitchen-y way.

I DIDN'T NOTICE STRAIGHT AWAY.

I mean, I work, right?

Yeah, I know, everyone works, everyone's busy, I obviously wasn't paying attention, whatever.

But I work a *lot*. Restaurant trade isn't like other jobs. You can't do it with half your mind, or half your heart. Everything's hot grease and hot pans and hot tempers, sharp knives and sharp words and the sour taste of adrenaline at the back of your throat from the time you sling the first pan in prep to the moment you walk out the door into the bite of deep, late night, a beer in one hand and a smoke in the other, and everything hurting. Your back, your knees, the endless assault of little burns and cuts and stinging scrapes. Or big ones, sometimes, but if your head's in the game that's rare.

We don't see daylight. We don't run errands. We don't have lives outside the damn kitchen, or not ones most people would recognise. People watch all these TV shows and think, yeah, it's all exaggerated, it's not really like that, it's all for the ratings and the drama. It's not. The shows are toned down, if anything. I mean, sure, you've got the seriously high-end kitchens with a dozen chefs fussing about with tweezers and eye droppers and half a leaf of parsley, where they're playing opera to the deconstructed, organic, hand-reared kelp and cumin cheesecakes, and serenading the single-malt strawberry gazpacho foam with piano concertos. They exist. So do the crappy, filthy holes staffed by one bored lad slinging boil-in-the-bag, pre-chopped, pre-cooked fish dinners into a microwave with a lemon slice while watching TikTok. There's glamour and grime in every part of the industry.

Most of us inhabit a kind of middle echelon, though. No eyedroppers or massaged beef, but we're hand-chopping every clove of garlic, picking through our lettuce for the decent leaves, losing fingertips to the meat-slicer and smashing through tray after tray of eggs for our panna cotta or tart au citron or whatever else is on the dessert board that week. And all of that takes time, and energy, and a warped sort of pride and blind dedication that makes no damn sense when you look at the wages.

Anyway. You're not here for a behind-the-scenes tour of the restaurant industry. Hardly important now, is it? All of that was just to say that no, I didn't notice at first, because life outside the kitchen tends to be conveniently hazy. We don't have the news on. There's no TV on the wall. It'd expire pretty rapidly amid the steam and the heat even if we did. We've got music sometimes, during prep and clean down, but mostly it's just the endless soundtrack of pans and knives and sizzling oil.

So the first hint I had that anything was *off* was when Marta, who you might call a kitchenhand if you felt like getting your ear slapped, came in with her hair in disarray, flopped over her forehead rather than fiercely spiked. Her lower lip was split, too, a dark line of red amid swollen skin.

"You seen what's going on out there?" she asked me, and I shook my head, not looking up from the carrot I was slicing rapidly into neat, uniform rounds.

"No. Black Friday or something, isn't it?"

"That was last month," she said, rolling her sleeves up over her tattooed forearms and setting one of the sinks to fill. "Where's your head at, Elle?"

"Here. Where else?" I flung the carrot into the stockpot and moved onto the celery, glancing at the hazed face of the clock on the wall. "Jack should be here by now."

"Not if he's on the bus, he won't be," Marta said, and I finally looked at her properly. I didn't ask about the split lip. I'd seen it before, even offered to help sort it out once, but it turned out not to be what I thought. Marta fought in low professional-grade MMA, and her compact frame was wildly muscled. She didn't need anyone sorting things out for her, no matter how good with knives they were. The hair was odd, though.

"What happened? You run out of hair gel?"

"I had to walk. In the rain. There's no buses." She sounded uneasy, put out, which wasn't like her. Marta was the calm in the storm in this place.

"Is there a strike?" I asked.

"Weird one if so. The buses are there, but they're not moving."

I didn't really care about buses. I cared about getting the pot au feu started, so as strange as it was for *Marta* to be fussing about transport issues, I turned back to my chopping. "Just sitting at the station, you mean?"

"No." Now she sounded *uncertain*. That stopped me mid-chop, the knife resting on the board, and I turned to look at her again. Marta was never uncertain. Focussed and sharp, or hyper and laughing, sure. Sometimes even pot-slinging furious, when some new hire treated her less-than for having her hands in the sink, cleaning up *their* mess (and the new hires never lasted long after that, if at all). All of these, but not uncertain. Never that. "They're just stopped in the streets," she said, watching the sink fill.

"The drivers left them at the stops or something?" I suggested. What were we now, France, with their endless strikes?

"No," she said, impatience flaring in the word with something like her usual self. "The drivers are there, and the buses are *in* the road. Not parked. They've just *stopped*. Blocking traffic all over the show."

I frowned. "And they won't move?"

"I saw a couple of coppers banging on the windows and door of one, and the driver never even looked at them. Just sat there staring at the windscreen. There were half a dozen passenger on board too, and they were the same. Didn't look up, didn't move. Nothing."

I rubbed the back of my neck, the skin prickling with goosebumps despite the heat that had already built up from the stove. "Weird."

"Yeah."

"Social media prank?"

She gave me a look that was fully Marta. "With an entire fleet of buses? You think we've got Jackass reboots in Leeds, kid?"

I shrugged. I didn't have time for social media. Didn't have patience, more to the point. The boss took photos of the plates, fussed with lights and angles and all that crap while the food got cold and muted with softly congealing sauces. He still ate it, so I suppose it was *fine*, nothing was wasted, but I hated the performance, and I hated even more how often I'd peer out into the restaurant and, instead of seeing diners eating the food we worked so bloody hard to make *just* right, to get to the tables when it was still as close to perfect as it could be, they'd all be there with their phones out like it was a paparazzi tour for sodding pasta. It was like the taste had become secondary to the likes, and the need to engage in that sort of behaviour was one of the reasons I never wanted to own my own place. That, and this way I knew I got wages in my account every month. That was never guaranteed when you owned somewhere.

I went back to my pot, throwing the last of the celery in with the onions and carrots and herbs, and lugging it to the stove. Marta was still staring into the sink as if it might contain answers. "Probably some sort of protest," I said, meaning the buses.

"About what, though?"

"No idea. But it got your attention, didn't it?"

She made a noncommittal noise, but started slamming pots about in her usual way, and then we were into prep proper, the rest of the crew crashing through the doors with apologies or excuses, or nothing it all in the case of Jack, who already had an apron on when he walked in, and simply grabbed a board and a knife and started, his woolly hat still pulled down to his ears and his eyebrows drawn tight. There was no time to worry about buses after that, and they hardly seemed important. Not with lunch bearing down on us with the single-minded brutality of an outback road train.

I DIDN'T THINK about the buses again until I was walking home in the rough edges of the night. We'd been done by midnight, cleaned down and squared away, and now I ambled along the silent streets with a couple of beers in me and a cigarette twining smoke into my breath, drifting in the still, crisp air. There were stars out, probably lots of them if you were in the countryside somewhere, but here was city sprawl and light pollution and urban foxes, so I had to settle for a few pinpricks glimmering in the distant dark.

I always walked, rain or not. It wasn't like I needed the exercise, not after sixteen hours or so on my feet in the kitchen, but the time outside helped me move from one world to the other, helped my head wake up at the start of the day and shut down at the end. I lived close enough that it was less than half an hour even if I was so tired I could barely navigate the kerbs, feet working on autopilot.

I wasn't that tired tonight, but my head was running on the next day's menu, so I wasn't actively looking for buses, but some part of my brain registered the lack of them anyway. There were still cars gnawing at the streets, but no relentlessly rumbling monoliths tearing paths through the night. No trucks, either. Just cars, and not many of those. The flow of traffic felt thin and hesitant, out of place in the emptied streets. I paused at the door to my building, taking a final draw on the cigarette before flicking it into a can by the door. The 24-hour store downstairs shed yellow light onto the pavement, and I could see Mr Patel behind the counter, reading a book with a cup of tea next to him. He didn't look around or move, and I went inside, climbing the stairs to let myself into my little one-bed flat. I showered then fell into bed, not thinking about buses.

I was halfway to work the next morning, clutching a mug of coffee and still not really awake, when the quiet seeped into my awareness.

Well, not quiet *exactly*. There were plenty of people on the streets, more than usual, in fact, all of them looking stressed and flustered. But the roads themselves were almost empty. A taxi and a delivery van were pointed in one direction, a low-slung, patchily painted old Volvo estate in the other, but none were moving. Their headlights gleamed on the wet tarmac, and I could see the drivers and the taxi's passenger staring fixedly though the windscreen. There was no sound of engines, not anywhere, and I watched the lights change from green to red and back again, while the vehicles just sat there. The pedestrians barely spared them a glance, and I turned in a slow circle, chin sunk into my coat. I could imagine the street shut off for an emergency maybe, but then why were the vehicles still on it, just sitting there with their occupants?

I hesitated, then stepped into the street, barely avoiding being run down by a cyclist, who hurled abuse at me. That, at least, was normal cyclist behaviour, so I ignored it and walked to the taxi. I knocked briskly on the window, leaning down to look at the driver. He didn't move, one hand on the wheel, the other mid-gesture. His eyes were on the rearview mirror, and his passenger had the politely neutral look of someone wishing they didn't need to engage with anyone. She had her phone on her lap, and a baggage tag on the computer case next to her. I tried knocking on her window too, but she was as unresponsive as the driver.

"*Huh.*" I straightened up, looking around the street. No one else seemed in the slightest bit interested in the unmoving cars, and I could see a few more vehicles beyond the next intersection, silent and simply *there*, like monuments to an age that hadn't yet passed, or art installations that meant something to the posh crowd, but which the average person regarded with only a mix of bemusement and exasperation.

"*Huh*," I said again, and turned to work. I didn't have the time to worry about it. I had a fish delivery coming in half an hour, and a lunch special to start on.

THE FISH DELIVERY was already there, sitting in damp, sagging boxes at the back door. No invoice in sight, nothing to sign for. Just the boxes blocking my way. I dragged them to the side and let myself into the dark kitchen, then lugged the lot straight to the walk-in fridge, hoping they hadn't been out there long. I didn't think they could have. The clock showed just after 8 a.m, so the fishmonger had been bloody early. Better that than the alternative, though.

I was still setting up when Marta banged in, wiping her feet brusquely and going to hang her coat up.

"Still no buses?" I asked when she reappeared.

"No what?" she said, swigging from a takeaway cup with a blurry, unfamiliar logo. A new place, or someone changing things up.

"The buses," I repeated. "They're still not running."

She gave me a blank look as she put on an apron, and I was about to ask if she needed a shot of something stronger in her coffee to kickstart her brain when the door was jerked open again, revealing the freckled kid from the veg supplier.

"Morning," he said, slinging an armload of large canvas sacks onto the nearest worktop and thrusting a sheet of paper at me. I took it automatically, frowning at the sacks.

"What, you run out of boxes or something?" It didn't

matter, not really, but the boxes made it easier to store every-thing, to stack them neatly in the walk-in and actually be able to find stuff without having to dig for half an hour and messing up the system.

"Eh?" the kid said.

"The bags?"

"Yeah?"

I gave up, scrawling a signature on the sheet. I wasn't emptying everything out to check it now, and I'd worked with Gill, the kid's dad, long enough to know he wouldn't send me any shoddy stock. Suppliers who did that to one restaurant didn't stay suppliers to any restaurants for long. I shoved the sheet back at the kid, and he gave me an affable grin and shambled out into the grey morning. It wasn't until the door swung shut behind him that I remembered I needed to put in an extra order for fancy mushrooms. The exotic ones needed a few days' notice, and I wanted to make a decent veggie wellington on the weekend. I ran after him, out into the alley, hoping I'd catch the van. Instead I saw the kid vanishing around the corner on a sodding *bicycle*, a cart wobbling behind it. I stared after him, thinking that Gill must be getting a little too caught up in the eco movement, then went back inside. I'd call him later.

Marta was already unpacking the veg bags and stacking everything into crates, the light smoothing softly over the royal blue globes of the tomatoes and the fat, glossy yellow peppers— I shook my head, and went to join her, peering into the tub and examining the produce.

"What the hell?" I said to her, holding up a tomato. The deep blues were variegated and multi-hued, turning it into a self-contained galaxy. It wasn't like one of the purple ones we got sometimes. It was a full-throttle *blue*.

Marta barely glanced at it. "Yeah, they're small at the moment. Weather's been bad for toms, apparently."

"They're blue," I said, shaking it at her, and she looked from it to me.

"Yes," she said, a question in her tone.

"What is it, some new varietal? I didn't order these. I just want plain bloody tomatoes for the caprese. What'm I going to do with sodding *blue* tomatoes? Smurf salad?"

Her brows drew down in concern. "You sleeping, Elle?"

"What the hell's that got to do with blue tomatoes?"

She looked as if she didn't how to answer, which unsettled me even more than the tomatoes, but at that moment Jack crashed through the door, wordlessly throwing a bag of pastries onto the worktop as he passed, and I went to kick the coffee machine out front into life.

Blue tomatoes and bicycles. Bloody Gill.

I SORT OF FORGOT ABOUT the tomatoes for a bit after that, slinging coffee for the three of us. Jack hadn't brought pastries after all, but instead individual servings of some sort of pink strawberry foam wrapped in green leaves. It tasted like kiddie bubble bath, and both he and Marta gave me weird looks when I asked where he'd got them. In the fridge by the coffee station the milk was a different brand to usual, with a strange gold tint to it, but it foamed up alright for the others, and I drink mine black, so it didn't bother me.

No, what bothered me was what happened when I went to get the cod for the fish special. I carted the box to my workbench then lifted the top off, the damp-softened cardboard smooth under my fingers as I folded back the plastic lining, ice still clinging to it gently. I glimpsed a flash of pale, unfamiliar flesh, and something glutinous and swollen, then *movement*, and I jumped back so far I lurched into the opposite bench, the edge biting my spine. I swore, the sound panicked and high to my own ears.

"Elle?" Marta spun toward me, a knife in one hand and luminously blue tomato juice dripping from the other, making me think, with a sudden, near-hysterical bubble of laughter, of Smurf salad again. I smothered it as Jack gave a grunt of surprise, looking up from his pastry bowl, and I pointed wildly at the box.

"What the *hell* is that?" I demanded. "What's going on?"

Jack ambled to my bench, leaning over the box to pluck at the plastic, and I waited for him to curse or flinch, or do anything. He was hardly the most expressive person I'd worked with, but *that* …

He looked around at me, eyebrows drawn so tightly together they'd become one unbroken dark line.

"Did you see it?" I demanded, and Marta joined Jack, poking the contents of the box. My gorge rose, the coffee making a comeback. "What the hell? I mean, *what the hell?*"

Jack and Marta exchanged glances, and it was Jack who spoke, his voice rough with smoke and disuse. "Elle, mate— "

"Don't *mate* me, you git. What's in that box? Is it a joke?"

"It's the fish order," Marta said, and she touched it. God, she *touched* it, the weird flabby folds and the coiled links and the still-pulsating, questionable *things* that might be organs or limbs or— I grabbed her, pulling her away, glancing quickly into the box as if normality might've reasserted itself, morphing the contents back into bland slabs of smooth scales and glassy eyes. It hadn't. The thing twitched, seeming to wink lewdly at me, and I slammed the top of the box back into place.

"What is it?" I screamed, the word tearing at my throat, because I'd seen tumours in slabs of beef and abscesses in the joints of sheep, worms in organs and parasitic freeloaders on the flanks of salmon, and never mind all the daily horrors of grease traps and blocked drains and industrial bins in summer, but that … What was in the box was beyond being gross, or nasty. It was *impossible*, and my head pounded with it, my chest tight and wheezy.

Marta tried to touch me and I pulled away, staggering to the walk-in to confront the crates of veggies. Stringy, waving lettuces had clambered out of the bins and were scuttling down the shelves, and mushrooms glowed in a kaleidoscope of fluorescent colour. Courgettes lay there being courgettes, and so did the onions, but the garlic whispered and bloomed and fired a screen of seeds as it dived for cover, while the lemons rolled in tight formation across the floor. I nudged a fat, orange-spotted aubergine aside with one foot, ignoring it snapping fibrous teeth at me, and turned to the meat shelves. We'd had a delivery yesterday, and I opened the nearest box tentatively, my shoulders tight. Inside, a clutter of individually packed steaks rubbed shoulders with a few vacuum-packed tenderloins, nothing moving or giving off weird vibes. Okay. That was okay. I eyed the fish section, where the rest of today's delivery was stacked. I didn't have to check it. I could hear things scratching and shifting inside, and the aubergine had called in reinforcements from the leeks. I backed out of the fridge, wiping my mouth with one hand.

Marta and Jack were both still watching me, and Jack fished in the pocket of his apron, took out his cigarettes, and lit one. I didn't even protest at him doing it in the kitchen, just took it with numb fingers when he handed it to me, and let him propel me out the door into the alley, where I alternated between panting, retching, and sucking down the smoke hard enough to make my head spin.

Marta followed us out a moment later, handing me a coffee cup half filled with whisky. I threw a gulp of it back, wheezed, and watched a horse trot past the end of the alley towing a two-person cart. A transparent sphere rolled in the opposite direction, a couple talking animatedly inside a central chamber which remained still while the rest rolled. I finished the whisky and found my own cigarettes in my pocket, lighting one without taking my eyes off the street. A spindly, spider-like thing scuttled past with a large carriage trailing docilely behind it, decorated with the logo of the local bus service. I pointed at it, looking from Marta to Jack, unable to even find the words.

"Go home," Marta said, not unkindly. "We'll manage."

"But," I said, and waved vaguely, encompassing the inexplicable vehicles and the nightmarish fish and the sodding galaxy tomatoes.

Jack shrugged. "Told you to take time off after Kate."

"This is not about Kate," I said, pointing at him. "Something's *happened*."

"You don't sleep, you don't eat, you work too much," Marta said, as Jack vanished back inside. "You *drink* too much."

"I don't," I protested.

"Not at work," she said, her gaze level, and I looked back at the street. Someone was jogging past, headphones in, just like normal.

"It helps me sleep."

"Doesn't seem to be working, from the look of you. We've all been waiting for you to hit a wall."

"Not a wall," I insisted, but I could feel that irritating bloody *endless* loss aching in my chest, trying to close up my throat. Not that it had been a surprise. Of course Kate had wanted someone who actually came home at decent times, and had weekends off, and didn't stink constantly of stale oil and old fish. Who wouldn't? And she deserved all that and more. I swallowed, then frowned. The *fish*. "I didn't bloody imagine the fish," I said to Marta, jabbing a finger at the kitchen door. "Something's wrong with it."

"Fish is fine." Jack said, reappearing with my coat and a coffee in a takeaway cup. I could smell the whisky in it. "You're not. Go home."

I looked from one of them to the other, pressing a hand to my forehead, then held a finger up. "Wait. My mobile."

"Mobile what?" Marta asked.

"My *phone.* We can look at the news. See what's happening."

They looked at each other, that awful, concerned glance that said nothing and everything. "You mean the newspaper?" Jack asked.

"No! My *phone.*" I took a step toward the door, meaning to get it, and Marta moved into my way, strong forearms crossed over her chest. I scowled at her. "Move."

"No. You're going home."

"You can't send me home," I snapped.

"No, but we'll both walk unless you go, and then what'll you do? Run service on your own?"

"Everyone else'll arrive soon." I protested, but that was weak, and I knew it. Jack was my second, and Marta was the pin the kitchen swung on. I could run a service without one of them, but not without both. Plus Marta would probably stop everyone else at the door and send them home, too. It wasn't like anyone was going to argue with her.

I swore, solidly and roundly, then snatched my jacket and the coffee off Jack and went stomping down the alley feeling like a cat with my back up and my ears flat. I didn't want to go home, to the empty fridge and an empty bed. But then again, maybe I *was* hitting a wall. Perhaps I was so strung out I was hallucinating. I had to be, right?

I IGNORED THE IMPOSSIBLE, fantastical machines on the street, bouncing and rolling and floating, filling the space where the vehicles had once been. I ignored the coffee cart on the corner where a smiling goat in a pastel apron slopped bright pink liquid into the waiting mugs, then tapped its hoof on the credit card scanner. I ignored the florist wrestling an escaping peace lily to the ground while a trio of cacti warred over the plant food. I ignored pigeons marching in strict formation toward a chattering, posturing phalanx of squirrels, while women in flat caps exhorted passersby to lay their bets. I ignored the signs in shop windows advertising mysterious brands, and the unknown music drifting from the doors, and the strange, sweet scents of foods I couldn't name.

I ignored all of it, and I didn't stop until I pushed through the door into the shop under my flat. Mr Patel looked up as the bell clattered, his eyes shadowed under big white eyebrows. He nodded at me gravely and took a packet of cigarettes from the display behind him, placing them on the counter. I set a couple of cans of baked beans and a loaf of wholemeal bread next to them, then pointed wordlessly at the vodka. The cheap stuff. I just needed it to work, not taste good.

Mr Patel got the vodka, then rang everything up laboriously on the old-fashioned till, and packed it into a paper bag without speaking. I liked that about him. He didn't waste time on chat. But as I watched him work, I realised something, and put a hand out, not touching him, just halting him. He looked up at me, eyebrows raised.

"These are the usual brands," I said.

"Yes. They are not good?"

"No. They're good." I let him finish, something easing in me. The beans were just beans. The bread was just bread. Things were okay. I'd had … a moment. Something. Overwhelm, burnout, whatever. I'd go home, eat beans on toast, and sleep it off with a little help from the vodka, then tomorrow everything would be back to normal. This proved it. Everything was going to be okay. I smiled at him, and he gave me a look I couldn't quite read, weary and worn.

He started to say something, and was interrupted by a scuffle in the corner by the fridges. We both looked around, and Tiff, the long-haired grey and white shop cat, leaped to the counter in a swirl of fluff. She had something in her mouth, and she dropped it in front of us with an air of satisfaction. Mr Patel and I watched a grape roll across the counter, twitching and bleeding, and Tiff purred.

Neither of us spoke, until finally Mr Patel said, "It is a new variety, maybe. I order red globe grape because Mrs Patel likes. She does not like these."

"No," I said, looking for my phone to pay. It wasn't there, but I found some crumpled bills and change in the pocket where it should've been. I handed him some, trying not to look at the unfamiliar colours and patterns on the worn paper, feeling that moment of relief drain away. He gave me my change while Tiff cleaned a paw, then tapped the grape again. It rolled over a couple of times, and spat a seed at me with a hiss.

"Apologies." Mr Patel dropped a cleaning cloth over the rogue fruit, and I looked at the door, then at him, wondering if I should say, *You remember, too. You know this isn't how it was yesterday. How has everyone forgotten? What do we **do?*** But then he smiled, a strained, strange expression, and said, "Have a nice day, chef."

And that was all there was. Either I was hallucinating, or the world had fallen apart, and in the end it didn't matter either way. I couldn't fix it, and Mr Patel wasn't going to suddenly become my mentor or comrade in arms or whatever, and it wouldn't have made any difference if he had. I made soufflés. I didn't change worlds, or stop them changing.

I needed sleep, was all. Maybe everything would make sense after I'd slept.

"Thanks, Mr Patel," I said, and went home. I poured a vodka, heated up the beans, then found the notebook I used for recipe ideas and wrote down everything I could think of that mattered.

The colour of *real* tomatoes, like the ones I'd bought by the bagful from Italian marketplaces, warm and round to bursting and wearing a sheen of dust.

The salt-fresh smell of fish when the boats come in.

The sharp snap of a lemon stem, plucked straight from a tree.

The pale, creamy taste of milk from farm shops, rich and fleeting.

The scent of Kate's hair, cutting past the stink of cigarettes and hot oil, light and fleeting and full of promise.

I wrote until my hand cramped up, then stared at my list. Because Marta didn't remember buses, and Jack didn't remember proper fish, and maybe it didn't matter.

But maybe it did.

After a moment, I wrote: *Red globe grapes aren't really red. They're the colour of red wine dried in a glass the morning after a party, or a bruise that blooms freshly after a fall, or old embers. They're purple, and pink, and a little dull, like stained glass seen from the wrong side, and pop when you bite into them like little bubbles of sunshine.*

I put my pen down and poured myself another drink. I didn't know if that was enough to remember them by, but I raised a glass to Mrs Patel anyway, then I went to bed.

Tomorrow's another day and all that. It just remained to be seen whether *an other* might be more accurate.

I thought it might.

My phone hadn't come back, and it had taken the TV with it.

19

WE GIVE THEM EVERY CHANCE

I went on a dating app at one point. It was an interesting experi-ence which yielded more than one entertaining encounter, as well as at least one good friend. But the thing with letting a writer loose on such things is that we really are a bit weird.

One very pleasant man told me about living in the far north of the world, and mentioned in passing that some people had been less than pleasant to him. To which I asked if he would like me to put them in a story and kill them off for him ...?

This is the story. And yes, we stopped messaging not long after that. Not sure why ...

THE POLICEMAN'S NAME IS JONAS, AND HE IS TIRED. THAT might be because it's three a.m., but in those long winters in the small village where the ice touches the horizon and the snow swallows the land, where the still-unfrozen waters in the centre of the fjord are as deep and dark as the sky and the stars drown there surely as they shine above, it's hard to tell what three a.m. really means. It's just another hour; it could be three p.m. and no one could tell the difference.

But mostly, he's tired because there's an investigator from Oslo staring at him across the desk with her arms folded over her chest. That sort of thing is *very* tiring.

The investigator is young and serious. Jonas is not very young, and he mostly wants a beer. But he has dealt with these investigators before. This has happened before, and he knows the dance well, so he merely folds his fingers together on the desk, gives a weary smile, and says, "I can't explain it to you any further. We have lost someone in the ice."

She taps her fingers against her arms. "I know that," she says. "I did read the report."

"So what more do you want me to say?"

"I want to know *how* you lost them in the ice."

Jonas shrugs. "It happens. Tourists, you know. We tell them. Every time, we tell them. We tell them the ice is treacherous, and not to be trusted. We tell them there's many kinds of ice, and until one has lived them, it's hard to tell one from the other. There's the ice for fishing, which is thick and hard and can be carved like a Sunday roast. There's the ice for skating, which is maybe not as thick, and it creaks and whispers, sending those who don't understand it fleeing for the shore. *We* know the sound it makes when our skates pass over it, though. We know it's safe enough. There's ice full of fault lines, which will shatter like glass without warning. Ice that's fragile as frost. And then there's the ice that lies. Ice that looks trustworthy but holds secrets."

The investigator frowns. "I do know about ice," she says.

Jonas thinks of a beer again, longingly. They all think they know about ice. "In Oslo, do you get proper ice?"

She smiles slightly at that, and he notices she wears dark circles under her eyes like the bruises of grim days. He wonders what she usually investigates. Not missing tourists in the ice, he imagines.

"Probably not the same ice as up here," she says.

Up here is within the Arctic Circle, *up here* is where the sun flees, where it deserts the land and the cold dark seas for weeks at a time, weeks that feel like months, *up here* there is only ice and silence and darkness, and it isn't somewhere the investigator is comfortable being. It isn't somewhere she *wants* to be. But her name is Nora, and as uncomfortable as she might be in the suffocating dark and the endless waste of ice and trees and snow and the weight of the eternal silence, she has questions, and she will ask them, because that is what she always does, even when they aren't good questions. Or rather, when the answers aren't good answers. The questions are always good. Or necessary, at least.

"This happens regularly," she says. "The vanishings in the ice."

Jonas shrugs. "We get more tourists than you might think. They come up here to feel the darkness. They want to see the Northern Lights. They want to ice fish, and swim in the fjords. They want to ride snowmobiles at midnight. They want to take a selfie with a polar bear."

"Really?"

"Really. I sometimes wonder that more of them don't vanish."

She gives him a sharp look, but he just smiles.

"Would you like another coffee?"

"Not really," she says, but then looks at her watch and nods. "But actually, yes. Please." It's too late – or too early – to worry about sleeping. She watches him get up, a tall rangy man with his beard neatly trimmed and his hair slightly longer than might be regulation for a police officer. He belongs here, carrying the landscape in his greying locks and sloping shoulders. "Other places get tourists," she says. "They don't lose as many as you do. On the ice."

Jonas gives her an affronted look as he pokes at the little coffee machine sitting in the corner of the cosy office. The night pushes tight to the windows, despite the yellow street-lights outside. "You can't blame that on us," he says. "We warn them. We tell them. They sign a form, when they rent the skates, or the snowmobiles, or the fishing gear. The form says they've been told, they've been made aware of the risks of the ice, it's all been explained to them. The safety precautions and how to look for rotten patches and what to do if something goes wrong. What more can we do?"

Nora makes a small non-committal sound and takes the cup of coffee he offers her. It's petite and dark and intensely strong, and she puts two cubes of sugar in it. "I'm not saying you could necessarily have done more," she says. "But every five years, this happens. Someone's out skating, and they vanish, and there's never any sign of them."

"The ice is hungry," Jonas says, and he isn't smiling this time.

The skin tightens on Nora's cheeks, and she shivers despite the well-heated room. She glances at the window, not that she can see much, not with those steady lights that hide the dark, but she can feel it. The ice that chokes the lakes and circles the fjords and creeps brittle and fierce across the waters, thickening and deepening with every night's breath, reaching down and down and down further still, turning the water syrupy and thick as jelly.

"Every five years," she says. "It's almost to the day."

Jonas shrugs again. "I can't explain that," he says. "These things happen."

She frowns. *These things happen.* Stubbing a toe on a filing cabinet twice in a row, or spilling coffee from a poorly placed mug three times over, or even bumping into the one insufferable coworker at lunch every week and not being able to hide, *those* things happen. Someone vanishing into the ice in a recognisable, predictable pattern, no. *That* doesn't just happen.

Jonas doesn't offer anything further, just looks at her, waiting. She knows somehow that he's waiting for her to ask the right question, the one that will unlock everything (if that's what she really wants, because somewhere behind that lock is hungry ice and biting cold and endless night, and something *other,* and does she really want that?), but she doesn't know what the right question is. She doesn't even know what she's trying to ask or why she's really here. No one told her to come, or asked her to. It was just that weird non-anomaly sticking out at her. Annoying her. Every five years, someone goes out on the ice, and they don't come back.

"Is it something to do with the skates?" she asks finally. "The rental skates, are they somehow … are they hazardous? Heavier, maybe? More likely to break through the ice?"

Jonas snorts, a dismissive sound that makes her cheeks heat up. "Are we renting deadly skates to the tourists? Wouldn't do much for our Tripadvisor rating, would it?"

She acknowledges that with a slight smile, reminding herself that she's still an investigator, and he's just a police officer at the end of the world. "Well, no, but I noticed all the rental skates are orange. All the same brand, too."

"Orange is easy to find," Jonas says. "You'd be amazed how many tourists just dump them by the side of the lake, thinking someone will come along and collect them. Like it's part of the service."

Nora's not convinced, but she doesn't push the idea,

either. It's not exactly much of a lead, after all. But none of the locals have that colour, she's noticed. They dress, whether it's skates or shoes or clothes, in greys and blues and greens, colours that mirror and blend with the dark sky and the snow-drenched trees and the ever-present ice, turning them into shadows and wraiths. For an instant she has an image of those orange skates as fishing lures, flashing above the heavy, silent water rather than in it, and she can't help but wonder what they could be fishing for.

"Can you tell me anything else?" she asks.

"Nothing," Jonas replies. "We've told the next of kin. There's really nothing else we can do."

She waves a hand dismissively. "That's not what I'm asking. I'm asking about the pattern. They all hired skates from the same place. Have you looked into everyone who works there?"

"There is only one place," he says. "They rent hundreds of skates every year, without any problems. They maintain their gear, and they give good briefings, thorough ones. They always recommend the tourists take a guide, someone who knows the nature of the ice, but none of them do. They all think they know better." He pauses, looking out the window, then drains his coffee mug and looks back at her. "We give them every chance."

Nora sighs. She doesn't have any more questions. She wants to go home. She wants to be in her own bed, with the rumble of the city outside. She doesn't want to be here anymore. Whatever she thought, whatever connection she imagined she saw on paper, it's not out here in the world. What did she think? Did she think she was Dana Scully? Off investigating mysterious goings-on in remote villages, solving for X? There's nothing here. He's right. Tourists are tourists. They don't listen. They don't understand the risks, no matter how many times things are explained to them.

They think they're invulnerable. And sometimes it catches up with them.

She puts the coffee cup down and looks at her watch. There's an early morning flight back to Oslo from Trømso, and if she leaves now she should make it. Suddenly that seems like not just the best option, but the only one.

"Alright," she says. "You'll call me if you find the body?"

"I will," he says. "But the fjords are deep, and the currents have their own lives. We've never found any of the others."

"Alright," she says again, and she leaves, going out into the sharp-edged, gnawing cold, the deep distant morning buried by the endless night of the Arctic winter.

NORA PAUSES before she gets into the rental car, aware of Jonas watching her from his office window. She pulls her coat tighter, tucks her scarf a little closer. She can smell the fjords. Salt and cold and secrets, and the ice like a pressure against her eardrums. The streets are empty and silent, the windows blind and dark under the yellow of the streetlights, and she walks to the edge of the frozen water and looks out.

The dock sticks out deep into the bay where fishing boats can still find a little clear water to reach it, a stark exclamation against the smooth sheet of solidified sea. The scars of skates skirt the shoreline, wheeling and circling. For a moment she wants to be out there, wants to be skating like she did when she was a kid, with her arms out and her scarf flying and the cold tearing her breath away, swooping across the ice, unleashed. There's a reckless exhilaration, something feral and untamed, about being caught between the night above and the night reflected below. But she doesn't move. She just watches, and her eyes are drawn again and again to the water where it meets the ice. She thinks she can see something in the shadows of the dock, something moving languorously beneath the heavy weight of the winter, maybe seaweed under the frozen surface.

She doesn't understand how she can see it because the ice is thick and opaque, and the night just as much so. She's mistaken. *Has* to be. There can't be anything. She's tired. She's had too much coffee. She needs to go home. She looks back up at the building, at Jonas standing silent at the window, his face hidden by the light at his back. She almost raises a hand to wave, but she thinks he's not actually looking at her. She thinks he's looking at the ice, too, and she imagines walking out onto its creaking, whispering surface, searching for that movement on the edge of the world. Strapping on orange skates and going out to see what comes.

As if hearing her, the ice creaks, and she looks back at it. There's no mistaking the movement now. It boils and curls, and it's not seaweed. It's not fish, either. It's nothing that makes any sense, except it *does* make sense here, in the dark and breathless cold. She catches its scent, dank and wild, and closes her eyes against the impossibility of it, thinking that she needs to see the doctor when she gets home. Or the psychiatrist. The winter is never a good time for her, and this one is maybe worse than others. She misses the sun.

Then she turns her back on the sea and the village and the police station, and climbs back into the rental car and switches an audiobook on, and tries not to think of the darkness stretching all the way to the horizon, all the way to the end of the world. Because it's just frozen water, and just winter, and just tourists, and she's not Dana Scully.

It's not until she's almost back to Oslo, a cup of lukewarm airplane coffee clutched in one hand, that she lets herself think of Jonas and his ice-dusted hair.

We give them every chance.

She pulls down the window shade and drinks her coffee

and doesn't look at the cold, frozen expanse sweeping past far, far below her. Let small towns keep their secrets. They have their own ways of surviving, and in the suffocating weight of the winter night, who is she to question it?

These things happen, after all.

2 0

CLOUDY WITH A
CHANCE OF SHEEP

This is not a Yorkshire village. Not quite.

Sure, there are drystone walls and hulking fells, green fields and winding waterways, there are ageing 4x4s and tea shops and clocktowers, farms and fields and rambling footways.

But those are just markers. Little links that point not to a sameness, but to a difference ...

TILDA STOOD ON HER TIPTOES, AS IF THAT WOULD REVEAL SOME hidden fold in the gently sloping field below her, a heretofore undiscovered nook or cranny amid the spring-vibrant grass and old grey stone.

It didn't, of course. She'd been farming these same fields for eighty-six years. They weren't suddenly going to develop extra dips and gullies of their own accord. Landslides were unlikely, earthquakes even more so, and while there was always the possibility of moles, they could hardly create a hole big enough to hide a sheep in. Other things could, of course, but Tilda had ways of guarding against those.

She whistled, the sound high and carrying in the clear air of the morning, and three lean, scruffy dogs of indeterminate breed who had been sniffing officiously around the rabbit holes and marking their territory on the drystone walls loped over to join her. One shoved his nose into her leg and she scuffed him absently behind the ears, her hands strong and heavy-knuckled.

"Let's take a look," she said, opening the sagging wooden gate and lifting it over a poorly placed tussock. The gate's frame was old yet solid, although the same couldn't be said for the hinges, which were held together with rust and a promise. Still, they worked, and there was no point replacing things before it was really necessary. That was just making work, and she had more than enough as it was.

The dogs stayed close as Tilda ambled into the field, hands tucked into the pockets of her faded corduroy trousers, her weathered waxed jacket hanging unzipped over them. The day hadn't had time to warm up yet, and at this time of year it might not bother, but the gentle nip of the morning didn't trouble her. The scent of damp earth waking from the winter, of new shoots stirring and old stone losing its chill rose around her, and she nodded in some vague and general satisfaction at the world.

Below her, mist was painted in soft swathes across the valley, swaddling the village and the river, and stands of old trees climbed stolidly out of hiding to meet the farm. Its fields ran out to either side of her vantage point before clambering up to meet the slab-sided fells, and up here the air was crisp and sharp-edged, the sky empty of even the smallest of clouds. Tilda had checked.

She surveyed the pale, woolly backs of the sheep drifting around the field, cropping grass and ignoring both her and the dogs. She counted them again, just in case.

"… nine, ten, eleven. Dammit." She'd counted right the

first time, of course, and the missing sheep hadn't reappeared. It just didn't make sense, though. *One* missing sheep. They were the ultimate followers, after all. If one had found a hole in the wall, they'd all be through it. She turned on her heel and started to circle the field, the ground soft and giving under her wellies. The dogs followed, ears twitching, and high above a skylark dropped its tumbling tune into the brightening day.

A circuit of one side of the field revealed no breaches in the wall, and no sign that her missing flock member had come to an unfortunate end. Not that there were any natural predators for sheep around here, but there was always the possibility of misbehaving dogs, or incursions of a less everyday nature. One could never dismiss such things entirely.

As they patrolled the bottom of the field her oldest pup, Dibs, snuffled around the abandoned stile, which was largely blocked with dislodged stones from the wall, then looked at Tilda and whined.

"Got something?" she asked, and went to join the dog. Plenty of her fields, as with all the farms around here, still had stiles from old footpaths that had fallen out of favour. Mostly ramblers stuck to the newer, marked tracks, with their wooden signposts and stone waymarkers, and Tilda tended to let nettles grow (or stones fall) on the ones she'd rather people didn't use. Occasionally she kept unfriendly livestock in the fields they crossed, too, if some of the old trails looked in danger of being resurrected. She didn't resent walkers, who were mostly well-behaved and decent sorts, but she didn't see any reason why they should be able to range over every part of her farm. That was just excessive, and came with its own risks to both her livestock and the ramblers.

This particular stile had a generous crop of nettles on the

far side to go with its barrier of broken stone blocking the way. A few pieces had tumbled into the shorter grass of the field, she saw now, and some of the nettles were bent, as if someone had been trampling through them.

Dibs's fringed tail wagged gently as she looked up at Tilda, and Tilda patted her side solidly. "Good girl," she said and turned back to the gate, where her quad bike was waiting. There was no point trying to find a trail over the soft grass of the fields. She might come up with the odd footprint in muddy ground, but what good would that do her? The sheep certainly hadn't gone over the wall of their own accord, and there were better ways to go about tracking such things.

Just to be sure, though – because sheep could be stubborn and fickle creatures – Tilda and the dogs spent the morning checking the land between the field and the edge of the farm. Unsurprisingly, there was no sign of the missing creature, but one had to be thorough. To that end, they took a pass through some of the higher fields, too, the ones where the rich earth and heavy carpet of grass gave way to rocky ground pocked with soggy blanket bogs. No one else seemed to be missing, which was a relief. The last thing she needed was some sort of multi-pronged escape to be dealing with.

TILDA MADE a cheese and pickle sandwich for lunch, eating it standing in the yard with a mug of tea in her other hand. The dogs didn't beg, just watched carefully, but Tilda didn't share. She had firm views on the sanctity of her cheese and pickle sandwiches. She did give them each a biscuit, though, and once she'd wiped off the breadboard and swapped her farm wellies for a pair of worn-down Chelsea boots, she went into the barn and started up her old 4×4, the engine grumbling and coughing as it warmed up.

"Stay," she said to the two younger dogs, who whined but sat down, ears back. "In," she added to Dibs, and the old dog jumped easily over her to sit on the passenger seat with her eyes bright and interested. Tilda shut the door and pulled her woolly hat down over her ears, flexing her fingers, then put the truck into gear. A trip out had not been in her plan for the day, but one had to be adaptable in farming. The days never went quite as expected.

It wasn't a long drive into the village, but the tracks were narrow, one-lane affairs tightly hemmed by grassy banks and stone walls, and Tilda took her time, still checking the fields even though she was sure the sheep was long gone. She only met one other vehicle, a faded red 4×4 even older than hers. It had only one headlight, the other an empty socket, and was driven by a diminutive man with a large beard, who gesticulated angrily at Tilda until she backed up, pulling in next to a gate to let him pass. She wound down her window as he pulled level with her, waving him to a halt.

"Alright, Giles?" she asked as he wound his own window down reluctantly.

He glared at her through heavy-lensed glasses. "What sort of question's that? Invasion of privacy, that is. You can't just go around asking personal questions of everyone!"

Tilda nodded amiably. "I've lost a sheep."

"Bloody careless, then, aren't you?"

"Have you seen anything?"

"None of your business what I've seen," he said, and shot an involuntary look at his own passenger seat. It would've been more suspicious if there hadn't been very clearly no sheep in sight, plus she also knew that Giles's interests tended more toward things that couldn't run away from him.

She was glad she'd left the other two dogs at home, though. She'd lost a weathervane and a chainsaw the last time Giles had gone past, plus three pairs of knickers that had been on the washing line.

"Let me know if you spot it," she said.

"I'm not your messenger boy," he snapped, and pulled away again, winding the window up frantically. Tilda spotted a mop and a birdhouse in the back seat, a squirrel still clinging to the birdhouse roof with a somewhat bewildered air. That was going to put him in a tizzy.

Even as she thought it, the squirrel leaped into the front of the car, and Giles swerved wildly, almost crashing into the wall before slamming the brakes on. She craned out of her window to watch, and a moment later Giles flung himself out of the 4×4, waving his arms and spouting a tirade of abuse. The squirrel didn't follow.

Tilda looked at Dibs, who tilted her head gently. Tilda nodded, put the car into gear, and headed off again.

Takes all sorts.

THE VILLAGE of Whistlewick was strung along the river at the bottom of the valley, the fields climbing to the fells on both sides, as if the houses had tumbled down the slopes to collect there. Cobbled streets curled between muddles of shops and houses with scant attention paid to order or logic, making way for trees rather than rolling over them, circling large chunks of green spaces full of benches and overstuffed flowerbeds, switchbacking and dead-ending and taking turns and bends at random, and generally turning the whole place into an utterly unnavigable town planner's nightmare, as well as leading to a lot of confused tourists in the season.

The river snaked in one side and out the other, barely

broad enough to justify the name and lined with moored canal boats and gravel towpaths and shivering willows. Tilda parked down by the lock, nodding at the long, low-slung passenger boat just making its way through, full of shoppers and a smattering of tourists. A big woman at the rear helm waved back at her, a line of spikes running down her spine to dive beneath her fleece, prominent teeth flashing.

"Tilds! You at the pub later?"

"Probably not," Tilda called back, not pausing.

"Aw. Friday?"

"Maybe." Tilda gave another wave then headed for the centre of the village, Dibs trailing after her with one eye on the ducks. Jen was always up for a drink, but she was at least twice Tilda's size and less than half her age. Tilda tried not to repeat her mistakes too often when it came to her choice of drinking partners. Not more than a few times a year, at least.

The slightly uneven tower of the town hall with its four-handed clock acted as a landmark, pinpointing the market square, which probably wasn't actually at the centre of the village but came close enough. It was surrounded by a clutter of shops selling everything from scented candles to hedge shears, plus two pubs, a glossy coffeeshop, and three near-identical tea rooms, only discernible from each other by way of their differently coloured gingham bunting.

Tilda strolled into the hall, Dibs still following on silent paws, and went straight to a heavy wooden door marked *Police*. It was unlocked, and she pushed through into a warm, softly lit room that looked like someone's parlour, complete with leather-bound books lining the walls, thick red carpets, and a couple of leather armchairs angled toward a hearth that held only a collection of melted candles. A slight woman in a pince-nez and a tweed coat looked up from one of the chairs, quirking an eyebrow.

"Hi, Maple," Tilda said.

Maple took a puff on a cigarette in a long holder, narrowing her eyes, and examined Tilda before she spoke. Tilda waited patiently, one hand on Dibs's head.

"Your boots are scuffed," Maple said finally. "Your hair is loose on one side but not the other. And …" She jumped up lightly and ran the couple of steps to Tilda, circling her, then paused to sniff her shoulder. Tilda bore it stoically, and Maple nodded, continuing, "You smell of fresh-cut grass. *Hmm.* I have it! You've been mugged by a landscape gardener." She sat back down, flinging one leg over the other and waving her cigarette extravagantly. "I'm right, aren't I?"

"No," Tilda said.

"Oh." Maple looked crestfallen. "Was I close?"

Tilda looked at her boots. "They are pretty scuffed."

Maple brightened, pointing the cigarette holder at her. "I knew it!"

"Any rogue weather reports?"

Maple thought about it. "Jimmy said the trout were swimming backward again."

"That's not weather-related. Also, they're not. He'll have been riding his bike past them, like always. Someone needs to explain relative motion to that lad."

"He did have his bike helmet on when he told me," Maple agreed.

"Nothing else?" Tilda asked.

Maple shook her head. "Why? What's happened?"

"Nothing much," Tilda said, already turning back to the door. "Cheers."

"It's *something.* I can tell. Your tread's heavy with concern, and you sighed when—"

"Just a missing animal. I'll find her."

"Can I come?" Maple called. "You might need my observational skills."

"You're all good," Tilda said, and closed the door before Maple could follow her.

OUTSIDE THE HALL, Tilda looked around the village square thoughtfully, then headed to the nearest tea shop. It had yellow bunting, and although there was no name on the door (none of them bore a name, simply blackboards proclaiming the day's scone and tea varieties), she knew it was called Steeped Dreams. More to the point, it was run by a pleasantly plump faun who was leaning over the counter as Tilda pushed through the door, whispering to a skinny woman with shimmering, scaled skin, who blinked her third eyelid lazily and licked her eyebrow with a long tongue.

"Hi, Tilda," the faun said, straightening up and adjusting her apron. It was yellow gingham as well, and inside all was sunflowers and rubber duck ornaments, smelling of lemon cake and thyme.

"Callie was just talking about you," the scaled woman said.

"I *wasn't*," the faun said. "You make it sound like I was gossiping!"

Tilda and the scaled woman both looked at her, and Callie sighed, touching her carefully curled hair. "*Fine*. Yes, I was talking about you. But nothing bad!"

Tilda could believe that. Inaccurate, probably, but bad, unlikely. It made it hard to resent Callie and her gossip. Plus, it was useful. "Any strange weather reports?" she asked.

"I just went past the school," the scaled woman said. "The head was running about waving an umbrella and yelling that he needed a plumber."

"That'll be it," Tilda said, turning back to the door. "Thanks."

"So it was you?" Callie called after her. "Why? What did he do? Was there—" The door swung shut behind Tilda, cutting off the barrage of questions. Tilda was sure the faun would make something up that was a lot more interesting than the truth. Not that she was sure what the truth was just yet, but the school? It gave her an inkling.

There was only one school in Whistlewick, and it was divided into two, split by the winding road. The primary school nestled on one side, a riot of bright colours painting the walls of its single-storey building, and the secondary school glowered at it from the other, drawn up to its full, vaguely imposing two-storey height. They were on the edge of the village, but close enough that Tilda walked rather than taking the 4×4.

She was fairly sure the primary school wasn't the issue, so she ignored it, examining the other instead. From outside, everything looked normal, a pack of teens chasing each other across the sports field, and the stone building's windows lit despite the bright day. Tilda climbed the steps to the front door and ambled down the hall with her hands still in her pockets, hearing a clamour of ducks behind one door as she passed it, voices raised in choppy song beyond another, and further off a small explosion that made Dibs yip. Everything smelled of stale sandwiches and whiteboard markers.

She found no one in the hall, but the school office held five people, two in wellies, one barefoot, and the other sloshing about in sodden trainers, even though the office itself was dry. Two of them were armed with mops and buckets, and the head's bald scalp was splattered with water.

"I know it was you," he was shouting at a dark-haired woman in wellies, who had her arms folded over her chest and an unimpressed scowl on her face. "This is sabotage!"

"*Sabotage* is you dragging me out of class in the middle of a practical section," she snapped. "By the time I get back someone'll have tried making the ethanol drinkable and someone else will have set fire to it, guaranteed."

That explained the explosions, then.

"Are you just going to stand there shouting, or are you going to help?" an older woman demanded, shaking a mop at the head. "Those sandbags aren't going to hold forever, and I'm meant to be demonstrating a Victoria sponge."

Tilda peered past them at the interior office door behind the head. Sure enough, there were sandbags on the threshold, holding back softly lapping water.

"It's already leaking downstairs," a man in a flannel shirt said, leaning on his own mop. "Do you know what stray water in an active cauldron can do?"

Maybe *that* was the source of the explosion. Or the Victoria sponge class. Tilda remembered very clearly her own school days, and someone using the wrong eggs for a meringue. They'd had to evacuate, and the school had been untenable for a week.

"Look," a woman in a polo shirt reading *Potts Plumbing* said, "There's no pipes in your ceiling to be leaking, and no toilets or anything upstairs to be causing it. This isn't my area. You've got some sort of unnatural nonsense going on."

"It's not nonsense," the head snapped. "And I want it fixed!"

"Then find someone who can deal with this sort of thing. If it's not pipes, I'm out." The plumber turned to leave, almost bumping into Tilda. She stepped aside to let the young woman pass. *Unnatural.* She never understood these anti-magic sorts. It was more natural than plumbing, when one came down to it. Older, anyway.

"Can I help you?" the older woman asked Tilda. "Are you picking someone up?"

"Maybe." Tilda strolled toward the head's office, thinking vaguely that she should've stayed in her wellies rather than changing into her town boots.

"Excuse me," the head said, stepping in front of her. "Where do you think you're going?"

Tilda gave him a vaguely surprised look. "Getting my sheep back."

"Your sheep? Why the hell would your sheep be in here?"

"Oh!" the man in the flannel shirt exclaimed, slapping a palm to his forehead almost theatrically. "I should've realised!"

"There's no sheep in there," the head insisted, putting a hand on Tilda's shoulder to stop her. She looked up at him, eyebrows raised, and Dibs growled, her worn teeth bared and still plenty sharp. The head dropped his hand hurriedly. "Why would there be a *sheep* in my office?"

Tilda examined him. "Students," she said, and walked on.

Inside, the office was ankle-deep in clear water, the carpet soft and algae-like underfoot. The walls, with their faded oil paintings and rows of old school photos, were untouched, as were a couple of incongruously modern, spindly armchairs and a coffee table to one side of the room. But above the heavy and somewhat grandiose old desk a downpour was underway, plastering notebooks and files to the dark wood, pouring in gentle waterfalls off the edges, and drumming steadily on the computer monitor, which was giving off a distinct scent of electrical defeat.

Tilda gave a grunt of recognition and waded around the desk, pulling a drenched leather chair out of the way so she could peer into the gap underneath. Pale blue eyes stared back at her expressionlessly.

"There you are," she said, and took a length of rope with a clip on one end from her coat pocket, along with a digestive biscuit. "Come on." She waved the biscuit at the sheep, keeping it just out of grabbing distance.

The creature looked from her to the biscuit, all four legs tucked underneath it. The desk had protected it from the rain, but the water on the floor was lapping about its chest. It gave a somewhat mournful bleat, then staggered to its feet, water pouring off its sodden wool. It followed Tilda as she backed away, then stood stolidly as she looped the rope around its neck before giving it the treat.

The head was peering in the door, and now he bellowed, "How the *hell* did that get in here? Who did it?"

"Pretty classic prank," the dark-haired woman said. "We put chickens in our head's office once." She examined the sheep, ignoring the head's outraged huff. "The whole water thing is new, though."

"Weather sheep," Flannel Man said. "Tilda's got the only flock in the county. Country?"

"I'm sending you the cleaning bill," the head snarled, shaking his finger at her. Dibs growled again, and he snatched his hand back, scowling at the dog.

Tilda ignored him and led the sheep out, the localised rain cloud following them. She pulled the hood of her jacket up over her head as she went, and the woman with the mop gave her a thumbs-up.

"Appreciate it," she said.

"Probably need to let the kids know they should check species before nicking any animals," Tilda said. "Old Hector's still got a couple of crocodile-llama crossbreeds on the other side of the valley, from when he was trying to create woolly dragons. They'll lose some limbs if they go for one of those."

"No one's stealing *anything*," the head snapped. "I'm giving the whole school detention until we find the culprit, then I'm handing them over to the authorities. I'll see them done for this. They'll never be back at this school, or *any* bloody school. I'm going to make a *proper* example of them. I'm going to—"

Tilda missed the rest, because she was already strolling down the hallway to the soundtrack of rain splattering on her hood, the other teachers following her. A worrying, pink-tinged billow of smoke roiled up out of the stairwell to the basement, and Flannel Man broke into a sprint, yelling, "Masks! *Masks!*" as he went.

Tilda gave the sheep another biscuit as they got outside, and it bleated at her.

"I know," she said. "We're going home now."

By the time she reached the 4×4 the rain had stopped, which was good. One unhappy sheep could fill the bed of the truck on the trip home, faster than the drains allowed it to escape, doing awful things to the suspension. She didn't need that. Especially not on a nice spring day like this.

They headed back to the farm, Dibs panting in the passenger seat and the sheep blinking at the scenery as the day grew steadily brighter and hotter. Tilda was glad the trip wasn't any longer. Never mind localised flooding – with the sheep enjoying the car ride that much, they'd have had the whole valley in drought given another ten kilometres or so.

Her good mood lasted only until she got home and spotted Giles's faded red 4×4 parked in front of her house, and the dogs lying outside the door to the chicken coop.

"Dammit," she muttered. Just because they looked like chickens and sounded like chickens didn't mean it was worth the risk of stealing their eggs. She leaned out of the car window, examining the coop, but nothing moved, not a single creature in evidence other than the dogs. She thought about it. Giles could wait a bit. She had the weather sheep to deal with first.

She parked in the barn and trudged off to get her wellies and the quad bike, a short solid woman with broad shoulders and white curls emerging from under her hat, her face wearing the passage of countless long days and wild storms and strange seasons. And *happenings.*

Because, honestly, there was always something.

There was always bloody something. Her lips tipped up in a smile.

And wouldn't it be boring if there wasn't?

2 1

FAE EYE

I didn't entirely plan for more stories to come out of Whistlewick, with its fields and fells, locks and canals, strangely identical tea shops and even odder police force, but I suspected it. Sometimes I have characters who turn up and won't leave me alone. Other times it's locations, which can be characters in and of themselves.

And, honestly, Whistlewick is weird. Even by my standards ...

JEN HUNCHED OVER THE TEA SHOP'S ONE WHEEZING COMPUTER, the chair creaking under her weight warningly. She kept telling Callie that the damn things were barely built for humans, let alone a river troll, but the faun kept declaring she didn't see size and everyone was beautiful. Which was a very nice notion, but Jen was fairly sure she was going to end up sitting in a throne of splintered wood one of these days if the place didn't get some reinforced furniture in.

She wriggled the mouse a few times, clicking randomly, then clattered some keys. They were too close together for her fingers and it made typing tricky, which was ridiculously annoying. She could tie fishing lures so delicate they'd make a sprite swoon, but typing a single line without laboriously backspacing and correcting half a dozen times was beyond her. Bloody small-centric contraptions, computers. Not that it mattered right now, because no matter what key she hit, the screen simply blinked a luminous green cursor at her, like a larva winking in the dim waters of the river.

"Callie," Jen called, starting to lean back in the chair and then freezing when it gave a screech of warning.

"Another smoothie?" Callie asked, popping her head around the corner from the tea shop's counter. The faun could barely see past the cake stands crowding it, all of varying heights and sizes, their neat glass domes encasing carrot cakes and shortbread slices and flapjacks and Eccles cakes, each neatly labelled with yellow cards.

"No, you're alright," Jen said. "What's happening with the computer?"

Callie squeezed out from behind the counter, stepping over a large grey rabbit snoozing on the rug, and came to peer over Jen's shoulder. She tried the mouse as well, and poked the keyboard a couple of times, but the cursor just blinked back at them smugly. Callie straightened up with a sigh. "It's glitching again."

"Has it got a bug?" a faery with sharp teeth and gauzy wings asked from one of the tables. Cards and a clutter of small items – cinnamon sticks and pretty shells and shiny buttons – were stacked on the yellow tablecloth in front of her, and an elderly man sat with her, shrunk deep into his purple cardigan, along with an even older woman with startlingly dark hair, red-framed glasses and a tight black choker necklace.

Jen vacated her chair rapidly, stepping back from the computer.

"Not that sort of bug," Callie said, while the old man snickered. "They're not catching."

Jen noticed Callie hadn't touched the keyboard again, though. "So it's not going to work?" she asked.

"Try restarting it," the woman in the red glasses said, picking up a delicate, stemmed glass half-full of sherry and throwing the whole lot back. "Or kick it. I did that once."

"Yes, and I had to buy a new screen," Callie said, frowning as she unplugged the computer from the wall.

"Worked, though."

"It would've worked sooner if I hadn't had to replace the screen."

The woman shrugged and folded her cards, tapping them on the table. "Are we playing, or just sitting around looking at non-functioning gadgets?"

The faery turned back to the table. "We're playing, Liza, keep your knickers on."

"I'd have to have them on to begin with. Got philosophical objections to that sort of thing, I do."

"Me too," the old man said, examining his cards. "Best to let things breathe."

"More information than I needed today," the faery observed, but laid her cards down. "Stuffed cottage."

"Dammit," the old man snapped, slapping his cards onto the table. "Are you magicking the game, Fiona?"

"No magicking in the tea shop," Callie said automatically, waving the unplugged computer cable at them. "It does things to the cakes."

"No one's magicking anything," Fiona said, sweeping up her winnings. "Grantham's just a poor loser."

"I'm definitely poor now," he muttered, but took a small nut out of his pocket and shook it, so the seed inside rattled. "Double or nutmeg?"

"It's not shiny," Liza said, frowning.

"I'll allow it," the faery said with a shrug. "Swap you a button for it if you win, Liza."

"Deal."

Jen tuned them out, watching Callie plug the computer back in, then poke the power button. The machine creaked and groaned, sounding as fragile as the chair, and Callie looked at Jen.

"Sure about that smoothie? I've got some kelp just in from the Shetlands."

"Go on, then," Jen said. She never could resist some good kelp. She followed Callie to the counter, picking out a large dandelion and honey scone from one of the cake stands. The computer would take ages to start up anyway. It was why no one much bothered with it, or with the one in the library. They were slow, and glitchy, and half the time when Jen decided to use one and venture into the green-tinged electronic wilderness they either expired with a whine halfway through loading the first page, or wouldn't start at all.

And it wasn't like there were more she could try. The only other place in Whistlewick that had them was the high school, and Jen doubted they were any more reliable. Last she'd heard, one had caught a bug and the computer teacher (who also did historical cursing and philosophy) was still trying to get the thing out of the attic. It kept scuttling off into dark corners and laying stacks of floppy discs in the rafters, which the cleaner wasn't too happy about. The other computer presumably remained unaffected, but Jen supposed it was only a matter of time before it caught something too, or the floppy discs got out of control and started spreading. And then what? Computers popping up all over town, maybe, which sounded unpleasant. No one needed a plague of the damn things. They were just fun for checking on the North Atlantic selkie feuds and the latest sea serpent sightings, was all. No real use to the damn things.

Well, almost no real use. She gave the computer an anxious look, but it still hadn't reached the start page yet, the screen flashing disconcertingly. All she needed was one quick look at her private messages. Just *one.* She should've checked yesterday, but the boat had been busy, and someone had shed a bunch of scales in the forward seating (why people couldn't pick up after themselves, she didn't know), and someone else had dropped an ice cream, which had attracted a load of sugar imps, and there had been an enquiry for a private cruise which she'd had to reply to, even though it was from the Uddershams, and everyone knew what *they* were like, and ...

And those were all excuses. She'd been *nervous*, and now here she was even more nervous, because one day was *playing it cool*, but two days would be just rude. And she had enough to contend with without being seen as rude, too. She sighed and plucked at her flannel shirt, as if her fashion choices were the issue.

"Jen?" Callie asked.

"What?"

"Do you want a plate?" The faun was looking at the scone Jen had clutched in one big hand.

Jen stared down at it too. She'd squished it, sprigs of dandelion leaves poking out the sides. "Um, no." She glanced at the computer, which chose that moment to settle on a stuttering blue screen. "I'll take it with me. And the smoothie."

"Right you are." Callie poured the smoothie into a large glass jar and screwed a lid on. "Are you alright, love?"

"Sure," Jen said, putting some money on the counter. "I might see if the library computer's working."

"Of course." Callie didn't say anything else, and Jen hurried out into the mellow sunlight of a Dales summer afternoon, her spinal spikes trembling with an uncomfortable mix of anxiety and anticipation. She *wasn't* alright, and she hated feeling so *unsettled*. It was rubbish. It wasn't worth it, surely? All this fuss and *uncertainty*, and having a nice chat and getting one's hopes up, and then someone sees a photo and just goes and vanishes. And never mind what happens half the time when someone hears the words *river troll.* She should just forget the whole thing, go home, catch some fish and drink a few beers. That would be the sensible thing to do.

She turned toward the library anyway.

In the cool, gently dim depths of the library, scented with old stories and strange worlds, no one was using the computer. There was a piece of paper stuck to the screen.

Got virus, it said, and Jen kept well back as she stared at it. Dammit. She looked around, and spotted a skinny, pointy-eared individual in half glasses re-shelving books with a look of grim determination on their face.

"Shouldn't this be quarantined?" she asked them.

"... *1-7-1-dot-2-3-8 The Art of Ethical Cursing* ... What?"

"The computer. Surely a virus is worse than a bug."

"I don't know," the librarian admitted. "I try not to know anything about it. It's an annoying thing. All ... electric-y." They waved vaguely, apparently indicating some mysterious force wafting off the computer to infect their books. Maybe there was. Jen didn't know how they worked. Computers *or* books, but books had power. Everyone knew that. Maybe the books had infected the computer, shutting it down before it could tempt too many people off the papery page.

"Is someone coming to fix it?" she asked aloud.

"Probably not," the librarian said, their voice thin. "Since I've not asked anyone to. No one uses it anyway, except to look at silly pictures, and if anyone wants those, there's plenty in the 740s."

"Oh," Jen said, and sighed. "Right. I suppose I'll have to wait until Callie's is working again."

"You could just read a book. Shocking thought, I know, but there it is."

"I do read books," Jen said. "I just wanted to read the computer today."

The librarian pointed into the stacks, the packed, uneven snickets and ginnels that ran every which way beneath the high, arched ceiling of the old building, the light from the tall windows flushing the still world in dusty glamour. "You can find everything you need here."

"Not quite," Jen said. "But thanks anyway." She turned and headed back outside, taking the scone from one of the cavernous pockets in her cargo shorts and munching on it disconsolately. She could go to the school, she supposed, but it was after hours, and she had no idea what staff would be there. If it was Abigail, she'd be sure to let Jen in, and probably share some of the gin she made in the back of the chemistry lab. Gordon would, too, even if he'd then talk to her endlessly about the lifecycle of the demented gnat, or whatever his latest passion was. But if it was the bloody head or someone like that she had no chance.

She sighed deeply, cramming the last bit of scone into her mouth and extricating the smoothie jar from her other pocket.

"*Psst.*"

She turned, startled, and spotted a thin young man – not much more than a boy, really – lurking on the library steps. Well, *lurking.* He was leaning against the wall, chewing on a leaf, but with the hood of his sweatshirt pulled low over his forehead he definitely gave the impression of lurking.

"Me?" she said.

"Yeah." He sidled closer, hooves clipping on the steps. He was too young to even have much need to shave his goatee yet, although he was evidently attempting to cultivate it. "You looking for a computer?" His voice was pitched low, a secretive mumble despite the fact they were alone on the steps.

"Why?"

"I can help."

"How? Can you get me onto the school computer?"

"Better than that," he said, grinning at her, then inclined his head toward the side of the building, where an alley dived between it and the tall old fence of the nearby park. "Come on. Somewhere more private."

Jen eyed him. "You realise I can crack you like a crab leg and shake your insides into the lake for the pike to eat?"

He blinked. "That was unnecessary."

"You're trying to lead me into a dark alley."

He looked at the sunny, cobbled side street then back at her. "Whatever. But if you want a computer, come with me." He turned and slouched off, radiating less an air of criminality and more the sense that his mum had asked him to do the dishes and he was skulking about, hoping she forgot.

Jen watched him go for a moment, then shrugged and followed, taking the lid off her smoothie for a slurp as she went. It was hardly a risk.

The young faun led her down the alley and through one of the park's side gates. They were only closed when the geese occasionally decided to nest around the duck pond, at which point the council would lock the whole place up until it was safe to venture in again. There hadn't been any bird-based incidents this year, so the gardens were looking lush and well cared for, the flowerbeds neatly weeded and the crowded plantings full of rich growth.

There wasn't really much in the way of grassy areas in the

garden, and instead gravel paths wound their way through a wilderness of foliage dividing it into different areas that represented a wide range of world regions and varying climes. The intention was that they stayed well-separated, but there had been some interesting and occasionally alarming accidental cross-cultivations here and there. They hadn't lost anyone since the sixties, though, when some hybrids occurred between plants of questionable origins that had been clandestinely introduced (no one ever claimed responsibility for either the introductions or the hybridisation, and it remained a village mystery). All the plants involved were subsequently removed rather rapidly, or as much as they could be, and the garden was usually quiet these days, although every now and then a dog or something might go missing, if their owner was careless. They fairly reliably reappeared uninjured, if sometimes slightly *altered*, but one had to live with such things.

The kid led her into the deeper reaches of the park, where the trees were old, crouching things that had been here long before the village, twisted and etched with the passage of frost after sun after storm. Their foliage whispered with an unfelt wind, and small creatures – squirrels of course, and birds, but other things too – watched them pass with sharp eyes and twitching tails. The branches trapped the rising green scent of cool, damp earth, along with a pleasant coolness, and a little waterway clattered and sparkled between mossy rocks as the kid stopped next to a fat-boled tree.

He checked around, then extricated a bag from a hollow within the tree's trunk, eliciting a yelp of alarm from inside, as well as some healthy cursing. He hurriedly threw a flap-jack into the hole, and the cursing gave way to happy mumblings.

Jen raised her eyebrows. "You're dealing with trunkles?"

"Twignuts," he said. "They're fine."

Jen didn't answer that. Let him find out for himself how fine things would be when he didn't turn up with the flapjack one day. Twignuts didn't have all those teeth for nothing.

The kid sat down on a lichen-encrusted bench and dug into the bag, and Jen sat next to him, slurping her smoothie. The kelp was excellent, if a little sandy. Callie was never very good at rinsing things. That's what came from having a half-goat stomach.

"Here it is," the kid said, holding something out to her in both hands.

She stared at it. "That's a watch."

"Not just any watch. It's a *Fatch*."

"What's that when it's at home?"

The kid did a very impressive double take that Jen would have bet he'd practised in the mirror for a good hour. "You've not heard of Fatch? The latest in wearable technology?"

Jen just sipped her smoothie.

"It's truly a breakthrough," the kid continued. "All the information in a computer, on your wrist."

Jen picked a string of seaweed out of her teeth. Always a problem with kelp. It never blended up entirely well.

"Imagine not having to go to the library! Or the cafe! You just do this"—he tapped the watch face twice—"and Fatch will answer all your questions. Like … Fatch, what's the weather in Whistlewick?"

There was a pause, while the flat face of the watch blinked like a large pink eye, then a reedy voice said, *"Warm and a little swampy, kind of like your nether regions, goat-boy."*

The kid growled and shook the watch violently, eliciting a thin shriek of outrage, and Jen took another sip of smoothie to hide her grin.

"I *said*," the would-be salesman insisted, "what's the weather in Whistlewick?"

There was a pause as the watch blinked, then it said,

"More promising than your chances with that sprite down at the lock."

Over the sound of the kid slapping the watch repeatedly against his opposite hand while it shrieked in protest, Jen said, "You know charmed tech isn't permitted in Whistlewick."

"It's not charmed," the lad said, a little breathlessly. He had both hands wrapped around the watch now, but Jen could still hear it screeching faintly, *"The wind's lighter than your intellect!"*

She ran a finger around the inside of the jar to get the last sticky scraps of kelp out, surprising a small crab, which she caught and popped in her mouth quickly, crunching with relish. "If it's not charmed, what is it?"

"It's a computer," he said, shoving the watch back in the sack.

"That's not a computer," Jen said. "Computers are desk sized."

"Not the new ones. Whistlewick's behind the times, is all."

Jen thought about it. It was true the village wasn't always up to the minute with such developments, but they weren't *backward.* They'd been one of the first places to have daily post drops via ParcelPixie drones, and the automated canal locks had been ahead of their time. Admittedly, they'd also been very unreliable, since the kraken who operated them kept getting bored and insisting the skipper of each boat arm-wrestle them to be allowed through. Jen had been one of only a handful of people in history to win an arm-wrestling match with a kraken, and after that he'd quit in a huff and they'd had to go back to operating the locks themselves. So it hadn't been *entirely* thought out, but it was still very advanced, as far as such things went.

"I've never had a computer insult me," she pointed out now. "I wouldn't be putting up with that."

"It just needs some training," the kid said. "It's Fae Eye."

"It's what?"

"Fae Eye."

"There's *fae eyes* in it?" Jen got up hurriedly, taking a step away from the bench. She might've won an arm-wrestling contest with a kraken, but she wasn't getting on the wrong side of the Fae.

"No! Not fae eyes. *Fae Eye.*"

"I don't care if it's just one or multiple. You get it out of the village right now, and away from you too, if you know what's good for you."

"No, it's new tech. *Faery Intelligence.* Fae I."

Jen blinked. "Fae *I*, as in the letter, not *fae eye?*" she asked, pointing at her own eyes.

"Exactly." He got up and held the watch out to her, silent now, but the screen swirling with waiting colours, reminding her of the blinking cursor of the computer in the cafe, promising connection to something beyond the village and beyond the dale. Connection to some*one.* "Go on," he said, his voice low and suddenly smooth. "Just try it. Everything you need. Everything you want to know. Every*one* you want to know. Right there on your wrist, any time you want."

No more hunching over the computer in the tearoom, hoping the chair didn't break, hoping no one was reading over her shoulder, fretting that she'd forget to log out of her messages and someone might see. Wondering every morning if there'd be a message that day, the swooping sickness when there wasn't, the bubbling, fragile delight when there was.

"It's all here," the kid said, taking a step closer to her, the watch glimmering on his palm. "Day, night, whenever you want. *You* get to choose, no waiting on ancient old electrics. More than that, it changes how you see yourself, you know? You get to be whoever you want with one of these."

"What?"

He leaned forward, holding the watch out to her, and it lit up with shimmering, multicoloured luminescence, a rainbow captured in miniature. She turned her own hand palm-up, and the faun placed the watch in it. It kept glowing, the light playing over her palms and turning the hardened grey-green skin soft and delicate. For one moment she imagined herself sylph-like, dancing to distant music through glades and glens, light-footed and graceful, sipping bubbly elderflower spritzers, ethereal and desired instead of earthbound and intimidating. Or *feeling* that way, which was almost the same thing.

"It's so much more than a computer," the faun said, pushing the sleeve of his hoody up so she could see his own watch. "Fae I. It's the future."

Fae I. Faery Intelligence. Jen took a deep breath. Damn faeries. She didn't understand the watches, didn't know how they worked, didn't know if they did any of the things the kid said, but there was no questioning what they *would* do. They'd do mischief, because that was what faeries did. She dropped the watch into her smoothie jar.

"Hey—" the faun started, and was drowned out by the watch shrieking.

"Oi! Mildred of the seas! You finned ogre! What d'you think you're doing? It stinks of fish in here, just like your breath! Even a rotting sea cow wouldn't smell as bad—"

Jen cut it off by the simple expedient of screwing the lid back on the jar, and put the whole thing in her pocket.

"You can't do that," the faun protested. "That's my merchandise, that is!"

"I'd advise you to take yours off and give it back to whoever's got you selling for them," Jen said. "And I'd do it now, because I'm going to walk into the town hall, show this to the sergeant, and tell her someone's selling faery traps."

"They're *not*. They're Fae—"

"They're faery traps, kid," Jen said. "Feeding you all the things you think you want, saying you can *be* anything you want, if you just sell one more. *Fae I.* You didn't see that coming?"

"Well," he said, scratching his arm. His watch was glowing an ugly red colour, and he gave it an anxious look.

"Give it," Jen said, holding her hand out.

"I mean … but it promised me a really good commission! I only had to recruit five people to sell for me and I'd get my own Fae I Vision!"

"I have no idea what that is, but please tell me you've not recruited anyone yet."

"I haven't," he admitted. "I sold a couple to kids at school, but Ms Marshall confiscated them and used them to demonstrate the effects of acid on fae-made tech."

Well done, Abigail, Jen thought, then frowned. "Hang about – Ms Marshall? You're bloody well still *in* school, aren't you?"

"Well, like, it's my last year. Almost. I mean, I'll be old enough to leave next year, and I want to be a tech entrepreneur, so—"

Jen grabbed him by the back of the neck, ripped the watch off his wrist, and jammed the thing into the smoothie jar with its twin, ignoring it screaming, *"Put me back! Put me back, or I'll curse your spines with ringworm and bone rot and leech spit and—"*

"Hey! That was *my* property!" the faun yelped, then his yelp became a howl as she grabbed one of his pointy ears and propelled him ahead of her toward the gates.

"You absolute *idiot,*" she said as she marched him along. "You silly child. Did you sabotage the town computers? And the school ones?"

"No," he said, rather unconvincingly, then added in a whine, "This is assault!"

"Absolutely. And it's well-earned," she said, driving him out of the park and onto the street. "I can't decide whether to take you to the police or the school." The school would be more likely to punish him. Knowing Maple, the town's police sergeant, she'd want to test the watches out herself, and next thing she'd be decreeing a new law saying the whole town had to buy them.

"No, come on, this isn't *fair*," the kid wailed. "I just wanted the Fae I Vision! And, like, it's so good for school and things! You can ask it stuff instead of having to read about it! You don't need books *at all!*"

Which was when Jen knew exactly where to take him.

"I DON'T LIKE HIM," the librarian said, staring at the faun, who was sniffling sulkily and reordering the 508 (Natural History) section into the correct sequence. "He looks like he dog-ears books."

"He probably does," Jen agreed, and the librarian gave her a horrified look. "But this is your chance to teach him better. He thinks *these*"—she held up the jar, in which the watches were still screaming faintly—"have more answers than the library."

"*Sacrilege*," the librarian muttered, and Jen felt a ripple of disapproval pass through the entire building.

"*Teach* him," she said. "Don't let me come back here and find out he's been eaten by 579 or something."

The librarian eyed her. "Fungi?"

"I still have nightmares."

"You used a *herring* as a bookmark."

"I was six, and it was a minnow. Herring are sea fish."

"Well, *excuse me*," the librarian said, and peered over their glasses at the faun. "Alright. But if he so much as creases a dust jacket I'm sending him into 424."

Jen frowned. "I don't remember 424."

"You weren't that bad. English language section, formerly thesauruses, now disused. Words gone feral, basically."

"Ouch."

"Exactly." The librarian straightened their cardigan. "Now off you go. I don't like those things being in here." They nodded at the jar. "They're making my sinuses hurt."

"Got it. Thanks, Glyph."

"Yes. Go away." They turned back to their books and the labouring faun, and Jen ambled out onto the library steps, squinting at the fading day. It was the right thing to do, of course. Nothing but trouble could come from these contraptions.

And yet.

And yet the idea of being able to get those messages whenever she wanted was *nice*. The idea of feeling light and delicate and attractive was *nice*, true or not. She held the jar up, and the two watches gave a burst of soft, enticing light, and she sighed. That wasn't her, was it? It was all lies and illusion, whispering charms and fakery. Besides, could some little dancing sylph arm-wrestle a kraken into submission? No. Of course not. She tucked the jar back into the pocket of her cargo shorts. She'd pay Abigail a visit and see if she had some more experiments she wanted to try out.

She was just passing the cafe when Callie popped out of the bright yellow door and called, "Jen, love?"

"Yes?"

Callie waved a slip of paper at her. "Got a Zephyr-drop message for you."

"Who from?"

Callie grinned. "*Well.* They didn't put their name, but ..." She flourished the paper, reading from it in a clear voice that was far too carrying on the quiet street. "It says, *This is for Jen who told me she uses the computer in your cafe. I'd like to buy her a smoothie, because she is magnificent, and if she wants to message me back this is my return address in case the computer doesn't work.* Then they've put The Crooked Cup in Mossford. It's a cafe too, I think."

"Oh," Jen said. "Fancy that."

"Well? Who is it? Are you sending something back? What're you going to say? Is this why you were worried about the computer? Who—"

"I need to pop over and see if Abigail's about," Jen said. "Thanks, Callie." And she headed down the street, tall and broad and spined, a grin spreading over her face. *Magnificent.* Not that she needed anyone to tell her that, of course, but it was nice, wasn't it?

Sod Fae I and all its pretty little tricks.

She was *magnificent.*

2 2

———

A LITTLE NOT-GOOD

Sometimes the smallest things can be doorways to another world.

In this case, trainers. Comfortable ones. Purple ones, with stars on ...

ED GUIDED HIS WHEELBARROW CAREFULLY ACROSS THE cobblestones, trainers scuffing gently. He was inordinately proud of his trainers. They were purple, and he had carefully appliquéd a large gold star to the back of each, as well as adding glittery gold laces to very pleasing effect. Plus they were very comfortable, which he appreciated. A lifetime of dodging imps and lesser demons, as well as the attacks of hapless heroes, had made his knees somewhat iffy, a condition not helped by the fact that said lifetime was unnaturally – and a *teeny* bit infernally – long.

"Morning, Ed," Abigail called. She was heading toward the school, wearing a pale blue cardigan over a high-necked blouse, the prim look rather offset by the large squid she had clutched under one arm. It writhed wildly, slinging its arms (legs? Ed was unsure of the classification) everywhere, and had already spat ink all down her side. She'd evidently dressed for the occasion, though, as she was wearing a translucent raincoat over her cardigan, and a shiny black PVC skirt.

"Morning," he called back. "Show and tell today, is it?"

"Interdimensional communication," she replied, not stopping. "Can usually raise a minor elder god, but the bloody kraken don't half make a fuss about the trip."

I am Kraken! the squid blared, the message arriving in Ed's head more as a concept than words. *Unhand me, puny human!*

"Look, I've got some nice koi at the school. It's worth your while," Abigail told it, striding on.

Are they the expensive ones?

"Yes, damn you."

Fine. But I want a couple to take home to the kids.

"You better put on a damn good show for that."

Ed smiled, and kept walking. He still remembered his first interdimensional portal, although it hadn't been at school. It had been on a barren, windswept hilltop, using a cursed book of lore he'd looted from a library he had no business being in. It had almost gone terribly wrong, but that was what being a kid was all about, wasn't it? Can't learn anything decent without breaking a few laws of physics and almost pitching the world into eternal, screaming darkness.

Early morning shoppers dotted the main street of Whistlewick, heading into the cheese shop or the butcher's, the fruit and veg shop or the bakery or the little corner store where one could get everything the other shops didn't offer (or, in the case of a certain ethereally beautiful faery called Lioren, where one could still get served after being banned from everywhere else for planting enchanted faery cakes among the stock). The four-handed clock in the town hall struck eleven in a needlessly complicated manner, and Ed lowered the wheelbarrow's handles, parking it outside one of the three tea shops that nestled together along the cobbled lane. None of them bore obvious names, and were mostly distinguishable by the different coloured gingham bunting. He chose the one with deep purple tones first, letting himself inside to the cry of a raven.

"*At the door!*"

"Hello, Kevin," Ed said to the bird, who tipped his glossy head.

"*Gimme four.*"

Ed obligingly tapped his fingertips to the raven's upraised foot, and ambled to the counter. There was no one else inside, and for a moment he just enjoyed the comfortable dimness, the sunlight filtering through gauzy black curtains to pool on the dark tile floor and heavy old wooden furniture. Flames guttered mellowly in metal lanterns on the walls, and a low soundtrack of chanting monks drifted from somewhere. In the short hall that led to the loos, Ed could see some new mugshots had been added to Grudge & Grinder's *Wall of Malfeasants,* which mostly consisted of customers who'd suggested *putting more lights on* or *cheering things up a bit.*

Ed soaked up the sombre stillness for a little longer, but when the room remained resolutely empty he looked at Kevin. "Where's Brian?"

"*Kitchen floor.*"

"What?" Ed leaned over the counter, with its display of dark red velvet muffins, the colour bleeding into the white icing, and black forest cupcakes studded with the round, glossy carcasses of fresh cherries. "Brian?"

"*Nevermore,*" Kevin intoned mournfully, and Ed gave him a dubious look.

"*Bah,*" a small voice said from his chest pocket. "Bird brain."

"I don't see him, though," Ed said, as a somewhat scraggly bat poked her head into view.

"Well, you're not looking, are you? You're just standing there peering around like an astigmatic gerbil."

"Are they unusually astigmatic?"

"I don't know. Do I look like a rodent optician?"

"You look like a rodent."

The bat hissed. "I am an agent of darkness and chaos, limited only by your ridiculous refusal to renew your contracts."

"You know I'm not going to, Margaret," Ed said firmly. "We're retired."

"You never consulted *me*," she said huffily, and launched herself into the air. She circled his head a couple of times, chittering venomously, and he sidestepped a deposit before she went to cling to the ceiling in the corner of the room and chatter at the resident spiders.

Ed took a dark red napkin from one of the tables and used it to clean up the mess, then ventured around the counter. "Brian?" he tried again.

"*Pantry door,*" Kevin suggested.

"I'm coming in," Ed called, in case Brian thought he was a thief and came out wielding a mace. It had happened before.

There was no answer, though, and no Brian, and no mace. Ed picked his way into the kitchen, catching a scent of burning. He checked the oven and found a tray of cheese scones going crispy at the edges, so pulled them out and set them on one of the workbenches. A half-finished mug of coffee had been abandoned next to a large ball of pastry and a rolling pin, and he called Brian's name again.

This time he was rewarded by a sharp knocking from under one of the benches, where stainless steel doors covered the front.

"Brian?" he asked uncertainly, and tried the door. It slid

open easily enough, and he was rewarded by the sight of the dwarf curled up inside, clutching a set of kitchen tongs and a wickedly sharp knife.

"Is it gone?" Brian asked.

"Is what gone?"

"*It.*" Brian tried to peer past Ed, and made a frustrated noise. "Move your giant form, would you?"

Ed stepped back so the dwarf could survey the kitchen properly before climbing out and smoothing the braids of his beard over a floury purple apron. "Are you alright?" Ed asked.

"*No.* Attacked in my own kitchen, I was!"

"By what?"

Brian started to say something, then stopped. "I didn't get a good look."

"Oh."

They were both silent for a moment, until Kevin screeched, "*Call the law!*"

A crash from the tea shop suggested the warning was well-founded, and Brian charged out of the kitchen, brandishing his knife and tongs. "*Get back here, you filthy wotsit!*"

Ed hurried after him in time to see tables toppling and chairs crashing to the ground, sugar jars and napkins and menus flying across the room. The devastation made straight for the front door, and Kevin flung himself in front of it in a swirl of feathers, squawking, "*Halt your paws, I guard the door!*"

The final table fell, and the tablecloth whipped off it, arrowing for the raven like a low-slung, deep purple ghost. Kevin managed one defiant squawk before the tablecloth hit him, and he was barrelled out onto the street in a cloud of feathers and colourful, non-rhyming cursing. Brian rushed after him, and by the time Ed arrived the tablecloth had drifted emptily to the ground, the dwarf was yelling curses in every direction, and Kevin lay sprawled on his back on the pavement, fluttering his wings feebly.

"Are you alright?" Ed asked.

"*Ow, the floor,*" the bird muttered.

"Thieving bloody imps!" Brian bellowed, shaking his fist at the world in general.

"It was an imp?" Ed asked doubtfully. He'd dealt with a lot of imps in his time, an unavoidable side effect of dabbling in the gloopier corners of magic. They were attracted to nefarious deeds like kraken to koi, but generally dealt in utter devastation rather than a few tipped tables, in his experience.

"I don't know! Bloody nuisance is all." Brian glanced at the wheelbarrow. "Give me five aubergines, a red cabbage, and a bag of tomatoes."

"Right you are," Ed said, handing them over. He didn't bother asking for payment. He'd put it on Brian's tab. It was difficult enough getting money out of the dwarf on a good day, let alone one he'd started in a pan cupboard.

MARGARET REJOINED him as he trundled the wheelbarrow to the next tea shop. It bore cool blue bunting, which somehow gave the impression it was merely deigning to appear gingham for the moment, as a grudging and short-lived favour, and would revert to something less clichéd as soon as it had the chance.

"That was fun," the bat said, trying to burrow into his beard.

"*Ow.* It wasn't *fun.* It was very destructive."

"*Ugh.* You'd have loved that not long ago. Trashing tea shops. Infuriating honest, hard-working business owners. Causing devastation and fleeing."

"That was before we retired," Ed said, wincing. "Can you stop? It feels like you're trying to rip my beard out."

"I'm making a nest."

"You don't need a nest. You're a bat. Go back in my pocket."

"It's boring in there, and too bright out here. Your beard's like Goldilocks's porridge. Lumpy and hot, but tolerable."

"Wonderful," he said with a sigh, but let the bat nestle into his beard anyway. It was a rather distinguished grey these days, and he'd been experimenting with purple dye on the ends. It matched his trainers.

The door of the blue bunting tea shop had a miniscule line of text in very plain, unadorned font stuck to it. It read *In/Fuse,* and Ed pushed the door open, stepping onto a welcome mat made of river stones. An understated chime, high and ringing, cut through the ambient harmonies of pan pipes and gentle melodies, and a sprite with painfully high cheekbones looked up from the counter, where she was using tweezers to put individual sugar crystals on top of a tiny, intricately folded pastry.

"Ed," she said, without smiling. Her structured linen outfit was even paler than the wood of the furniture and floor, matching her hair and skin, and the only colour in the place came from succulents standing in the exact centre of each table. A woman in a well-tailored grey suit was sitting in the corner of the room, sucking on her finger, so Ed assumed she'd tried to move one of the plants. They didn't like it.

"Tove," he said, nodding at her gravely and trying to remain as proud of his purple trainers as he had been a moment ago. They felt a little gaudy and gauche in here.

"I have had a disaster," Tove said, raising one eyebrow minutely.

Ed blinked at her. In twenty years, the only time he'd seen

her expression alter was when Brian had thrown a tourist through his own front window for patting the bottom of one of his staff. Tove's mouth had turned up very slightly at the corners, then she'd set the local kelpie to chasing the man out of Whistlewick. So a raised eyebrow meant things were serious.

"What's happened?" he asked.

Tove didn't answer. She just set her tweezers down and went into the kitchen while he looked at the sign on the counter. It read *Re/Fuse*, with nothing else below it. He'd never dared to ask if it was her business motto or a warning. Maybe both.

She was back a moment later, holding a tub out in front of her at arm's length. "Look."

Ed peered warily into the tub, wondering if the mysterious havoc-causer from Grudge & Grinder had made it in here and been disapproved to death. Instead, a succulent sat sadly at the bottom, bearing a bunch of bright pink blooms. "I don't— *Oh.* The flowers?"

"Why are there flowers, Ed?"

"I don't know?"

"You are meant to be the horticulturist."

"Well, yes." He took the succulent out of the tub and examined it. "They're very elegant flowers."

"*They are pink.*" Tove gestured in a manner that approached agitation. "Do you see anything *pink* in my shop?"

"No."

"You supplied me with these plants. I hope there will not be any more surprises."

"Of course. I'm sorry." He tried to put the succulent back in the tub, but she jerked back.

"Remove it."

"Right." He held up the soft cloth bag he'd brought in. "Salad leaves?"

She glared at him with fierce, light eyes. "I hope there are no edible blooms in there."

"Well, no—"

"That was a joke."

"Oh." Ed decided he was better not to speak, and just offloaded the cucumbers, courgettes, green peppers, green tomatoes, celery, and spring onions without further comment.

In the corner of the room, the woman in the tailored suit called, "Hello?"

Tove's pale gaze lifted to her, her jaw tightening. "Yes?" she said, her voice barely a whisper.

"Hi. Can I have … do you have some caramel syrup or anything? This coffee is very bitter. And maybe some strawberry jam for the scone? Just butter is a bit boring."

"You can pay me later," Ed said, and all but ran for the door. He had no desire to see a murder today. When he wasn't directing them they were always a little boring, anyway.

IT WAS ALMOST a relief to step into Steeped Dreams, despite there being so much yellow – bunting and tablecloths and cushions and sunflowers and an extraordinary collection of rubber ducks which seemed to constantly change – that it made his eye twitch, and Margaret had an instant, hissing tantrum in his beard.

"Do you want to wait in the wheelbarrow?" he asked her.

"*No.* Some spawn called me *cute* the other day. Cute! I am of the night! The darkness! The chaos that lurks—"

"Do you want some carrot cake?"

"Yes. I'm still the darkness, though."

"I know." Ed set his box of fruit and veg on one of the tables since the counter had no space, crowded as it was with cake stands and cookie jars, all labelled with multicoloured penwork and decorated with plenty of exclamation marks and squiggly flowers. A few uneven vases of sunflowers took up any remaining space, and Ed nodded in satisfaction. He'd been right to bring some more. These ones were almost done.

A giggle in the corner caught his attention, and he turned to see Maple, the town detective, sitting on the lap of a very large, broad-shouldered man, his long hair spilling over his shoulders to mix with his beard. She kept running her fingers through it. Ed squinted at them. It was very bright in here, and unreasonably cheery, but—

"Yes, it's Gavin," Callie said, her voice low. "I have no idea what's going on, but they basically had bluebirds singing around their heads when they saw each other."

Ed blinked at the faun. He hadn't even seen her appear at the counter. "But he's—"

"I know. Prime suspect in all that weird fae tech that's been going around. But the whole town's lost their minds, and it's not even lunch!"

"What?"

Callie did a funny little head-jerking thing toward the back of the room, and Ed realised Maple and Gavin weren't the only ones canoodling in a corner. A very elderly werewolf called Isaac was lying under one of the tables with a dryad stroking his fur and crooning gently. His tail thumped the floor softly, and his clothes were puddled around them.

"Isaac just changed in here?" Ed asked.

"Yes! Not even a by-your-leave. All his bits waving around the tiffin slices until the fur came in properly. No one needs that over their morning cuppa." She came out from behind the counter to inspect the box. "No kiwi? I've been doing some wonderful kiwi smoothies."

"They're taking some time to come ripe." They weren't, but Jen from the ferry had begged him not to let Callie have any more. Given Callie's goat-stomach, she didn't seem to think it necessary to peel fruit, and Jen wasn't a fan of the resulting hairy smoothies. The pineapples that went in with their spikes still attached were bad enough, apparently.

"Boo," Callie said now, and picked up a fig. "These look good, though."

"They're excellent this year."

"It was the goat I sacrificed under the blood moon to the decaying shades of harvests gone," Margaret said.

Ed bopped her on the head with one finger, and she tried to bite him. "Sorry," he said to Callie.

"Of course," she said. "Fancy some hummingbird cake?"

"*Nooo,*" Margaret snarled.

"Carrot," Ed said apologetically. "It's the cream cheese icing. Sends her silly."

"*I am not **silly**! I am the evil that lurks in the hearts of men! And women! And fauns! And—*"

"Tea?" Callie said. "That lovely herbal blend of yours is going down well."

"Just regular for me," Ed said, and took a seat well away from the amorous couples, taking his sunglasses out and settling them on his face. He *was* retired, but it was still far too bright for any self-respecting warlock.

ED DIDN'T DELIVER to the tea shops the next day, but he did take a load of potatoes, carrots, and leeks to the pub for the Tuesday darts night shepherd's pie, and two more full barrows of potatoes to the fish'n'chip shop down by the canal, and three replacement loads of flowering plants to the town hall, to replace the ones that had been eaten at the last council meeting.

It was as he was delivering them that he spotted Brian standing outside his shop with an oversized hammer in one hand, shouting at Tove, "Keep your bloody anaemic geckos to yourself!"

"I do not have *geckos*," she said, her arms folded over her immaculate tunic. "I only have Smör, and he is staff."

"He's a creepy bloody ghost, and he's trashing my place!"

"Smör has no more interest in your squalid hole than I do."

Brian growled, and jabbed a thick forefinger at her. "You lot have too many weird vowels and it's gone to your head."

"*My* head?" she said, the words cool and precise. "*You* need to keep your … *stuff* to yourself."

"What stuff?" he demanded, shouldering the hammer. His muscles bulged dramatically under the cut-off sleeves of his black T-shirt.

"*Colourful* stuff." She stepped toward him, tall and spare, the movement liquid as water, and dropped a rose just to his side of the property line between the two shops. "*Red.*"

"That's not mine," he spat. "You think I'd send *you* a rose? All the same, you sprites. Think too much of yourselves."

"And dwarfs think only of their stomachs," she said. "Your apron's looking a bit tight, Brian."

He pressed one hand to his leather-clad front. "At least I enjoy myself! No wafting around looking like I've got a stick—"

"*Stop it!*" Callie yelled, bursting out of her shop door, and Ed thought she was talking to the squabbling tea shop owners. Instead she launched a jug of water at a well-dressed elderly woman and a young man who seemed to have lost his shirt. They were entangled on the chairs outside Steeped Dreams, and the woman shrieked as the water hit them.

"*Callie!*"

"If you want to do that, do it on your own front step," Callie shouted. "This is a family establishment!"

"*Ooh*, I love a good bit of conflict," Margaret said. "Can we have cake?"

"No," Ed said, and turned the wheelbarrow for home. It was the heat, he supposed. Everyone always went a bit funny in the heat.

Although, the day was a perfectly reasonable temperature for early September, as far as he could tell.

WEDNESDAY MEANT a return to the tea shops, and Ed found himself slowing as he approached the main street, shifting his grip on the barrow's handles as he walked.

"Come on, come on," Margaret chittered, peering out of his breast pocket. "Why're you walking like an old man?"

"I *am* an old man."

"You wouldn't be if you renewed your contracts."

"You'd still be a troublesome rodent, though."

She hissed, digging her claws in a little harder than was necessary as she clambered into the shelter of his beard. He winced but didn't complain. There was no point making her day better.

It soon became clear that, if he'd hoped things would be quieter, he was sorely mistaken.

They turned into the main street to find it unusually busy, a small crowd collected around the tea shops. Abigail had a kraken in each hand, pointing them at Glyph, the local librarian, like they were loaded guns.

"I'll rewrite your bloody *face*," she shouted.

Glyph pushed their glasses up their nose. "Your late fines just started accruing interest. *Backdated.*"

"You … you're just a footnote in the index of the biography of a D-list celebrity—"

"*Where's Maple?*" Brian bawled. The entire contents of his shop appeared to have been emptied into the street, heavy dark wood tables keeled over next to chairs upholstered in red velvet, and skull candleholders and fat red candles and black menus that had to be read under blue light all thrown together unceremoniously on the cobbles, tangled up with more purple tablecloths. He'd swapped his hammer for the mace, and half his beard had come unravelled, a sole surviving bow clinging desperately to the end of one plait. "*Maple!* Stop dribbling over Nadia and do something about these sodding *imps!*"

"Nadia? Wasn't it Gavin the other day?" Ed asked, and Margaret snickered.

Tove swept out of her shop, her hands held high, as if begging the world to stop. "*Pink!*" she shrieked. "*Everything is pink!*" She pressed a hand to her forehead, and for a moment Ed thought she might actually swoon, like a storybook maiden, but instead she recovered, marched to Brian's clutter of furniture (and in the sunlight even her usually pristine clothing did have a rosy tint, as did her sleek hair) and grabbed a decorative lance out of the jumble. She whirled around to face the little crowd on the street. "Come, dwarf! We will *destroy* those who would destroy us!"

"*Bring it on!*" he roared, stepping up next to her with the mace at the ready.

They stood shoulder to shoulder, glaring about as if expecting to be attacked by imps wielding fabric dye, and for a moment all was still, no one seeming to have any answer to the situation. Then yelling exploded out of Steeped Dreams, and everyone swung toward it. Half a dozen people in various states of undress scrambled out of the door, pursued by Callie, who had evidently hooked a garden hose up out the back and was drenching everyone indiscriminately.

"*And stay out!*" she bellowed. "I don't have a licence for that sort of behaviour! I don't think there even *is* a licence for it! *And* it's contravening at least half a dozen food and hygiene rules!"

"*Maple!*" Brian bawled again.

"Callie!" Tove shouted. "Is this you? Have you turned everything *pink?*"

Callie waved frantically at her own door. "*Pink?* I'm more worried about disinfecting my *entire shop!*"

"Oh dear," Ed muttered, setting the wheelbarrow down.

"*Amazing,*" Margaret said. "Glorious. I love it."

"Margaret?"

"What?"

Ed grabbed the wheelbarrow again, turning to go back the way they'd come.

"What're you doing?" Margaret demanded. "I want to watch!"

"You are the worst familiar ever."

"I *am*. I'm incredibly terrible. You're lucky to have me."

Ed got the wheelbarrow moving, and took two paces before a large form loomed into his path. He looked up to find Jen staring down at him, her heavy arms crossed over her chest. The river troll's spinal spikes gleamed in the sun as if she'd been polishing them.

"Morning, Jen," he said, trying for breezy.

"Where are you going, Ed?"

"I forgot the aubergines?"

An aging border collie ambled up to Jen, and she leaned down to scruff its ears. Ed's heart sank, and he looked around as Tilda wandered toward them, hands in the pockets of her old trousers and her short grey hair tousled in the sunlight.

"Can I interest either of you in some rhubarb?" he asked hopefully.

"How's that new herbal tea of yours, Ed?" Tilda asked.

"The tea?" He didn't have to fake the bewilderment in his voice. "It's just mint and liquorice."

"Does this look like mint and liquorice?" Jen asked, nodding at the street. One of the kraken had shot ink all over Tove's wide-legged linen trousers, and she was chasing Abigail around Brian's furniture while he and a faery in a twinset yelled increasingly intricate threats at each other.

"Well, no, but why would you think it was my tea?"

"Only new thing on every menu," Tilda said. "Jen and I have been having a little poke around, since Maple's somewhat indisposed."

"But it really is just mint and liquorice," he insisted. "It can't do this."

"Are you sure?" Tilda asked. "You've not been dabbling?"

"I'm retired. You know that. I wouldn't risk—" He stopped, closing his eyes. "*Margaret.*"

"What?" she asked.

"What did you put in the tea, you winged harridan?"

"Only what you should've done. You've gone soft, and it's *so boring.*"

"We're *retired.* No more cursing people. We promised!"

"*You* promised. And it wasn't a curse. Look at them. They're having a great time!"

"To be fair, Meredith *does* seem to be enjoying herself," Jen observed, nodding at a woman with a tightly set white perm gyrating against a hulking troll, who seemed to be enjoying the attention, even if he'd gone the red of igneous rock.

"No," Tilda said firmly, and pointed at the bat. "Unacceptable behaviour."

"*You* can't do anything," Margaret said. "You're just some decrepit sheep farmer."

"Jen," Tilda said, and Ed braced himself. The river troll plunged her heavy hands into his beard, fishing for the bat with the same nimble skill she used to catch minnows in the weeds.

"*Nooo!*" Margaret shrieked. "No, hands off, you great lump!"

Ed winced as Jen pulled Margaret free, along with a fair amount of his own chin hair.

"Sorry, Ed," Jen said.

"No, my fault," he said, and it was. He should've kept a closer eye on the bloody bat.

Margaret frothed with fury, doing her best to bury her fangs in Jen's tough skin, and Tilda leaned forward, a small spray bottle in her hand. Ed caught a strong whiff of garlic extract as the woman gave Margaret a spritz, and he winced.

"*Ow! Owowowowow!* You *monster!*" the bat wailed. "How *dare* you? I am of the night! I am of the pit! I am darkness incarnate! I am a hell-beast—"

"You're a nightmare," Ed said.

"Yes, I am! And you're a *disgrace*. Call yourself a warlock—"

"Retired."

"You used to be worthy of the name. Now you're nothing but a washed-up gardener! Edgarth Blackroot the Night-dread, you—"

"Just Ed," he said.

"Give her another one, Tilds," Jen said. "She's still trying to get through the skin."

Tilda gave Margaret a slightly more vigorous spritzing, and the bat spluttered.

"Are you trying to *drown* me? Garlic won't kill me, you know. I'm not a vampire."

"Always calms down you creatures of the night, though, doesn't it?" Jen said. "Like a little camomile for the darkness of the soul."

"I'll give you camomile," Margaret muttered, but she wasn't frothing anymore.

"Was it the tea, then?" Tilda asked.

"Yes," the bat said sulkily, rubbing her face on Jen's finger to wipe off the worst of the garlic spray. "Just a touch of dreamthistle and tanglewort."

"You'll ruin my business," Ed said with a sigh, and Jen patted him on the shoulder with her free hand, heavily enough to make him stagger.

"You're alright, Ed. Everyone knows you're a good 'un."

Margaret made a dramatic gagging sound.

"Is it going to wear off?" Tilda asked.

"Maybe," the bat said.

"Honey cream infused with cinnamon and cloves," Ed said. "That'll sort everyone out. Always a good antidote to mild cursing."

Jen handed him Margaret. "I'll get on it." She jogged off, and Ed put Margaret back in his pocket, where she crawled to the bottom to sulk some more.

"Sorry, Tilda," Ed said. "I missed it completely."

She nodded, looking at Tove and Brian, who were rummaging through his furniture, shouting at each other enthusiastically and drinking from large tankards of beer. Brian had the rose tucked behind one ear, and Tove was wearing a black woolly cap with a purple skull embroidered on it. "Never mind," she said. "Doesn't hurt to shake things up here and there, does it?"

She ambled off, hands back in her pockets, and Ed watched her go, then picked up the handles of his barrow again, turning for home. No one would be interested in more stock until things calmed down a bit. He'd come back in an hour or so to help clean up, without the damn bat. He should've sent her back to the deep realms when he'd broken good, he supposed. He just kept forgetting to get around to it.

"Come *on*," Margaret hissed, peering out of his pocket. "That was fun, right?"

"No," he said firmly. "You're a horrible creature."

"Thank you," she said smugly, nestling down out of sight again. "I knew you'd appreciate it."

Ed sighed.

That was the worst of it. He *did.*

It was really hard to be good after centuries of being bad. And vegetables did get a bit boring.

He probably shouldn't have added the rampant ragweed, though. Margaret's own mix would've been enough on its own, and accidentally overdosing the whole village wasn't going to get them anywhere.

Although, without it, who knew if the shenanigans in Steeped Dreams would've been quite so … well, *shenanigan-y?*

He hummed a merry little dirge as he headed home. They hadn't done anything *bad,* as such. Just a little *not-good,* and he'd never promised to retire from *that.*

He really did have to make sure they didn't both behave in a not-good manner at the same time again, though. Unless they planned it, of course.

THANK YOU

Lovely people, thank you so much for taking a chance on this curious little collection of tales. Thank you for recognising there's a strange and beautiful magic in these brief whispers shared in the shadows, no less so than there is in the fireside saga of the novel. Thank you for your interest in strange lochs and deep fjords, in hidden valleys and lost worlds. It's truly a joy to share them with you.

And if you did enjoy these stories, I'd very much appreciate you taking the time to pop a review up at your favourite retailer or on Goodreads (or both, if you're feeling particularly generous).

Reviews are a different sort of whisper in the dark, secrets passed from one reader to another. *Try this,* they say. *I promise the bite is sweet.* They're arrows drawn in the snow, twigs broken to mark the path, signposts to something unseen. They're how you, lovely reader, get to share magic with a stranger, and isn't that such a lovely thing?

Plus they mean the world to writers. Not just to our egos (which are fragile beasts), but because they say to the retailer, *hey, this one's okay.* And then the retailers pass your whispers on to new readers, and maybe they listen, and follow your breadcrumbs into a book. And that means more stories for all of us. So reviews are always deeply appreciated.

But that is all for now, lovely people. If you'd like more short stories, you may want to check out the Familiar Society, inside the Toot Hansell Auxiliary community. There's a shiny new tale every month, as well as other fun things to discover.

If you'd like to send me a copy of your review, theories on where the shed came from, or anything else, drop me a message at <u>kim@kmwatt.com.</u> I'd love to hear from you!

Until next time,

Read on!

Kim

Bringing you the inside scoop from the undead realms!

Just because you're in thrall to a Queen of the Night is no reason to abandon your self-development goals, deadly dolls! Hanging around crypts gets old *fast*, and when everyone you talk to's been dead for three centuries, of course you're out of the loop.

But I got you, bestie. Grab your downloadable sample from the exclusive VA Diaries now, before I go fully VIP. (Or dead. Honestly, it could go either way.)

Stay unbitten, stay fabulous! 💋

The VA xx
(Vampire Assistant)

Scan above or use the following link for your free download:
https://BookHip.com/DVBRKTC

"What've we got?"

"Tigers. Snakes. Alligators. Tears in the skin of the universe." Susan shrugged. "I think I saw a kraken in the sink, too."

We were only hired to find a book. No one said anything about void-monsters, sink-krakens, or saving the world from a plague of niceness.

And there was *definitely* no mention of dentists …

Join Leeds' best (and only) magical PIs in the first Gobbelino London book!

Scan above or head to https://readerlinks.com/l/4797062

ACKNOWLEDGMENTS

As ever, I can never thank everyone who has helped bring these stories into being. The list is endlessly long, and the page is rather small. So this is only a small selection of the people who have supported, cajoled, inspired, and prodded me into getting the words onto the page in some semblance of order. If I have missed you, I'm sorry. I love you all anyway.

To my *amazing* Familiar Society members (also known as the weirdwolves, at least in my head), formerly Ko-fi members, who are the reason these stories are here at all. Not just because of the membership support, but because you've grabbed every monthly story with such glee that I can't *not* want to write more. You are amazing. Thank you for supporting weird, feral stories, and the writers who produce them.

Every time, to Lynda, the least scary editor (TM), and amazing friend. Sharing giggles in Word comments while editing is its own sort of magic. As always, all good grammar praise goes to her, while all mistakes are mine. Find her at www.easyreaderediting.com for fantastic blogs on editing, grammar, and other writer-y stuff.

To my lovely friends, online and off, quite a few of whom have actually read my stories and despite that are still friends with me. It's astonishing, and I love you.

And to you, lovely reader, sharing these tales with me. Maybe last in the notes, but never last in my mind. These stories are always for you. I hope we can share many more to come.

Until next time,
Kim x

ABOUT THE AUTHOR

Hello, lovely person. I'm Kim, and in addition to the DI Adams tales I also write other funny, magical books that offer a little escape from the serious stuff in the world and hopefully leave you a wee bit happier than you were when you started. Because happiness, like friendship, matters.

I write about baking-obsessed reapers setting up baby ghoul petting cafes, and ladies of a certain age joining the Apocalypse on their Vespas. I write about friendship, and loyalty, and lifting each other up, and the importance of tea and cake.

But mostly I write about how wonderful people (of all species) can really be.

If you'd like to find out the latest on new books, learn about giveaways, discover extra reading, and more, jump on over to www.kmwatt.com and check everything out there, or join me on the membership site for monthly short stories and weekly updates.

Read on!

amazon.com/Kim-M-Watt/e/B07JMHRBMC

goodreads.com/kimmwatt

bookbub.com/authors/kim-m-watt

facebook.com/KimMWatt

instagram.com/kimmwatt

youtube.com/@KimMWatt-yd1qb

"It's a no-brainer to recommend this one to anyone who enjoys cozies. Or laughing. Or paranormal stuff. Or sarcastic wit. Or great writing in any form."

– Amazon reviewer

Short Story Collections

Oddly Enough: Tales of the Unordinary, Volume One

"The stories are quirky, charming, hilarious, and some are all of the above without a dud amongst the bunch …"

– Goodreads reviewer

Need more stories?

Join the membership site for monthly, member-exclusive short stories, behind-the scenes content, early access to ebooks, and more!

Free stories!

The Cat Did It

Of course the cat did it. Sneaky, snarky, and up to no good – that's the cats in this feline collection, which you can grab free by signing up to the newsletter. Just remember – if the cat winks, always wink back …

The Tales of Beaufort Scales

Modern dragons are a little different these days. There's the barbecue fixation, for starters … You'll get these tales free once you've signed up for the newsletter!